A Stranger's House

A Stranger's House

Clare Chase

Gripping edge of your seat reads!

Copyright © 2017 Clare Chase

Published 2017 by Choc Lit Limited
Penrose House, Crawley Drive, Camberley, Surrey GU15 2AB, UK
www.choc-lit.com

A CIP catalogue record for this book is available
from the British Library

ISBN 978-1-78189-347-0

MIX
Paper from
responsible sources
FSC® C018072
FSC
www.fsc.org

Printed and bound by Clays Ltd

*To Mum, who convinced me
to move to Cambridge. (Do you
remember the walk along
Brookside?!) And also to Dad.*

Acknowledgements

Huge thanks to my beloved family as ever, Charlie, Georgie and Ros, as well as my wonderful parents, brother, wider family, friends and colleagues, for all their tremendous encouragement. Special thanks, too, to the Westfield gang for the best book signing ever!

I'd also like to thank the writer friends I've made, IRL and online, for all their friendly support, and the book bloggers I've got to know, whose generosity has been amazing.

And so to Choc Lit, and warm thanks to the readers on the Tasting Panel – Hrund, Olivia, Sigi, Siobhan, Linda Sy. & Jen – who gave *A Stranger's House* the thumbs up! Massive thanks also to the entire Choc Lit team who are truly fantastic to work with; their friendly, professional and attentive approach is second to none.

And last but definitely not least, thanks to my fellow Chocliteers. It's wonderful to be part of such a kind, sociable and supportive gang.

Author's note

I've tried to remain generally true to the layout of Cambridge, but as locals will notice, I've altered the arrangement of houses on Midsummer Common that face the river. North Terrace, which exists in reality, is replaced by my fictional row. I've also inserted a new college, St Audrey's, in the centre of town!

Chapter One

I stood in the shade cast by River House. There was a lot of it, thanks to its three storeys, but it didn't affect the temperature much. A wave of heat rushed over me, which was partly down to the oppressive weather, and partly to anxiety. The place looked formal and unfriendly, with its sombre navy door and lion's head knocker. The rooms inside were in shadow, so glancing through the windows gave nothing away. I wasn't even sure if Nate Bastable had arrived yet. Could a place look that deserted and yet contain a living being? Images of Bookman's Cottage filled my head, though I tried to push them aside – its bright, informal feel, so familiar after ten years of living there with Luke. The idea that I might never call it home again was almost too much to take in. For a second my eyes prickled. I blinked quickly; time to take a deep breath and get ready to make a good impression. Staying at River House was my chance to get away from the village gossips and hunker down.

I put the lion's head into action, without really expecting a response, and jumped when the door opened almost immediately.

Nate Bastable was nothing like I'd expected. I'd never met the owner of a house-sitting business before, but within seconds I realised I'd conjured up a detailed picture of what one would be like, and Nate wasn't it. He was wearing a charcoal-grey shirt – its sleeves rolled up – and scruffy jeans. His dark hair was tousled and, although he was a good few inches taller than me, there was nothing lanky about him. Rough and ready was the phrase that sprang to mind. I'd expected the owner of a house-sitting business to be ready, but ready with polish and a duster, rather than anything else. And if he was going to be rough at all, then I'd imagined this would be with something like a Brillo pad. Nate Bastable was smiling at present, but he looked like someone you'd back in a fight.

For a moment I felt self-conscious, and peered behind him, hoping Steph had made it to River House before me. She'd insisted on coming along to introduce us, which I'd felt was mollycoddling at the time.

At that moment I spotted her, standing in a doorway in the shadows. 'Ruby!' She darted forward and hugged me round the middle, since she can't reach any higher. Not that I'm a giant, only five ten, but she's four eleven to the top of her bouncy, ginger curls.

After she'd let me go she stood back, and her sympathetic expression hardened slightly. I could imagine why. She doesn't approve of my black jeans and DMs at the best of times, and probably thought them especially inappropriate for a first meeting with a new employer. I hadn't compromised on the number of earrings in each ear either. No point in pretending to be something I'm not.

'I presume you have brought some other clothes with you?'

I took a deep breath – there wasn't time to count to ten – and twisted slightly so she could see the rucksack on my back.

After a second she seemed to recover enough to do what she'd come for. 'Ruby, this is my cousin, Nate Bastable. Nate, this is my best friend, Ruby Fawcett. I know she looks like a squatter, but it's just a front.'

I'd get her for that later.

There was a twinkle in Nate's blue eyes as they met mine, but then his expression changed, and I had the sensation of being read; as though all I'd been going through was laid bare. To be fair, he probably wasn't relying on mind reading, thanks to Steph and her motor-mouth. A wave of humiliation washed over me, heating my neck and cheeks. I'd only just clapped eyes on the man, but I was already quite clear I didn't want him knowing what was in my head. Yet somehow I couldn't pull my gaze away.

'Come on in,' he said at last. 'I'll show you round and then we can sort out signing the paperwork if you're happy with the contract. There are a few instructions from the owner too.'

As he backed into the hall, I took in my surroundings. An umbrella stand contained a walking stick I thought might be made of cherry, with a dog's head at the top. Black beaded eyes looked mournfully out at us. 'Spindly as hell, isn't it?' Steph said, following my gaze. 'No one could use it for actual support. I think the house-owner's big on antiques.'

I noticed she'd taken off her Birkenstocks, leaving her feet unadorned except for some coral nail varnish. Through a doorway, in what looked like a drawing room, I could see an expensive-looking rug in front of a fireplace. I wondered for a second about taking off my own footwear, but the removal of Docs is hard to achieve in a dignified manner, and Nate was still wearing his boots. He led us into the drawing room, and I made sure I walked on the floorboards.

'Take a seat,' he said, handing me a file full of information. 'I'll get us all a drink. Coffee?'

'Thanks.' Steph and I both nodded and he headed back through the hallway.

I perched on the edge of a delicate-looking Georgian sofa, and Steph took the piano stool. The nice glossy folder in my hand felt like the sort of pack you might get at a holiday let, but that was where the similarity ended. The first sheet told me I was to sleep downstairs in the room we were currently occupying. I glanced up and spotted my bed: an ancient-looking, folding contraption. It was narrow and covered by a woollen blanket; not the upmarket, soft sort, but the kind that was old, matted and prickly. Not good qualities in bedclothes. Still, there was a thinnish sheet to go between me and it, and I hadn't been sleeping well lately anyway.

I got up for a closer look. Why had the house owner jammed it between a glass cabinet and an armchair like that? I was going to have to go through major manoeuvres each time I wanted to go to the loo. Plus, the chances of me not putting an elbow through one of the cabinet doors were pretty slim. Perhaps I could get Steph to help me move it somewhere else. It was light enough to drag, but I didn't fancy the owner's reaction if I scuffed his beautifully varnished oak floorboards. Between the sofa and the baby grand might be better. It would make it more obtrusive, but it wasn't as though I'd be inviting people in for tea.

The bed's foot stopped just short of the posh rug, and as I stared down at it, I noticed a dark stain on its fringe. I was pretty sure it was dried blood. If it had been in the kitchen I wouldn't have turned a hair, but it's less easy to injure yourself in the middle of a sedate drawing room.

'What is it?' Steph asked.

'Just a stain.' I peered back at the instructions again. Apparently the house owner, Damien Newbold, felt it was a much better deterrent having someone sleeping on the ground floor. Hmm.

I explained the arrangements to Steph.

She'd got up to join me and peered down at my so-called bed. 'Blimey. I hadn't noticed it squashed in there. You think he wants you to know your place then, this Damien guy?'

'Looks like it. Though he claims it's just to make sure I'm handy should he ever be bothered by intruders. Shame I haven't done any self-defence classes. If I do come across a burglar I'll just have to throw the blanket over their head and hope the dust sets off an asthma attack.'

Nate was taking a while with the coffee. I suddenly wondered if he was stalling on purpose, to give me time to read and digest my instructions without pressure. I sat back down and reapplied myself to the task. Damien Newbold wanted his pound of flesh all right.

The last page of the instructions included things like the code for the burglar alarm, the login details for broadband, and information on bin day.

Eventually Nate returned with a tray loaded with three mugs, a jug of milk and a bowl of sugar. He put the lot down on an occasional table between me and Steph, took a mug and went to perch on the sill of the window facing Midsummer Common. 'What do you think of the list of duties?' he said.

'I'm not sure I've taken all of them in yet.' I put down the papers and picked up one of the remaining coffees.

He gave a hollow laugh. 'There aren't normally quite so many pages. The standard company rules are fairly straightforward, but everyone booking has the option of tailoring our service to what they need. Damien Newbold appears to have taken full advantage.' His blue eyes met mine again. 'Does any of it bother you?'

I shook my head. 'It's no more than I'd be doing in my own home.' Well, that was a big, fat lie. I would have categorised several of the weekly cleaning jobs as five-yearly tasks.

There was a trace of amusement in his eyes; he clearly recognised bullshit when he heard it. I was glad really; only a weirdo would do that much housework voluntarily, and that wasn't the impression I wanted to create.

'So, I think Steph mentioned that this job is for ten days in the first instance.' He paused for a moment. 'You'll have seen your bed, and the instructions about sleeping downstairs.'

I nodded.

'I'm afraid the burglar alarm is an old-fashioned type that doesn't have a night setting but you'll need to activate it when you go out. And there are locks for each of the windows, which I know will be a pain in this weather. Lots of fiddling about. And you're aware of the agreed number of hours you need to spend here in the house each day?'

Twenty-one. I'd noticed that. I nodded again.

His expression turned serious. 'I don't want you to take this job unless you're completely happy. It's not too late to say no.'

But it was. I didn't have anywhere else to go. I couldn't stay with Steph, bang opposite our old house. Not after what had happened. I'd already spent five nights in a B&B in Newmarket, but that was unsustainable on cost grounds and the owner had clearly picked up on my state of mind too. Her look of concern over breakfast each morning made me squirm. Great; the prickling sensation was back in my eyes, and Nate was looking right at me.

But at that moment he stood up, walked over to the mantelpiece and picked up a set of keys.

'If you want to go ahead, then let's sign the contract and I'd better give you these. Yale and mortise for the front door, and mortise only for the back. There are bolts on the inside to use at night too. The keys for the window locks are on the sills.' He put the main set down on the tray next to the milk jug.

I found a pen in my rucksack, signed the contract that was at the front of the file and passed it to Nate. I watched as he rested the paper on the edge of the occasional table and added his signature. For just a second, a frown crossed his face, but then it was gone.

'Let me know if you have any trouble connecting to broadband,' he said, folding the contract and putting it in his pocket. 'I gather you need to be wired up for your regular work. Steph said you write books about social issues? Sounds interesting.'

I glanced at her, wondering if she'd just happened to mention the particular topic I was working on at that moment. She was looking at the floor. I could feel myself flushing again.

'That's right,' I said. 'But it's nothing terribly intellectual or world changing. I write for the general reader and use lots of anecdotes alongside the facts and theories.'

He looked at me again, and then suddenly he leant forward and shook my hand, something he hadn't done when I'd first arrived.

'My business brochures say all my house-sitters are personally vetted,' he said, 'so I felt it was essential I should at least take the time to say hello. I imagine you'd prefer to know who you're working for too. I'm glad we've met.'

He took his coffee mug out to the kitchen and then reappeared in the hall where Steph and I joined him. I'd been nervous about the meeting, but he was obviously about to go, and in the end he hadn't faced me with any difficult questions. Perhaps he valued Steph's judgement enough to take me on trust.

'I'll come out with you,' Steph said to Nate as he opened the door. 'See you off.' She turned to me. 'Back in a sec.'

I stood and watched them go. The heat outside was like a wall, and the bright sunlight was startling to my eyes after the dim interior. Steph trotted along after Nate, turning right along the footpath that separated River House from Midsummer Common and then right again down the passageway between my new bolthole and the next villa in the row. I paused for a moment, looking down at the long grass a few feet in front of me, still in the unshifting air, and then glanced up towards the area of the Common where sweating men, bare to the waist, were preparing for Strawberry Fair, Cambridge's free festival. Barriers were being erected between the smart houses of the well-to-do of the neighbourhood and the beginnings of a large marquee. Out in the centre of the grass more workers were wrestling with the front panels of what was set to be a large stage.

I was reluctant to close the front door, quite sure that Steph would be making the most of her opportunity to chat to Nate, now that I was no longer in earshot. If I could just think of an excuse to go and interrupt them ... some last-minute query would do it. But anxiety and the need for speed made my mind go blank. I decided to follow them anyway, hoping for inspiration along the way, but as I neared the alleyway – Midsummer Passage – my mind was still empty and I couldn't see them up the lane ahead. That left Brunswick Lane, which cut off to the right, behind River House. I was just about to round the corner, turning a right angle past the back wall of Damien Newbold's garden, when I heard Steph's voice, and froze.

'They were trying for a baby, you know.'

Hell, Steph. I definitely wouldn't have thought that came under the category of essential information relating to Ruby Fawcett. I crept forward so that I could peer at them.

'It's probably six months since they decided to go for it, but no luck so far, of course.'

Hmm, nice level of detail.

'Probably just as well as it turns out.'

You are my best friend Steph, but sometimes I hate you.

'Will she be okay here, on her own?' Nate said, pushing a lock of almost-black hair out of his eyes. 'I had my reservations about it as soon as you explained the background. It might not be the best thing for her right now. It's tough being housebound for so many hours a day.'

'She's stable.'

Well, thanks. The make-up must have worked then.

'She just needs somewhere quiet to get her head together and pick up the pieces,' Steph went on, helpfully. 'If she can at least keep her writing ticking over then she'll have something left for the future.'

Good grief.

'It's nice of you to be concerned for her,' Steph went on, her eyes raised, head on one side.

Nate shrugged, looked down at the pavement and folded his arms. 'Of course, I don't want to make things worse. But there's the business to consider too. The last thing I need is someone who's falling apart.'

I felt all the air go out of me.

There was a long-ish pause before he added: 'The guy who owns the house ...'

Something in his tone made me listen all the more intently.

'What about him?'

He was silent for another second, but then he sighed. 'Actually, forget it. It doesn't matter.'

Nate was thinking so hard about Ruby Fawcett as he drove home that he lost concentration. Not great on Newmarket Road, which was thick with buses, and cyclists that wove between the lanes of traffic. He shook himself and tried to focus on the matter in hand. Shame the air conditioning had packed up; a cool blast would have helped him snap out of it. Instead, he'd wound down the window, and a fug of fumes hung in the air. The Volvo didn't owe him anything; he'd run it into the ground. Safer to drive a beaten-up, nondescript car than something more eye-catching. Nate leant over to switch on the radio, which, miraculously, still worked.

He should have told Ruby to go home. The thought came

back to him, blanking out the news report currently on air. And he'd known that, standing there opposite her, watching her glance at Damien bloody Newbold's list of dictates. From what Steph had said, house-sitting for some control freak was the last thing she needed. Hours on end on her own, with a list of monotonous duties for light relief. If you weren't already down that would do it for most people.

He thought again about the wad of instructions. There wasn't anything fundamentally wrong with any of them individually. He'd had plenty of clients before who'd wanted a house-sitter to occupy a specific room, or who'd been obsessive about what they could or couldn't use. It was the combination that got to him in Newbold's case. Didn't want Ruby to use the upstairs bathroom, did want her to clean like a skivvy, and sleep on a rickety bed that looked like it had been made from *Scrapheap Challenge* leftovers. Some people enjoyed exercising power, showing what their money could buy – not just services but compliance.

It would have been satisfying to have told Newbold to get lost, but the instructions had come at the last minute; he'd still been digesting them as he'd driven over to Cambridge. Before he'd left River House he'd wondered again about letting Ruby stay, and if she'd even want to. But her discomfort when he'd told her she could still reject the job had been obvious. Nate could see her expression now; the look in her eye had made any change of heart impossible. He hadn't wanted to be the next person to pull the rug from under her feet. Though, in fact, she struck him as a survivor; he just didn't want to be the one putting her strength of character to the test.

Nate suddenly realised it was the first time in eighteen months he'd made a decision that wasn't based on reasoned argument. And he knew what could happen if you dropped your guard. His mind strayed back again to the comment

Newbold had made when he'd seen Ruby's photo ... then he remembered Jack Jones, his old mentor's advice: 'Never ignore your gut instinct. We're animals and we've developed it for a purpose.'

All well and good, but Nate was no longer reliable. The events of eighteen months ago meant he couldn't differentiate between his gut and paranoia.

Chapter Two

I managed to make it back inside River House before Steph knocked at the door again. If I'd been on better form I might have opted for a full-scale row, but as it was I didn't have the energy. Far simpler to pretend I'd never heard.

'He really liked you,' she said, shutting the door behind her and smiling her perky little smile.

'Oh come on. He was only here for forty minutes. Admittedly, I managed to avoid any of the classic mistakes: running round in circles clucking like a chicken, that kind of thing. But as for liking me …'

Steph turned and walked back through to the drawing room, moving over to one of the windows facing the Common. 'You managed to turn off the flippancy, so that was a bonus.'

I gave her a look from where I'd perched on the sofa.

'I know you just do it in self-defence, but other people might think you're shallow. And, anyway, you don't need to do it with me. I've known you since you were five, for God's sake.'

'It is actually just my nature, not a front.'

She rolled her eyes. 'Yeah, right. There's no need to be so prickly. I know it's not nice being checked out, but you can't blame him. You'd do the same.'

I shrugged, but she was right, of course.

'Besides, I know Nate,' she went on, 'and I'm quite sure his desire to see you was more to do with settling his own conscience than protecting Damien Newbold's interests.'

'I'm sorry?'

'He wanted to know you'd be okay here.'

And that I wasn't going to crack up on the job, of course.

Steph's eyes suddenly lit on a photograph in a silver frame sitting on a shelf near the sofa. She wandered over to get a closer look. 'God, do you think that's Damien Newbold? He's quite a looker. A moodier version of George Clooney, wouldn't you say?'

I stood up to peer over her shoulder. The picture showed a man with the smooth yet slightly dangerous good looks popular in Hollywood. He was receiving some kind of award – for something businessy, I reckoned. The various suited executives standing to his left and right had that feel about them. I guessed the photo's main subject might be somewhere in his late forties. He had a fair amount of grey in his hair.

Steph moved on towards the bookcase, which covered one whole wall of the room, up to the high Victorian ceiling, and stroked the spine of something red and leather bound. Her eyes flicked over to the baby grand. 'I do like the idea of a man of culture. Robin never really gets beyond the likes of *Cowboys and Aliens*.'

'You're doing the banter thing now, Steph. You might get a sense of proportion, at least in my presence.' The idea of sitting through *Cowboys and Aliens* was almost painfully harmless compared with Luke's recent choice of entertainment. 'Tell me more about my new boss instead.'

She stopped book fondling and moved over to the sofa, perching on the edge of it as I had, as though one wrong move might make it fall to bits. 'Nate keeps himself to himself. He's been through a lot over the years, to tell you the truth.'

'What kind of thing?'

She gave a little shudder. 'Difficult stuff. It's—'

'What?' She was always doing this.

She shook her head, again with that small shivering movement. 'I shouldn't even have mentioned it.'

I was starting to wonder what on earth *it* could be. 'No, you shouldn't, if you were going to clam up afterwards.'

'It's no good. It would be all wrong.' And, for once, she did look as though she meant it, and wasn't just after a pleasant little tussle before letting the gossip flood out. 'The trouble is, once people know, they can never relate to him without focusing on the associated baggage. It wouldn't be fair. He'll tell you himself if he wants. Ask me about something neutral instead.'

I tried to think and eventually managed to slip back into the mundane with: 'How long has he had the house-sitting business?'

'Got to be almost eighteen months now. Seems to be growing all the time.'

'It was nice of you to arrange this for me.' I sat down opposite her on the piano stool. 'It's saved my bacon, having somewhere to stay until I get sorted.'

'My pleasure,' she said. 'And as for the job, it was pure luck, really. I hadn't spoken to Nate in a while, but he called to let me know one of our great aunts had died. We had a bit of a catch up and, apropos of the house business going from strength to strength, he told me about this Damien guy who'd requested a sitter, right at the last minute. He said how he was going to have to turn him down, he was so booked up. Thought I might as well throw your name into the ring. Of course, you're not at all his usual sort of contractor.'

I raised an eyebrow.

'He normally makes use of mature, well-built, ex-police officers, or as close an approximation as he can manage.'

'Makes sense.'

'But, as I said, this guy needed someone urgently and I was able to assure Nate you were the right sort.'

'I have to say,' I said, 'he doesn't look like your average

service industry worker. What did you say he did before he set up the business?'

'I didn't,' she replied. 'As a matter of fact, he has always been in the service industry.'

'What is it you're not telling me? Come on. I am working for him.'

She sighed. 'All right; he used to be a private investigator. If you think about it, house-sitting's a natural off-shoot of that. Lots of security work involved.'

'But less action, I imagine.'

She put her head on one side and paused. 'Look,' she said, eventually, 'it's actually best not to ask him about it, okay?'

She went back to the window to look out again, possibly to stop me beseeching her for information with my eyes. 'So it's Strawberry Fair on Saturday,' she said, a slight note of distaste in her voice. 'Do you think that was one of the reasons old Damien didn't want to leave his house empty?'

'Looks like it, from his notes.'

'Maybe one of the reasons he took off too. Must get pretty noisy here when the whole thing's up and running.'

'A ringside seat, I'd call it.' I'd been lots of times myself, and liked the range of bands. 'I won't be seeing much of it this year though.'

'No?' She glanced at me over her shoulder.

I pointed to my sheaf of instructions. 'The rules say I have to keep the house in sight on the day of the Fair, so there'll be no lurking in beer tents. In general I'm not supposed to go out for more than three hours a day, too. Not that I'll want to.'

'You're worried about running into Luke?'

Saxwell St Andrew, where I had lived with Luke, with Steph and Robin as neighbours, was only fifteen minutes' drive from Cambridge, but still I shook my head. 'He hardly ever comes into town. I just think I'll appreciate being able to hole up and get on with things, that's all. It's lucky that I'm at the writing-up stage with this book.'

Though quite how I'd tackle its subject matter, given what had happened, I wasn't sure.

Steph left, with the promise of another visit soon, in spite of all my hints about the value of personal space. The trouble is she's an author-illustrator of children's books, so neither of us has a strict work timetable to adhere to.

After she'd gone I drank some Coke I'd brought in from the car. It was depressingly warm, as well as being slightly flat, but Damien Newbold's Smeg fridge freezer had an ice dispenser that improved things.

I was ridiculously hot in my black jeans and boots, and, now that I no longer needed to goad Steph, I went to the downstairs cloakroom to swap them for loose white linen trousers and sandals. There was a mirror above the basin, and I flinched as I saw the reality of me, standing there in such strange surroundings. There wasn't much physical sign of what had happened. The face that stared back at me, framed by dark, feathery, shoulder-length hair, was pale, except under the eyes where there was shadow. At least the red rims had gone though. The constant crying I'd been giving in to had been replaced by a sort of numbness. I was managing to keep all my feelings locked away again. Most of the time. But when I suddenly came up against reality – my face in the mirror, for instance, or a sympathetic friend on the other end of the phone – then the feelings came rushing back. I felt myself flush, as though someone had slapped me hard on each cheek. The cause was a feeling of deep and aching sorrow, mixed with a sharp sense of foolishness. And then there was the shame – that was a significant part of it – for Luke's actions. It didn't seem fair to have to cope with that, on top of everything else.

Time to get what little else I had packed from my car.

I went via Midsummer Passage to Midsummer Lane, the road beyond. The scent from a bank of honeysuckle covering a weathered brick wall mingled with the food occupying number four's green bin.

I looked at the haul I'd managed to grab from mine and Luke's house when I'd walked out. I'd barely been aware of what I was doing that day; certainly had no idea where I'd end up until I finally saw a B&B on the outskirts of Newmarket. All in all, I reckoned I'd done well to gather the basics. At least I'd got a wash kit, a few clothes and books, my own digital radio and my laptop. For a moment my mind strayed to the rest of my stuff, stranded back in Saxwell, but I pushed the thought away. Way more than I wanted to cope with right now. Eventually, maybe I could send Steph in as an emissary to help with extracting a few more bits and pieces.

Back in the drawing room I slipped off my sandals and tested the bed. I cursed myself for having forgotten to ask Steph to help me move it, and the bloody thing was seriously uncomfortable too, not to mention noisy. Springs creaked with every muscle I moved. When I lay on my stomach my feet reached beyond its end, my toes knocking against the metal frame. I turned on to my back, and gazed up at the seascape over the mantelpiece. It looked weird there; it was too small.

I wasn't any more comfortable in my new position than I had been on my front. My feelings of irritation towards Damien Newbold were intensified by the fact that he'd probably spent over a grand on that fridge freezer of his, but had saddled me with a five pound, junk-sale bed. I was never going to be able to sleep on it.

I woke up with a start, the room in near darkness. For a moment I couldn't think where I was and reached out in the normal direction of my bedside table, bashing my arm on the cabinet as predicted. Luckily for the glass, I only connected with its wooden corner. Once I'd extricated myself and switched on the drawing room light I glanced at my watch. Hell. I'd slept for five hours straight; the longest stretch I'd managed since I'd left home. I must have been making up for lost time.

I suddenly realised how hungry I was. I'd been intending to go out and shop for food, but the moment had passed. If I went to find an eight 'til late now it would be midnight before I got anything to eat. Instead, I went back into the hall and found a phone book, sitting on a mahogany side table that smelt of polish.

Safe in the knowledge that a pizza was on its way, exploring the house became a priority. I couldn't believe I'd fallen asleep without checking all the rooms first. That surely went against some kind of animal instinct. Looking up the stairs into the shadows I felt an inexplicable moment of nervousness and shook myself to clear the irrational sensation. At last I found a light switch and made my way up, my feet sinking into the thick burgundy stair carpet.

The first-floor landing had three mirrors and, whenever I turned, unexpected movement caught my eye. I knew my brain was just being tricked by the layout, but it gave me an unpleasant feeling, as though there was someone else there with me. The series of closed doors became intimidating and I wondered what secrets they had to give up. I had my hand on one round, brass doorknob, ready to go in, when, once again, I felt that little shiver of apprehension. For no good reason I turned to the second flight of stairs instead, flicking on the halogen lights for the attic.

The first thing that hit me as I went up there was the heat. Through four enormous Velux windows I could see clouds scudding across the night sky now, but during the day there would have been none, and the sun must have flooded the space. The room was impressive, and the bed was already made up. It would have been ideal for your average house-sitter, thank you very much.

Back on the middle floor I took myself in hand and started at the rear of the house, finding a guest bathroom, spacious and luxuriously tiled in marble, as well as three guest rooms, two with en suites. Gradually I made my way forwards, towards the master bedroom, which I could see must be large, spanning the width of the building.

I was aware that Damien Newbold was expecting me to visit each of the rooms at River House – after all, his list of cleaning jobs involved delving into every area of his home – but slowly opening what must be his bedroom door still felt like prying. Perhaps that was what made me hesitate. I felt as though I might be caught, even though I wasn't actually doing anything wrong. The house didn't feel empty; its owner still seemed like a palpable presence, with indications of his personality everywhere I looked.

For a moment I stood in the doorway. The curtains of the bay windows were drawn back, leaving blank eyes looking out onto a dark world. And then I flicked on the light switch.

Bits of Damien Newbold's bedroom were just as I would have expected. He had heavy linen sheets, a quilt that was no doubt filled with the finest goose down, period bedside lights, and an en suite wet room.

What I hadn't anticipated were the paintings. There were studies of female nudes on each of his four bedroom walls: one over the head of his bed, one opposite that, between the two windows, one to the left of the wet room door, and one to the right of his wardrobe.

Nude portraits are obviously not normally shocking – the female body is a beautiful thing – but four? Wasn't he being just a trifle greedy?

I stood there, joking to myself about it, but there was something peculiar about the quality of the paintings, and the way they'd been placed. They faced one another like the leaders of opposing armies, staked out across a battlefield. Damien Newbold's bedroom. I felt my skin prickle.

There was no mistaking the physical resemblance between the women too – superficial, but apparent all the same: dark hair, reaching well below their shoulders, blue eyes, and petite curvaceous figures. It was their expressions that marked them out as individuals. The one to the left of the wet room looked eager to please, a tentative smile on her slightly parted lips, her eyes almost pleading, whereas the woman on the wall opposite, next to the wardrobe, simply looked shy, her eyes cast down, arms crossed over her torso, partly obscuring her breasts.

The woman whose portrait hung opposite the bed, between the windows, exuded happiness. The look in her eyes spoke of love, unsullied and simple, and a kind of joy radiated from her. If Damien Newbold inspired such pure, uncomplicated emotion in any woman he was lucky, I thought, looking round at the indications of his complex sex life.

But it was the woman whose portrait hung over the bed that stood out. Her hair was tousled, and there was a look of fiery challenge in her wild eyes. If Damien Newbold was playing her for a fool, you got the impression he might get his fingers burnt.

20

Chapter Three

Nate spent a couple of hours delving into Damien Newbold's Internet presence. He was playing catch-up; it was normally the first thing he did before signing up a new client. Admittedly, the lengths he went to varied, depending on who he was dealing with. When he'd first started the business, he'd researched everyone's background equally. And, of course, the elderly, well-to-do of East Anglia didn't make much of a mark on the web, so he'd enquire elsewhere. As the months went on, he gained a bit of perspective, and became more selective about the research he did. He didn't spend much time on people like the vicar of Little Haxstead. The chances of him having any link to the crooks whose paths Nate had crossed were on the slim side.

As for Newbold, he came across as a standard rich businessman, working for one of the hi-tech Silicon Fen companies that abounded near Cambridge. The way he'd tailored the house-sitting contract marked him out as a tosser, but you could hardly hang a man for that. There were no untoward connections in his past that rang alarm bells.

Nate got up to switch on the light. It was after nine and the shadows of the trees on the paving outside had lost their sharp edges. Probably time for some food. He walked across the quarry tiles to the aging fridge freezer. Inevitably, Speck sauntered in at that moment and rubbed herself against his legs.

'Cupboard love, you treacherous cat.' He bent down to stroke her all the same. No wonder she'd adopted him. He was a soft touch where she was concerned.

He hadn't remembered to go shopping, but there was still half of the crusty loaf he'd bought the day before. Nate hacked off chunks and ate it with cheese and pickle, washed down with a couple of cans of Adnams. He was half-conscious of the trees and pathways that made up the gardens at Two Wells Farm, as the greys turned to indigoes and purples. Most of his mind was taken up with the day. He ought to have asked Steph more about Ruby Fawcett. She'd got as far as telling him about her work, and the fact that she'd trust her with anything from the care of her pot plants to her life, if the need should arise. That had been sufficient, but, having met her, Nate found he wanted to know more. She and Steph were an odd match, chalk and cheese on the face of it, yet they'd remained close friends since childhood. Dim and distant snippets of information came back to him now. Hadn't Steph mentioned something about Ruby on one of the family holidays they'd shared, way back when they were kids? Something about her best friend's mother having taken her off travelling? He vaguely remembered Steph sounding fed up about it. But maybe it had been some other friend. It was all too long ago to remember clearly.

After he'd finished eating, he did his usual walk, once round the perimeter of the house, looking out along the lane that led towards the village. Better safe than sorry.

Something woke Nate with a start around two in the morning, but he could see through the curtains that the security lights hadn't come on. For a moment he focused on listening, but he was distracted by memories of the dream he'd been having. Ruby Fawcett still filled his mind's eye. He lay flat on his back and let the image and its effects fade. Then he turned over, and closed his eyes. Hell. Was that why he hadn't wanted to turn her away?

It went without saying that it wouldn't do, for a myriad of reasons. Nate pressed his face into the pillow. Her recent break-up was probably the least of them.

Whether it was because of Damien Newbold's paintings, my long early evening nap, or my pizza binge I wasn't sure, but I didn't sleep well that night. When my mind wasn't on the pictures it strayed back to Luke, floating between an image of him laughing, after we'd come back from our last bike ride together, to the look in his eyes when he'd had to explain to me what he'd done. I wasn't sure which made me more miserable.

It was hard to banish the thoughts, and they almost made me forget physical discomfort, but not quite. It was incredibly hot. Eventually I caved in and slid the sash window open at the top, issuing an invitation to every no-good roaming the Common to come on in and see what was on offer at my place. Once again I rued the fact that Damien Newbold had told me to sleep downstairs.

Before I returned to bed I pulled the curtain back for a moment to look out into the night. Dim lights lit the Common's footpaths, both right next to the house, as well as over on the other side of the grass, by the river, but between these little pools of comfort there were vast shadowy areas – peppered with caravans, half-erected tents and stalls – where anyone might be lurking.

Disconcerted, I went back to bed and lay there, my ears straining for the possible sound of someone outside, easing up the bottom sash.

Thanks to only achieving sleep by three or so, I woke late and lay there in my so-called bed, stretching so that the springs creaked and moaned. It was only a knock at the door that ensured I got up at all. Hell, who could it be?

I was still in my night things and this now seemed a bit embarrassing, given that it was ten past ten on a weekday.

I had contorted myself around the furniture, and was making for the hall at top speed, when I felt a sudden pain in the sole of my right foot. The knocking came again, firmer this time, so I didn't stop to investigate, but limped along to open up.

'Sorry to disturb you,' Damien's postman said, a smirk spreading across his face. 'Package for Mr Newbold that wouldn't go through the letterbox.' He handed me a jiffy bag, together with a couple of junk mail envelopes, and sloped off up the path to the house on the other side of Midsummer Passage, turning once to look back at me over his shoulder.

I put the post down on the hall table. What had happened to my foot? Each time I put my weight on it, pain shot through my heel. I sat down in an ungainly position to find out what was wrong. It didn't take long. A piece of glass, broken into a sharp shard, and quite a decent size too. My mind strayed back to the blood on the rug as I picked it out and deposited it in the drawing room bin.

I must have been near the fireplace when I'd stepped on it. I went over to check for any other stray bits that might be lurking there. Before long I found a second, jammed in between two of the floorboards. My DMs were clearly essential on health and safety grounds.

The shower Damien Newbold had instructed me to use was downstairs, next to the cloakroom where I'd changed the day before and a boot room, off which came a back door to the garden.

The boot room was full of mud and spiders, so I was braced for the horrors that the shower might present. In fact, all was well. The new day was already beginning to heat up, like the one before it, and the one before that. The sun penetrated the shower room's obscured glass, making the clean, white wall tiles gleam. I adjusted the water temperature so it was warm, rather than hot, and let the jets run over my head, closing my eyes.

In the kitchen, I decided to eat before I did any clearing up. Although I hadn't been food shopping, I'd got a banana and a reasonably inoffensive cereal bar in my rucksack, so I fetched those, and made myself a coffee using a spoonful of Damien Newbold's instant. He had some little canisters and a machine for making proper stuff, but the complexities of this seemed too great at the moment.

It occurred to me that Damien Newbold might have left some milk in the fridge, given how hard it always is to make sure everything's finished off before one goes away.

Well, opening the fridge door was interesting. Damien had certainly found this aspect of waste-free housekeeping particularly challenging. Not only was there milk in the door – a two litre bottle, three-quarters full – there were also two packets of smoked salmon, an unused pint of double cream and two punnets of strawberries. Inside the dairy drawer there were packets of Brie, Stilton and Roquefort. Not to mention champagne on the fridge's bottle shelf and some posh pâté.

I shoved all his stuff on to the top shelf; then at least I could isolate some space for my food, when I got it. As I moved the smoked salmon I glanced at the use-by date. Monday 8th June, three days' time. Given he hadn't just gone for the weekend, it, plus most of this other stuff, would be off by the time Damien Newbold got back. Crazy. I was tempted to go freegan and pinch it for my own use, but it seemed too dishonest. And anyway, I didn't much fancy eating his food.

Back at the kitchen table, nibbling at my cereal bar, it occurred to me that if Damien Newbold's fridge contents was anything to go by, he must have walked out of his life in very much the same way as I had: right in the middle of things.

In the end, I didn't fancy the banana after the cereal bar. In the heat of the room it came to me that the kitchen bin smelt bad. I went to investigate. Hmm, mackerel skins. On top of a lot of other rubbish. That would explain it. To be fair, I hadn't even thrown away my takeaway pizza box yet. I went to grab it, then wrenched the overstuffed bag out of Damien's Brabantia bin, and made my way through the boot room to the back door.

Outside, sunlight saturated the view, bouncing off the pale Cambridge bricks of the garden wall and the flagstone paving. Large pots were dotted around. One contained a cistus, its hot pink flowers in full show, another a clematis which sprawled over a trellis. A long trough was crowded with lavender, its scent filling the air as I brushed past.

Damien had three wheelie bins, each labelled with instructions from the council. After scanning them, I dumped the pizza box in the green one, then lifted the lid of the black bin, hoisting the rubbish bag up. I was just about to let it drop when something caught my eye. I paused for a moment.

More glass. And not just glass, but a broken mirror. The shard I had stepped on had been ordinary glass, and there in the bin, on top of the mirror frame, was a broken whisky tumbler. My mind flicked to the mantelpiece, with the seascape above it that looked so out of place.

I put my bag of rubbish in at last and walked slowly back into the cool of the house.

Chapter Four

Nate spent the morning with a prospective house-sitting client, Pippa Craven. She had an Elizabethan place just outside Bury St Edmunds: a real Aladdin's cave, full of paintings, statues and wall hangings. He put her at around forty. She was very smart, with a perfectly executed pixie crop and a well-cut purple dress. It turned out she was considering relocating to Paris, to be with her boyfriend of six months, but wanted to try out living together before burning her boats. As an art collector, she couldn't risk letting to tenants. Touching that she had such faith in his outfit. Nate imagined someone like Barry, one of his regular sitters, plonking around amongst the canvases. Perhaps not. But Jamie was lighter on his feet. He'd do.

Nate got back into the Volvo on the shingled drive, thinking of Pippa's determination to check things out before selling up. Had some kind of past trouble made her cautious? Funny to think how cavalier he'd been on the subject of risk just a few short years ago. When Jack had taken Nate on to help with his PI business he'd told him to take more care. Nate had laughed it off, thinking it was only his personal safety that was at stake.

Once he got back to Two Wells Farm he called Steph. He wanted to know if Ruby was the childhood friend she'd talked about, all those years before.

'Wow – you've got a good memory,' she said. 'But you always were one for details. Yes, that's right.'

'And I remember you were cross because her mother had taken her off travelling.'

'So I was. Blimey, I'd almost forgotten that myself, it was so long ago. I think we'd made plans to do things over the summer, but then Eve – that's Ruby's mum – dragged her away and ruined everything.'

'So does she come from a rich family? Were they off somewhere exotic?'

Steph sounded surprised. 'Oh no. It wasn't like that. They were sort of middle class, I suppose, like us. Ruby's grandparents were both teachers. Eve had Ruby very young, before she was ready to settle down, so Ruby spent a lot of time living with them. But every so often, Eve would reappear and take Ruby off, claiming she was ready to start afresh. Then after a bit she'd run out of money, and they'd end up sleeping on one of her friends' sofas. And then Ruby would arrive back at her grandparents' place again.'

'Shit. That must have played havoc with her schooling.' And perhaps that was why he'd sensed Ruby was tough, too. She'd have to have been.

'Yes, she did well academically, considering. That was thanks to her grandparents being able to coach her.'

'They sound great.'

There was a pause. 'They were,' Steph said. 'They were killed in a car crash whilst Ruby was at university. You can imagine the effect that had.'

He could. Ruby had spent an awful lot of time fending for herself.

I don't know what sent me back upstairs to Damien Newbold's bedroom. I suppose the two discoveries I'd made since I'd arrived – the broken glass in the bin, and the nude paintings – were linked in my mind because they triggered the same reaction: that feeling that there was more to come. And that it wasn't going to be pleasant.

The day before, I'd been glad to leave the bedroom behind. Now I wanted to look at the pictures more closely. Who had the artist been? It must have been someone commissioned by Damien Newbold, of course. What on earth must they have thought of him, each time he presented them with yet another female to commit to oils? Though perhaps it might depend on just how often he put in a request.

But there were no dates on the paintings, and no signatures either, except on the one between the two windows. Someone called 'Nico' had signed the picture of the happy woman, and now I looked more closely, the style of that painting was quite different from the rest. I peered at his signature. He'd made a strange little mark, like a hat, next to his name. Not that that told me anything and, in any case, I didn't know what I was expecting to find out. Suddenly, standing there on the north side of the house, I felt chilly and was glad it was time to go outside and do something mundane, like food shopping.

There was a good deal of everyday reality to help me feel better out on Midsummer Common. Two women were trying to put up a large, red tent, each struggling to push an end of the same bendy pole into separate holes. Finally, one lost her grip and fell forwards onto the grass, which left them both roaring with laughter. A little further on, one man was cleaning Portaloos whilst another checked some cables that ran through a channel under the path that criss-crossed the grass.

Then I reached Riverside. A lady with ash-grey, corrugated hair, tied back in a loose ponytail, flew past me on her bike, followed closely by a man in a cream coloured sunhat riding a tricycle and staring intently at a handlebar-mounted GPS. You wouldn't get that in Saxwell St Andrew.

It was on my way back from the supermarket that I got Steph's text: Coming over to see you. Presume you're in?

I sent a message back: No need. Really. Everything fine.

Quick as a flash another one popped up: I shall presume for the sake of our friendship that you want to see me really. Be there at half-two. Steph.

It felt as though I'd only just beaten the shopping into submission when Steph turned up. As I steered her through to the kitchen I noticed she was holding something in her left hand and wearing the same expression as a traffic warden about to issue a parking fine.

'What is it?' I asked, keen to get any unpleasantness out of the way before we started on the tea and chat.

She grimaced. 'Sorry. It's from Luke.' She put the envelope on the kitchen table between us as she sat down, and then pushed it a little further towards me when I failed to pick it up.

'When did you see him?'

'He came over and knocked at our door yesterday evening.' She looked across at me. 'It has to be said, that shows how keen he was to get a message through to you. I don't imagine he thought he'd get a friendly reception from me. I was tempted to chuck a bucket of water over him.'

'A bucket of water?'

'Well, obviously, I'd have considered sick, if I'd thought I could get it. But water would be to hand, in a way that sick wouldn't. Anyway, the point is, I didn't go inviting him in, or suggesting he get in touch, or anything like that.'

'Good.'

'Everyone's being foul to him, I expect you can imagine. Judy's even banned him from the village shop, and you know how keen she always is to maximise sales. I should think she'll miss his beer money. He's had a couple of people abusing him in the street too.'

'Did you see all this happening?'

'Well, no … He told me most of it.'

'Hmm. You must have been out chatting on the doorstep for quite some time.'

Steph made a face. 'He did try to keep me talking, but I don't honestly think he was looking for sympathy; trying to glean information more like.'

I raised an eyebrow.

'About you, of course. He wanted to know where you were staying. And don't look at me like that. If you even have to ask whether I told him or not then our friendship is at an end.'

'Okay. So why are you looking so shifty then?'

She sighed. 'It's nothing really. But I think he must have talked to Robin, too. He knew I'd nipped over to see you yesterday.' She leant forward and rested her forehead on her right hand. 'So I think he at least guesses that you can't have gone far, and, of course, Cambridge is one of the nearest towns you could have chosen to get lost in.'

I went over to the kitchen window and opened it wider, not that it made much difference to the heat. I could feel my trousers sticking to my legs. When I turned back towards the room Steph's brow was still furrowed.

'God, don't worry,' I said. 'He's not going to go trekking round the whole of Cambridge looking for me. And I could be in Newmarket or Bury St Edmunds for all he knows. In any case, he's not likely to push it. It's true that I don't want him in my sight at the moment, but when all's said and done, if he did come looking I'd just tell him where to go and stuff himself. Heck, I'd enjoy it, in fact. You can stop agonising.'

'Do you think you should read his letter?'

I recognised that look now. The brow had smoothed out and the eyes were alight with interest. 'No.' I shoved it into my back jeans pocket. 'Let's have some tea instead.'

I'd bought a coffee cake, and we sat there, stuffing

ourselves, whilst I wondered how tea could still seem like the best drink in the world when it was thirty degrees outside.

'Nate hasn't contacted you again about me being here, has he?' I asked. I'd been worried he might have second thoughts, after what I'd overheard him say to her.

'He called to thank me for recommending you.'

I gave her a sharp look, but couldn't detect any dishonesty. 'You two aren't a bit alike to look at.'

'I know.' She took a sip of her tea. 'His Mum's Irish – that's where he gets his colouring from.'

'You seem close.'

She nodded. 'Definitely my favourite cousin. Our parents used to take us on holiday together until we were about ten. But then Nate's mum had a difficult pregnancy with his youngest sister, and it all stopped.' She sighed. 'I got the impression his mum and dad's marriage went through a rough patch around then. They came through it, but I think that was a factor too.'

'Shame. Does he have kids himself?'

She shook her head. 'Confirmed bachelor.'

I gave her a look.

'There have been women in the past. And he certainly doesn't lack eager candidates, but ... well, he prefers his independence.'

I wondered. It wasn't normally as straightforward as that in my experience.

'It's no use you looking at me like that,' she said, catching my expression. 'It's just the way he is. No psychoanalysis required.'

Behind Steph's back, as we chatted, I could see the house on the opposite side of Midsummer Passage. Like Damien Newbold's place, it had a pair of bay windows facing towards the Common, but whereas the door to River

House faced that way, towards the river, the door of this other place, Oswald House, opened onto the passageway. It meant I could see any comings and goings from the kitchen.

The night before, when I'd popped in for a glass of water, I'd spotted a girl with dark hair talking to a man on the doorstep. And then a girl with curly, blonde hair had come out whilst I ate my lunch, just before Steph had arrived. I quickly realised that having this view from the kitchen, along with the entertainment of the fair from the front of the house, was a bonus. Once you know you're housebound for most of each day, things like that become significant. It was in my nature to want to find things out – I'd made my living from it, in fact – and it was automatic to start probing for information. And then there was Damien Newbold himself. If I'd known of his existence earlier I could probably have put him in my latest book. He was shaping up as a likely candidate.

'So what do you think?' Steph said, looking at me suddenly.

I sprang to attention. 'I'm so sorry. I had a really rough night last night. I think I was drifting a bit. What did you say?'

'Oh, it doesn't matter. I mean I can just stop if I'm boring you.'

'Go on.' I gave her puppy eyes. 'You know you have to forgive me when I'm at a low ebb.'

She sighed elaborately and took another swig of tea. 'I was asking what you thought of this place. And of Damien Newbold. I mean it's my dream, to take on a job like this. I love looking round other people's houses. I keep talking to Robin about moving, but it's not really because I want a new place. Our house is fine; I just want the excuse to go burrowing round other people's homes.'

So I filled her in on everything I'd found out so far, though

I had a feeling it might be against Nate Bastable's company ethics. 'It's probably all covered by some house-sitters' oath,' I said. 'In fact, you're not even supposed to be here really. It says on page two of my instructions. "No visitors whatsoever without prior agreement from the owner."'

'But you took no notice.' Steph curled a strand of hair round her left ear. 'That's really touching.'

'Well, since Nate let you in yesterday I thought there was no going back.'

'I see. Thanks.'

'Oh,' I said, my eye caught by movement just over her shoulder, out in Midsummer Passage. 'He's there again.'

Steph turned in her chair, following my gaze. 'What are you on about?'

It was the man I'd seen the night before, saying goodbye to the same girl on the doorstep of Oswald House.

'She's quite a stunner, isn't she?' said Steph. 'Gorgeous colouring; such clear, pale skin with that dark hair.'

'I'm trying to work them out,' I said. 'The people that live there, I mean. I think the stunner, and a blonde girl I saw earlier, must be students, sharing the house. But what about that man who's leaving now?'

Steph shrugged. 'Looks too old.'

I nodded. 'But too young to be a parent. And it's not quite the end of term yet, so too soon for him to be coming to pick up her stuff, anyway.'

'Blimey, Ruby,' Steph said. 'One day in River House and you're turning into Miss Marple, stuck in your own little microcosm.'

'Well, I haven't got much choice as far as that goes, have I?' I picked up a stray walnut from my plate and popped it into my mouth. The man and the girl were still talking on the doorstep.

'He could be anyone.'

'I know,' I agreed. 'But she looks sad, doesn't she?' And there was something odd about him too. The way he leant against the house wall; that eager stance. He was rather closer to her, physically, than he needed to be.

'All right; she does look sad. A bit like you, in fact, but without the snippy attitude. She might have just been chucked off her course for all we know. Perhaps he's broken the news. Let me guess. You were wondering if there was something going on between them?'

I nodded. 'He's clearly hanging around.'

'Well, he looks respectable ...'

We both knew that meant nothing. She was right though; he did. He was wearing a herringbone suit, for heaven's sake. And bicycle clips. No one wearing that kind of kit could be up to anything too nefarious.

Steph leant forward and squeezed my shoulder with a hot hand. 'You don't think maybe your view's a bit skewed at the moment?'

I decided not to dignify that question with a response. It would be a shame to come to blows. Instead, I asked her about her work, and then we chatted about everything and nothing for a few minutes.

At last she got up to leave, though she made me show her the nudes before she went. As she looked at the paintings she shuddered. 'You're right, you know, Ruby. I'd say there is something pretty odd about Damien Newbold.'

When she had gone, worry drove me to my laptop. I'd hardly looked at the material for my book since I'd found out about Luke, but I couldn't funk it forever. I had a contract to fulfil and there would be bills to pay. More sizeable ones, now that I wasn't going to be sharing them. Hell, what a mess.

I hadn't written up any of the material from my most recent set of interviews. I'd hardly been in the mood. It was immediately after I'd got back from my last research trip that all the upset blew up. Well, if you go away for three whole days, what can you expect?

As I sat down at the computer I was conscious of Luke's envelope in my back pocket, but I still didn't want to open it. I felt a huge, boiling rage. Did he really have so little sense of what he'd done that he thought I'd be receptive to a letter? I wanted to go on ignoring the whole thing, altogether, for a long while yet. Not easy with the book to write.

'I don't give a damn what you have to say on the subject,' I muttered under my breath, attempting to banish Luke from my mind as I opened an email from my publicist. But the contents of the message made our recent history even harder to ignore, and my head started to pound. What had just happened could get me a whole load of media attention of the sort I'd rather not have. I wondered what to do, and spent some time trying to order information; I couldn't manage anything more creative.

By nine o'clock the creaky bed loomed large in the drawing room, in spite of its diminutive size. The time for me to try to sleep in it was drawing nearer. I was determined to stay up really late, in the hope that I'd be able to drop off more easily. I thought I'd begin by making use of Damien Newbold's piano and went hunting for some sheet music. The bookcase nearby seemed the most likely place, but when I pulled out some promising-looking publications they turned out to be upmarket magazines with swanky, matt covers. Then I noticed that the piano stool was the sort where the seat lifts up, but the space underneath was empty. No music – unless it was very well hidden. So much for Steph's fantasies about a man of culture. I tried playing 'Clair de Lune' from memory but kept hitting the wrong keys. The piano itself must have been tuned recently though. All the notes were in perfect order. I put Newbold down as a man who kept up appearances.

In the end, I went to explore the basement, which I would have done later anyway. I'd poked my head round the door the day before, after I'd eaten my pizza, and it had looked quite inviting. The uncarpeted wooden stairs descended into the middle of a vast, open-plan room, taking up the entire area of the house. Damien Newbold had set it up as a sitting-cum-recreation room and it was as relaxed and slouchy as the drawing room was formal. There were lots of lamps dotted around: tall standards with white paper shades, and squat angular ones sitting on side tables and shelves. As I put them on, one by one, the duskiness outside took on the appearance of a velvety, midnight blue in contrast.

A huge, squashy sofa ran along half the side of the room nearest the Common, with a window over it that reached to just above ground level outside. At the other end, a row of windows looked out onto a small paved area, with French windows in the middle, opening in front of steps that led up to the back garden. I'd seen them from above, and they emerged just behind Damien Newbold's study, well to the right of the boot room. The corner under the boot room itself was home to a look-at-me, state-of-the-art TV and I flopped down on the sofa, ready to take full advantage.

I flicked through endless channels, trying to find something that would remove Luke from my mind. How like life that one of the films showing happened to be *Parenthood*. Not something I wanted to focus on right now; to have gone from trying for a baby to this in a matter of days made me feel hollow. More flicking produced little choice. There was a game show where people were wobbling round on giant, slippery balls; a documentary about the mis-selling of insurance policies; and something about the secret life of snails, which ought to have been soothing, but wasn't. I pressed the standby button and went to a long bench with cupboards in the base. It had DVD storage written all over it. When I looked inside I found Damien Newbold was even more organised than I'd hoped. He'd made a list of all the films he owned on the inside of the cupboard door; lots to choose from, and lots of recent stuff I hadn't managed to catch at the cinema. It was hard to read the handwritten inventory at an angle in the half light, but I could see it was only stuck to the door with Blu-Tack, so I pulled it away, ready to bring it over to one of the lamps for a better look. It was as I touched it that I realised the texture of the paper was odd. It felt familiar, but out of context. The moment my fingers came into contact with its glossy reverse side, I knew what it was. Damien Newbold had written his DVD list on the back of a photograph.

I turned it over, and the face that looked back at me was a face that I knew. It was the woman who beamed down from between the windows in Damien Newbold's bedroom; the one who had been painted by Nico. This new portrait homed in on her head and shoulders, but even so you could see she was clothed. The photo revealed part of a V-necked dress and she was wearing a hat with an exaggeratedly broad brim. She was laughing to the camera, as though perhaps the photographer had got her to strike a dramatic pose, and she found it a huge joke. The paper was far better quality than you'd get from most processing services, and the whole thing had a classy feel. It was arty, and the woman it depicted definitely had a touch of star quality. Just as in the bedroom portrait, she looked happy, caught up on a wave of bliss. And yet there she'd been, her face hidden from view. I was about to put the photo back, although it seemed entirely wrong for it to be down there, when something else caught my eye. Halfway down the list of DVDs, on the reverse side, some writing had been crossed out. The person wielding the pen had made a thorough job of it, and the words had been obliterated.

I played the whole of *Skyfall* without taking any of it in, despite the fact that I'd chosen it especially as easy watching because I'd seen it before.

How many people write lists of all their DVDs? Wouldn't you normally just go and look, if you wanted a reminder of what was there? Was it possible that Damien Newbold had whiled away an evening writing on the back of the photograph, simply to indicate his disdain for its subject? As a way of saying, you are nothing to me, and here's what I'll do with your picture? But, if that was the case, then why did he have a painting of that very same woman in pride of place on his bedroom wall?

And so it was that I lay in bed in the drawing room once more that night, as sleepless as ever, listening to three of Damien Newbold's antique clocks counting their way into the small hours. I'd opened the window again, and that was turning out to be a mixed blessing. Friday nights in Cambridge were noisier than in Saxwell, I discovered. People came past quite regularly, sounding steadily drunker as time wore on; presumably students and young career types, making their way home to grotty digs or yuppie flats, further up the river. As a backdrop to the occasional shouts and bursts of laughter, there was a smattering of traffic noise. Sirens periodically screamed their way along Victoria Avenue or Elizabeth Way.

The events of the day whirled round in my head, but at last the reflections became blurred at the edges, the sounds outside less distinct, and reality started to fade away.

The noise jolted me awake again with a start. Ringing. Hell, what time was it? I reached out and scrabbled for my bag, under the armchair by the bed. As I tried to find my mobile, my mind became focused enough to realise that the noise wasn't coming from there.

House phone? I scrabbled with the blanket and hoisted myself off the low bed, but when I reached the hall, the extension there was quiet. I had to pause, steady myself and think. Behind me. It was coming from somewhere in the drawing room after all. I was fully awake now, and at last I was regaining some sense of direction. Somewhere beyond the piano. Finally I had it: a mobile, which had been left, balanced on top of one of the books in the bookcase.

'Hello?' I must have got to it just before voicemail kicked in.

There was a moment's pause before a woman's voice came on the line, deep and slurred: 'I might have bloody known ... And who the hell are you, bitch?'

Chapter Five

The woman who'd called rang off before I could answer her. I'd wanted to explain that I wasn't, in fact, some one night stand of Damien's; had never even met the man and was beginning to wish I'd never heard of him either. Because she must have been imagining just the opposite, of course. She had naturally assumed that where Damien Newbold's mobile was, Damien was too. Ergo, I must be with him, in the dead of night, close enough to his side to pick up his phone and answer for him.

Well, I couldn't blame her for latching onto that conclusion. Most people do, after all, keep their mobiles with them. It is their *raison d'être*, when all's said and done. But dear Damien hadn't taken his. Maybe after the row he'd had, involving the glass and the mirror, he'd decided he'd prefer not to be encumbered with it. He might have had the consideration to turn the bloody thing off though. Or he could have just taken it with him and screened his calls. Instead, he'd landed me with his crappy fallout.

I veered between anger and anguish over the case of my mistaken identity. I didn't like the idea that someone I didn't even know was wishing me ill.

By four o'clock in the morning I was sitting in the kitchen, drinking hot chocolate and eating Damien Newbold's strawberries. Bugger him. I was definitely owed after my stay in his house so far. And since I was up anyway, I was thankfully not asleep when the next interruption occurred. An alarm going off – nothing as loud as a burglar or smoke alarm, instead it was a persistent chiming. If I hadn't known I'd already switched Damien Newbold's phone off, I'd have thought that was the source. For some reason the noise didn't even set my heart racing, whereas the phone ringing earlier had thrown me into a panic. This time I just dragged myself to my feet, pushing my hot chocolate to one side, and padded back up the hallway towards the front door.

It was soon clear where the noise was coming from. The parcel I'd taken in for Damien Newbold that morning was still on the hall table, where I'd left it whilst I pulled the glass out of my foot. Whatever was inside stopped bonging, just as I reached it. Right.

I wasn't sure if it might give a repeat performance and I hovered next to the table, wondering what to do. The strawberries were one thing, but opening someone's private post didn't feel right. And what else might be in the packet, along with the alarm clock or phone or whatever it was? If there was any other little message for Damien, I didn't want to be on the receiving end.

At last, I made up my mind and marched back down the stairs to the basement, already bathed in the early morning light from the French windows. I stuffed the package in the cupboard with the DVDs and the photo, putting a couple of cushions over the top of it for good measure.

When you only begin your night's sleep proper at five a.m. it's a considerable disadvantage to have an all-day festival going on outside your bedroom window the following morning. I managed to sleep until the first bands started up, with only the occasional jolt into brief consciousness before then, when some sudden or violent noise occurred.

Once the band called Blood Metal came on there was no hope for it. I admitted defeat and got up. Peeking round the drawing room curtains to get an idea of what was going on, I met the gaze of a small child, her face decorated with tiger stripes. Yet another shock to the system and a cue to shape up, get clean and into coping mode.

I was going to have to call Nate Bastable; that was the decision I came to as I stood in the shower, shampoo suds streaming off my hair and down my arms. I didn't want to go running for advice but, realistically, I needed to know what to do about the phone. Okay, and partly I just wanted to make a point too. I was still quite convinced that Damien had abandoned it to avoid dealing with awkward callers, and why should I have to put up with the results? Not in my job description, thank you very much Mr Newbold.

And then there was the parcel. It came to me that I didn't actually know where Damien Newbold had gone. If he was in the Bahamas, he would no doubt prefer to deal with his post when he got home, but if he was away on business in London, he might want things forwarding. Admittedly, probably not practical joke parcels that woke you up in the middle of the night, but ...

And again, I felt that undeniable desire for revenge. I wanted to forward him a parcel that would disturb his night's sleep. Serve him right. And presumably someone else had felt just the same way, which was why the bloody thing was here in the first place.

If sending it on wasn't an option, I wanted to get permission to open it, or destroy it. Otherwise I'd be constantly listening out, expecting it to do the bonging thing again.

Standing in the kitchen, my hair drying rapidly in the warm room, I picked up my phone and dialled.

Nate smiled when he saw Ruby's number on his mobile; the worry about why she was calling came a split-second later. He dragged one of the wooden chairs out from under the scrubbed oak table, and reached for his half-drunk coffee as he pressed the green button.

Things moved fast in Newbold's household. Already

an abusive phone call in the middle of the night, and the delivery of what Ruby called a 'prank' package, with its alarm call. Nate leant forward in his seat as she talked, elbows on the table. He could tell from her tone she wasn't spooked – just irritated and venting. But there was something in all this that made him uneasy. 'I don't much like the sound of any of that.'

There was a moment's pause, but then she spoke quickly. 'I was just having a rant; it's no big deal.'

'Ruby—'

'Seriously.'

Nate leant back in his seat and closed his eyes for a moment. She shouldn't have to put up with this, and if he let her, then it was his fault as much as it was Newbold's. And as it happened, he'd had a message from Barry to say he was unexpectedly free. He'd been on a break at Cromer, but had driven his wife home early when his sister-in-law had called to say she'd broken up with her bloke. Now – Nate gathered – both wife and sister were installed in his two-up two-down, talking twenty-four seven about why all men were bastards. Barry was keen to take on any work available, as soon as.

'What if one of my other sitters took over? I've got someone available now. You might be more comfortable with family.'

Nate heard her draw in a sharp breath. It was followed by a long pause. Well, maybe not then. After what Steph had told him, it probably figured. Her grandparents were dead, he hadn't heard any other relations mentioned, and who knew what her mum might be up to.

'Or it goes without saying that Steph would have you.' Hell, he'd have her. The thought came unbidden.

'It'd be like being in a goldfish bowl, with all the village cats staring in at me.'

Which Nate had known already, before he'd suggested it. And things tended to get more expensive when you suddenly found yourself single. Staying in a hotel for a few weeks wasn't likely to be an option. 'You said the woman on the phone sounded drunk?'

'As a lord.'

'And did you manage to explain who you were, or that the charming Mr Newbold wasn't in residence?'

'She hung up too fast.'

He was less than happy about that, but before he could reply Ruby added, 'It's really nothing I can't handle.' She was aiming for breezy again. 'Might it be worth just talking to Damien Newbold to see what he says about the package and the call? Assuming you can get hold of him, that is.'

Nate's resolve was ebbing away, like sand around his feet being pulled by the tide. How could he possibly chuck her out? 'I can get hold of him,' he said, eventually. 'Already spoken to him on a mobile number since he left, in fact, so presumably he has more than one.'

'Maybe he's taken his work one with him, and left his personal one here.'

'Quite possibly.'

'Shall I wait to hear back from you, once you've spoken to him?' Ruby's voice conjured up her image, those eyes, and the high cheekbones.

Bugger. 'All right then. But Ruby?'

'Yes?'

'You will tell me if anything else strikes you as odd, won't you?'

'Of course.' But she said it too quickly.

The conversation hadn't put me in a great mood for work. I could tell Nate pitied me, and didn't really think I should stay at River House. Ironically, it was also out of pity that

45

he was keeping me on. It shouldn't matter, of course; having a roof over my head was what counted. Officially. I put it out of my mind and went to search for somewhere to set up camp with my laptop.

Damien Newbold's study seemed made for the purpose, just along the hall, behind the drawing room. I'd hardly been in there, but now I looked properly I found a large desk, side on to the window, with a bulky wooden swivel chair, for those who reject the more comfortable, modern sort. Damien had chosen dark green, swagged curtains for the room. They covered at least a third of the glass and I tugged at them, feeling irritated. They refused to be pulled back properly, so I had to submit to wandering round in fish-tank gloom, peering at the set-up. Everything was tidy and subdued. The desk had a pile on it, but it was a neat pile – one that had been arranged and left just so. An A4 leather-bound address book sat on top of some other stuff. I sat down for a moment, ready to push the heap aside, but the room was too much somebody else's. The kitchen would do better. I went out again, closing the door on the dust motes and silence.

Trying to launch back into my work felt similar to dipping into a cold, stagnant lake. But I hadn't got time for niceties. The deadline was looming and I was already way behind schedule. The process of going through the interviews I'd done filled me with a sense of self-loathing. I'd never faced up to it before, but I knew all my books had been voyeuristic. Whether I was focusing on weird parenting, or sibling relationships, I was always delving into people's personal lives for my own benefit. It was just this current one that had taken my research to a higher level of prurience and made me see my work for what it was. I should never have embarked on the topic – the moment I'd done the first interview I'd realised I'd taken a wrong turn, but by then it had been too late. And, now the subject was one I found personally difficult, there was all the more need to tackle it without flinching. The business with Luke felt like a punishment; my just desserts.

I put in a couple of hours but the need to eat broke my concentration. Over a plateful of toast I began to browse the web. Typing 'Damien Newbold' into Google was irresistible. I had a strong desire to know what made him tick.

Well, money for a start, evidently, though that wasn't news to me. You could see as much by looking round his house. The Internet filled in some of the background to his riches though, telling me he'd made a mint working for a technology consultancy called TomorrowTech. Naff name, but it was clearly doing the business as far as investors were concerned. There were several interviews with Damien in the local business press, commenting on various innovations, and the company's successful launch on the stock exchange.

I carried on scrolling through the Google results and eventually found something that had been posted on a technology blog only a day earlier.

'According to our informant, Damien Newbold of TomorrowTech is about to hit the industry press headlines again. There's talk of a significant new invention which could lead to record profits for the company next year, spelling great news for shareholders and sealing Newbold's reputation as TomorrowTech's greatest asset.'

So, Damien Newbold might be a weirdo, but he was a clever weirdo.

Then I Googled his company, and found it was based on a science park, just to the north of Cambridge. I scanned the media section for information on his rumoured new innovation, but TomorrowTech's latest press release dated back three weeks, and there was no mention of his 'significant new invention' in any of their recent news.

Could the rumour and his going away be related? Perhaps he was at some test lab somewhere, working on his new idea in secret. Maybe he was the sort that dropped everything for work, and he had simply flown out of the door, leaving smoked salmon, mobile phones and irate girlfriends without another thought. I let my mind drift away, mulling the package and the phone and what it all meant.

My attempts at doing more proper work were half-hearted and in the end I spent the rest of the afternoon investigating my list of chores. By eight-thirty I'd cleaned the bathroom, using a special brush to push non-existent gunk out of the Jacuzzi-style spray holes; vacuumed each of the middle-floor bedrooms; paused for a bolognese supper and then dusted some bookcases. It was slightly galling, particularly since it all looked spotless anyway. Then again I was being paid to do a job, and, if I did it well enough, maybe I could get other house-sitting work to tide me over until I'd decided what to do.

I was about to start dusting the basement for a change of scenery when there was a rap at the door. I opened up and found Nate standing there.

'I had to drop off a contract in Cambridge,' he said, 'so I thought I might as well stop by instead of ringing, if it's not inconvenient.'

I was edgy, just at the sight of him. It didn't help that having a roof over my head was under his control. 'No, it's fine.' I stood back so he could step into the hallway. 'Would you like a lager?'

'That'd be great,' he said, following me through to the kitchen.

I fumbled about with glasses, and poured us each a Beck's. 'What news of Mr Newbold?'

He pulled out a chair and looked up at me from under his fringe. There was a twinkle in his eye, and my fears of being chucked out receded. 'I hope you've got a strong stomach.' He took a swig of his drink.

'Explain.' I sat and swigged too. A bit too eagerly, in fact, as is my wont when I'm nervous.

'Newbold's just fed me a load of bullshit, and I'm about to pass it on to you.'

I took in his half-smile, and the wry look in his eyes.

'As far as the mobile goes, he was very apologetic.' He paused for a moment. 'As well he might be. He says he thought he'd left it on the train, and he tells me he's been on the phone to First Capital Connect's lost property desk almost constantly ever since.' His tone and the pausing said it all. 'Where exactly did you find the phone?'

I explained. 'I suppose you *could* accidentally leave your mobile on top of some books in a bookcase,' I added. 'If you were looking for a particular volume, and happened to have it in your hand.'

'Hmm,' Nate said.

'Still,' I went on, not giving him time to chip in further, 'if it is just girlfriend trouble then it's not likely to affect me. And I've got a thick skin. It'd take more than that to cause me any upset.' I'm sure the threat of losing my job enhanced my acting skills. 'So, what should I do with the phone?'

'He said keep it switched off, and he'll respond to any voicemail when he gets back.'

'Yeah, right.'

Nate smiled. 'And as to the package, he says it sounds like a silly prank and, once again, he's "terribly sorry you had to deal with it".'

'My turn to say hmm.'

'He says to take the thing outside and chuck it in the bin.'

'He doesn't even want me to open it? Or to see what's inside himself?'

'No,' Nate said. 'I think it's odd too. My guess would be he's had similar before and so there's nothing to find out. He certainly sounded genuinely laid back about it, as though it was run-of-the-mill stuff. It was only his attitude that made me relax, really. If he'd sounded edgy, it would have been another matter.'

But it had still bothered him, I could see that. It wasn't just that he didn't want me upset; he was on high alert too. I wondered why. Still, the main thing was, he'd decided to let things lie for now. 'So everything's okay then. That's great.'

He did another one of his pauses, his eyes on mine, so that I had to look away. Something told me he still wanted me gone. I was going to have to tread carefully.

'It's just a matter of seeing what happens next,' he said at last, draining his lager. 'Right, I'd better get out of your way.'

I walked him to the door. He turned for a moment. 'Ruby?'

'Yes?'

His glance met mine again for a second, but then he looked away. 'Actually, it doesn't matter. I'll see you soon.' And then he was gone.

Nate's visit left me feeling unsettled, but at least it answered what to do about the package; there would be no waiting for it to go off that night. I went down to the basement, opened the DVD cupboard and took the jiffy bag out from underneath the cushions.

If it were me, I'd have wanted to check inside at least. Still, there it was. I walked over to the French windows, undid the bolts and used the key from a small hook near the ceiling to open up. I'd got as far as climbing the steps to the bins, but paused before I chucked it in. The fact was, it *was* me. The package might have been addressed to Damien, but it was I who had had to deal with it. It still felt personal, even though it wasn't. And, now that Damien Newbold had said he wanted me to chuck it out, opening it up didn't seem so dishonest. I was just looking at something someone else had abandoned as trash.

Hmm. So I was planning to plunder another person's rubbish ... But it was too late now. My fingers were already sliding underneath the sticky fastening of the envelope.

It was a mobile. I turned it over in my hand, and then peered inside the jiffy bag, but there was no note. The outer screen was the sort that would show the number of an incoming call but it was a model that flipped open to reveal a larger interface. I fiddled about until I found the calendar function and there was the alarm, set to go off every morning at four a.m.

Of course, if Damien Newbold hadn't been away he would have opened the package and, assuming he was mystified, he would have explored it, just as I was doing, trying to find out what the game was. I was quite sure he would have seen the booby trap well before it disrupted his night's sleep. But maybe just knowing someone was trying to get at him would have been unnerving.

I looked up at the house from where I stood by the bins, thinking of everything I knew about its owner. I couldn't imagine him getting spooked by something like that.

Who had sent it? That was the question. I checked the phone's address book and looked for any other calendar entries; there were none. But there was one other obvious place to dig for information.

And that was where I found the message. The text said, simply: Made you look.

I caught my breath. It wasn't meant for me – of course it wasn't – but the mocking ill will hit home all the same.

Chapter Six

Nate stood in the kitchen back at Two Wells Farm. What was Newbold playing at? He wished he'd asked Ruby to show him the package now, but if she had, he wouldn't have been able to resist opening it. That would have been the action of a PI, and broken every rule in the house-sitting book. He took a deep breath. No use chucking in the game if you were going to get drawn back in at every second turn.

The game … That was exactly what it seemed like. Newbold hadn't sounded perturbed or surprised when Nate had told him what had been going on. He'd sounded amused.

I did throw the phone away after I'd read the text. Half of me felt I should keep it, in case it was ever something I wanted to show someone, but the other half knew I could never admit to Nate that I'd gone ahead and looked at it, against instructions. I noted the sender of the text's number before I ditched it, all the same. I wasn't sure what I was planning, but it seemed sensible not to burn my bridges.

Suddenly the house felt claustrophobic, as though there was something uneasy trapped in there with me. Outside the deep thud of music from the main stage still filled the air. I decided to walk up and down along the pathway, well within range of the house as per Damien's instructions, and get some space. I locked up and set the alarm.

The day had become overcast, and I was glad of the jumper I'd pulled on over my jeans. Strawberry Fair mid-evening is scuffed around the edges, losing its colour. The face-painted children, clutching their Pegasus helium balloons, had long since gone home in tears. Earlier, through the window, I'd seen a hairy-legged man dressed up as a fairy on top of a pair of stilts, but there was no sign of him either. Audiences for the music had thinned out, with most people huddled round the bars and food stalls, or lolling on the ground. A man dressed all in white was talking earnestly to himself as I went past.

At the first stage I came to, a woman with long black hair, save for one pronounced streak of grey, was dancing alone. She nodded to the music, dipping her knees in time to the beat. As I watched, one of the bangles she was wearing slipped from her wrist onto the ground, but she didn't seem to notice.

I needed to eat, and staying out here to get something seemed preferable to going back inside and brooding over everything that had happened that day. I went to join the queue for crêpes, peering round at River House as I stepped over a guy rope holding up one of the tents. I was keeping it in sight, complying with the letter of Damien Newbold's instructions. The bottom half of the house was masked by a caravan, a tent and a bouncy castle, deserted now in the gathering dusk. Even so, there were still a number of people around, and it didn't seem likely that anyone would do anything worse than having a pee in the front garden. The queues for the Portaloos were still long. All that beer had to go somewhere.

At last I reached the front of the crêpes queue and watched as the lady running the stall poured the batter over a large, round hotplate, swishing the mixture neatly into shape with her spatula. Hot fat hissed and steamed into the cooling air. She filled my crêpe with cheese and mushrooms and, as soon as I'd handed over my money, I turned to face towards the house again. I could move just a little closer, then eat and watch the world go by at the same time.

I sat down on the grass, hard up against a tent in my own

little space, away from a group who were lying on their backs, looking up at the sky, passing a cigarette between them. The smell of canvas, crêpe and tobacco filled my nostrils.

Suddenly my attention was caught by a couple holding hands. The female half was the girl with curly blonde hair from next door. She leant her head against her boyfriend's shoulder like someone who'd had too much of a good thing. I glanced around, but I couldn't see the sad housemate with the long, dark hair. My mind flicked to Mr Herringbone Suit. Perhaps she was holed up with him, somewhere in that big house of theirs. I pictured her – rather fascinated by his seriousness and maturity – and him ... Well, I knew what he would be fascinated by.

The noise of someone throwing up jolted me out of my reverie; the sound was uncomfortably close to where I was sitting. I glanced round and shifted further way. Thank God I'd already finished my crêpe.

In spite of everything going on around me, the text message kept creeping back into my mind. I should never have looked. It was as though I'd walked into Damien Newbold's life – stepped into his shoes almost – and I wasn't enjoying it. Should I dial the message sender when I got back? Not using my mobile, certainly; that wasn't a direct link I wanted to set up. I could use the house phone. But then whoever had sent the package would assume that Damien was there, and had got the message. If they answered, I could tell them what was going on, and where to stuff it, but if they just let it ring they'd be thinking they'd won, and he'd taken their bait.

And then maybe they'd make their next move ...

Always assuming the message had been meant for him. At the back of my mind something nagged. Could someone have known I was coming? Someone who sent the package knowing that Damien Newbold was never going to be the one receiving the parcel, getting woken by the alarm?

It was time to go back to the house really, but I put it off, and went to get myself a hot chocolate from one of the vans. The woman at the hatch yawned as she took my money, rubbing her eyes with the back of her hand before chucking the coins into a tin. The wind was high now, making me shiver, and I cupped my hands around the drink, grateful for its warmth.

I was being paranoid. It was unlikely that Damien had bothered to tell any of his contacts I was at River House, and Steph was the only person I'd told. Other than that it was just Nate who knew.

But still I wondered. Made you look. It was the wording that did it. Damien Newbold would have been bound to look. There would have been no triumph for the sender in achieving that end. What else was he going to do? If he'd opened the thing at all he'd quickly have seen all there was to see.

But in my case it was different. The package hadn't even been addressed to me and, as a result, the alarm had worked a treat. And then I'd been unable to resist opening it up at last; reading the message, allowing myself to get intimidated. Now that was a reason for the sender to crow.

Made you look.

And suddenly I thought of Luke. It was his fault I was stuck here, the stupid, shallow, selfish little shit. So on top of everything else, for whatever reason, I was now starting to feel scared. My eyes stung, and I blinked away the beginnings of tears as I finished my drink. My watch said quarter to ten. It really was time to be getting back.

Moments later I was standing at the top of the steps to the door of River House, fumbling with the lock. Inside, my hand hovered over the keypad for the alarm, my brain trying to make sense of something that jarred.

It took me a second to get it. The alarm wasn't sounding its warning beep, the one that tells you you need to key in the number to deactivate the system.

I paused there in the doorway, my brain trying to make sense of the situation. I couldn't have set it when I went out. Except I was sure that I had.

I looked around the hallway in the gloom. Everything was still. Perhaps the alarm had malfunctioned. Well, that would be just typical. I smiled inwardly. That must be it, because I was damn sure I had set it.

I closed the door behind me and switched on the hall light, taking off my boots and tucking them under the side table.

It was as I put my jacket back on the coat stand that I heard the noise. The tiniest sound: the faint creak of a floorboard. I stood motionless. Someone was in the house.

I was still within a few feet of the front door. I could make a dash for it. Get outside and use my mobile to call the police. I was turning on the ball of one foot, trying not to make a sound, when the study door started to open, slowly, silent on its hinges.

A woman stood looking at me: long, wild dark hair, her eyes flashing with amusement and malice. She held a cigarette in one hand, and a torn scrap of paper in the other. 'So I know who you are now,' she said, waving her cigarette in the direction of my file of information from Nate Bastable, which sat on the hall table.

And I knew who she was too. Woman number four. The woman not to be messed with. This was the woman in the portrait at the head of Damien Newbold's bed.

Chapter Seven

'I'm so glad we're talking in person this time,' the woman said, 'rather than over the phone. Much more convivial.'

She was wearing an arty, black cotton dress with a plunging neckline, and a large, green, perspex ring on the middle finger of her right hand.

'I had no idea Damien Newbold had left his mobile here until you called last night,' I said, catching up with the implication of her words. I hadn't recognised her voice, although I might have guessed if my adrenaline levels hadn't been distracting me.

'Damien Newbold, eh? Very formal. You've never met him then?' She didn't wait for an answer, but went on: 'I already knew he'd gone away. Told me he would, but neglected to mention where to, or that he was cutting off communications.' She raised her eyebrows. 'I didn't know he'd installed you, though. When I watched you coming out of the house earlier I was quite convinced he was here after all, and he'd just told me he was going to put me off the scent. Thought I'd come on in and give the faithless bastard what for.'

'Well, now you know it's not what you think.' She didn't seem in any hurry to go and I badly wanted her out. 'And if you've read my house-sitting file, you'll be aware that I'm not allowed to let any visitors in without the owner's prior consent.'

'All right, all right,' she said, waving the cigarette again. It now had a centimetre of ash on the end. 'I don't need to be here any more anyway, so there's no need to get your knickers in a twist.' She put the scrap of paper she'd been holding into her pocket. 'I've got what I came for, and I can let myself out.'

'I'm Ruby, by the way,' I said.

'Are you now?' the woman replied. 'How nice for you.'

As she walked through the hall I said on impulse, 'You didn't send Damien Newbold a parcel, did you? It arrived yesterday.'

She rolled her eyes. 'I'd hardly be likely to, would I, given that I knew he was going to be away?'

And then she walked out through the front door, without me even discovering her name. Though Damien Newbold would know who she was, of course, once I'd been through the embarrassing process of explaining what had happened to Nate Bastable.

Mechanically, I went to find a dustpan and brush from the under-stairs cupboard and swept up the spilt ash. Then logic reasserted itself and I went to bolt the front door so that any other girlfriends with keys wouldn't have the range of the house. My legs suddenly felt like jelly, and I sat myself down at Damien Newbold's study desk.

What kind of a man leaves a house-sitter in charge without bothering to warn her that other people might come barging in? A man just like Damien, of course: selfish, thoughtless – used to getting his own wishes granted without considering anyone else's needs.

And if he was so concerned about security, why give girlfriends he was going to upset his house keys and even the code to his burglar alarm, for heaven's sake? Presumably he'd done it in the first flush of the relationship, when things were still rosy.

If he'd only warned me I could have stayed in. Or surely the alarm code could have been changed. So? Well, presumably he hadn't cared if she did turn up. All very well for him; for me personally, I'd have preferred not to have come face to face with her like that. I glanced at my watch. Eleven thirty. At least Damien Newbold's attitude helped me make up my mind about whether to leave calling Nate until the morning. He clearly hadn't cared about the possibility of his girlfriend popping in, so I assumed it wasn't an emergency to let him know his defences had been breached.

In front of me on the desk the A4, leather-bound address book I'd noticed earlier was still present, but now it was open, its pages held wide by a stapler, used as a makeshift paperweight. Down the inside of its spine lay one of those tassels publishers sometimes attach to books as a built-in bookmark. The page marked was for contacts beginning with E, and there was only one official entry there: an Elizabeth Edmunds, with an address in Newmarket written neatly in blue ink. Off this entry, though, a line had been drawn leading to another address, scribbled in black biro: The Cottage, Burnham End, Little Boxham. I knew Little Boxham was near Newmarket. The same black biro had underlined Elizabeth Edmunds's phone number a couple of times, as though the pen holder had been doodling, perhaps whilst talking to the said Elizabeth on the phone. Next to the address for the cottage was scribbled: available Weds 3rd June.

Glancing across the desk I noticed Damien Newbold's blotter pad. One corner of the paper had been ripped off, revealing the black leather underneath. The woman had found everything she'd needed here, even stationery to hand. She'd got what she'd come looking for all right; no doubt drawing just the same conclusions as I was now. Elizabeth Edmunds was clearly a contact of Damien's with a cottage to let, and that was where Damien Newbold was now. Simple as.

I was awake by seven the following morning but put off calling Nate until half-past. He answered on the second ring; the sound of Dave Brubeck floated down the line.

'Morning, Ruby,' he said. 'Something tells me you're not calling about a blocked drain at this hour.'

I wondered how long he'd been up. 'Your instincts haven't let you down,' I said, and filled him in. There was no way of skirting over the details, and his reaction was much as I'd feared.

'This isn't making me feel any better about you being there,' he said at last. 'I'm going to take it up with Newbold right now, but then you and I have to talk.'

I sat there stewing, trying to eat some Weetabix, but it seemed to stick in my throat. I looked at my options. Inevitably, my mind strayed to my grandparents first. It was over ten years since I'd lost them, but the grief felt as raw as ever. I took a deep breath and tried to focus on the here and now. Other than Steph, it was really only my mother who could put me up, and that would never work. Even if she had a room spare, I couldn't face sharing her place with the bunch of eccentric house guests she'd collected. As for my father, well, if I'd ever known who he was, he might have been a possibility.

One way or another, I needed to make independent plans. I hadn't currently got enough money to rent somewhere if Nate cancelled the job. Certainly not anywhere near Cambridge, that was for sure. My mind flicked to ways of boosting my financial situation. The one thing of value I had to sell was my Mini, but the moment the possibility of parting with it crossed my mind I felt tears well up. Crazy. As though I was considering selling a beloved pet, rather than a car. That's the trouble with Minis, of course – they are lovable.

My nerves were jangling, and I really wanted to offload. By nine forty-five I decided I could risk calling Steph without waking her.

'So sorry,' I said, after I'd given her the gist. 'I really need to talk to someone.'

'Well, of course you do,' she said, her voice almost brimming over with enthusiasm, 'and that person's definitely me.' Gossip gathering was, admittedly, one of her favourite roles. 'Who'd have thought a simple move to the city would put you at the centre of such intrigue,' she added, a touch of envy in her tone. I think that, for a moment, she'd forgotten the reason behind my change of location.

It seemed that talking over the phone wouldn't do from her point of view. 'Robin's gone off to play five-a-side with the gang from Elm Heath, so I'm stuck here on my lonesome anyway. I can pop over to you and still be back home in time for a late lunch. Then we can chew everything over properly.'

Whilst I was waiting for her to turn up, Nate rang back.

'What did Newbold say?' I asked.

'I might as well tell you about it when we meet.'

'We're going to meet?' That smacked of a serious set to, where he could tell me the bad news.

'Newbold wants the locks changed today, so I'll come over with the locksmith around four and catch you then. Okay?'

I was glad Steph would be gone again by that time. If Nate was going to boot me out I needed to be able to deal with it on my own. Tea and sympathy can occasionally make things worse, I find.

She arrived all in a bustle, as though she might have missed some new development. 'I've brought chocolate digestives,' she said as she pulled off her shoes. She always likes to intensify the pleasure of a good gossip by accompanying it with food, and who am I to argue?

'So first those weird nude paintings,' she said, marching into the kitchen and hunting for a plate, 'and then the photo in the DVD cupboard and the funny phone call.' She tipped the digestives out and put the lot on the table. 'And *then* the mobile that was set to wake you up at four a.m., not to mention the accompanying text message, and now this rough woman turning up unannounced.' She sat down and helped herself to a biscuit. 'You could have called me sooner to tell me about the latest stuff, you know.'

'I was rather busy dealing with it,' I said. 'Tea?'

'Please.' She waved the biscuit at me. 'You had all day yesterday to give me the goods on the package and the phone call.'

'Well, if things are going to happen this often it's probably best if I save it all up for an omnibus edition every couple of days.'

It was clear she didn't agree, but she let it rest. 'So, now you've had a chance to think it all through, what do you reckon?' she asked.

I poured boiling water onto the teabags and shrugged. 'That there's something going on I don't get.'

'No shit Sherlock!'

I pulled a face. 'The nudes and the photo are beyond me, apart from the fact that I'd say Damien Newbold's a misogynistic git, but I don't suppose I'd get a prize for coming to that conclusion.' I went to get the milk from the fridge.

'And did you believe the rough woman when she said she didn't send Damien Newbold the mysterious mobile?'

I paused, the milk suspended above my mug. 'Probably. She said she knew he'd be away, so why would she bother? In the ordinary way it would just have gone back to the post office and bonged to itself each night.'

Steph leant back as I put her mug down in front of her. 'Thanks. But you said she'd begun to suspect he hadn't gone away at all, but was holed up here with you.'

'Yes.' I sat down. 'But by the time my presence aroused her suspicions the parcel had already been sent, so that doesn't really alter things.'

She sighed. 'You're right.'

'I bet she's responsible for the broken glass I told you about in the wheelie bin though. She looks just the sort to throw a whisky tumbler in anger. And then perhaps Damien announced he was going away in retaliation. Not that I think he was frightened into hiding – he's clearly not the type. My guess is it amused him to go and leave his girlfriend dangling. And for all I know the woman who owns the cottage he's renting is another lover. I'm sure that would add to the entertainment.'

'No doubt. And then last night?'

'Last night the regular lover turns up wanting to find him, and stumbles across his address book, sitting conveniently in what was probably the first place she looked. She wouldn't have had to do much searching.'

Steph glanced up at me over the top of her mug. 'You think he wanted her to find it?'

'A five-year-old could have tracked it down. The page was even bookmarked for God's sake.'

'You didn't say you thought that on the phone,' Steph said, accusingly, as though I'd been holding out on her.

'The information's been gradually settling in my mind. I think he's leading her in a carefully choreographed dance, and I'm the mug who's caught up in it.' I drained my tea and asked the inevitable. 'Anyway, what's new in the village? Has the gossip died down?'

She took my hand and gave it a squeeze. 'Not really, if I'm honest. Luke's keeping a very low profile, but I'm quite sure he's suffering for what he's done.'

I gave her a look. 'At least there's some justice in this world.'

When Steph had gone, I wondered again about the mobile that had been sent to Damien Newbold. I was still debating whether or not to call the number using the house phone and it was playing on my mind. What were the chances of someone answering? The idea of being able to talk to them – and tell them the phone had missed its target – was still tempting. Not knowing who was behind it made me edgy. I took the number I'd noted down out of my bag and sat there looking at it. I got as far as taking it to the hall table, picking up the phone and dialling the first four digits, but then I got cold feet.

Turning back to the kitchen, I worked a bit more on my book, but it was hard to concentrate. I'd thought house-sitting would slot neatly alongside my writing, but it was proving to be thoroughly disruptive. I went through the motions for a while, but what I really needed was something mindless to do. There were several outdoor jobs listed on the itinerary of domestic chores, and getting some fresh air would distract me from panicking over Nate's impending visit. I started off in the walled garden at the back, but Damien Newbold's notes were particularly insistent about some pernicious weeds that grew along the sidewall of the house. Apparently they worked their way into the mortar and compromised the damp course. I took the small green compost bin from the kitchen and set to work, crouched down, wiggling away at the roots.

It was only a couple of minutes before I heard the door to Oswald House open behind my back. I glanced over my shoulder and saw the blonde, curly-haired girl coming down the steps.

'Hi,' I said. It seemed appropriate, since I'd caught her eye.

She blanked me and made as though to walk towards the Common, her mouth stretched taut. God, was this because I was at Damien Newbold's house, and people therefore assumed I was associated with him? It seemed far-fetched, but I couldn't think of any other reason for her refusal to acknowledge me. 'I'm new here,' I said to her retreating back. 'House-sitting for the owner.' Who I've never met, and am sure I would hate, I almost added.

The blonde girl turned for a moment. 'You're a friend of his then?'

I shook my head. 'Just an agency employee; I've never met him.'

The girl's shoulders relaxed and she came over to me. 'I'm Fi,' she said. 'I house share next door. I'd shake your hand but ...'

'I'm very muddy,' I said. 'Yes, I know, don't worry.'

She smiled. 'I'm sorry I pretended not to hear you before. I assumed you were maybe a girlfriend of Damien's and, well, to be honest our household's had a bit of a falling out with him.'

'I see.' I was dying to draw information out of her, but the only obvious way to get her to confide was to start gossiping about him myself, and there were limits. At least chatting to Steph was keeping it in the family. This Fi girl was another matter.

'You're off out then?' I said instead, so that she could take her cue and carry on without embarrassment if our conversation was at an end.

She nodded. 'There's only Emily in just now – my housemate – and she needs a bit of space.'

It seemed odd that Fi should have to go out to give anyone a bit of space in a place the size of Oswald House. It was just as big as Damien Newbold's pad. At that moment though, Mr Herringbone Suit turned up. I'd swear his eyes narrowed when he saw me too, standing by Damien Newbold's open back gate. But perhaps it was my DMs.

Fi explained what I was doing there, and then he too unbent.

'I'm Paul,' he said, also eyeing my hands.

'Ruby,' I said. Personally, I had not unbent and didn't intend to. I still wasn't sure what he was up to, but visiting this Emily girl and requiring a whole houseful of space seemed to confirm all my suspicions.

Once he'd gone inside I said, 'Ah! So that's why Emily wanted space!' in a horribly phoney, girls-together, nudge-nudge, wink-wink voice.

'Oh, no,' Fi said, surprised into laughing for a moment. 'It's nothing like that. I mean, he's old enough to be her dad or something, isn't he?'

He hadn't looked all that old. Probably not much older than me. 'He'd have to be a pretty young one,' I said, bristling slightly.

'No, but you know what I mean. Anyway, there's definitely nothing like that going on. He's actually from our college, St Audrey's; he's Emily's tutor, so he's her first port of call for welfare issues. That's why he's here, to be honest. Em's been going through a bit of a rough patch lately.'

'Oh,' I said, all my theories pushed aside. That was a relief in one way, but it still meant there was something wrong. The memory of Emily's sad eyes replayed in my head; they were the kind that looked tired out by the number of nights they'd spent crying. I recognised them.

'He's been terribly correct, as a matter of fact,' Fi went on. 'Always sees Emily in the communal sitting room, and he usually asks me to sit in if I'm there.'

'And that's why you're escaping?'

She blushed. 'Yes. Emily doesn't want me watching her every move; she's admitted that. And I just get embarrassed.'

On the spur of the moment I said, 'Do you fancy a cup of tea?'

She hesitated.

'Don't worry – no obligation. It's just that I was about to stop for one myself, but if you've got somewhere to go ...'

'I haven't really. It would be nice – just so long as I'm not spotted loitering or Paul Mathewson might drag me back in again.'

So we sneaked through the gate and sat in the garden of River House, which I felt wouldn't be breaking Nate's rules about visitors.

'Is it usual for women students to see male members of staff when they've got problems?' I asked.

'It depends what stage things get to. Dr Mathewson's in the front line, and he'd be the person to refer Emily on to one of the university counsellors, if that was required.' Fi accepted one of the chocolate digestives Steph had left behind.

'I'm glad it hasn't been.'

Fi pulled a face. 'Actually, I think it's just what Emily could do with, but she's not having any of it.'

I raised an eyebrow.

'The fact is, I called Paul Mathewson in without asking her. She's going along with it – thanks to his gentleness and tact, I think – but she's not willing to take the next step. On the upside, he takes his responsibilities seriously. He's done some kind of short counselling course himself, I think.'

'I'm getting to know his face,' I said, pushing the sugar bowl in her direction. 'Not that I'm meaning to be nosy.'

She took a sip of her tea, giving the sugar a miss. 'Yes, he's been round quite a lot. She was in a hell of a state when I first contacted him, and I actually think he really cares.' She leant forward and lowered her voice. 'I'm not sure how much good he's doing though.'

'I suppose some things just take time,' I said, wondering what it was all about.

'I'm sure you're right.'

'Does she have family nearby?'

Fi rolled her eyes. 'I've only met her mum, but I don't think she'll be any help.'

'There are some things it can be very hard to discuss with a parent,' I said. I knew I sounded as though I was probing now. It was force of habit.

Fi smiled. 'True, but that's not the root of the problem with Saskia – that's Emily's mum. You'll soon see, I expect. I gather she's been threatening to come round.'

'Sounds like a treat in store!'

Fi grinned. 'As a matter of fact, it's a family house we're staying in. Emily's grandmother's. She's supposed to be nice, but she's abroad unfortunately.' She paused suddenly. We'd both heard footsteps on the other side of the garden gate.

I nipped into the kitchen for a moment and checked through the side window. 'No sign of life from your place.'

'They'll probably be a while yet. I'd better go, and leave you to it, but thanks for the tea.'

After she'd gone I pretended to myself that I was going to do some more gardening, but I was sick of the weeds. Before long I'd decided to stretch my legs. A trip to Boots called; I'd run out of shampoo.

As I cut back from the Grafton shopping centre down Midsummer Lane I saw Paul Mathewson in the distance, coming out of Oswald House. Emily was on the doorstep again to see him off. And then he began walking in my direction, stopping next to a black bike with a willow basket that was D-locked to a lamp post.

He bent to deal with the lock, but looked up as I crossed the road towards him. 'Oh, hello again,' he said.

'Hi.'

I made to walk past but he stood up straight as though he had more to say. 'I'd heard from the girls at Oswald House that Damien Newbold had gone away, but neither of them realised he had a house-sitter in.'

'I think it was all rather last minute.'

Paul nodded. 'I gathered something of the sort. I expect he was escaping all the chaos.' He waved his hand at the remains of Strawberry Fair.

'Could be,' I said.

Suddenly he surprised me by grinning. 'I rather like Strawberry Fair,' he said as though confessing a guilty secret. He held out an arm and indicated his sleeve. 'The suit's my day-job uniform. I had to go to a college chapel service this morning, so I had my gown on as well. But yesterday I found a scruffy old T-shirt and holey jeans and came along to the Fair in disguise. I doubt my own students would have recognised me.' And then he laughed. It was amazing how it transformed his face. He went from being a rather quirkily old-fashioned bloke with a weird taste in clothes, to someone with an alter ego, who was quite capable of sharing a joke.

I told him I'd been along too.

'I imagine you managed to blend in much better than I did,' he said, and then added quickly, 'I meant that as a compliment.'

He got on his bike, wobbled slightly as he waved me goodbye, and disappeared onto Maid's Causeway.

Back inside the house I tidied up my bed and the kitchen, ready for the arrival of Nate and the locksmith. Three-forty. Still twenty minutes to go. I paused in the hall by the telephone again, staring down at the number I'd left there earlier. And then at last, without acknowledging what I was doing or considering what I'd say to anyone who answered, I dialled.

I held on for what felt like ages, hoping I could at least leave a voicemail message, but no answerphone kicked in. There was to be no resolution.

Nate found Bill, the locksmith, in the passageway outside

River House and they walked round to the front door together.

Ruby opened up quickly when Nate knocked, and gave him a lopsided smile before turning to walk through to the kitchen, her shoulders hunched. Bill set his toolbox down in the hall, ready to get to work, but Nate followed Ruby.

When she reached the far side of the room she put the kettle on before turning to face him again. 'Nate, I know what you're going to say.'

He thought she'd probably tackle things head on this time – it was more her style – so he followed suit. 'This man's a pain, Ruby, pure and simple. The only thing I'm not sure of yet is the degree of shit he's likely to throw in your direction. And however much it is, it'll be more than you could do with right now.' He leant back against the work surface and folded his arms. 'Steph told me a bit about your circumstances.'

'A bit?' She gave him that half-smile again as she turned to reach for a couple of mugs.

'Well, we both know Steph, your best friend, my favourite cousin … Anyway, what she gave away makes me all the more uneasy about your being here. Seems to me you've had enough to deal with recently.'

She looked round at him, one eyebrow raised. 'Are you seriously saying you don't want me to do this job any more because I've come face to face with one of Damien Newbold's girlfriends wearing loud make-up and waving a threatening cigarette?'

Nate couldn't suppress a smile, just for a moment.

'Now the locks have been changed I won't even have that sort of excitement to entertain me.' She gave a deliberate sigh. 'Things are going to be so dull. Coffee, or tea?'

She was doing it again. He suddenly realised he'd unfolded his arms. 'Coffee, thanks.'

'To my mind,' she went on, sorting out the cafetière, 'everything that's happened so far is probably down to this one woman. Now that she knows he really isn't here, it's going to be plain sailing from my point of view. I wouldn't fancy being in Newbold's shoes though.' She was looking at him from under her long lashes and Nate felt his smile creeping back.

It wouldn't do. He needed to lay down some ground rules at least. 'If anything else crops up I need the full story, straightaway, whatever time of the night it is, and however insignificant it seems. Clear?'

He watched her nod, but she was pouring the coffees, which was a good excuse not to meet his eye.

'Crystal. Did you ever find out the name of my unexpected visitor? If you don't mind me asking?'

'No problem. It's clearly not a secret.' Newbold had patently enjoyed telling him all about it, in fact. The pleasure was all his. 'Name's Maggie Cook, apparently, and I gather she's a reasonably well-known actor if you happen to watch something called *Mike's Friday*. She's also a semi-precious girlfriend of his.'

Ruby raised one dark eyebrow a fraction as she put the coffees on the table.

'He didn't put it quite like that, but that was clearly what he meant.'

'I knew they had a connection,' she said, running a hand through her hair and glancing to one side as she took a seat. 'There's a revealing painting of her in his bedroom.'

Nate joined her at the table. 'Why am I not surprised?'

'And how did he take the news of her coming in, and finding his temporary address?'

'Cool as a cucumber.' The memory of Newbold's off-hand drawl set his adrenaline pumping all over again. 'Apologised that you'd had a shock – without sounding remotely concerned about it – and said that, given he'd told her he'd be away, he'd had no inkling that she might pop round. Why should he?'

Her eyes were on him again now, and there was a sparkle in them he hadn't seen before. 'Because she's after his blood. He must have a pretty thick skin if he hasn't realised that.'

Nate felt himself smile.

'Well, he must know she's after him now at least, since she came looking for his address,' Ruby went on. 'But from what you're saying he wasn't angry about her having found it?'

'If anything he sounded satisfied.' He'd been wondering whether Newbold enjoyed their fights, and the passion they unleashed. He'd come across that before. And seen it get out of hand. Ruby was nodding. None of it came as a surprise to her either, apparently. She'd obviously been drawing her own conclusions, cooped up here on Newbold's home territory. He wondered what other clues she might have unearthed. He had a feeling she was the sort who'd have noticed … He opened his mouth for a second, and leant towards her. She shifted in response, leaning forwards too. It was almost a reflex action to move in closer still … But he pulled back. She'd only leant forwards to hear what he was going to say.

'In any case,' Nate said, after a moment, 'he made it plain that now we'd brought the matter to his attention, he didn't want Maggie Cook back in again. He simply told me to get the locks changed "without fail" today. And that was that.'

'He sounds like a charmer.' She tucked a strand of hair behind her ear.

'I do occasionally find "service with a smile" a bit of a strain. I'm not sure when I'll crack in Newbold's case.'

She paused for a moment. 'Do you ever miss your old work?' She shrugged in response to his raised eyebrow.

'Well, you know Steph: my best friend, your favourite cousin ... In your case, though, she really did tell me almost nothing.'

Nate felt his jaw tighten – an automatic reflex – and got up from the table. 'That's because there's nothing to tell. I'd better go and see how Bill's doing.'

And he turned and left the room, so he didn't have to say any more.

I found it hard to focus on supper. I kept replaying the scene with Nate in my mind. That amused appraising look had left his eyes the instant I'd asked about his old work. And then I remembered the feeling as he'd turned his back on me, cutting me out. I closed my eyes for a moment and felt shocked at how much I minded. Of course, I was at a low ebb. Making a member of the opposite sex turn away in disgust wasn't great, even if he was just a work contact.

I was jolted out of my reverie by my mobile, letting out its perky tune. I ought to change it for something more appropriate to my mood.

'Hiya!' It was Steph. 'I'm just calling to let you know there's no need to update me on your latest meeting with Nate.'

'Oh right, very noble of you.' I refused to rise to the bait and ask her why. 'There's nothing to report, anyway.'

'Really? I had a call from him, wanting to know if I thought you were okay.'

I waited for her to spit it out.

'When he mentioned you'd told him this Maggie woman featured in one of Damien's paintings,' Steph went on, 'I assumed you must have told him about the rest.'

'Oh God! So you mentioned them?'

'I didn't know it was a secret. Why was it, anyway?'

'It wasn't. I just didn't want him to think I was shocked,

73

or that I'd been standing there staring at them or something. Oh hell. He asked me to tell him about anything that struck me as peculiar. Now he'll assume I've been holding out on him.'

She laughed, which set my teeth on edge. 'Oh, I'm sure he won't. He only asked you to mention anything out of the ordinary. He'll just presume you regarded their presence as completely normal, and that you habitually surround yourself with nude portraits too.'

'Oh hell,' I said again and took a deep breath. So he'd think I was both nosy and a perv. 'What made him worried about me, anyway? Now the locks have been changed things should be safe enough.'

'Oh yes, sure, it wasn't that. It was just Damien Newbold's reaction when he told him about Maggie Cook.'

'What do you mean?'

'Oh no, didn't he tell you?'

'I don't think so,' I said, wracking my brains. 'Nothing that would make him worry about me, anyway. But you're going tell me, Stephanie. I won't sleep for wondering otherwise.'

She sighed.

'I mean it, Steph. The last thing I need right now is more mystery.'

'Well, it was something and nothing,' she said. 'I'm sure it doesn't mean anything. Nate always does notice every detail. He just mentioned that Damien seemed very interested in your reaction to finding Maggie Cook standing there. He said,' she paused, 'well, he said it was as though he enjoyed listening to the answer.'

Chapter Eight

I had more important things to think about than my landlord and his stupid games.

After I'd showered on Monday morning I made myself consider the future. Damien Newbold's absence was open-ended. If, as I suspected, he'd just gone off for a few days for his own entertainment, then he could decide to come home any time. I was booked for ten days initially, but there was nothing to stop him going back on that. At first, I'd been too numb to consider making plans, but I knew I couldn't put it off much longer if I wanted to keep a roof over my head.

Unless I went back to Saxwell St Andrew, of course. I still hadn't read Luke's letter.

Without really concentrating I went all the way up to the attic and opened one of the Velux windows. Out across the Common I could see boats on the river: students grabbing the chance of an early morning practice before the next lot of races.

Above me, swifts issued their high-pitched calls as they swept across the mackerel sky. A cool breeze blew round my shoulders, ruffling my shower-damp hair.

Yes, I would have to talk to Luke, engage, sooner or later.

I shut the window and fished in my jeans pocket for his letter. I couldn't stop my hand shaking as I slid a thumb under the seal. I knew what to expect from the heavyweight ivory envelope. The message he'd sent was on one single sheet of the copperplate headed paper he'd bought in celebration of our tenth anniversary together at Bookman's Cottage. I remembered how I'd felt when he'd given me the box of stationery. It had been such a short time ago but a world away from where we were now. As I began to read, a tear fell down onto the paper.

Dear Ruby

If I could only convey to you how sorry I am. I've just made the most stupid mistake of my life and I want to do my best to explain how it happened.

Though Daisy Buchanan's only seventeen, she's anything but innocent.

It was true that she was singularly ill-suited to the name of Daisy, with its connotations of dewy freshness. Nonetheless, she was still a child as far as I was concerned. Not old enough to drink in a pub or see an eighteen film for freak's sake.

The first time she showed an interest in me was when you were away in Dorset in March.

When, by my reckoning, she would still have been sixteen.

She came and knocked at our door, saying her father wanted to borrow one of your weirder gardening implements – which was apparently true – but by the time we got round the back I could see the reason she'd offered to come and do the asking. You can believe me when I say I made it very clear that the whole thing was totally unsuitable.

What did he want? Congratulations?

When you went away this most recent time she came round saying her parents were out, but that one of the taps had come off their bath, and the water was rushing everywhere.

Everywhere. Presumably mainly into the bath in fact, which was quite a good place for it.

And please would I see if I could fix it. I honestly didn't see what else I could do. It would have been churlish to leave her to it. I went and found their stopcock,

76

If only that had done what it said on the tin …

turned the water off and managed to get the tap back on. Daisy had been getting ready to have a bath and was standing behind me in a dressing gown when I finished the job.

God. How much detail was he going to go into? Did he think this was helping? Did he expect me to call him and say, well yes, I do see that faced with her in only a dressing gown you could hardly leave without shagging her senseless? Otherwise it would obviously have been churlish, which would never do.

She made a dead set at me, telling me her parents wouldn't be back for ages, and who was to know but us? Then she let her dressing gown fall open and said she'd fancied me for months.

Of course I shouldn't have gone for it. If you'd been there at home I certainly wouldn't have.

How touchingly loyal.

But it suddenly seemed to me that you'd been away a lot lately. And, of course, sex between us has changed. It hasn't been the joyful old scramble for the bedroom it used to be, has it? Ever since we started trying for a baby it's become a case of where are we in the month, and is it better at this time of day or at that, and will this time be the one?

Being presented with totally uncomplicated sex, from someone who simply wanted the pleasure of a stolen half hour, was incredibly tempting.

I don't want you to think I was off on some macho trip, introducing a lovely young virgin to the experiences of womanhood. Daisy told me from the outset that she'd first had sex when she was fourteen, and she certainly seemed very experienced.

That was why I thought it would be harmless.

I couldn't carry on reading the rest. Uncomplicated

sex. How was having sex with the teenage daughter of a neighbour uncomplicated? I was willing to bet it had seemed bloody complicated when Daisy's mother had walked in on them. And did he think the fact that she'd already had a bit of fun with a few other teenagers meant it didn't matter throwing his thirty-one year old self into the ring? Didn't he see there was a difference?

And yet his end conclusion had been that she was tempting, and since sex with me had become a chore, he thought he might as well go for it. At seventeen she was probably more energetic than I was. And to cap it all, he'd made the point that I was away too often, in a letter that he'd tried to pass off as an apology.

And the bastard had done all of this when I was in the middle of producing a book on men, women and the midlife crisis.

Even after what had happened, it was really me that he blamed. And if I went back, I'd have the pleasure of seeing Daisy wafting around with low-cut tops and belt-sized skirts, glancing at Luke under her eyelashes.

Except we'd never be able to stay in Saxwell St Andrew after what had happened. He'd burnt our boats there. It would be some other town or village, and the temptation would be some other nubile, young thing.

It was stupid, but I cried harder over the letter than I had when I'd first found out. It made it so horribly apparent that a future together would never work. The thought of the wasted years we'd had ... Images of the past skimmed through my mind: me jumping down off a wall in a ball dress into Luke's outstretched arms; us both snorting with laughter, huddled up in our tiny tent, listening to a couple next door having noisy sex; hiding behind the sofa together in Saxwell, when his awful Uncle Basil had turned up on the doorstep unannounced.

And then the memory of returning home after my last work trip: seeing the neighbours looking at me oddly as I stood on the doorstep, rummaging for my keys. And lastly, Luke's face as he'd told me what had happened, and how, overnight, we'd become the talk of the village.

When I'd cried until my head was thudding I got up, dragged myself downstairs and went into the back garden. I needed some time to let everything sink in, and then I would write back to Luke and arrange to meet and talk. But I knew after reading the letter that I could never go back.

The thought set me off again, and I went to the shed, still shuddering with misery. The sky was louring as I got busy with a trowel, removing the weeds from the various pots. Then I used a knife to poke out more from between the paving stones. The wind – quite bracing now – had a strangely soothing effect, as though it was blasting away everything but the nature that surrounded me. Perhaps I could keep up the feeling of being in a bubble, and shut the bad stuff out.

After I'd made a decent job of the garden weeds I remembered I'd never finished the ones along the bottom of the wall, outside in Midsummer Passage. I nipped into the house to check my face in the cloakroom mirror and splashed my eyes with cold water. I looked as though I'd been up all night, but you couldn't necessarily tell I'd been crying now.

Out in the passageway I planned to work my way along from the front end of the house towards the back, and then along the garden wall. I was halfway through when I heard the door to Oswald House open again. It was the girl, Emily, coming down the steps.

Chapter Nine

She smiled hesitantly at me. 'You're the house-sitter?'

I nodded and waved a muddy hand in greeting. 'Ruby. And I gather from Fi that you're Emily?'

She nodded. 'Emily Amos.' And then she walked across the lane towards me and I unbent and stood up. 'Did Fi explain about me?'

'She said you were her housemate.'

'And I know you saw Paul Mathewson.'

'That's right.' I hesitated. 'She told me he's one of the tutors at your college.'

'It's okay,' she said. 'Fi admitted she told you he's been helping me through a rough patch.'

I leant back against the wall. 'He seems nice.'

She nodded, running a hand through her long, dark hair, and suddenly I saw her afresh. Her blue dress was figure-hugging, showing off her petite, curvy outline. A familiar physical type. The feeling of knowing what was coming next was eerie. 'Your trouble was with Damien Newbold?'

She looked at me and then lowered her eyes and nodded. God, so it wasn't just Luke who ran after younger women. Okay, so Emily wasn't quite as young as Daisy, but it was all familiar territory.

And in spite of being at least a year older, since she was already at university, Emily looked a lot more vulnerable than Daisy did. There were huge dark rings under her eyes and she seemed hollow, as though someone had dug all the life out of her. It must be playing havoc with her studies, let alone her life in general. Standing there I suddenly felt a surge of rage against Damien Newbold. How dare he go about mucking up people's lives like this?

I took a deep breath. 'Has it been helping, seeing Paul Mathewson?'

She shrugged. 'He's very nice, and I can tell he really does care, but somehow that almost makes it worse.'

'How do you mean?'

'I suppose you really need someone who's completely detached and totally calm. I don't mean I want someone uncaring,' she paused for moment, 'but someone who can listen without getting upset *along with* me. Do you see what I mean? When I tell him what I'm feeling I can see the sympathy in his eyes, and that makes it harder.'

I nodded. 'I suppose a professional counsellor would have more training in listening without getting involved.'

She gave me a look. 'I can tell you've been talking to Fi. She thinks I should see someone officially, but I can't bear to. And Paul Mathewson is kind.' She looked up at me then, her eyes pleading. 'What would really make a difference is to see Damien and get things straight. Only he's cut himself off.'

A dusty, black cat wove its way between us, rubbing its back against my legs. Even fickle animals were more reliably affectionate than men, if my experience to date was anything to go by. I wondered how I could possibly convince her Damien Newbold wasn't worth it.

'He'll be back,' I said, mentally adding, unfortunately.

'You see, what happened between us ...' She paused.

'You don't have to tell me if you don't want to.'

She rubbed her forehead as though it ached. 'I won't go into details, but the thing is, I just went way over the top at the wrong moment.' She was still looking away from me. 'I think he does have feelings for me, but I'd got the impression they'd moved on further than they really had. And meanwhile I'd – well – basically, I'd fallen in love with him. Sounds pretty stupid and old-fashioned.'

'Nothing wrong with falling in love per se, but maybe Damien Newbold's not—'

She cut across me. 'He has another girlfriend you see. Nearer to him in age.'

I was willing to bet he had several more on top of that too, probably of all ages.

'Anyway, it was stupid of me, but I didn't realise how involved they still were. He'd given me the impression ... Well, anyway, it doesn't matter. And then I found out it was all very much still on. And I went a bit nuts. I behaved like a toddler, not a nineteen-year-old. And now the girlfriend – Maggie – has been in touch with me, telling lies, getting abusive, that kind of thing.' She shuddered. 'It's all rather horrible.'

I couldn't stay quiet any longer. 'Emily, it sounds to me as though you have nothing to be ashamed of. It's Damien Newbold who ought to be doing the apologising. He's a heck of a lot older than you are, and he ought to know better.'

She was looking at me again now. 'That's Paul Mathewson's opinion too. He doesn't say so, because he's remembered that he's not meant to pass judgement, but I know it's what he thinks.'

Go Paul.

She began to pace up and down along the lane. 'I don't mean to be rude, but, you see, neither of you was there, and you don't understand.'

I couldn't think of a neat way to answer that one. 'You're right, of course, that I don't know anything about your particular case,' I said. 'And I don't want to interfere. It's just that having lived in Damien Newbold's place for a few days, I do get the impression he has quite a lot to do with several different women.'

She frowned.

'I'd hate you to get hurt – more so than you already are, I mean,' I said, trying to rescue the situation. 'I just wish there was something I could do to help.'

Her expression loosened again and her shoulders relaxed. 'As a matter of fact, I was thinking that perhaps there might be. That was really why I came to talk to you.'

Hell. What was coming?

'I wondered whether you might possibly be able to get a message to Damien for me.'

I could see her taking in my expression.

'I know you think it's a bad idea, but if we can just get together to talk I'll be able to keep calm this time. And then, even if it's all over – or if there never was anything and it's all in my head – at least I'll know where I am. That's what's going to make me feel better.'

I wasn't at all sure that that was true. I'd seen Emily's kind of obsessive love before; remembered it from my own teenage years, in fact. Anything would feed it. If Damien Newbold gave her the slightest reason to hope, she'd be in even deeper than she was already.

'I'm afraid I'm only the house-sitter,' I said, using my get-out-of-jail-free card. 'We don't get given information on where the house owner's staying.' Which was true, as far as it went. I tried not to think of the address book, sitting in the study. 'My boss would know,' I added, 'but he'd never be allowed to give the information out without permission.'

'But he could at least forward a letter.' The pitch of Emily's voice rose slightly.

I shook my head. 'I'm sorry. I'm sure he'd be on your side too, but he'd never be able to agree to that, under the circumstances.'

She stood there for a moment, and I could tell she was trying to think of another solution.

'I really am sorry,' I said, meaning I was sorry for her

situation. I wasn't sorry about refusing to put her in touch with an egotistical womaniser.

It took her a moment to answer. 'What? Oh yes, I know. I do understand. Anyway,' she lifted her head and put her shoulders back, 'I'm pretty sure he hasn't gone far.'

'What makes you say that?'

'I called his work. The woman on reception told me he was away from the office, but only after I'd given her my name. I didn't believe her. It was like listening to someone who's been given a script to perform but hasn't learnt it by heart. Do you know when he's due back here?'

I shook my head. 'My understanding is it's open-ended.'

She nodded. 'Well, I think I'll go crazy if I just have to wait on him.' Her eyes were intense. 'I'm going to find out where he is.'

As she walked back up the steps of Oswald House the first raindrops, thick and heavy, smacked down on the tarmac, the water mingling with the summer dust.

I spent a lot of the following twenty-four hours wondering what could be done for someone like Emily. From memory, it was usually the arrival of some replacement love interest that wiped away the pain of that sort of infatuation. That, and the support of a good friend, or a mother. Fi had clearly already tried and, from what she had said, the mother was a dead loss.

For myself, I was now feeling almost aggressively dry eyed, as though reading Luke's letter the previous day had somehow switched off hope, leaving me feeling deadened, yet more certain now of the planning I would need to do for the future.

When I'd had enough of cleaning, I decided to set off into town for an hour. I'd yet to take advantage of the rule that said I could actually be gone for three, but this stipulation hadn't been revoked – in spite of Maggie's little visit – and I was really desperate for a change of scene. I could maybe find an estate agent or two, and start thinking about my options.

Getting as far as King Street felt like a rush of oxygen after surviving for days in thin air. As I walked past the St Radegund pub I began to feel more relaxed. I straightened my back and breathed in deeply, enjoying air that wasn't tainted by Damien Newbold's presence. Crossing over, I was assailed by a series of smells, beginning with smoke and beer from the King Street Run, where two pot-bellied men were standing outside, puffing away. Loud sports commentary leaked through the pub's swing doors.

Those smells were overtaken by garlic and seared meat from a Turkish restaurant – making my mouth water. Further up the street, the scent of tea and coffee wafted out from a shop with lots of jazzy teapots in the window. By an Italian cafe I was sure I could detect cake too, a sweet chocolatey aroma. Perhaps I would have to visit later. Laughter rang out from inside, overlaying a cacophony of cheerful voices. It all sounded so normal and reassuring.

Regent Street is estate agent territory in Cambridge. I started at the town end, and peered in at the first window.

Blimey. I half closed my eyes to see if that made the prices look any less scary, but really it was a job for a general anaesthetic. I moved past the doorway to a second window that displayed properties to let, instead of those to buy. The houses in Cambridge were particularly notable for being beyond my means. The village properties didn't look quite so impossible, but I'd still need to organise some steadier income if I was to have a hope of securing something. Perhaps if I kept to a diet of grit and river water I might be able to rent someone's shed.

The woman inside had me sat down before I'd really

thought what I was doing. I knew full well I wasn't ready for any of this yet. How long would it take her to realise I was a time waster? Still, there was no harm in seeing what was on offer.

'These locations are all very convenient for the A14 if you need to be able to come into town,' the lady said, handing me a sheaf of pamphlets. I presumed 'convenient for the A14' was putting a positive spin on 'bordering a massive dual carriageway', but didn't say so.

'It would be handy to be somewhere with shops and a railway station,' I said, and another sheaf was produced, with a higher average price tag. At least I'd have something to focus on when I got back to Damien's place. It might be as well to start trying to narrow down an area. Somewhere where I'd still be within reach of Steph, in a region I knew reasonably well, but without the daily danger of bumping into Saxwell St Andrew-ites.

Back at River House I made tea and sat browsing through the house details. Shelford looked lovely. It wasn't an awful lot cheaper than Cambridge, though. But what about Ely? From the details I'd got it looked as though it was big enough to have a greater range of accommodation and I loved it there. The cathedral and the river were beautiful, and there was that great bookshop.

I flicked open my laptop and Googled some images, reminding me just how nice it was. Thank God I could take my work anywhere, and at least it brought in some kind of a living. With that thought I settled down to write up more material for my book and focused on it properly for the first time since I'd arrived.

By the time I'd eaten supper I was feeling more positive, and decided to take control. I wasn't going to sleep downstairs tonight. It was ridiculous, pandering to Damien Newbold's stupid stipulations. I needed relaxation, and then a good night's sleep. I made for the guest bathroom first and filled up the film-star style tub, setting all the jets going for good measure. I'd cleaned them, so it was only fair that I should get to enjoy them too. As I lay amongst the bubbles I heard the rain start to beat against the window. The climate had changed completely since the weekend.

Just as I was well and truly settled, the house phone rang, but I didn't bother getting out to answer it. If it was anyone who actually wanted me, they'd call my mobile. Damien's friends could bloody well wait until he got home. I stretched back, letting my body float in the water, and smiled. I hoped he would find a whole load of really offensive messages on his return.

As I padded across the landing I could hear that the wind was getting up. It squeezed itself through the gappy sash windows and moaned as it pushed its way down the chimney in one of the spare rooms.

Upstairs in the attic the noise of the rain was louder, pounding on each of the four windows, but I didn't care. I was marching to my own tune now, doing what I felt like.

I put my book down on the bedside table, switched on the little lamp that sat there, and pulled back the duvet.

Underneath, written on thick cream paper, was a note.
Thought you'd end up here eventually.

I'd gone to bed ridiculously early to try to catch up after my disturbed nights, but I found it very hard to get to sleep. My attempt to escape Damien and his plans for me had brought us together again. I felt like a puppet, dancing on the strings he was pulling. I stayed upstairs, but when I closed my eyes I saw the face of the man in the silver frame, laughing at me. What kind of person played these sort of mind games? And why?

It was the phone that woke me, jolting me out of a deep

slumber so that I sat up in less than a second with my heart racing. In spite of the tensions of the evening, I'd been in the throes of a vivid dream about Nate. My cheeks went hot when I thought about it. Where had that come from? And then, when I reached for my mobile, I realised it was him calling.

As I picked up, the bedside clock's illuminated hands caught my eye. It was only eleven fifteen.

'Ruby?'

His tone pushed the dream from my mind. 'What's wrong?'

'Thank God you're okay.' He paused for a moment, as though catching his breath. 'I'm sorry to call you this late. I thought it was best you knew straightaway. I guess the police will be round to see you tomorrow morning anyway.'

Foreboding and shock made my voice unsteady. 'The police? What's happened?'

'I'm afraid it's Damien Newbold. He's been murdered.'

Chapter Ten

Nate waited for her to take it in, listening to her strained breathing. It brought back his own past; his body was still reacting too.

'What happened exactly?' Ruby said at last.

'I've just got off the phone with the police. They didn't go into much detail, but they're coming to talk to me in person. They found information about the house-sitting service where Newbold was staying, and my number as a missed call on his mobile. I rang him around eight.' He closed his eyes for a moment. 'Now I know why he wasn't picking up …'

There was a long pause. 'Shit,' she said at last. Then, after another moment, 'The police were quick to call you.'

'They wondered why I'd called him. And they wanted to know if I'd heard anything was amiss at River House.' He'd had to sit down where he'd stood when they'd told him they'd called and got no reply. 'They said they couldn't raise you. I think they were worried that if someone was after him, they might have tried his permanent address first.'

'Just like Maggie did,' she said. Her voice was uneven. 'God, I'm sorry,' she added as though suddenly coming back to the present. 'Nothing's happened here. I heard the house phone go, but I was in the bath at the time, and I guessed the call wouldn't be for me.'

Nate could hear the acoustics change, and the sound of her movement. He guessed she was checking round the house, and fought the urge to tell her to be careful. There'd be no one there now, and anyway, she would be.

'So who found him?' she asked.

'The woman who owns the cottage he was renting,

apparently. She popped round mid-evening. I may be able to tell you more tomorrow, once I've talked to the police again. And they'll want to get round to River House quite quickly I imagine; talk to you, look through Newbold's stuff.'

'God. They'll want to see the address book Maggie found.'

'Yes. Though she wasn't the only one on his tail. I was returning a call of Newbold's when I tried to get him this evening. He'd left me a message about some other girlfriend who'd been trying to track him down through his work. For some reason he wanted to talk to me about it.'

There was a long pause on the other end of the line. 'I sense this isn't news to you.' Hell. What was she playing at? 'God, Ruby. It might be good if you stopped pissing me about. I know you don't want me to chuck you out, but this is getting a bit counterproductive.'

He heard her draw in a sharp breath, but Nate was through pussyfooting around.

'Newbold had a love-sick student neighbour,' she said at last. 'He probably guessed she'd try to pump me for information and wanted you to warn me off.'

'Right.' The adrenaline was making something of a comeback.

'I did wonder whether to mention her to you, but she's only just crossed my radar, so I hadn't had the chance to think it through properly. Besides, she's just a kid.'

He wished he was there with her. Over the phone was no good. 'Murderers come in all shapes and sizes.' Nate realised he was sounding like some kind of movie cop, but all the same, it was true. Then he heard her house phone ringing, as distant as she was. 'You go. We'll talk tomorrow. Call me if there's anything to report.'

The phone call was from the police again, checking up on me for the same reasons as Nate. They said they'd be round as soon as they could the following day so I set the alarm for six-thirty. After they'd rung off, I thought again about Emily, and what Nate had said about murderers. I wished I'd told him about her straightaway. It was as though by keeping her secret I'd made her seem guilty. And what about Damien Newbold? Maybe he'd recognised something in Emily that had unnerved him, something that might have unpredictable consequences. I guessed he knew damn well he could deal with Maggie and her rages and her passion, but Emily might have been a more uncertain proposition.

I sat on the edge of the bed in the attic, shivering, and wondered how he'd died.

I didn't manage to sleep until after three and woke up confused about where I was, but the fact of Damien Newbold's death hit home again in seconds, leaving me feeling as though I'd been punched.

By seven a.m. I was at the kitchen table attempting to eat Weetabix once more. The estate agents' details were still heaped up at one corner and, as I glanced at them, I realised with a jolt that I might need them sooner than I'd realised. What was my position, now that Damien Newbold was dead? I could be homeless within days. I'd need to ask Nate, but it felt horribly self-centred to be considering my housing needs when Damien was lying on a trolley in the local mortuary.

I got up at last and clattered my bowl into the sink, ready to go back upstairs to do my make-up.

My foot was on the bottom stair when I heard someone putting a key into the front door. Someone with an old set, who didn't know that the locks had been changed.

Chapter Eleven

I felt my heart thudding uncomfortably and my stomach tightening. The key was taken out, put in again and the turn was attempted with more force. I could hear the person outside swearing quietly.

Someone coming to River House after killing Damien Newbold? Someone with something to find, or tracks to cover?

I stole back into the hall and crept towards the door, putting my eye to the spyhole. A woman's distorted face came into view. No one I'd met before. Her dark hair was flying in the breeze and she looked mystified. Her face disappeared from view for a moment as she leant forward, perhaps to examine the lock. She was turning the key over in her hand now. Then she moved away from the door and, as I stepped back and glanced into the drawing room, I could see that she was peering in through the window. Moments later she returned to the front door and began clattering the brass lion's head.

I paused for a moment, trying to think logically. In my panic my mind refused to engage properly, but I held onto the fact that if she was knocking, she wasn't trying to come in in secret.

I went and opened up and, now that I could see her face to face, she was familiar. It was like collecting cards in happy families. This was the woman who had looked pleading and eager in Damien Newbold's nudes collection. And presumably she had no idea that he was dead. In my initial panic I hadn't thought about the much more likely possibility of her being an innocent bystander. What the hell was I going to tell her?

She was looking at me with her head on one side, her mouth set in a grim, straight line. 'I'm sorry,' she said, 'but, if you don't mind me asking, who the hell are you? And,' she looked down at her key, 'what the heck's going on?'

How many of Damien Newbold's girlfriends had his door keys for heaven's sake? What would he have done if they'd all turned up at once? Enjoyed the spectacle probably.

I explained my presence.

'House-sitter? I had no idea.' Her eyes were fixed on a dark corner of the hall, but I didn't get the impression that she was taking in what was in front of her. Her look was far away, focused on piecing together a puzzle she didn't understand. 'I knew Damien was going away, of course. And he told me to come in as usual, so everything would be in order when he got back.'

My mind grappled with her words. 'In order?'

She nodded. 'I come in and set Damien's home to rights.'

'A sort of housekeeper?'

She nodded again, and raised her eyes to meet mine, but then her shoulders sagged. 'Or indeed glorified dogsbody, cleaner, bottle washer. Call it what you will. When I want to feel good about myself I liken it to being a kind of household PA. Damien would describe me as "the woman who does".'

That was exactly how he had referred to her in his notes in fact. And judging by the painting, she definitely had done. It was interesting to note that he had asked her to come in as usual during his time away, when he'd told me that he'd called her off, since I was there to do the work instead. 'I think I've been fulfilling the same role,' I said, then added hastily, 'well, almost.'

'I noticed the folding bed through the window.' Suddenly she laughed, her hair falling over one eye. 'I think that's why I wanted to share. Dogsbodies of the world unite.'

'Why don't you come in?' I said. 'I think it might be handy to have a chat, if you don't mind. There are a couple of things it would be useful to check.'

She nodded. 'I'll need to get on and do my jobs, anyway. I hope I won't be in your way. My name's Tilly by the way; Tilly Blake.'

'Ruby.' It was all so friendly and polite and – on the surface – normal.

As she came into the hall, I went towards the kitchen, but she stepped to one side and poked her head around the drawing room door. 'I thought my eyes must be playing tricks on me when I looked through the window,' she said, 'but he really has put that seascape up over the mantelpiece in there. It's normally in his bedroom. I wonder why he's swapped it with the mirror. Seems a bit odd.'

'I found the remains of the mirror in the bin,' I said as she followed me through to the back of the house. 'Broken, I'm afraid. So he must have brought the seascape down from upstairs.'

She nodded.

Well, the seascape hadn't left an obvious gap on his bedroom wall. Did that mean he'd re-arranged his other paintings too? And how could I carry on producing chit-chat about paintings and cleaning routines when I knew he was dead? And she clearly didn't.

'Tea?'

'Thanks,' she said, perching on one of the chairs. 'It would be nice to have a drink before I start.'

And, as I filled the kettle, I knew that I had to tell her, whether it was officially the right thing to do or not. However, my mind went blank when I tried to call up the words. I must have looked like a goldfish, my mouth forming a shape and then letting it go again as I abandoned each phrase I'd thought of starting. As I poured boiling water into our mugs I said instead, 'I was quite surprised by the paintings in his bedroom.'

Tilly rolled her eyes. 'The one of Maggie Cook, you mean?' she said. 'It is a bit "in your face", isn't it? She and Damien have had an on-off thing going for years. He says it's mainly off these days, but I'm not so sure.'

I turned my back on her to get the milk out of the fridge.

'He certainly doesn't seem to want to take her picture down, anyway.' She sighed as I put her drink in front of her. 'Thanks. Maggie's an actor you know. Lives up to the dramatic stereotype too.'

'And what about the other paintings?' I said.

Tilly shrugged. 'I'm no expert, but I quite like the still life. Why do you ask?'

My mind was still working on what she'd said, so that I didn't reply for a moment and she continued with her next train of thought. 'Where will you want to be this morning, by the way?'

'I'm sorry?'

'I was just wondering what order to do the rooms in, so I don't disrupt you too much.'

'Oh, I see.' I suddenly saw my moment. 'Tilly, look, I don't think you need to do the cleaning today. I couldn't work out how to tell you, but I'm afraid I had some awful news last night. Really awful …'

I suppose there's no mistaking someone's meaning when they utter words like that. Even if one hasn't had to deal with them in reality, one's seen them uttered on a hundred different television dramas. I was sure Tilly knew what I was going to say before I said it, but it seemed precious little in the way of preparing her for the shock.

She looked up at me, her eyes suddenly wide and scared. 'What is it?'

'I'm afraid Damien Newbold's been found dead.'

'What happened?' she asked at last, her voice almost a whisper.

I explained the call I'd had the previous night. 'I'm so very sorry. I'm expecting the police here this morning, to come and look through the house.'

I was glad that I hadn't had to tell her about how Damien Newbold had deliberately double booked us, ensuring that I did cleaning I didn't need to, whilst she had a wasted journey. Bad enough that he was showing her how little he cared by failing to tell her about my presence, worse still if she'd found she'd been deliberately set up like that.

'I can't believe it's true,' Tilly said. She looked at me with eyes still forced wide by shock, her face blank and white, and then at last she started to cry: large, silent tears.

It was some time before it seemed right to speak again. When she'd regained some control I said, 'When did you start working for him?'

She blew her nose on a tissue. 'Just after I'd been made redundant from TomorrowTech. You know that's where he worked?'

I nodded.

'Well, Damien sympathised with my situation and asked me out for a drink. He said then that he had some work in mind for me.' She let out a rather bitter laugh. 'To be honest, I thought he meant something to do with marketing. That's what I'd done for the company. But it turned out he needed a cleaner. We ...' she paused and tears filled her eyes. 'We had a bit of thing together at the time, and he said how nice it would be to have me around the place. We used to combine my visits with ... well, with other things. Otherwise I'd have said no. But the job market's been crap recently, and although I've got some freelance work since I left, I needed the extra cash.'

'To be honest,' I said, 'I was pretty sure you and he must have been close, at least at some point.'

Tilly looked up at me, a glimmer in her wet eyes. 'Really?' she said. 'Did he say something about me?'

The woman who does. Hell. I wondered what to do. 'Well, it sounds as though you're not aware of this,' I said, wondering how best to put it, 'but when I arrived, Maggie's wasn't the only nude image on Damien Newbold's bedroom wall.'

She looked at me, frowning. 'What do you mean?'

'He'd put your painting up there too.'

'My painting?'

I nodded.

'I need to see.'

Which wasn't ideal, given the other two I hadn't yet mentioned. But Tilly was already making her way towards the hall, striding up the stairs.

We stood together in the doorway of the master bedroom as she took in the scene.

'I had no idea,' she said at last.

'You didn't sit for the portrait?'

She shook her head. 'He did once take some photos of me. He must have had it done from one of them, but he never said, and when we were together ...' She paused, unable to go on for a moment. Eventually she managed to add, 'When we were together, Maggie's was the only nude portrait he had up here. He used to say I shouldn't object to the presence of a beautiful image, and that it didn't mean anything.' She looked at me. 'But I always knew that it did.'

So Damien Newbold had set up this little exhibition especially for me. My head swam for a moment. He'd engineered so much: my meeting with Maggie, the trail that led her to him, and now my meeting with Tilly. And had he envisaged this scene in his bedroom too?

'Do you know who the other two women are?' I asked.

She shook her head. 'I've never seen that one before,' she said, pointing to the shy nude next to the wardrobe. 'But there's a photograph of that one downstairs.' She indicated the painting of the joyous woman that faced Newbold's bed and I noticed she was shivering.

'You mean the one in the DVD cupboard?' I asked.

She shook her head. 'If there's one there, then it's another,' she said. 'I'll show you the one I know about.'

And I followed her down the stairs and into Damien Newbold's study. Tilly took me over to the wall opposite the door, which I now saw was rather damp. She leant behind a dark, mahogany chest and, as I peered over her shoulder, I could see a photograph frame, right down next to the skirting board, turned to face the wall.

'I asked him why he'd left it like that, and he said she was out of favour. He was a bit weird that way.' She shivered again. 'I found it when I was cleaning, but he told me never to dust down there again. He wanted it left, he said, because she hated spiders, and he wanted as many cobwebs down there as possible.'

'That's sick.'

She nodded. 'Even before I knew about that photo I was aware he could be obsessional.' She looked at me as though willing me to understand. 'But it was too late by then. I'd already fallen for him, hook, line and sinker. It seems awful, but when he showed me that photo I was just glad that it wasn't me he was treating like that. I think for a while I stopped seeing things in the round.'

She glanced at her watch. 'It's nine o'clock. I guess the police'll be with you soon. I'd better go.' She swallowed. 'I suppose they'll want to talk to me too, especially with that painting hanging upstairs in Damien's bedroom.'

I nodded and she got out a piece of paper, scribbling

down her number. 'Perhaps you could give them that,' she said. 'My number's not in Damien's address book. I made the mistake of looking once.'

After she left I went into the dining room to wait for the police to turn up, taking the photograph with me. There wasn't much for them to look through in there – assuming they weren't interested in Damien Newbold's sideboard contents – so I should be safely out of the way if I kept to that room.

When I'd dusted off the glass that protected the photograph I could see clearly that the woman pictured was beautiful. Her hair fell in long, full waves over her shoulders and she was wearing a knitted dress with zigzag patterns on it in browns and orange. Her look was fashionably retro.

What was it all about? I glanced at the back of the frame, which had clips you could turn through ninety degrees to release the backing. Once I had it out, I could see the reverse of the photo. It was signed by the same artist who'd done the portrait. Nico. And once again he'd drawn that little hat symbol next to his name.

Inspiration suddenly struck and I fetched my laptop, pacing the room as I waited for it to boot up. If this Nico did photographs and portraits that he signed in that flamboyant way, maybe he was well known for his work.

I keyed 'Nico', 'artist', 'photographer' and 'hat' into Google. If I could track him down, I might possibly be able to identify his subject.

It was surprisingly easy. Wikipedia came up with the top link and provided the information I needed in its first summary paragraph. Nicholas 'Nico' Sidorov. Russian-born artist and photographer, sought after by society and celebrity clients during the late 1960s and 1970s. Born June 1939. Died of pancreatic cancer, November 1981.

Chapter Twelve

I felt the hairs lift on my arms. What an idiot I'd been, thinking the photos were arty and retro. Of course they weren't, they were genuine period pieces. I thought back to the image in the DVD cupboard: the wide-brimmed hat and the Carole King hair. Transparently 1970s if I'd had the eyes to look. Only I hadn't seen it because I'd been convinced that all of the women in Damien Newbold's paintings were recent lovers.

I looked again at the photograph Tilly had found for me. How old would its subject have been there? Somewhere in her late thirties, maybe? And that meant that now she would be – I counted in tens on my fingers – somewhere around seventy, depending on the exact dates. And that put rather a different complexion on things. If she wasn't a lover …

I walked back through to the drawing room. I knew what I was looking for now, and I'd seen them, that second night when I'd been looking for the piano music. I remembered them being somewhere on the bottom shelf.

I crouched down to scan the row of albums, running my fingers along them in turn. When might Damien Newbold have been born? I'd put him in his late forties. The albums were labelled by date, so I pulled one out that had ''61 to '65' written on a label, stuck onto its spine.

The first pages were mainly holiday photos: clear white sunlight in exotic locations, whitewashed, flat-roofed buildings with ornate arches. North Africa? Morocco, perhaps? A younger version of the woman I was interested in appeared in many of them on her own, smiling at the camera. She looked happy here too, but perhaps a little bit less relaxed. Maybe that easy joy was something that came with the passing of years; it spoke of some kind of inner confidence. After a couple of pages there was a picture of the woman with a man. He looked older than her; attractive, dark glasses, his arm around her shoulders. Just behind them was a camel being held by a man in long robes, and the woman was laughing, but with an edge of nervousness showing in her eyes. Perhaps they were about to have a ride and she was feeling anxious.

I carried on turning the heavy pages of the album and was about halfway through when I found what I was looking for. A photograph of the woman holding a baby. After this there were lots of photographs of the woman on home territory, and at this point someone had begun to add captions to the images. Neat ink italics on pale blue squares of paper. It was an indication of the obsessive joy and interest that overwhelms new parents, I guessed. I could empathise; I was sure I'd be the same. The thought tugged at my heartstrings.

The first annotated photograph was labelled: 'Bella with Damien, November 1964.'

His mother. It had suddenly seemed like the most likely option, once I'd understood the dates. I'd written about men with odd relationships with their mothers, although none as odd as this appeared to be, admittedly.

I scanned the rest of the album, which included many more baby pictures. There was an image of what must have been Damien's first Christmas. He was surrounded by family, thumping a thick rug with a wooden hammer. Then there was one taken in February 1965, with him engulfed by a traditional christening gown, held tight by his mother. A pretty snow-covered church stood in the background. The man I assumed must be his father – Harry, according to the caption – hovered nearby. The following spring he was pictured lying on a rug in the sunshine and by August 1965 he was sitting up, laughing, on a sandy beach next to a sophisticated castle someone else must have constructed. And yet in the end he had been screwed up, dysfunctional and destined to die before his time.

What could Damien's mother have done to make him despise her so? And where was she now?

I glanced at my watch. The police were sure to be here soon. It was nine-twenty already. I probably didn't have much time, and a sense of urgency overwhelmed me. There was clearly more to find out, and I didn't want to be deprived of the chance to investigate. What if the police wanted to take away personal items like the photograph albums? I pulled out the 1966 to 1970 instalment. Everything I saw there spoke of a happy childhood. At the very end of that book another baby arrived, Samson in May 1970.

I pushed that album back and reached for 1971 to 1975.

There were two things that struck me about that batch. Firstly Damien's father, Harry, only featured in a few photographs, right at the beginning. After that he disappeared until one brief appearance in February 1974. The other was that there were far fewer photographs of Samson than of Damien, though of course Damien was almost six years older than his brother. He was bound to be more actively involved in proceedings. Where a third-party had taken a photograph of Damien and his mother they still looked close. Often they seemed to be catching one another's eye, and they each shared the same mischievous, conspiratorial grin.

I had my hand on 1976 to 1980 when the door knocker went.

Chapter Thirteen

The lead officers that came to look over the house were both men: a DI Johnson, greying and tall with hollow cheeks, and a DS Brookes, who was stocky with red hair and looked disconcertingly like my old biology teacher.

Although I'd imagined simply keeping out of their way as they went through Damien Newbold's stuff, it was soon clear it was me they wanted to focus on first, whilst some of their colleagues took care of searching for other evidence.

It was too grotty to take them into the drawing room, with its folding bed, and the kitchen felt unsuitably informal, so I led them back to the dining room.

'Nice photograph,' DI Johnson said, wandering over to peer at Bella's image.

'Damien Newbold's mother,' I said, picking it up and putting it on the sideboard. 'I was just wondering if she was still alive.' I found myself raising a hand to cover my eyes for a moment. 'Unbearable, the thought of her having to deal with the news about her son.'

DI Johnson looked up at me. 'Our information is that the next of kin is a brother.'

'Can I get you some tea?' I asked, and went off to the kitchen with their orders. I already felt I'd kept something from them by not explaining Damien Newbold's weird relationship with his mother, but then what bearing could it possibly have on his murder? In the next-door room they were strangely quiet and when they did speak it was in voices so low that I couldn't make out the words. For some reason butterflies were flitting round my stomach as though they were on speed. What must it be like for a guilty person? I tried to steady my hand as I poured milk into both teas, but managed to knock the teaspoon against the side of the mug as I added sugar. The work surface was scattered with spilt grains, but that would have to wait until later.

Back in the dining room DS Brookes was standing near my laptop. 'You wanted to find out more about Mr Newbold?' he said, accepting his mug with a nod of thanks and a smile.

'I'm sorry?'

'I was judging by the browser tabs you've got open on your laptop.'

I glanced at my computer. Was he allowed to just look at what I'd been doing like that? Then again, he was a detective, and I had left my computer just sitting there. I supposed in fact it was probably in his job description. Still, I was convinced he must have deliberately knocked the glide pad. Otherwise the screensaver would have been on.

Into the pause DS Brookes said, 'I see you found the same technology blog we did.'

I nodded. 'The one that mentions the rumour about some whizzy new discovery Damien Newbold was supposed to have made? Yes, I did. It all seemed a bit hazy though.'

'True. You took a look at his company website as well?'

That tab was still open too, labelled TomorrowTech Newsroom, at the top, so he could see full well that I had. Anyway, it wasn't a secret.

'Yes,' I said. 'I was wondering about him, what his background might be and so on. It's quite odd, living in someone else's house. You get immersed in their environment, yet you know very little about them.' Look, I'm just a nosy parker, please don't make me babble on like this.

'And so you looked to see if the company had made any announcement about the rumoured discovery,' DS Brookes finished for me, homing in on how specific my enquiries had become.

I raised my eyebrows.

'Well, presumably that's what you were checking for, if you went to the section for press releases,' DS Brookes said. 'We did exactly the same thing ourselves as soon as we started to look into Mr Newbold's background.'

The obvious difference between us being that I wasn't a police officer, so why had I been looking? I knew he was waiting for me to comment.

Again he spoke into the gap I'd left: 'People do acquire a certain notoriety when they've died a violent death, of course. Cambridge will be full of people Googling Damien Newbold to find out more as soon as the news breaks.'

'I wasn't Googling out of some kind of morbid interest,' I said, realising as my voice rose that DS Brookes was playing me like a fiddle. 'I looked at those sites several days ago now.' Which was just the information he'd wanted to elicit. 'When I put my computer away at night I tend to hibernate it, rather than shutting it down, so any web pages I have up stay up, unless I deliberately close them.'

Both officers were sipping their tea and waiting for me to go on.

'I started looking into Damien Newbold because of the situation I found myself in. I was minding his house, plonked down in the middle of all his physical stuff, of course, but increasingly getting drawn in to his everyday dealings and all the ...' I couldn't think quite how to put it '... all the entanglements he seemed to have. It was a disconcerting feeling, and it made me want to know what kind of person he was.' My throat felt rather dry, and I took a sip of tea. 'I was interested when I saw the piece about how successful he was at work, because some other aspects of his life seemed ...' I paused again '... well, a bit dysfunctional. Truth to tell, I haven't done this sort of job before. I'd imagined it would be a bit like staying in some impersonal holiday flat, when in fact it's been like setting up an uncomfortable tent next to a nest full of angry wasps.' This last bit came out in a rush and I felt myself blushing. A nest full of angry wasps? Talk about a drama queen. Damien Newbold had just been murdered and here I was, getting a bit hysterical over having to deal with the odd abandoned girlfriend.

DI Johnson was talking again now. 'I'd heard that this was your first house-sitting job. My understanding is that Mr Bastable, who runs the business, normally hires people with some kind of security or police training. You're the first contractor he's used who doesn't match that profile. Could you explain to us how you came to take on the role?'

And so, of course, I had to go into details about my circumstances, and how Steph was Nate's cousin and had put me forward for the job. Naturally, I knew that Nate was well aware of the entire story, thanks to Steph, and so presumably he had already related it to the police during his interview too.

'And Mr Bastable didn't express any reservations about taking you on?' DI Johnson said.

I thought of the words I'd overheard. He'd had reservations all right. 'Steph had vouched for me.'

'He must have a lot of faith in his cousin's judgement,' Johnson said. 'Well founded, I'm sure,' he added, smiling at me. But in spite of his friendly tone, and my innocence, I could tell he thought the situation was odd.

'Nate Bastable had to get someone in at short notice,' I said, 'and so I suppose his choice was limited. He came to meet me on the day I arrived—'

'On the day you arrived? That really was last minute, wasn't it?' DI Johnson was still smiling, but I felt under attack. Adrenaline pumped round my body, and its effect was overlaid with a sense of disbelief. He seemed to be using everything I said to show that either I, or the house-sitting business, was wanting.

'The whole thing *was* very last minute, as I said. Nate didn't have many options. But anyway,' I tried to keep my voice steady, 'he came to meet me to satisfy himself that I was suitable. I assume he must have had Damien Newbold's go-ahead, and that would have been the main thing, surely?'

'Of course,' DS Brookes said. 'I imagine he must have admitted your lack of experience to Mr Newbold and, for whatever reason, Mr Newbold decided to proceed regardless.'

'He probably didn't imagine there would be so many complications,' I said, hearing how ridiculous that sounded. Complications. That hardly covered it. But DS Brookes merely nodded.

DI Johnson stood up and wandered over to the window to look out onto the Common, then turned back into the room to face me. 'You were saying that Mr Newbold's life came across as dysfunctional,' he said. 'Could you explain, please, what gave you that impression?'

Well, where to start? It was probably best to include everything now; even those things I hadn't highlighted to Nate. 'The first thing that struck me was the paintings on his bedroom walls.'

'You've been into all the rooms, have you?' He raised his eyebrows for a moment, but then let them relax. 'Part of the job I suppose.'

I agreed, and explained about the cleaning tasks I'd been set, and he nodded.

'So the paintings? Perhaps it would be easiest if you showed me.'

We went upstairs to the front bedroom in silence, and I let them go in ahead of me to see the display Damien Newbold had put on, apparently for my benefit.

'I see,' DI Johnson said.

'I know who three of them are now,' I said. 'I expect you've heard from Nate Bastable about Maggie Cook, who let herself in to this house whilst I was out.'

Johnson nodded.

'That's her,' I pointed. 'And that one is Tilly Blake, Mr Newbold's cleaner.' I saw Brookes raise his eyebrows in a way that told me he'd like a cleaner like her. Hmm. 'And that,' I said, pointing at the painting opposite the bed ...

'Is Mr Newbold's mother?' DI Johnson capped my sentence. 'I recognise her from the photograph you showed us downstairs. Not the sort of face you'd forget in a hurry.'

We were all silent for a moment.

'But I haven't identified the subject of the fourth picture yet,' I said, and indicated the woman with her eyes cast down.

Johnson and Brookes exchanged a glance. 'Oh, don't worry,' Brookes said. 'We know who she is.'

I wished I could ask.

As we went back downstairs I explained about Tilly's visit, and how she was able to tell me that Maggie's painting was normally the only nude hanging in the bedroom. 'And somehow, that didn't come as a complete surprise. It had seemed to me, more and more, that he was having a game with me. Setting up situations that would embarrass me – and the women in his life – for his own amusement. It wasn't a very nice feeling.'

'And yet you stayed on,' Brookes said.

'I don't like giving up. And I don't actually have anywhere else to go, as you already know.'

Brookes looked down at his feet and I felt as though I'd scored a point at last.

After that, they got me to recap all the other 'incidents' that had made me feel uncomfortable: the picture of

Damien's mother in the DVD cupboard, Maggie's phone call to his mobile in the middle of the night, the package someone had sent him, and every detail of Maggie's unexpected visit.

'You say it all seemed staged,' DI Johnson said. 'As though Mr Newbold wanted you and Maggie Cook to come face to face.'

I nodded. 'And he wanted me to have done his cleaning, only to find Tilly Blake was booked to come in and do it anyway, and I needn't have bothered. And equally, I think, for Tilly to turn up and find someone else had taken her place.'

'You'd think she'd be glad,' Brookes said, 'to find someone else had done her work for her.'

I shook my head. 'I know it seems weird, but I've written about that sort of situation before. She was pleased he still needed her, whether it was for sex or for washing the floor. I didn't want to tell her he'd double booked us. I could see it would hurt her feelings.'

DS Brookes looked mystified. As well he might.

DI Johnson said, 'And each time one of these incidents took place, you reported them to Mr Bastable?'

'Well,' I said, 'I did whenever it was something I thought needed to be reported back to Damien Newbold. If it was just an oddity, like the paintings or the photo in the cupboard, I obviously didn't bother saying anything.'

He nodded. 'But when you felt it warranted it, you went through Mr Bastable?'

'Of course.' Why the repeat question?

'And you've never met Damien Newbold personally?'

'No.'

He looked at me. 'I was just wondering why it was then, that you tried to make direct contact with him whilst he was away.'

'Direct?' My confusion must have shown on my face. 'How do you mean?' I paused for a moment. 'I didn't.'

Johnson glanced down at his notebook. 'I've got a record of a call made to a mobile found at the cottage Mr Newbold was renting on Sunday 7th June at three forty-two p.m. The call went unanswered. It came from this house.'

It took me a moment or two to get it. The mobile in the package. God – Damien Newbold had sent it himself. Of course, now that I'd been told, it made perfect sense. He knew damn well I'd leave it for him to open when he got back, and so I'd get woken by the alarm. He was the one who'd made me look, and no doubt sat there watching the mobile ring when I'd called. I should have known as soon as I'd got the note tucked into the attic bed. Both acts had the same hallmark.

I explained to DI Johnson. Of course, I couldn't produce the mobile with its text, given that I'd finally thrown it away as instructed and the bins had been emptied since then. That and the fact that I had to admit my nosiness in opening the package were demoralising, but at least the basic story fitted with Newbold's taunting modus operandi. And, of course, Nate would be able to confirm my call about the mysterious package that had woken me up in the night. I wished he didn't need to know about my having opened up the parcel.

'Have you still got the bit of paper you wrote the number down on?' DI Johnson asked.

I fished in my jeans pocket and gave it to him. 'You might want this too,' I said, handing over Tilly Blake's number.

'And we'll have the mobile that Maggie Cook called, please,' DS Brookes said.

I went into the drawing room to fetch it from the bookshelf where it still lay, switched off. The detectives followed me.

'And where were you yesterday evening between, say, six and nine p.m.?' DI Johnson said.

'Just here on my own. That's mostly the case at the moment.' I handed him the phone.

'Yet you didn't answer when we telephoned.'

I could feel the heat creeping up my neck, the flush spreading to my cheeks. 'I told you when you called the second time; I was in the bath.'

'So you did.'

We re-crossed the drawing room.

'Officially,' he went on, 'there were only two people who knew where Mr Newbold was staying: Elizabeth Edmunds, who owns the cottage he was renting, and Mr Bastable.' He walked through the hall and went over to lean against the dining room wall by the window. 'Then Maggie Cook let herself in and found the address, and, of course,' he paused, 'we understand you saw that address too, after she'd left.'

DS Brookes sat back down at the table and I followed suit, my legs wobbling.

'Naturally,' Brookes said, 'we've no way of knowing who else he may have told, but in general it looks as though he kept his whereabouts fairly quiet. His work didn't know where he was staying, for instance. Of course, he was still in the office each day, so they had no particular reason to ask.'

At that moment my mobile went. Nate. Johnson inclined his head, indicating that it was all right to break off for a moment. So long as I had whatever conversation it might be in his hearing, of course.

'Are they still interviewing you?' Nate said as soon as I picked up.

'Yes.'

'Jeez. Right. Call me when they leave?'

'Okay.'

And that was that. I hoped it left my visitors feeling frustrated and curious.

I turned back to face them. 'I'm so sorry. You were saying?'

Johnson looked at me. 'About how few people seem to have known where Damien Newbold was staying. It's important for us to talk to anyone else who had that information. We'll be checking with Maggie Cook, of course, in case she passed the address on. What about you?'

I shook my head. 'I haven't told anyone,' I said.

Brookes leant back in his seat. 'And has anyone been asking?'

I paused, not because I was intending to lie, just because I really didn't want to be the one to put the police onto Emily Amos. She'd started to confide in me, just a little bit, and it felt wrong to be casting suspicion on her. 'There's a student next door,' I said at last, and explained the background. 'But I never gave her any clue as to where Mr Newbold was staying, so I don't see how she could have found out.'

'Thank you.' Johnson nodded. 'We'll look into that.'

My head was aching. 'God,' I said, 'she won't even know Damien Newbold's dead yet.'

'Probably not,' Brookes agreed.

His choice of words only struck me as they went off to look through the contents of the house. They sent a shiver down my spine.

DI Johnson, DS Brookes and their colleagues were still at the house, sifting through papers and belongings, at twelve.

Whilst they'd been working, I stayed in the dining room feeling sick, unable to put my mind to anything. I was still reeling, images spooling through my brain: Maggie in the house, Emily's haunted eyes, Damien Newbold's mother, a defeated Tilly. A thick mesh of unhappiness, fury and passion stirred up for all the wrong reasons.

When, at last, Johnson and Brookes left, I leant against the front door. Thank God I didn't have to answer any more questions. For the time being at least. I could guess the detectives' next port of call though, and nipped through to the kitchen. Sure enough, they were knocking on the door of Oswald House. I saw Fi answering, and the puzzled expression on her face as she led them inside. After that I could only imagine the scene as the news came out.

The rest of the police team were gone by two, and it was only then that the feeling of being under siege really receded. I waited for five minutes until I'd stopped feeling sick, and then called Nate.

Ruby opened the door quickly, and Nate wondered if she'd been looking out for him. He followed her into the kitchen.

'Would you like something cold? I've got Coke.'

'Thanks. How were the police?'

'Very unlovely.' She explained how she'd opened the package addressed to Damien with its mysterious alarm, and how she'd found the 'made you look' text, and eventually called the sender's number. 'And it turned out that that was none other than Newbold himself. Not knowing the background, they wondered why I'd been trying to contact him direct. They're bound to ask you about it. I told them you'd be able to confirm I'd received the package at least.'

'And that Newbold asked that you throw it away unopened.'

She looked at the floor. 'Um, yes. That too.'

But Nate couldn't wind her up after she'd had such a tough morning. 'Relax. I'd have done the same. Ever thought of going into PI work?'

The ghost of a smile crossed her lips as she took the Coke cans out of the fridge. 'Steph calls me "understandably curious".'

'That's one way of putting it.' Nate leant against the worktop. 'Well, it certainly confirms my feelings about Newbold. One screwed up git. Anyone who'd go to those lengths to pull someone's strings is definitely way off-beam.'

'I suppose that might tie in with what's happened; he pushed someone over the edge. He was certainly out to taunt me.' As Ruby took down tumblers and poured their drinks she told Nate about the note from Newbold that she'd found in the bed in the attic, when she'd decided to decamp there the previous night. She looked at him over her shoulder. 'Serves me right for going against instructions, really.'

Nate shook his head. 'I reckon most people would have cracked sooner. So, have you decided to start sharing things with me? It would have been good to know about the student next door with the older man fixation. And Steph told me Maggie's nude portrait isn't the only one on Newbold's bedroom wall.'

She was dispensing ice from the fridge freezer. 'I did think they were weird, but not enough to make a thing about it. Not in comparison to everything else that's been going on, anyway.'

'I guess I can understand that. But from now on, take it as read that I'm "understandably curious" too. Plus, sharing can sometimes make things less stressful.'

She glanced at him over her shoulder for a second, then looked away, and Nate wondered what she was thinking.

'So what else did the police want to chat about?'

'There was definitely nothing chatty about it.'

'Ah. I was afraid of that.'

'Every comment they made set me squirming.' She put the glasses on the kitchen table, and they sat down. 'It was clear they thought it was really weird that you'd given me this job in the first place. They treated me as if I was some kind of imposter. And when I told them about the paintings upstairs, it was as though they thought I'd been ransacking the house for personal details.'

'I'm sure they don't really view you as a suspect though.'

'Why not?' She leant forward, hunched over her drink. 'As the police pointed out, I'm one of only four people that definitely knew Damien Newbold's whereabouts.'

'We're part of an exclusive gang. I'd like to know what motive they could dream up for you.'

She shrugged, and raised an eyebrow. 'I'm a woman in emotional turmoil, with every reason to hate men at the moment. I've admitted I was being taunted by Damien Newbold; perhaps it was the straw that broke the camel's back. Something finally snapped and I strode out into the evening air to wreak my revenge.'

'It's nice and dramatic, I'll give you that, but you'd have to be pretty far gone to kill him for that reason.'

'They might think I am,' she said. 'But then I can imagine other reasons why I might have done away with him too.'

This was getting interesting. 'Such as?' Nate asked.

'Well, this house is full of valuable stuff. What if I'd gambled that no inventory existed, gone off to kill Damien and then removed a few of the choicer items before the police turned up, assuming no one would be any the wiser?'

Nate must have smiled, and when he saw her smile back it brought the feelings he'd been trying to shut down to the fore. 'You should definitely be a PI. Being able to think like a criminal's a prerequisite. But it would be pretty risky to assume there was no record of the house contents.'

She shrugged. 'People take risks all the time. And the police might reason that I'd be very glad of the money, given that I now have no home to call my own.'

'And your conscience?'

'They'd assume that it would be calmed by the fact that

Damien Newbold was clearly a nasty man who treated women badly.'

'Neat.'

There was a moment's pause. 'Do you know how he died?'

Nate shook his head. 'The police weren't keen to share that with me, though it'll be in the papers soon enough. You're thinking the method might provide a clue as to who killed him?'

She nodded.

'Listen, Ruby, even if this murder was entirely personal, I'm not happy with you being here. And I don't know where Newbold's death will leave this house-sitting job anyway. I gather his next of kin is his brother. If River House goes to him, it'll depend on whether he still wants the place minded.'

She nodded.

'Obviously, I know this is more than just a job for you—'

'Yes.' Her green eyes locked onto his. 'Look, I'll be fine, honestly. Whatever's going on, it doesn't seem to involve me. I can just sit tight, assuming the brother wants me to stay on.'

Nate leant forward, resting his elbows on the table. 'I don't want those to turn out to be famous last words.'

'Well, amen to that.'

'Look, if you really want to stay then fine, but I'm going to stay too.' Nate couldn't help noticing her startled look in response to that. Not flattering. 'Damien's got enough spare bedrooms to shelter a team of house-sitters, and I'm no longer convinced that this is a one-person job. I know you're capable and tough; you've proved that. It's just ... well, safety in numbers, that's all. I'd be planning exactly the same thing if it was one of my regulars, Bill Morris, sitting in your place. He's ex-army and six foot five, but I still reckon he'd regard it as a sensible precaution.'

Ruby bit her lip. He could tell she wasn't overwhelmed with joy at the idea, but he couldn't back down. Especially given her habit for digging up information and then keeping it to herself. Digging dirt when there was a murderer on the loose tended to be a hazardous pastime.

'Besides, although I've no intention of going back to PI work, old habits die hard, and the experience might yet come in handy.'

'Okay,' she said at last. 'That does make sense. At least now when I hear creaks in the night I'll be able to imagine it's you, going to the bathroom, rather than a hammer-wielding maniac.'

Nice to know he was preferable to that option, at least.

Chapter Fourteen

I waited alone at River House whilst Nate went home to pick up what he'd need for his stay in Cambridge. Truth to tell, it was comforting to think there'd be someone with me overnight from now on. All the same, it went against the grain to admit it, so I'd tried to sound casual about the whole thing. I didn't want him to think I couldn't cope.

Now that I was alone again, I found it hard to settle to anything. My nerves were strung taut after the news of Damien Newbold's death. Time for some distraction. I went back to the bookcase in the drawing room and knelt down beside it. The albums were still there. I picked up where I'd left off and pulled out 1976 to 1980.

The photos of Bella, Damien and Samson continued: both boys in school uniform, Damien towering above his brother; Bella and Damien lost in conversation, captured by a third party; Bella and Damien in a shiny car, with Samson in the back seat. I wondered what the occasion was. Perhaps the car had been new. Then I noticed that it was Damien who was in the driver's seat. Bella had her hand on his upper arm, as though she'd been rubbing it, in an encouraging, or congratulatory way. She was looking at him, rather than the camera, pride in her eyes. I glanced at the caption: August 1977. He'd only been, I counted, thirteen. Behind them were trees, and the car was on grass. Perhaps she had taught him to drive early, on private land.

It was midway through the 1978 photos that I found the first picture stuck into the album face down. It had clearly been glued in the right way round at one time. The back showed signs of tearing where someone – I could only assume Damien – had detached it from its conventional position before reversing it.

Okay, so Nate had understood why I'd opened up Damien's package against orders. As I fetched a knife from the kitchen drawer, I acknowledged he might not be quite so relaxed about my next action. All the more reason to get on with it quickly, before he returned. I went back to the album, and edged it under the centre of the photo, trying to ease the paper free by moving the blade towards the loosest corner. It was a slow process, but at last I separated it from its backing. It wasn't perfect – there were sections of the picture that were covered with a layer of the backing paper that had refused to come away – but I could see enough.

Bella was standing in a cocktail dress in some grand room with ornate columns. She wasn't the only woman in the photograph, but the others were chattering away, not facing the camera. Only Bella looked in the direction of the photographer, her eyes sparkling as brightly as her diamond earrings. Her look matched the one she bore in the bedroom painting. The joy was there, without that indefinable reservation that had been present in her early marriage photos.

Across the bottom corner of the picture was scrawled, 'The only woman in ...' The next bit was obliterated by the glue and backing paper, but just below I could see part of the word 'Nico' and a kiss.

I might have looked further, but at that moment I realised I'd missed a text from Steph. A wave of guilt washed over me. I should have called her before. The news was bound to have got out, and she was probably frantic.

She answered on the second ring, and I filled her in on everything that had happened, and how Damien had got me dancing to his tune by mailing me his own mobile. 'And judging by the line-up on his bedroom wall he could have been doing the same sort of thing to a lot of other women.'

'Too true,' she said. 'And given that they were much more intimately involved with him, I suppose one of them might have snapped.'

'Yes, that's what Nate and I were thinking.'

'How did he seem?'

'Nate? Okay. But all this is a bit extreme; not what you'd expect given his new line of business. He's going to come and stay here at River House so he can keep an eye on things. It must be hard for him.'

'Really hard,' Steph said. There was something in her tone that struck me, but before I could say anything she added, 'Do you know though, I think he's almost relieved?'

'Relieved?'

She paused for second. 'Don't get me wrong. He's not dancing a jig at the news of Damien Newbold's death, though it's clear he wasn't a fan. But ever since that prank package turned up, I think he's been worried about what might happen next.'

'He was worried something might happen to me?'

She sighed. 'He thought he was being paranoid. He's always trying to fight against taking things too seriously and, after all, there wasn't much to go on. All the same, it was on his mind. He said it seemed like more than standard nastiness.'

'I suppose he must see the worst in every situation, having worked as a private investigator.'

Steph paused for a moment. 'Something like that. Speaking of men who treat women badly, did you ever get round to reading that letter of Luke's?'

'Yes.'

'Sorry,' she said. 'Wrong thing to ask on a day like today.'

'It's okay.'

'Do you know what you're going to do?'

I could hear the anxiety in her voice, which made it worse. 'I can't go back, Steph. It's no good.' And I explained how he'd effectively blamed me for what had happened. 'And it's not just him,' I said. 'Daisy Buchanan's mother caught me in the street when I was chucking stuff into the car on the day I walked out. She said something like, "Such a shame you were away, otherwise it might never have happened." And then she went on about Luke having taken away Daisy's innocence.'

Steph snorted. 'If she really thinks that, she's a bigger fool than I took her for. And I took her for a pretty huge one, I can tell you.'

'But the fact remains, even she thinks I'm partly responsible. How the hell did that happen?'

'For her it's old-fashioned-woman syndrome, I'm afraid. Thinks we really can't expect men to keep their hands to themselves if they're left unattended for five minutes. It's probably personal experience; I've heard quite a few things about her husband ...' She coughed meaningfully. 'But, as far as Luke goes, you don't really think he blames you, do you?'

'Probably not, deep down. It's just guilt putting him on the defensive. But he ought to be able to rise above that at a time like this. Anyway, that's all immaterial. It's still no good. It's too much of a betrayal. He didn't just risk damaging me and her when he slept with Daisy, he put our whole life in Saxwell on the line.'

She sighed. 'I understand. I'll really miss you, you know.'

I had to take a deep breath to keep my voice steady. 'You won't get rid of me that easily. I'll have to visit Saxwell St Andrew in disguise, that's all.'

Nate arrived back at around seven. I opened up and he stepped into the doorway, loaded with carrier bags. He followed my eyes and gave me a wry smile. 'I wasn't sure what food you'd got in, but I had a feeling shopping might not have been uppermost in your mind.'

'Spot on, as a matter of fact.' I turned towards the kitchen and he followed me, dumping the bags on the worktop. Once he'd offloaded them, I noticed he was wearing a rucksack too.

'I can unpack the food whilst you go and sort out your stuff, if you like.'

'Thanks.'

I opened the first bag. Prosciutto, Parmesan cheese, mini plum tomatoes, aubergine and spaghetti. Hmm. I suddenly realised I was ravenous. That, and the fact that I was glad Nate had done the shopping; I couldn't have picked better myself. The second bag had onions, garlic and herbs and a couple of bottles of red. Better and better.

'When did you last eat?'

I hadn't realised he was back in the kitchen. He moved quietly for someone of his size.

I had to think for a second. 'Breakfast.'

'And given that you had a police visit hanging over you, I'm guessing it wasn't a hearty one?'

'It's amazing how far you can go on a spoonful of cereal. Though I can't pretend I'm left entirely cold by the contents of your shopping bags.'

I glanced at him for a moment, taking in the unruly hair and the eight o'clock shadow. I wondered if he'd slept the night before. He scrubbed up all right for someone who was up against it.

'Glass of wine?' I said. 'I've got some in, but yours looks superior.'

'After today, I'm not sure I'll care about the quality, but yes, please. Bring it on.'

I reached for a corkscrew whilst he got down some

glasses. It felt so weird to be using Damien Newbold's things, now that he was dead. As though we were somehow trespassing. I shivered for a moment and caught Nate watching me. He nodded. 'It takes a while for it to sink in, doesn't it? I've read what little the news sites have to say on the Internet now, but it still doesn't feel real.'

'I know he wasn't a nice man—'

'But that just makes it all the more confusing? Because you feel guilty, at the same time as seeing the horror of it?' He took the corkscrew from me and opened the bottle I'd put out.

I nodded.

'It's not unnatural.' He handed me a full glass. 'Or at least, I bloody well hope it's not, because that's exactly how I've been feeling. By the way, Damien Newbold's brother, Samson, has been in touch now. The family solicitors have contacted him; turns out he's his brother's sole beneficiary, and also an executor. In principle, he'd like us to carry on overseeing this place. But he's coming to check on arrangements tomorrow.'

His tone said it all. 'You don't like him?' I asked.

'Probably a bit of a snap judgement, given that it's based on one phone call, but no. I have a feeling we won't hit it off.'

'I guess the signs weren't good, given his family connections.'

'Quite.'

'Would you like me to chop an onion?'

'No.'

I raised an eyebrow.

'I'd like you to top up your wine and go and sit in the garden. I wouldn't have chosen to put you through all this. Cooking you dinner won't exactly make up for it, but my options are a bit limited at the moment.'

I did as he asked and topped up my wine, which was

obviously stupid, given I hadn't eaten anything for over twelve hours. Let's just say I was past caring.

Being outside accentuated the feeling of unreality. It was drowsily warm, the heat of the day having abated, and a blackbird was singing. I sat on the bench and a bee buzzed around the climber by my shoulder. It seemed unbelievable that Damien Newbold would never look on any of it again. I wondered how Emily was doing. I could only imagine the effect his death would have on her. For a second I listened for any sound from Oswald House, but it was quiet.

Through the window, I could see Nate, crossing back and forth, from the kitchen sink to the cooker.

After ten minutes or so, I got up to go to the bathroom and found my head felt a bit swimmy.

By the time I'd finished, Nate had fetched my glass from the garden, refilled it, and was dishing our pasta and sauce onto plates at the kitchen table. It smelled like heaven.

I sat, and he dropped into a chair next to me and took a swig of his wine.

I found it hard to come up with conversation. My mind was taken up with everything that had happened that day, and I wanted to ask what he thought about the murder. He was bound to have an opinion, given his past experience as an investigator. But remembering his reaction when I'd asked about his old job, I held back. I thought again of how he'd walked out of the room.

He glanced sideways in my direction, a forkful of food halfway to his mouth. 'What?'

'Sorry.' And then the thoughts that had just been running through my mind came straight out. It must have been the wine.

He sighed and leant back in his chair. 'I'm sorry I was so rude when you asked me about my PI work.'

'I knew you must have your reasons.' And of course, I'd wondered what they were, but I wasn't going to ask. Not now.

'I have, but it doesn't excuse me being foul about it. So, to answer the question you asked back then, yes, I do miss my old job. But I can't go back to it.'

His tone told me the subject was closed. We both ate for a moment, but then he put his fork back on his plate and looked in my direction.

'In spite of that, it doesn't mean we can't talk about Newbold. God, it'd be pretty hard not to under the circumstances.'

'I just wondered what you thought about who might have done it.'

'You've probably got a better idea, after living in this place.' He topped up my wine again, before I'd thought to object. 'But the women on his bedroom walls all seem like possibilities on the face of it.'

'Except one.' I explained I'd found out that one of the paintings was of Damien's dead mother.

'Interesting. Okay, so not her then.'

'And I've met another of the nudes now, Tilly Blake.'

He raised an eyebrow. 'It's as though you're collecting them. I take it she was dressed on this occasion?'

I let out a laugh that surprised me. 'Thankfully, yes.' I explained how Tilly had turned up out of the blue that morning. It was hard to believe it was the same day.

'Sounds as though her shock was genuine.'

I remembered her reaction to the news. 'It certainly seemed that way. Poor woman.'

He caught my eye and for a second put a hand on my arm. He didn't say anything, but I could see he understood. 'Whereas Maggie Cook?'

'A firebrand. But then again, that means she wasn't bottling anything up.'

'There is that.'

'And then there's the fourth woman, who the police clearly know about, but I don't.'

'And we can't discount your young student friend, I'm afraid.'

I looked down at my plate. 'I suppose not.'

'Cheer up. There's Samson to consider too. If he's inheriting this place, plus its contents he's got a nice, fat motive.'

'Let's say it's him.'

After we'd finished our food, I dared to ask the question that had been on my mind. 'What was it that made you worry about Damien Newbold, right from the start?'

He raised an eyebrow.

'To be honest,' I said, 'I overheard you talking to Steph in the street, that first day we met.' I sat back in my chair.

He looked across at me slowly. 'You did?'

'I'm afraid I guessed she might be passing on the gossip in a little more detail than was strictly necessary, so I followed you both out, in case I could distract her.'

He raised an eyebrow again. 'I see.'

'And I heard you start to say something to her about Damien Newbold. Do you remember?' He looked down. His dark fringe had fallen over his eyes now, and he didn't answer, so I went on. 'You were going to confide in her, but then you stopped and said it didn't matter.'

'Ah, yes,' he said as though he was regretting it. 'Now I do remember. And I wish you hadn't got such a good memory. Or such an inquisitive personality. Do you always go about sleuthing like that?'

I wasn't going to let him off the hook. 'It tends to stand me in good stead, both for the books I write, and in everyday life.'

'I can imagine.'

'Anyway, after all that's happened, I wondered what you were going to say.'

He sighed. 'The truth is, I was surprised at how readily he'd agreed to you minding his house. He could have gone to other agencies, found someone with more experience.' He looked me straight in the eye now. It was clearly his trademark approach when he had to tackle anything tricky. For a second my mind flitted to Luke, staring at the floor as he'd told me about Daisy. 'He'd asked me for background details on you, of course,' he went on, bringing me back to the present, 'and as part of that I directed him to your website. It was what he said then that worried me.'

'Why?'

He gave me a wry smile. 'Your photo's up there, and he said you *looked* perfect.'

'Hmm,' I said. 'The guy clearly had more to him than I'd realised.' God. Where had that come from? Bloody wine. I felt my cheeks go hot.

There was a sparkle in Nate's blue eyes. 'I certainly wouldn't dispute his judgement,' he said, turning sideways to face me. 'But those high cheek bones don't strictly qualify you as an expert house-sitter, so I wondered if he was keen for the wrong reasons.'

We sat there for a moment, then he leant forwards, and I found I had too. We were only a couple of inches apart. He put his hand to my cheek and his touch sent a rush of static round my body. Then suddenly we weren't a couple of inches apart any more. He was kissing me hard, his arm round my waist, pulling me to him. And, oh boy, was I kissing him back ... It was only at that point that I realised my dream wasn't just some embarrassing trick of the mind. It had been trying to tell me something, only I'd been a bit too preoccupied to acknowledge it, what with one thing and another.

Either way, it was all quite satisfactory from my point of view, until suddenly, after what was only probably a second or two he pulled away.

'Shit, Ruby. I'm so sorry.'

'It's okay.' When I said it was okay, I meant great.

'No, it's not. I was completely out of order.' He got up and put his empty wine glass on the counter. 'I'm out of it on adrenaline, I think. There's no way I should have leapt on you like that.'

He wasn't facing me any more, but I'd seen the look of dismay in his eyes. Had he leapt on me? Or – horrible thought – had I, in fact, leapt on him? I'd made that stupid comment about Newbold having good taste in admiring my looks. Well, that had put Nate in a position where he'd had no option but to pay me a compliment in response. The only alternative would have been to ignore my lame little remark, and leave me looking like an idiot. I knew he was too much of a gent to do that. And then … Well, then everything went a bit hazy. I remembered leaning in towards him, but had he leant first? He'd gone for it, once we were in such close proximity, but once again, I'd probably put him in a position where he couldn't politely do otherwise. He'd taken the hit, but then pulled back as soon as he could, and pretended it was all his responsibility. I couldn't fault his manners.

'I'll go up to my room,' Nate said. 'Give you some space. The last thing you need is me mucking you around, as well as everything else.'

Shit. He'd be regretting his decision to move into River House now. And there was no way I could turn back the clock.

Chapter Fifteen

Nate couldn't believe he'd allowed it to happen. He'd been caught off guard – laid into the wine too enthusiastically. But he knew what the after-effects of adrenaline were like. He should have guarded against it. Hell.

And how would it seem to Ruby now? He'd basically insisted on moving in with her, then made a pass at her, all in one day, for God's sake. Nice one, Nate. And now, he couldn't think how to handle it. She didn't have anywhere to go, and to chuck her out after what he'd done would be totally wrong. But equally if he now decided he had to leave, he'd be abandoning her because of his own selfish actions.

Nate wondered for a second about asking Jane Trask to come and take his place. She was on another job at the moment, but he could swap with her. Or he could offer to pay to put Ruby up in a hotel. Which of course, she'd never accept, so pointless even raising it, except for show.

He was going round in circles. He'd kissed her – and she'd kissed him back. But he'd plied her with wine beforehand, she'd had practically no food all day, probably precious little sleep in the last thirty-six hours and the shock of Newbold's death to deal with. He'd seen her reaction to the idea of him moving in. It wasn't the one of someone secretly hankering after him. No. She'd just kissed him back because of the state she was in.

Shit.

There were no sexy dreams for me that night. I tried to push the incident out of my head but it was impossible. A terrible, creeping embarrassment weighed in my chest. In Nate's mind I was no doubt the desperate lady, abandoned by her partner and on the prowl for fresh meat. Hey, subconsciously I was probably looking for someone to father a child for me, too. Great that he knew that little detail. And when it came down to it, I couldn't rely on my feelings. Luke and I might be washed up, but I'd still been crying over him that very day, after I'd spoken to Steph on the phone. Basically, I was all over the place. And the most humiliating thing of all was that I was now staying in River House thanks to Nate's charity, and performing no useful function. How he must be wishing I'd got somewhere else to go. I know I was.

I wasn't sure what time Nate had had breakfast, but I didn't clap eyes on him during the hour I sat at the kitchen table. A little later, when I was up in the attic, he called from the landing to say he was off to fetch Samson Newbold.

I decided to get outside for some fresh air whilst I'd got the chance, and my feelings were instantly put into perspective. I bumped into Fi, standing beside Oswald House, smoking a cigarette. The squally weather whipped at her curly hair, blowing it across the lighted end, so that she had to tug it out of the way. She looked momentarily guilty when she saw me watching her. 'I don't really smoke any more,' she said, 'but the last twenty-four hours have made a temporary relapse very appealing.' She looked at me. 'It's been appalling.'

'I can hardly begin to imagine. How's Emily?'

'Completely crazed. God it was awful when the police told her. She went totally silent and white for a moment and then she ran out of the room. We could all hear her throwing up. She only made it as far as the hallway.' She took another deep drag and offered to pass the cigarette over to me, but I shook my head. 'Whilst the police were there, she just sat staring into space. She managed to answer their questions, but she sounded as though she was in a trance.' She looked at me, her eyes wide with remembering. 'I tried to help her get cleaned up, before the interview began, but there were still bits of sick in her hair.'

'How were the police? Were they sensitive?'

She exhaled. 'As much as they could be, I guess. They had to do the telling, of course, but that was out of the way pretty quickly. They really wanted to talk to her because she'd called Damien Newbold's work; tried to find out where he was hiding. It was clear they were wondering about her as a possible suspect. After they'd let her go upstairs to rest they asked me more about their relationship. What did I know? How acrimonious had it really been? How had Emily reacted when Damien went away? Basically whether I'd felt the balance of her mind had been upset. I suppose that was what they were getting at.'

She raised her eyes to mine. 'It's funny, isn't it? Makes you realise how economical we are with the truth, most of the time. I could imagine answering exactly the same questions, from – oh, I don't know – one of the college tutors, say, who was checking up on Em's well-being, and I'd have had all the right patter to allay their concerns. I'd easily have smoothed everything over and made it seem like nothing. And that would have felt like the right thing to do, too. After all, I know Emily's just been going through a bad crush, and that she'd have got over it in her own sweet time.' She leant back against the wall of the house. 'But you can't do that when it's the police asking, can you? Suddenly you know you've got to tell the truth, warts and all. And I did, and it sounded awful. Telling it, in cold blood like that, made her sound capable of anything.'

'I think it's the way the police ask their questions. I felt they suspected me too and it took me completely by surprise. They were very suspicious about the last-minute way I got this job, and the fact I hadn't done any house-sitting before.'

She stubbed the cigarette out against a brick. 'Crazy, isn't it? When it comes down to it, life's just like that. Sometimes things do happen in a haphazard way.'

I nodded. 'And as for Emily, the police must be aware of how intense teenage crushes can be. It's just a stage.'

'You're right, but I'm still worried they suspect her.'

'I'm sure there are lots of people higher up their list.'

'Having known Damien, I expect you're right,' Fi replied. 'I still feel like a proper little Judas though.' She took out another cigarette. 'I'll tell you something. I'd swear Emily never did get hold of his address. She'd have told me if she had; everything's coming straight out with her at the moment.'

Back inside I tried to put the thought of Emily out of my head for the time being. I needed to focus on the meeting with Samson Newbold. That and how I was going to manage to behave normally round Nate.

The clothes I'd brought with me were just those I could fit into my rucksack and a small holdall, so I hadn't got much of a repertoire. It was a cooler day so I could put on something more formal without overheating. I grabbed a jersey dress and went off in search of an iron. If I could just get him to think Nate and I were best cut out to mind the house, then I could put off the evil hour when I had to make my next move.

I looked at myself in one of the long mirrors on the landing and hastily took out the extra earrings Steph had disapproved of. Now a sombre woman – neat and reliable – looked back at me.

Nate couldn't look at Ruby as she opened the door of River House, which meant he watched Samson Newbold instead. Unlike him, Samson had no trouble meeting her eye. He didn't try to disguise the nature of his up-and-down look either; his tongue was practically hanging out. Nate had intended to give Ruby as wide a berth as possible; he still couldn't believe how he'd lost control the day before. All the same, it was instinctive to put himself between her and Samson to perform the introductions.

Newbold junior had a drinker's face: the whites of his eyes were veined with red, his nose had the telltale discoloration, and he'd gained weight that his elder sibling had managed to avoid.

Nate saw Ruby battle the urge to flinch, as the murdered man's brother came within a few inches of her. The smell of stale alcohol and cigarettes hung in the air.

He glanced at her for just a second, but she was looking determinedly at the floor. Understandable. If she'd had anywhere else to go she'd probably have walked out of her own accord already.

'How funny to be back,' Samson said, striding into the drawing room as though he owned the place. Which of course he would, very soon. 'It's been years.'

Ruby cast him a questioning glance in response.

'Our guardian helped let the place after our mother died and we got packed off to boarding school,' Samson explained. 'Damien made the most awful fuss about it, but he only got stuck there for a year. I had seven. He, I may say, got off lightly.' He drawled out his words and looked up at her from under his lashes in a horrible parody of coyness.

'I've heard some places can be pretty tough,' Ruby said.

Nate would have shot her a warning glance, if she'd shown any signs of looking in his direction. She was probing, and that wasn't part of her role. He cursed inwardly, but, in fact, Samson seemed too wrapped up in himself to notice anything untoward. He raised his eyes to heaven in response to Ruby's comment about his school.

'Ours was appalling, but unfortunately it was also the alma mater of our guardian, who couldn't see anything wrong with it at all.'

'It must have been a relief when it was over. I expect it was good to come home again.' She locked her glance onto Samson's, smiling as she spoke. Nate supposed it must be automatic with her, trying to get more information. Same journalist's instinct she'd use when researching her books. Well, she certainly knew how to work Samson, and it worried him to death.

He watched as the murdered man's brother wandered round the room, taking in the scene. When he replied, his tone was careless. 'Oh, but we didn't come home; not back to Cambridge, I mean. The house stayed let whilst Damien went off to Oxford, and then to the States. He made a lot of money by keeping the place full of tenants. Only came back here when he got the job at TomorrowTech. As for me, this is the third time, precisely, that I've been back since I was eleven. I remember attending a party next door, and seeing strangers occupying this place. It felt odd, let me tell you.'

He looked down at the folding bed set out for Ruby by his brother. 'So he put you down here,' he said.

Something in his tone and the way he looked from the bed to Ruby told Nate exactly what Samson was imagining. He made the effort to unclench his fists.

'Well,' Samson went on, running a tongue over his full lips, 'that seems sensible, given the things that are in this room. I'm sorry though; it can't be all that comfortable.' He turned to smile at Ruby, and this time she looked away.

'I thought you'd come to that conclusion, too,' Nate said. 'Now that I've seen the poor quality of the folding bed, I've asked Ruby to move upstairs. The contract your brother signed says that all sitters must be provided with a reasonable standard of accommodation.'

Samson hesitated for a moment, but then shrugged and gave a wry smile. Even if he'd been tempted to argue, it seemed the lure of his future possessions was enough to distract him. He began to walk around from antique to antique. His hand shook slightly when he reached out to touch one of the clocks, putting Nate in mind of a drug addict having his fix dangled in front of him before he'd paid up.

Then, slowly, Samson manoeuvred into a squatting position to examine something in the treasure cabinet. 'Good God,' he said, his eyes watering slightly, 'I didn't know old Damien had this.' It was a large enamelled porcelain vase; Chinese and well over a century old, at a guess, unless it was a good fake. 'Well, that really is having your cake and eating it,' Samson murmured, 'given that it belonged to Nico. I remember it in his London flat. He must have left it to mother when he died.' He was talking almost to himself. Eyes on the prize. 'And then Damien got it when she went, along with all the other good stuff. So much for high-minded principles; obviously went for nought when there was something valuable involved.'

Ruby seemed reluctant to drag herself away, but at last she offered them drinks. Samson agreed to coffee, but was clearly disappointed she hadn't suggested anything stronger. She glanced over her shoulder as she left the room and made her exit as slow as possible. Once the kettle was on, she hovered in the doorway, rather than waiting whilst it heated.

They went to the dining room for their drinks. Samson's eyes lit on a photograph, sitting on the sideboard. 'Well, well, well!' he said. 'I didn't expect to see Mother staring back at me. Thought he'd thrown all the pictures from that period away.' He picked up the frame, showing no emotion except surprise. 'Was this in here when you arrived?' he asked suddenly, a shrewd look in his eye.

Ruby paused for a fraction of a second before she replied. 'Damien asked me to clean for him whilst I was here. He was rather particular about how thorough I needed to be.' She gave Samson a little smile. 'I found the photo behind a chest, on the floor in the study, covered in dust. I think it must have fallen down there a while back, and been overlooked.'

'Good of you to rescue it,' Samson said, looking at her intently. He put the photo back down again. Then, suddenly, he spun round to face Nate. 'So, we know Ruby can keep house, but what about security here? That's my concern. Can she hold her own when it comes to protecting the place?' He was talking about Ruby as though she wasn't there now.

Keep house … Nate took a deep breath and consciously leant back against the sideboard. 'You're anticipating trouble?'

'Well,' Samson said, 'not specifically, of course, but isn't that why anyone hires a house-sitter? Because of the outside possibility of burglars?'

'Well, yes.' Nate tried to squash the tone of exaggerated patience out of his voice. 'You're right. Because it's relatively common for empty houses to get broken into. But it's much less usual when you've got someone around for twenty-one hours out of twenty-four. In those circumstances, trouble becomes significantly less likely.' In theory. Unless there was something Samson wasn't telling him …

He looked unconvinced. 'But then uncommon things do still happen. Look at what's just befallen my dear, lamented brother.'

Ruby walked towards Samson. 'I'm currently dressed for a business meeting,' she said, folding her arms across her chest. 'My normal outfit involves jeans and a T-shirt and heavy-duty boots. I can take care of myself and your house. And besides,' her eyes moved in Nate's direction for a second, 'Nate's decided to spend the nights here too, just to be sure – given what's happened.'

Samson's eyes popped. 'Well, I hope you don't imagine you can up your fees for that. I don't require two of you.'

Nate saw Ruby flush before she turned and moved towards the window to look out over the Common.

'No extra charge,' he said. 'We're delighted to beef up your protection for free.'

Samson's eyes narrowed, but he clearly couldn't work out whether or not he should take it as a jibe. 'All right then,' he said. 'I'm reasonably satisfied with the arrangements here. I'll have to run it by the other executor but I'm sure so long as I'm happy, he will be. I've got a small bit of business to take care of round the corner. I'll be back here, ready to go home, in, what, an hour?' And with that he walked out of the room and let himself out of the house.

It was a moment before Ruby spoke. 'What do you think the "business" is?' She was still looking out of the window, rather than at Nate.

'He'll have gone to check out the local boozer.'

'Seriously?'

He nodded. 'I had an uncle who was an alcoholic. He was just the same if he had to visit anywhere where there was no drink on offer. Always "just had to nip out" somewhere. And Samson's almost inseparable from the Red Tavern in Newmarket. It was all I could do to drag him over here when he realised he'd miss opening time.'

Ruby shuddered. 'The Red Tavern ... I can just imagine what sort of a place that must be. Probably full of dirty old men, with lap dancers in the basement.'

Nate wanted to avoid confrontation but there were limits. 'Whatever it's like, it's none of our business.'

Ruby turned to face him at last. He could tell that his sharpness had annoyed her, but he didn't care. 'I don't like the way you're playing around with this, Ruby; asking your questions, leading him on.'

'Only because the information we get back might pay dividends.' She held her head high, her green eyes unflinching.

'I'm worried the payback might be of a different sort.' He walked over to the mantelpiece, to put some distance between them, but then turned to face her again. 'What did you think of him?'

'He made my skin crawl.'

'Agreed. And why is he so panicky about protecting the house, do you think?'

'Wants to make sure no one else gets their mitts on his nice, new acquisitions.'

Nate nodded. 'He certainly seems very aware of their value. So given all that, doesn't it occur to you that he must be one of the most likely suspects for Damien Newbold's murder?'

He caught her give an involuntary shiver. 'Of course, I knew he must be up there on the list.'

'This isn't some kind of game, Ruby. If I were you I'd make damned sure he never suspects you're interested in him and his activities. If he is guilty and thinks for one moment that you're onto him ...' Nate let the sentence hang. 'He's asked for a key to this place – one of the new set – and as he's an executor I assume I have to give him one, but I don't like the idea. There'll be nothing to stop him letting himself in any time he wants. And there's no knowing whether he – or anyone else – might try to catch one of us on our own. So forgive me if I suggest you let the police get on with their job whilst you get on with yours.'

She looked angry, but Nate knew he was right.

'In the meantime, do me a favour? Bolt the doors, front and back, when you're alone in the house. I'm not patronising you. I'm planning to do the same.'

Chapter Sixteen

In a way, the run-in with Nate had been a good thing. I'd been furious at the way he'd spoken to me, but at least it had put some distance between us. The fierce look in his blue eyes came back to me again. He'd got past the way I'd behaved the day before; business had taken over. Eventually, Samson reappeared, ready to be chauffeured home, and Nate and I managed to stay out of each other's way for the next few hours.

By the time I went out to buy a paper that afternoon someone had laid flowers, wrapped in cellophane, by the front iron railings. Word must be getting around. The wind was still high and the bouquet shifted in a sudden gust, so I propped it up in the lee of the front steps. A couple on the Common looked at me curiously as I walked away up the path.

At the newsagents on Fitzroy Street I saw Damien had made the front page of the local daily, with promises of further coverage on pages six to eight. I paid up, tucked the paper into my shoulder bag and walked back, past the elegant townhouses on Maid's Causeway and along Midsummer Lane.

Paul Mathewson was standing outside Oswald House, facing away from me, his shoulders hunched against the wind as he did up his jacket.

'Hello,' I said, and he turned in my direction. 'How's Emily doing?'

His look said it all. 'Completely distraught. I've just left her. She's bent double on the sofa now and I can't get anything out of her. When I arrived she was still upstairs, making the most pitiful noise. It went right through me.' He shivered. 'She sounded like a wounded animal.'

Paul looked dreadful too, his face white and pinched, eyes rather blank. 'To be honest,' he said, 'I don't actually know what to do.'

I didn't imagine the short course Fi said he'd taken covered offering solace following the murder of the client's heart's desire. 'Presumably the university's counselling service will step in to give you some backup now,' I said, 'if Emily's willing to see them.'

He nodded. 'I think I've talked her round. And they'll be much more adept at providing what's needed, but all the same ...' He paused, his eyes wide. 'I don't know that they'll get through to her. I mean we both know, don't we, that Damien Newbold would only ever have caused her more pain.' He looked to me for support and I nodded. 'But she can't see that at the moment, and she feels as though her life's over.'

I put a hand on his arm; he looked so lost. 'It's such early days. It's going to take time.'

He shook his head. 'I can see that makes sense. But I'm starting to realise that his death's actually taken away her chance to move forward. She'll probably always think they could have been happy together, if only they'd had the chance.'

'Whether she thinks that or not, she'll still come to terms with it, eventually. She's young. It will always be a dreadful incident in her life, but she'll still grow up and blossom.'

He nodded slowly.

'I'm sure you've done all the right things,' I said.

He looked at me as though he'd realised who I was for the first time, like someone coming out of a trance. 'Thanks. I'm sorry, it's just that it's hard not to get involved, you know?'

I nodded.

'Once you're on someone's case you feel you should be

able to wave a magic wand and come up with all the right answers. And students often think you'll be able to do just that, against all the odds. When I find I can't – well, it just makes me feel bad.'

'I'm sure that's only natural,' I said, smiling at him, 'but not justified. What's just happened isn't exactly run-of-the-mill stuff, is it? I think most support staff would be somewhat challenged, under the circumstances.'

The ghost of a smile crossed his lips and he took a deep breath. 'True.' He put a hand on my arm for a moment. 'Thanks for listening.' Then he got on his bike, and cycled slowly away.

Back inside the house, I made a cup of tea and spread the newspaper out on the kitchen table. The front page covered all the most important details of the murder. Damien Newbold's body had been found at eight-thirty on Tuesday 9th June by Elizabeth Edmunds, owner of the cottage where he'd been staying. She'd apparently arranged to meet him there for a drink – yeah, and the rest – and had let herself in with her own key. The body had been towards the back of the house, in the kitchen, slumped on the floor. Damien Newbold had been beaten over the head – the police were guessing that a hammer (or similar) might have been the murder weapon, though nothing had been found.

The victim had been at work until six that evening, so the time of death was somewhere between six-thirty or so, when he would have arrived back at the cottage in Little Boxham, and eight-thirty when he was found.

I took a sip of my tea and scanned the article to see if there'd been any sign of a break-in. Hmm. Apparently not. The police thought that he must have known his assailant, and have invited them in quite willingly. When he was attacked he'd been in the process of getting glasses out of a cupboard below the work surface, enabling the murderer to take him by surprise, and from above.

There was a quote from DI Johnson which read: 'This was a vicious and frenzied attack. The person who committed the crime is therefore even more likely to have made mistakes than someone operating in a cold and detached manner. I would urge the public to search their memories for anything relevant they might have seen at any stage on Tuesday. It's important that they should come forward to the police with their input, however insignificant they think their information might be.'

Vicious and frenzied. The awful thing was, I couldn't imagine Damien Newbold having been killed in any other way. He'd taken such pains to make sure each of his human instruments were strung up nice and tight and then twisted the tuning keys further and further, almost as though he wanted to see which one would snap first.

There was a picture of the cottage he'd been renting, and the caption described it as 'an idyllic hideaway turned house of horror'. It looked as though it might be relatively isolated. The photograph showed a field to one side. Would Elizabeth Edmunds ever be able to let it out again?

The article noted that the police were keeping an open mind as to the motive for the killing, but did confirm that Mr Newbold's laptop was missing. It went on to note that unconfirmed rumours had been circulating recently about a new discovery he had made, which might be worth a lot of money, and that some industry commentators were speculating – off the record – that this could have provided a motive for the crime.

Would someone become vicious and frenzied when killing in a case of industrial espionage, though? That didn't sound right.

The inside coverage really went to town. There was

a box containing information about Damien Newbold's working life, with the headline: 'Damien Newbold – Impassioned Genius.' They'd used the same awards photo that was framed in the drawing room. The article estimated how much money he'd earned TomorrowTech as its head of research, and talked about his impact on what it termed 'Silicon Fen' and the 'Cambridge Phenomenon.' There was a quote from the Chief Executive of TomorrowTech which talked about Newbold's extraordinary creativity and vice-like mind, which could latch onto any problem and produce a result. I noticed that he hadn't felt moved to mention any attractive personal qualities. The article said he was unable to comment on the rumour about Damien Newbold's latest discovery.

I left off reading for a moment to think. What would Damien Newbold have been like to work with, when it came down to it? What if he'd schemed against colleagues who got in his way, and then bragged to one of them about some new discovery? Perhaps then the frenzied attack might be more believable.

Underneath the article on TomorrowTech came one about Newbold's social connections with the headline 'Affairs of the Heart.' Yuck. And there was a photograph of Damien and Maggie Cook outside some kind of premiere in London; the opening of *Why I Loved Larry*, apparently. It didn't sound familiar, but there was lots in the article about Maggie's acting career and her ongoing starring role in the TV show *Mike's Friday*.

It described their affair as 'volatile' and told of a very public row they had had at the Savoy Grill, where Maggie had tipped a glass of red wine over his head and he'd slapped her across the face. They'd managed to produce a photo to prove it: Damien, still seated, his hair plastered flat on his head and wine dripping down a pristine white shirt.

The thought made me shiver. Knowing what I did of his personality, I could barely begin to imagine his reaction to such public humiliation.

The article also described Damien as 'popular' with women – presumably something they'd deduced by the number he seemed to have had affairs with, a fact that might also have made him unpopular with each individual woman, as the affairs came to light. Next to this bit of commentary there was a photograph captioned 'Elizabeth Edmunds'. Now I understood why the police had recognised the fourth woman in Damien Newbold's nude collection; it was the lady who owned the cottage in Little Boxham. Oddly, she was standing in exactly the same position in the newspaper photo as she was in her portrait – looking down and to one side – but in this instance her hand came right up to cover her eyes. There was no comment on her relationship with Damien, but the positioning of the image, next to the 'Affairs of the Heart' section, gave a huge hint.

They'd also produced a section on Little Boxham itself, saying that Damien's was the first recorded murder in the village since 1794, and talking about the cruel intrusion of violent death into a society more used to cricket on the village green and tea at the vicarage.

Finally, they moved onto Damien Newbold's family, noting that he was the son of 1960s society beauty Bella Carrington and renowned Cambridge academic Harry Newbold. Under a 'Troubled Youth' sub-heading they went on to say that Damien had been an orphan by the time he was seventeen, when his mother had been killed in an horrific car accident. Apparently there had been some speculation at the time that it might have been suicide.

That was something new. Where had that rumour come from?

Then the section went on to talk about the boarding

school Samson had mentioned. Apparently it had been a place of extreme austerity that hadn't drawn the line at beating sixth formers, on top of which, Newbold had found it hard to fit in because he'd arrived so late in his school career. The newspaper had done its homework, managing to track down some old school friend to say what an awful time Damien had had there. The classmate, one Max Williamson, was quoted as saying: 'I think his treatment made him all the more determined to succeed in life. Every time someone got the better of him you could see the look of determination on his face. He was vowing to get his own back.'

Nate nipped back to Two Wells Farm after he'd dropped Samson off in Newmarket. As soon as he'd got rid of him, he'd opened the windows of the Volvo as far as they'd go, but the smell of stale booze, cigarettes and aftershave lingered.

He spent some time dealing with a pile of letters that had turned up at home – it was amazing how many of his clients still preferred to communicate that way – and then did some intensive placating of Speck before he headed back to Cambridge. Nate wanted to make sure he was in residence again by evening, but he knew Ruby would be glad of his absence until then.

When he let himself back in to River House, it felt strangely still, and he wondered if she was out, except the alarm hadn't been set. He stood in the hall for a moment and, at last, heard the faint creak of a floorboard up above.

In the kitchen, he found a copy of the local paper she must have bought, got himself a beer and sat down to scan the murder coverage. There was a photograph of the fourth nude from Damien Newbold's wall. So that had been Elizabeth Edmunds, the woman he'd been renting the house from. Given their likely relationship, perhaps it had been a case of borrowing rather than paying for his accommodation. And if she was a current lover, that added up to quite a collection.

Nate thought again about Newbold's words when he'd seen Ruby's photograph. She looked perfect. And yet he'd gone ahead and served her up for him anyway. Newbold had played games with her, clearly wanting to control her, just as he had all the rest. Not by seducing her, but with Newbold it seemed as though it was all driven by the same impetus: the desire to get women where he wanted them. What had made him like that? And was it one of them who had finally taken back control?

A sound from the hall made Nate look up, and at that moment Ruby came in. She raised an eyebrow. 'I see you're just as bitten by this mystery as I am, underneath it all.'

'I never said I wasn't. I expect half of Cambridge is poring over all this ...' He tapped the paper. '... wondering who did it, and yes, sure, I'm probably all the more curious because of my background. But trawling through the details, and speculating about it, is different from investigating. Do you want a beer?'

She shook her head.

'Ruby, I think I've made us both being here impossible. I meant what I said: this is a two person job now, but that second person doesn't have to be me. I could call a female member of my team to take over.'

'But it's not really a two person job, is it?' she said, her tone fierce. 'You just need one professional. You've kept me on out of charity, and I'm well aware of it.'

'That's certainly not true at the moment. I've got a business to run, and commitments during the day. The house would be unattended for far too long if you weren't here.'

She didn't reply.

'If you don't believe me, think about it. Do you imagine I was just sitting at home, kicking my heels each day before I moved in?'

She made a face. 'No. I suppose not.'

'And I wouldn't ask any of my regulars to watch the house of a murdered man on their own.' She was still silent. 'So, do you want me to swap someone in?'

At last she shook her head. 'There's no reason to. We were both overwrought last night. And I was drunk too, for that matter. None of it meant a thing. Given that, I'm sure we can get along okay. I was just still smarting because you told me off earlier.'

And she turned on her heel, and walked out of the room.

Great. Nate downed the rest of his beer, and sat there feeling ridiculous.

Chapter Seventeen

In spite of the awkwardness between us, it felt safer when Nate and I were both at River House together. Unfortunately, as he'd pointed out, he kept having to go out on business which meant the moments of calm were few and far between. I was convinced he was partly just avoiding me. Either way, he was always back by six in the evening, ready to do his guard dog bit again.

During the day, if I was alone, I fidgeted, not knowing whether it was better to be in or out. It was stupid, but when I went into the garden I kept worrying that the back gate might open – there was no lock on it – revealing Samson on the other side.

Being properly out was okay. Then I knew if he turned up at least I wouldn't be there to face him. I was lying in bed on Saturday morning, wide awake, and worrying, so I decided to get up and go for a run along the river. I'd already heard Nate go out. The day was bright, with mist just shifting off from the grass on the Common, and all the signs were that it would be hot later.

I ran up towards Jesus Lock. To my left a tramp searched an overflowing litter bin, his grizzled head hung low over an open bag, ready to store anything useful. A woman on a moored narrow boat to my right was out on deck, soothing a fretful baby. The roof of her vessel was covered in terracotta pots spilling over with aubretia, a mass of purples, pinks and white. It looked idyllic, but I could imagine what hard work it must be. What would it be like in winter, when the baby wanted to get up at five?

Past the lock, a city council worker was clearing rubbish on Jesus Green, addressing an area where the imprint of a group had been left: a circle of burger wrappers, empty drinks cans and cigarette ends.

Up on the boardwalk the punting stations were still quiet, but I tried to focus on the beauty of Magdalene College and take an interest in the other comings and goings. A couple of drunks were following a cleaner into the loos on Quayside, intent on a good-natured chat she probably didn't want to have.

But the tapestry of Cambridge life was losing its effect. I didn't want to jog through the busy city streets and, in any case, I was running out of steam. It was time to turn round and head back to River House. The thought made me feel instantly sick; clammy tendrils of fear, born of paranoia, clutched at my insides. Samson could be there now, waiting for me. And each time I let myself back in that would be the case. Stupid. He had no reason to visit, and I had found nothing damning about him.

All the same, Nate's words of warning had hit home, once I'd got over my irritation and embarrassment. From what I'd seen of Samson, it was entirely possible that he might have killed his brother, even if there was no positive evidence. He obviously had a lot to gain financially, and there was clearly no love lost between them. My mind strayed back to the photograph albums. No secret, of course, that Damien had been older than Samson, but when you looked at those images you could see what a practical difference that age gap had made. When Samson was seven, Damien had been a teenager, his mother's confidante, learning to drive, the apple of her eye. That was the kind of dynamic that could foster serious resentment.

But then Damien's bond with his mother had broken down. Had it been the photographer, Nico, who had caused that dreadful rift? And if the relationship was in ruins, perhaps that might have ironed out any resentment on

Samson's part. But then I thought of what I knew of him, of his sly smile and the calculating look in his eye as he'd taken stock of the goods in Damien's house. What was it he'd said about the things his mother had left in her will? Something about Damien having got 'all the good stuff'. If Samson had been resentful of Damien, I was willing to bet it was over who had been left what, rather than a mother's love.

I was so engrossed in my thoughts that I overshot River House. I had to run back across Midsummer Common, using one of the paths that struck off diagonally from Cutter Ferry Bridge up to the row of villas. The single bunch of flowers left in Damien's memory had grown to a mound, and the sight of them struck me afresh as I ran up to the front door. I wondered which of the contributors had actually known him. Not many, judging by the messages, but Emily had left one: a bunch of white lilies, with a note that said, 'I'm sorry.' I was sure she was referring to the final row she'd told me about, but it could obviously be misconstrued. It was clear she was far too shaken to think of that, even for a moment.

The flowers were forgotten as I stood on the doorstep, holding my breath as I turned my key in the lock, Samson's image filling my head. But the moment the door swung open I heard the familiar alarm warning tone and keyed in the number, sighing with relief. A sense of my own ridiculousness welled up inside me.

As I showered I sifted through the information I had so far about Damien, Samson and Bella and my thoughts left me wanting one thing: more information. It was a plus that trying to get it was a harmless way of passing the time whilst I shut myself up, doors bolted, hidden away from the world.

I set myself up in the kitchen and opened my laptop.

Time to Google Damien's dad, Harry Newbold. Presumably he ought to feature somewhere if he was such a renowned academic as the local paper had claimed. Good. Wikipedia had him. That was a start. I clicked on the link. There was quite a bit. I scrolled down the page to get the measure of what was there: early life, career, personal life – excellent – and a list of publications.

I decided to save the academic stuff for a spare moment later and went straight to the section that revolved around family.

'Newbold's ten-year marriage to society beauty Bella Carrington resulted in the birth of two children, Damien in 1964 and Samson in 1970. However, pressure of work increasingly kept the couple apart, and the marriage began to falter as early as 1969. When Newbold was offered a professorship at Harvard in 1971, the marriage was effectively at an end, and a new relationship, with actress Matilda Wentworth, quickly followed. In 1973 Newbold and Bella Carrington were divorced, freeing Newbold to marry Wentworth soon after. The couple were childless.

'Newbold made frequent return visits to England for academic conferences, but never regained full contact with his children, making only one visit back to the family home in 1974.'

I wondered who had put that detail in. Anyone could add to Wikipedia, I knew. I imagined either Damien or Samson keying in the accusatory words.

'Tragedy struck in 1976, when, aged just 46, Newbold was killed in a plane crash on his way to a conference in Australia. The incident cut short an astoundingly impressive career and left his wife heartbroken.'

So there it was. Bella had been left to bring up their children alone, and had been doing a good job of it, if the photographs in the album were anything to go by. But then, presumably, Bella had met Nico. That photograph he'd signed with a kiss. The nude in Damien's bedroom. Oh yes, she'd looked happy, joyous even, but perhaps it was that joyous look – directed at a new man, Nico – that selfish Damien couldn't take. He'd been his mother's right-hand man for years, the one she relied on, and then suddenly he'd felt supplanted. Was I being fanciful? But that was the way it looked from the photographs. Not just the adoring way in which Bella had looked at her older son pre-Nico, but also the expression in *his* eyes. As though she'd somehow put him in charge after his father had left. That might have changed when a new lover arrived on the scene, and I was quite sure he wouldn't have taken demotion lightly.

Poor Bella. Deserted by horrible Harry, she had remained a devoted mother, holding things together for her family, but all the time she'd been unwittingly building Damien's conviction that he was top dog. And then she'd seen her chance of happiness: the loving Nico, ready to adore her, to help with the burdens she'd shouldered for so long, and instead of being happy for her, Damien hadn't wanted to share his mother with another man. By the look of things she hadn't let him get his own way, and he'd never forgiven her for it.

What about Bella? What had happened to her? I went to fetch the 1980–1985 photograph album and brought it back to the table. Throughout the 1980 section there were more of the reversed photographs and then, late in 1981, they stopped. When Damien was seventeen; when Bella had died.

Suddenly I heard a knocking from outside. A woman was standing at the door of Oswald House. She was glamorous – I could tell that, even from behind. The sort of person who always dresses with the opposite sex in mind. Slit skirt, but classy, not tarty; expensive looking. She had a neat waterfall of platinum-blonde hair, behaving exactly as it should in a well-controlled bob. It was Fi who let her in.

I turned back to the photo album. How far should I go? I'd already eased out one picture. I got up to get the sharp knife from the drawer again, hesitating for a moment. What with this and peeking at next door's visitors, I really was letting my nosiness run away with me. I hoped Steph would agree that I wasn't normally this bad. But under the circumstances it seemed only reasonable to try to find out the background to this business. After all, I was the one who might have to deal with Samson at any moment. The more knowledge I had of his background, the better prepared I'd feel.

With the image of Nate in my head, his blue eyes boring into mine, appalled at my behaviour, I set to work, but in the end I wished I hadn't.

I'd Googled Nico again, to check the date he'd died, and then homed in on November 1981 in the album. It was horrible. The first photo I investigated was of Bella with the children, caught on camera as she struggled to carry on with normal life, but the sadness in her eyes was like nothing I'd ever seen. I only looked at a couple more after that: one where she was standing alone in the snow in what was clearly the back garden here in Cambridge, and one that someone had taken of her and the children. Damien was looking up at her in much the same way as he had in the pre-Nico pictures, but although she held Samson's hand, I had the impression that she was hardly aware that either of them was there.

And then what about the car crash the newspaper had mentioned, and the possibility that it had been suicide? The woman pictured certainly looked utterly without hope, but I was sure she would still have hung on for the sake of her children.

Of course, I hadn't Googled Bella. I tried it then, and found she was actually mentioned on Nico's Wikipedia page as well as on Harry's. I'd been so caught up in the chase previously that I'd only read the first paragraph. Under a section on his personal life, there was information on 'a passionate and deeply happy love affair with divorcee, Bella Newbold, cut tragically short when Nico succumbed to cancer'. And there, as far as the Internet was concerned, both his and her story ended.

And I had no way I could think of for getting at the truth.

I jumped about a foot when the door knocker went; a loud peremptory sound of someone who didn't want to be kept waiting. My heart thumped as I walked across the hall. Through the spyhole I could now see the front half of the same woman who'd knocked on the door of Oswald House earlier. Viewing her at this angle confirmed what I'd gleaned from her rear view. Good looking but hard with it, showing a carefully polished exterior. I guessed she must be in her mid- to late-forties – her hair had been touched up perhaps – but her skin had very few lines and I imagined her figure was still as it had been when she was eighteen.

What on earth did she want? Better open up and find out.

She smiled a smile that didn't reach her eyes and introduced herself. 'Saskia Amos. I gather from my daughter that you're one of the people she's been confiding in since this business with Damien Newbold began.' She already had one foot on the hall mat.

'I'm afraid I'm not supposed to entertain visitors here,' I said, not quite believing she was about to barge her way in. 'It's nothing personal, just strict house-sitting rules.'

She shook her head, ostensibly to get the very tame hair out of her eyes, but really, I thought, as a way of disguising a moment of anger. 'Surely under the circumstances you can invite the respectable mother of a grieving neighbour into Damien Newbold's precious house,' she said, and, of course, I did see her point. Horrible though she reportedly was, she was presumably angry with Damien for leading Emily a dance, and the last thing she wanted was someone being obstructive in his name.

'I'm really sorry,' I said. 'Damien Newbold's brother's in charge of this place now, as one of the executors of the will, and he's very particular. He's keeping an eye on me to see if I'm up to the job.'

Saskia Amos gave me a look that told me what she thought of both me and Samson.

'Why don't we talk in the garden?' I said. 'It's a halfway house, and, after all, it's a lovely day.'

She followed me through the hall saying, 'How you can describe today as lovely under the circumstances I'm not quite sure.'

Outside, I led her over to a bench by the lavender. We had to sit uncomfortably close together, but it was better than getting Damien's reclining deckchairs out of the store and us both having to lounge around practically prone, as though we were on holiday.

She refused a drink and so I waded in, wanting to get the talk over with. 'You wanted to speak to me about Emily? Because she's been talking to me about Damien Newbold?'

She nodded, crossing one slim leg over the other, her lined skirt shifting neatly to adjust to the new position. 'It sounds as though you've been very sympathetic,' she said, 'but in fact, what I want you to do is stop.'

Okay. Interesting. 'Stop?'

'Oh, not just you; the whole lot of you, I mean. I understand Paul Mathewson's involved on behalf of Emily's college and, of course, Fi Parkinson's been dancing attendance too. Not that her sympathy will be boundless; I can tell she's losing patience already, very understandably. Emily really needs to pull herself together, and having a whole load of people hovering about, clucking over her isn't going to speed the process up.'

At that moment, I caught a flicker of movement at the kitchen window, which was open. Nate had come back.

It took me a second to formulate a reply. 'But Emily only heard of Damien's death three days ago. Her grief's still very fresh. Surely it's a bit soon to be trying to jolly her out of it.'

Saskia waved a hand, clear nail varnish gleaming at the end of slim, elegant fingers. 'The death's a fresh thing, of course, but her reaction to it is a continuation of the same problem.'

I must have frowned and she was irritated by my slowness.

'I mean it's an extension of her gauche and rather embarrassing obsession with Damien Newbold. I'm certain the whole thing only existed in her mind. She's not at all sophisticated; a man of Damien Newbold's maturity would never have given her a second glance.' She shifted her legs again, clearly cramped, and then sighed and got up from the bench to walk around the garden. Beyond her, in the kitchen, I could see that Nate was still standing where I'd spotted him before, presumably taking it all in. It looked as though he was indulging in a cool drink, too. Hmm. Nice for him.

'Emily's my daughter,' Saskia went on, 'and I know her better than anyone. She's always been rather self-obsessed. If Damien Newbold had smiled at her across Midsummer Passage she'd have thought he was giving her a come on. The result is these histrionics over an invented love affair.' She caught my eye. 'I'd rather speak the truth than pussyfoot around. The fact is, you're not doing her any favours, any of you, especially Paul Mathewson, from what I've been told. What an old woman. Awful mawkishness. The sooner she stops being the centre of attention, the sooner she'll calm down, you mark my words.'

She sat back down on the bench again and smoothed her hair. A strand of it caught in the setting for the ruby she wore on her ring finger.

'Of course, you don't have children,' she said. 'You don't yet know what it's like. Once they reach adolescence they may seem quite adult, but believe me they're well short of the mark. Bags of unreliable hormones.' She raised her eyes to heaven. 'I once worked at the Philip Radley School and I remember it well. When I started, my children were still young and I was green around the gills. But I soon realised that those almost-adult students were very far from being grown-up.' She made a disparaging little noise.

'So did you leave teaching?' I asked. I couldn't imagine her in the classroom for one second.

'Oh, I wasn't a teacher,' she said. 'I was the headmaster's right-hand woman. A manager, effectively. But I didn't really need to work, of course. I decided to devote more time to my growing family and my husband's household instead. Managing a place as big as ours is a full-time job in itself. There's only so much organising one person can do.' She got up. 'I must say, I've never met a house-sitter before. What an interesting career that must be.'

I could feel her putting inverted commas around the word career, and decided to see her out of the back gate as quickly as possible. It was all I could do not to give her an encouraging shove.

I would like to say that I rose above her ridiculous words, but it would be a lie. Instead I was busy stewing over what she'd said, like a six-year-old, when Nate came out into the garden.

I raised an eyebrow. 'Finally decided to join me have you?'

'You were doing such a good job with her, I thought it was best not to interrupt. Even though I'd love to have been introduced.' The corners of his mouth twitched.

'Hmm.'

'I did consider coming to hold you back when she made the crack about house-sitting. The look in your eye was scary. Why didn't you tell her this isn't your regular work?'

'I decided she wasn't worth the effort.'

Nate announced his intention to go and shop, so I offered to cook once he was back and gave him a list of ingredients. After he'd left the house, I continued to brood over what Saskia Amos had said. The worst of it was, it should have been the awful way she'd talked about her own daughter that had got to me. But in fact it was still her taunts about my 'career' that left me full of impotent rage. Not very becoming. I hadn't been quite honest with Nate. In reality I had two reasons for not telling her about my regular work. For a start, it would have made me sound defensive, as though I cared one way or the other what she thought. And also, didn't 'Oh, I write pseudo-scientific books about things like midlife crises' sound pretty worthless? Making money from letting other people offload their woes, when later on, after their first flush of emotion was over, they might wish they hadn't. My work ... Well, I was out of love with it at that moment. But, hey, at least it wasn't going quite so badly as my relationships. I was shocked to find that my mind flitted immediately to Nate when I thought this, rather than to Luke. His tousled look and penetrating blue eyes came vividly to mind ... but then that image morphed, and I saw again his acute embarrassment after we'd kissed, and his anger at my nosiness. The feeling of shame was back in my stomach. I considered what Saskia Amos had said again. I supposed she was right, and house-sitting would be an unusual career choice, but, of course, no one started off their working life looking after empty properties. Presumably some had taken early retirement from the police, and perhaps some were on career breaks for whatever reason – maybe when the stress of a job working in frontline security got too much. I wondered again about Nate. What had made him crack and take on his current role? He didn't look like the sort to buckle under pressure, physically or mentally.

I got myself a glass of water, packed with ice from the posh fridge freezer, and as I cooled down, I made up my mind. Everyone's got a web presence. Internet research had worked well in the case of Harry Newbold and Nico Sidorov, and now it was time to try to find out more about my employer.

Of course the first hits on Google were all for the house-sitting service. I hadn't actually looked at the website much, beyond a quick glance when Steph had first mentioned the job to me. Now I saw that it was clearly quite common for people to request a house-sitter after a death, as probate went through. There was a special section devoted to it on the 'How we can help' page. Nate's face stared back at me; he looked unusually well-shaven and tidy. I was determined not to keep flicking back to peer at him again, like a teenager.

The hits further down the list of results were interesting. There were a couple of links to ads in the *Bury Free Press* and the *East Anglian Daily Times* relating to his old business. The services offered were comprehensive; everything from surveillance to computer forensics.

I clicked the back arrow on the browser window and carried on scanning the results page, noting that he'd obviously somehow avoided Facebook, LinkedIn and all the rest of it. Maybe you developed an instinctive caution about detailing your life online if you knew how easily hackers could plunder your history.

And then I found something that brought me up short, the hairs on my scalp lifting. There was a link to an article in the *East Anglian Daily Times*, dated eighteen months earlier. The headline read, 'Fire at Two Wells Farm was Arson, Police Confirm.' Under the headline, the by-line read, 'Victim's death to be treated as murder.'

Two Wells Farm? Wasn't that Nate's home? Hell, I was sure it was. I went back to his house-sitting website and clicked on 'contact us'.

Two Wells Farm.

I clicked back to the results page and hit the link, not ready for whatever information it was going to give me.

The article was long, but I scanned the page at high speed, wanting to get the worst over with. 'The victim is believed to be Susie Bastable, sister of the house owner, private investigator, Nate Bastable.' God, this was horrific. When Steph had said Nate had been through a bit of a rough patch recently, I was imagining girlfriend trouble, or a blunder at work, or, well … certainly not this.

I navigated back to the results page again and tried to find a follow-up to that first article. What had happened next?

There was another. The headline this time read: 'The Wrong Place at the Wrong Time – Was Brother Intended Victim of Two Wells Farm attack?'

I felt goosebumps rising all down my arms and scanned the page once again.

'Police have reason to suspect that Nate Bastable might have been the intended victim of the arson attack that took place at his home in Little Nighting on December 23rd. It has emerged that it was only a lucky last-minute change of plan that kept Bastable, a private investigator, away from home on the night of the attack. Sources say that his sister, Susie Bastable's visit was also unplanned, in this case with tragic consequences.'

I could only begin to imagine what he'd gone through; the guilt, as well as the grief. It put a whole different complexion on the warnings he'd been giving me, too – and on his concern when Damien Newbold had seemed to be under fire from so many people. He'd already seen the results of a bystander getting in the way of a killer. I thought back to my huffy reaction to the telling off he'd given me. He'd been thinking of his dead sister and I'd stuck out my metaphorical bottom lip, like a kid.

And who had been after Nate? Someone he'd crossed in his work?

I searched several more pages of results after that, finding that the story of the fire had reached some of the nationals too. But I didn't find any further information; no details of an arrest or a trial. It looked as though Susie Bastable's murderer was still out there.

Chapter Eighteen

I'd been intending to get on with my writing whilst Nate was out, but I couldn't settle after what I'd discovered. I was pacing round the ground floor of River House when a hammering at the door jolted me back to reality and filled me with the usual sense of foreboding.

Through the spyhole I could see it was Maggie Cook, looking distinctly the worse for wear. Wonderful.

I opened up and got her in greater detail. She had mascara running down her cheeks and her hair looked as though it hadn't been washed since she'd heard about Damien. 'Ruby?' she said. 'You did say it was Ruby?'

I nodded.

'You've got to let me in.' She wasn't crying now, but her voice was high and desperate.

I made to answer but she put up a hand as though to hold back my response, stumbling slightly as she did so. She reeked of alcohol and cigarettes. 'Don't,' she said. 'I know. You're not allowed to have me in. I remember you told me that before, when I went into Damien's study. But it's different now.' She looked at me, her eyes frighteningly intense. 'You must see that.'

I shook my head, drawing myself up to full height. 'I'm so sorry for what you're going through, Maggie,' I said. 'But Samson Newbold's given me exactly the same rules as Damien did, and I can't go breaking them; least of all at a time like this, when everyone's overwrought, and no one really knows what's going on.'

'You mean you don't know who you can trust!' She spat the words out and a fleck of saliva shot from her mouth, landing on my sleeve.

'There is that too,' I said.

'But you let Samson Newbold in.'

I could feel my eyes roll before I got them under control. 'Well, I didn't exactly have much choice, given that he's Damien's heir, and his executor.'

Her eyes flashed and her mouth opened, ready to say something, when I saw her visibly pause and think – something only obvious in the very drunk – and then change tack. 'Look, Ruby,' she said, 'there are things in River House – things that belong to me – and I want them back.' She cried a little now, and it came across as very theatrical. She would probably have done it better if she hadn't been hammered. 'They're things I had when Damien and I were together. All I want is to see them again; they're all I've got left now. The police must have searched the house by this time.'

I nodded.

'And if they have, then where's the harm? Surely you can't grudge me this?' Her tone was veering haphazardly between wheedling and threatening now, the extravagantly acted tears forgotten again.

'What kind of things did you leave?' I said, trying to sound calm and reasonable.

'It's none of your fucking business!' she suddenly snarled, shocking me with her unexpected ferocity. I could feel myself reeling slightly, when I noticed movement beyond her. Someone was wheeling a bike across the Common from the direction of town.

'Everything all right, Ruby?' Paul Mathewson said, frowning as he got close enough to see what was going on.

I gave him a wry smile. 'Just another average day. It's okay though, thanks, only something that needs a bit of sorting out.' Which, thinking about it, wasn't calculated to soothe my visitor.

'You're damned right it does,' Maggie said, her voice grating. She looked round to see who had caused the interruption.

Paul ignored her and looked at me. 'I thought I'd pop in and check on Fi and Emily, so I'll probably be around for five minutes or so. If you want any assistance, you've only got to knock on their door.'

I was confident I could cope, but that didn't stop it being nice to have someone fighting my corner. 'Thanks, Paul,' I said. 'I really do appreciate it.'

He grinned. 'I'll see you around, anyway.'

'Who the hell was that little shit?' said Maggie, squinting after him.

'Paul Mathewson is not a little shit, or even a shit of any kind,' I said, suddenly feeling inexplicably jolly and flippant. 'Not all men are like Samson and Damien Newbold, thankfully.'

The last bit of my sentence was a stupid comment to make, and I could see her reacting, but then once again the expression on her face changed. She was going to have another go at being nice. The smile she adopted sent shivers down my spine.

'Come on, Ruby,' she said, trying to cajole me, like a small child asking for an ice cream just before supper. 'You can do this for me. You've lived in his house. You know what he's like. I loved him for God's sake, even though he was a bastard.'

'If you told me the things you need to collect, maybe I could go and look round the house for them, gather them up and bring them outside. I'm sure no one could object to that.'

And now she started to cry again, big heaving sobs, her whole body shuddering with emotion. I wasn't sure what to do, but I was quite certain the tears were genuine this time.

On impulse I grabbed the front door keys, set the alarm, and stepped out of the house, pulling the door shut behind me. 'Let's talk,' I said, and set off on the path across the grass.

Midsummer Common itself wasn't crowded, but the pathway along the river was still busy. 'Maybe we should just sit down where we are,' I said, looking again at her face. She wouldn't want to be paraded past a load of bicycle commuters, heading home from work. And if anyone recognised her we'd probably have the press out.

She tried to descend into a sitting position and ended up half falling into the long grass.

'What did you really want?' I asked.

She looked me. 'I think there was probably a shawl in there, and maybe some scent ...'

I went on staring at her, my eyebrows raised.

'Oh, all right,' she said, taking out a handkerchief and blowing heavily into it. 'I wanted to look for some paperwork.'

'Paperwork? What do you mean?'

'Before he died,' Maggie said, 'a little while back, Damien and I had a really good patch.' She put a rather snotty hand on my arm and I tried not to flinch as her fingers slid towards my wrist. 'We fought,' she said. 'Everyone knows we did – like cats and dogs – but that can be part of a relationship. If you have two people with personalities that feed off drama, and highs and lows.' She took her hand away again and leant to one side on the grass. 'Six months ago Damien started to say things like, "I'm beginning to think you're the only girl for me, Maggie." He actually said that. It was just after a row. Our slanging matches always seemed to make him feel ... exhilarated.'

Creepy. And where was this leading?

'And then one day, he told me he wanted to leave me

everything.' She dropped the words out, giving them each an individual emphasis.

'He was going to make you the sole beneficiary in his will?'

She nodded. 'He said he was going to alter it to make sure I had a comfortable future, and that none of it would go to his brother. I know it sounds crazy, but it probably makes more sense when you know about his relationship with Samson.'

I looked across at her.

'Hated him,' Maggie said. 'It was all to do with their mother. Damien adored her, but she let him down, and then their relationship collapsed completely. It wasn't directly to do with Samson, but Damien was jealous of him because by the time it all happened, Samson was a fairly biddable eleven-year-old who still took his mother's side. Damien couldn't seem to connect with either of them.' She paused. 'Then the mother killed herself.'

'It really was suicide?'

Maggie's unfocused eyes showed surprise. 'Well, she got drunk and drove herself, very fast, head on into a large brick wall. I think officially they might have called it an accident to protect the feelings of the family, but you work it out.' She paused again, and twisted her legs round so that they were tucked under her skirt. 'Well, Samson blamed Damien for that.'

'Why?'

'Said he'd goaded Bella into it. Bella was devastated because her lover had died. Damien, on the other hand, was delighted. I don't suppose he made a secret of the fact either. He told me he'd hated the lover and assumed that family life would return to normal once he was out of the picture.'

'But it didn't?'

She shook her head. 'Bella was grief-stricken and Damien was left out in the cold, even more than he had been when

166

she was caught up in the love affair. Then one night, so Samson says, Damien found her crying again and told her she was absolutely no use as a mother, and if she was going to carry on like that it would be better for everyone if she was dead, like the lover.'

'God. And that was when she killed herself?'

'Couple of days later. Damien denies the conversation ever took place, and says her suicide was simply the last in a line of selfish acts, a sort of final abandonment of him.' She looked at me. 'Poor Bella. Damien was warped, wasn't he? Really messed up. I knew that. But that was what made him interesting. And that was why he needed me.' And she started to cry again.

A couple walking their dog were staring at us, but looked away quickly when I caught them at it. I waited for Maggie to recover herself and then asked, 'So, do you think Damien really did draw up another will?'

Maggie nodded. 'He said he was determined to do it. Hated the thought of everything going to Samson, but up until then that's what would have happened. No other relatives to leave it to.' Her hand was back on my arm. 'Samson killed Damien,' she said. 'Or had him killed. Doubt if the slimy, little shit would do it himself. He probably thinks he got in in time, before Damien made the new will, but I think the new one will be in the house somewhere. Or at least, there'll be some hint that it exists; letters or something. And if they do go ahead and process everything using the current one, I'm going to contest it.'

I didn't think she'd have much luck, with no bit of paper and no witnesses. And anyway, I was losing track. 'Hang on,' I said. 'How would Samson even have known there was a danger Damien might change his will?'

Maggie looked down at the grass. 'I told him,' she said, quietly. 'It's because of me that Damien's dead.'

'I don't understand.'

She looked up at me, still squinting slightly although she was obviously sobering up. 'Damien and I were at Newmarket racecourse, around four weeks ago. Damien was in an exceptionally good mood – he'd really dressed up for the occasion – and I'd gone to town too. I was wearing a low-cut satin dress and I'd bought myself a good hat. I remember Damien was unusually demonstrative, putting his arm around me all the time.' The tears were back in her eyes again. 'He wasn't usually much of a romantic. The local paper took our photograph and the caption afterwards called us a handsome couple.' She sighed and looked at me. 'We were good together,' she said, nodding.

'It was when we were going off to get some food that we saw Samson. He was drunk, of course, always is.' She caught my eye. 'I know, I know, pot, kettle, black. Anyway, Damien was in the sort of mood when even bumping into his brother couldn't dampen him down. We all went to eat together and Samson put away the best part of a bottle of champagne that Damien had actually paid for.' She rolled her eyes. 'Everything was going okay, until Damien saw some people from work, over at a table on the opposite side of the restaurant. He nipped across to say hello.'

'And you and Samson got talking?' I said.

She looked at me and pulled a face. 'He made a pass at me.' She was physically squirming at the memory. 'It was fairly full on. So much so that I was pretty forthright in my put down.'

'And I don't imagine he liked that.'

'He was livid. How he could have thought that I'd … Well, anyway, he turned on me, smiling, and said, "You'd be better off with me, you know. Damien can't form proper relationships with women – been like that since school days." And then he said, "You look like our mother, you know. Damien hated her and you can take it from me he hates you too."'

'Blimey.'

She nodded. 'That was when he told me that Damien had goaded his mother into killing herself. Anyway, I said, "If he hates me so much, how come he chooses to spend his time with me?" But Samson didn't even have to search for an answer. He said, straightaway, "Because he wants to control you. He couldn't control our mother, but he's damn well determined all other women in his life are going to stay firmly under his thumb." It was horrible.'

I could see goosebumps coming up all over her arms at the memory. And then I thought of all the games Damien Newbold had played with me after I'd arrived at his house. It fitted with his desire to control women. I was too tall to resemble his mother, but my hair and face were more or less right.

'What happened then?' I asked.

'Samson leant forward and breathed in my face,' Maggie said. 'I can still remember exactly what he said. "You're like a beautiful butterfly, stuck on a pin in Damien's collection, only you're still alive and writhing." And I think I hated him all the more because he was right. Even though I loved Damien – because I loved him – that was exactly the way it was.' She paused. 'And that was when I told him. "If he hates me so much," I said, "and wants to control me, then why is he planning to leave me all his money?" I had his attention then, I can tell you. I can still see that smug smile falling away; his horrible, jowly jaw going slack. And then I rubbed it in. "That's right," I said. "*You* were expecting that little prize, weren't you? If you're lucky enough to outlive him; which, the rate you're going ..." And then I looked down at that gut of his and the booze in his hand and let the sentence hang. "But Damien's planning a little alteration in my favour. Sorry to disappoint you." Truth is, I'd been drinking too, and I was hell bent on denting his revolting air of superiority.' She put her head in her hands. 'It was so stupid of me. In the normal way of things Damien would've been around for decades, so the will thing wouldn't have made much difference. But he'd had a scare recently. His heart.' She shrugged. 'I didn't know if Samson knew, but, if he did, he was probably already looking forward to the day when he might inherit. And for me it was symbolic – a way to score points that happened to come to hand. Anyway, there's no doubt he knew all about Damien's intentions, and it's my bet he always thought he could call on the cash any time he needed by helping Damien on his way. Then suddenly he was in danger of losing that security.'

Would Samson really have been willing to go to those lengths for cash? Even if she was right, I was still sceptical. How could she be sure Damien had actually gone ahead and made the change?

As though reading my thoughts, she said, 'I can see you're not convinced. If you let me into River House, maybe I can provide you with evidence.'

'Maggie, you know I can't. But, believe me, I'm sorry.'

I expected her to be angry, but instead she looked thoughtful, as though she was working out her next move.

Nate caught sight of Ruby sitting on the grass on Midsummer Common talking to a woman as he came back from Tesco. He was pretty sure it was Newbold's actor girlfriend. He recognised her from the news coverage of the murder – that and the painting in the master bedroom. He might have gone over to join them if he hadn't been loaded up with shopping. Also, he had a feeling Ruby would think he was interfering. He was unpacking the food when she let herself back in.

'So how was Maggie Cook?'

She did a double take. Clearly she hadn't seen him pass by them out on the Common. He wasn't surprised. Things had looked rather intense.

'Pretty awful, to be honest. She was drunk again. Not that she doesn't have an excuse, under the circumstances.'

'What was she after?'

She paused for a moment. 'She wanted to come inside. Said something about having left a shawl here. I promised I'd look for it, but I wouldn't let her in, of course.'

Nate gave her a look. 'Of course. And then she unburdened herself?'

'Yes. She told me all about her relationship with Damien. Apparently its volatility gave them both a buzz. And she knows Samson, too; says he made a pass at her recently when she and Damien bumped into him at Newmarket Races. Actually, a pass is probably putting it mildly. Seems he's got the same womanising instincts his brother had, but is rather less successful.'

'Hmm. All in all, it doesn't sound like you were having much fun out there.' He thought of offering her a G&T, but then remembered the consequences of too much booze the last time. Instead, he ripped open a packet of cashews, and they got halfway down it before he uncorked the wine.

As they sipped their drinks, Ruby stayed quiet. She walked to and from the fridge, fetching the ingredients she'd asked him for: onion, garlic, chicken, yoghurt and peppers. Then she went to a cupboard for spices and got busy with some kebab skewers. Every so often Nate caught her looking at him. The moment their eyes met though, she looked away. The third time it happened she was biting her lip, too. It was starting to make him nervous.

'Are you all right?'

She nodded quickly. 'Fine.'

'Can I do anything?'

She shook her head, and turned to face the chopping board she'd taken from under Newbold's counter. A few of the cashews and some dried apricots were going into the meal.

'Do you really think Samson might be guilty?' she asked eventually. It somehow smacked of 'making conversation', but Nate went with it.

'I don't know. The house and its contents provide him with quite a motive. He's planning to sell the lot, by the way.'

'No sentimental desire to move back into the family home then?'

Nate took another handful of the remaining nuts. 'I doubt Samson Newbold's got a sentimental bone in his body. But even though he's keen on realising his assets, I don't know about the murder. There's something cold and reptilian about him. All that business about the frenzied attack ... I couldn't see him working up the energy somehow, could you?'

'Probably not.' Ruby was glancing at him again.

'But I could be wrong. Who knows what went on between them in private? And whether he's a murderer or not, I'd stake my life he's up to something.'

'What makes you say that?'

'Instinct. That and the fact that he's far too bothered about having someone in the house. As though he actually expects someone to come and swipe his new acquisitions from under his nose. That worries me.'

They sat down to the food Ruby had prepared. She served it up on rice, with a green salad.

'Looks good,' Nate said.

'Thank you.' After all the glances earlier, she wasn't meeting his eyes.

'Um, Ruby?'

'Yes?'

'What's up?'

'Nothing. By the way, I'm sorry I got cross when you told me off about pumping Samson for information. I can see from your point of view it must have seemed reckless.'

From his point of view ... 'Wait a minute. With your instinct for investigation, have you, by any chance, been looking me up on the net?'

The characteristic blush tinged her cheeks. 'Well ...'

For just a second Nate was angry. He didn't want her knowing, didn't want her to see how he'd failed a member of his own family.

'I'm sorry.'

Her tone brought him to his senses. 'Don't be. I should have told you myself.'

She seemed to read his mind. 'It wasn't your fault.'

Nate sighed. 'If you're a PI and you can't even protect your own sister, it's your fault.'

She put her fork down. 'Do you know who did it?'

He shook his head. 'Eighteen months on, and I'm still in the dark. And until I find out, I don't know what I'm dealing with. If Susie was targeted to get back at me, then anyone else I'm close to might be in danger. And I'm sure she must have been – either that or I was the intended victim all along.'

I lay there that night, my mind spinning after my conversation with Nate. My thoughts rushed from what he'd been going through, to what he'd said about anyone he was close to being in potential danger. It explained Steph's comment about him being a confirmed bachelor, and the way she'd gone all tight-lipped about it afterwards. Those thoughts were followed by waves of guilt at my selfishness for even considering all this, and minding, at least in part, for my own sake. And then, after I'd wrestled with all of that for an hour or so, my mind turned back to Maggie Cook. Cue more guilt, because I hadn't admitted to Nate that she thought Damien had made a new will. And what's more, that Samson was aware of the fact. Nate had said he thought Samson expected trouble. Maybe he was worried Maggie might break in, in order to search for the document. Hell. I should have been open. But the truth was, I felt sorry for Maggie, and I hadn't been able to think quickly enough when it came to working out how much of her story to pass on.

As I'd got our supper ready, I'd thought again about what she'd said. I was sure she hadn't killed Damien. She'd been pretty drunk when she'd first told me about the will, and was quite clearly convinced she'd given Samson a motive for killing his brother. I didn't reckon she could have acted so convincingly with that blood alcohol level. And anyway, the timing didn't fit. She'd been hot with rage when she'd found his address at River House. If she was going to go and bash his brains out she'd have done it then, not waited a few days. She wasn't the sort to plan the thing out coolly in advance.

But might she attempt to break in to find the new will, now I'd sent her packing? My head started to ache. It was two in the morning, and sleep seemed utterly out of reach.

I pulled on a jumper over the top of my nightshirt and stepped out onto the attic landing. All was quiet below. Of course, the stairs creaked as I made my way down. I kept stopping to listen for any sound from Nate, so my progress was slow; all the more so as I crossed the middle floor landing. Moonlight showed my reflection in Damien's mirrors.

I reached the ground floor and went to the study. I could at least check the obvious places for any sign of a new will.

I sat down in the chair by the desk and tried to be systematic. Step one, check the files. He had the cardboard sort that hang from metal hooks. Each section was tidy and organised; none of your papers spilling everywhere, or having to shove files to one side with all the force you could muster to drag out one section. He really had been weird. I looked under w, for will, l, for legal, s for solicitor, f for finance and then did a general once over, checking for any section that looked as though it contained a thicker than average document. I was pretty sure wills were full of standard clauses and legalese that meant they bulked up. But there was nothing.

And yet, as I sat there thinking, I felt more and more certain that he must have told her he'd gone ahead and seen a solicitor. And it had probably been recently, which was why she wasn't saying as much to me. It would certainly make her a prime suspect. Damien Newbold wasn't the kind of man to stay constant in his affections. If she had wanted the money, killing him soon after he'd made a new will would have ensured he didn't get the chance to change his mind.

I believed her when she'd told me she'd loved him, but I knew what Nate would say to that. Hers must have been a love that could easily have tipped over into hate and despair. What if I was wrong about Maggie? Perhaps after years of being belittled and snubbed, taunted and strung along, she'd finally snapped.

Chapter Nineteen

Nate didn't have to go anywhere the following day, so he suggested I should take some time out in town. As I left the house Maggie Cook was still uppermost in my mind. Twice I was on the point of admitting what I'd kept from Nate, but knowing he'd send me straight to the police held me back. That, and the idea of explaining why I hadn't been honest in the first place.

Instead I tried to distract myself by looking round the shops. I still hadn't been back to Saxwell, so I was pretty short of clothes, and even though I was trying not to spend too much, I could afford the odd T-shirt to tide me over.

It was in the Market Square, standing next to a stall selling tie-dye stuff, that I saw Daisy Buchanan. She must have clocked me first. By the time I looked up she was nudging the leggy brunette next to her, and looking in my direction, laughing. I turned away, feeling heat rush up my neck. I moved quickly along the row of stalls, not taking in what was in front of me. It was a couple of minutes later when I realised one of Daisy's gang had come over to join me.

'Daisy says your Luke won't leave her alone. She wonders if you'd have a word with him. It's – like – getting a bit heavy now.'

I didn't answer her. I could feel hot tears of fury and humiliation welling up in my eyes. In the middle of the sodding Market Square. Great. I stumbled away blindly, past WHSmiths and Fat Face, keeping my head down, letting my hair fall forward over my eyes.

It was a warm day and the tourists were out in full force. Outside Boots a man in a purple shirt, green waistcoat and trousers was singing Mozart arias. A crowd had gathered and the hat he had laid on the ground was full of coins.

A man and woman walked past me, he in flip-flops, T-shirt and surf shorts, she in a black vest top and sarong. They were eating ice creams.

A carefree summer's day in Cambridge. There were probably tramps as well, begging for money, but I didn't see them. Didn't want to. Didn't want company in my misery. Instead I looked at a hundred happy people, flitting before my eyes, and rubbed salt into my own wounds.

I'd got past Emmanuel and the bus station when I realised someone was staring at me. Well, hey, probably loads of people were staring at me, but – oh the luck – this was someone I knew.

I should have thought how close I'd wandered to St Audrey's. 'My goodness!' Paul Mathewson said. 'What on earth's happened?'

I shook my head. 'I'm sorry,' I said, welling up afresh at his concern. 'It's not a great time to be honest. I'm not in a brilliant state.'

I tried to carry on walking up the pavement, but he put an arm round my shoulders. 'So I gather, but you don't have to walk through town like this.'

'I'm sorry?'

'I live in college. You can come in and get yourself together. I'll make you a drink, and then, when you're in a fit state, I can walk you back to River House.'

I looked at the crowded street, and swiped at the tears cascading down my cheeks, but more arrived to replace them.

'Come on,' Paul said, steering me round, away from the road, and under a stone archway. 'Give yourself a break. You've had so much to deal with.'

'I'm sorry. I just don't feel like talking.'

He walked me across a court, to the bottom of a flight of uncarpeted wooden spiral stairs. 'Don't then,' he said. 'Why don't we just sit for a bit and take it one step at a time?'

It was the very last thing I wanted. I could feel him using his counselling experience on me, switching into responsible adult mode, taking care of the vulnerable, befriending the unfortunate. It made me squirm with embarrassment.

At the same time I knew he'd been going through a crisis of confidence about his dealings with Emily, and I couldn't think of a tactful way to reject his offer. And in any case, it was true: I didn't want to parade my misery for all the town to see. Who knew, I might bump into Daisy and her mates again.

He unlocked an oak door and ushered me into his rooms. Then I sat in an easy chair, next to a mullioned window, and he went to the sink to make me a cool glass of lemon squash. Outside, I could see the college gardens, awash with colour – roses, lavender and honeysuckle. How ironic that I should be spending such a beautiful afternoon in this way. I would just have to endure it until he felt he'd done his bit. Then I could go home again, and find something indestructible to kick for light relief.

We did sit in silence at first, but then we graduated to stilted small talk. I had a feeling I needed to move to this stage, so that Paul would feel I'd 'opened up'. He was probably used to formal college dinners where he had to be polite to strangers for hours. He had no problem coming up with neutral topics to keep us going.

I told him all about how I'd stayed in Cambridge as a child, but I was careful not to stray into genuinely personal territory. Before long I was able to turn the conversation.

'What about you?' I said. 'Where were you brought up?'

'I lived in Barnsley until I was ten,' he said.

I was surprised. 'You'd never guess it, from your accent.'

'My parents had to move down here, and then I got a scholarship to an independent, co-ed school on Huntingdon Road. I lost the accent pretty damned quick. Self-preservation, weakness, call it what you will. Some of the staff thought I was a curiosity; the kids were worse. It singled me out for attention,' he said, pausing for a second, 'one way or another ... But I got past all that eventually, and by that time I'd got a taste for the city. I stayed here to study for my first degree.'

'I don't even know your subject.'

'I read politics, psychology and sociology here at Cambridge, and followed that up with a PhD in social anthropology at Yale. Then I came back here again as a post doc.'

'You really do love Cambridge?'

'I thought it would do me good to leave ...' He let the sentence trail for a moment, his eyes far away. 'But it was a mistake.'

'You didn't like Yale?'

'Oh, it was great,' he said. 'I met some fantastic people, and I loved New Haven as a place, but I, well, I just love Cambridge more. Warts and all. Once I knew I wanted to stay I applied for a lectureship, and settled here at St Audrey's last year.'

When we'd exhausted our upbringings I asked about Fi and Emily, and Paul quizzed me about my interview with the police, and about Damien himself.

'Such an incredible thing,' he said. 'Not what you think you're going to have to deal with. Obviously, I'd got a pretty poor impression of what Newbold was like after Emily's dealings with him, but to attract that much hatred ...' He looked at me. 'It must have been hard for you, living in his house. Did you get any inkling that he might have engendered those sorts of feelings?'

179

I sighed. 'To be honest, the more I've seen, the more I've been able to imagine any one of a number of people wanting to finish him off.'

Paul nodded, as though it confirmed what he'd already thought, and I sipped my squash.

'God, I'm sorry,' I said. 'That was an awful thing to say.'

'It can't be awful to speak the truth,' Paul said. 'And at least …'

'At least?'

'Well, obviously, it's always appalling when anyone dies before their time, but I suppose – being brutally honest once again – it has to be less appalling if it turns out the person concerned spent their life hurting others.'

'In terms of it being less hard for everyone left behind to bear?' I said, clarifying what he was saying in my own mind. 'Yes, that has to be true, really.'

He picked up the squash he'd made for himself. 'When I saw you were upset,' he said, 'I guessed it must be to do with this business. I wondered whether it was something that woman who called last night had said.'

'Maggie Cook?'

'Was that her?' He raised his eyebrows. 'I didn't recognise her. She seems to be a tartar. I think Emily had a run-in with her over the Damien Newbold business.'

'I shouldn't imagine she's the sort to take kindly to a potential rival.' I remembered Emily mentioning something about Maggie having been in touch, and that she was 'telling lies'.

'Might she be on the list of murder suspects, do you think?'

'One of the many, I'd guess. But it wasn't she who upset me.'

And at the thought of Daisy, the floodgates opened again. I don't suppose Paul knew what had hit him. I hated myself for letting go, but once I'd started I found I couldn't stop.

'Just tell me,' he said. 'You'll feel much better, and it won't go any further.'

And between sobs I found myself reeling off the whole sorry story of Daisy and Luke. Even down to the fact that Luke and I had been trying for a baby. All the pent up anger and sorrow just exploded out of me. I think it was from having bottled it up for so long.

Paul's face fell, and there was real pain in his eyes. 'That's unspeakably awful, Ruby. I'm so sorry.' He put a hand on my arm and gave it a squeeze. 'Has he been in touch?'

I let out an undignified snort. 'Oh yes.' I found myself taking the letter Luke had written out of my handbag, and pulling it from its envelope. 'This is his idea of an apology. He just doesn't see what he's done, either in terms of betraying me, or the effect it might have on Daisy. See for yourself. I can't go back to him.'

Paul took the letter out and studied it for some time, frowning, and then looked up. 'Counsellors aren't supposed to pass comment, but I think you're right. There's no way you should try to patch things up.' He folded the paper, slipped it back into the envelope and passed it to me again. 'I'm glad you've told me. You've had a lot to cope with recently. Do you feel a bit better for having shared?'

I nodded. And I did, even though opening up went totally against the grain.

'I'll walk you home then, shall I?'

'It's okay. I'll be fine.'

He shook his head. 'I insist. It would be a pleasure.'

Nate was in the kitchen when he saw Ruby walk back along Midsummer Passage. She wasn't alone. A guy he hadn't seen before – rather formally dressed in a brown suit – was with her. They seemed to be deep in conversation. Outside the student place next door – Oswald House – they stopped, and Nate wondered if this was the tutor guy Ruby had said was looking after Emily Amos. Maybe they'd bumped into each other in Midsummer Lane. But then Mr Suit put a hand on Ruby's shoulder and drew her in to give her a hug. What was that all about?

Nate stood in the kitchen doorway as she let herself into the hall.

'Nice time in town?'

She raised an eyebrow. She looked – dishevelled somehow. Her eyes were in shadow so it was hard to read her expression.

'I spotted you out there.' He nodded towards the window. 'That was the tutor guy?'

She nodded. 'Paul Mathewson. I ran into him in town.' There was a pause. 'He, er, he wanted to talk about Emily. He was, well, he was just sympathising because of what we've all being going through.' She turned and went upstairs.

Sympathising, huh? It had looked like a bit more than that when he'd seen the expression on Mathewson's face. Well, it wasn't any of his business anyway.

And Nate kept telling himself that for the next hour and a half as he caught up with some business admin at the kitchen table.

I couldn't bring myself to admit to Nate that I'd told Paul all about Luke. I was already seriously regretting my weakness on that score. No doubt Nate knew most of it already, thanks to Steph, but having to refer to it myself was another matter – plus he'd think it odd that I'd been washing my dirty linen in public. The fact was, Paul was a good listener and, because he was one step removed, I'd found it easier to unburden myself in his presence.

I didn't feel hungry at suppertime, so I excused myself,

had a slice of toast and went up to my room. All I could think of was Daisy and her friends, and how it seemed I was now expected to talk some sense into Luke. What's more, even though his letter of 'apology' hadn't done the trick, I had at least believed him when he'd said he knew he'd made a mistake. But if what Daisy's friend had said was true, he was still pestering her. Talk about hedging his bets. Either way, someone was lying. So once again, I lay there in the attic, sleepless. After an hour or so had slipped by, I decided to get up. I went and looked out of the velux that faced north. It gave me a good view of the Common, the river glinting in the light from the boathouses opposite, shadowy narrow boats lining the water's edge. Badly lit cyclists flitted across the dark expanse like outsized bats, presumably on their way back from clubs or parties.

I wanted to do something productive that would take my mind off Luke, so I set myself the task of finding out about the fourth woman on Damien Newbold's bedroom wall: Elizabeth Edmunds.

I went down to the study, intending to start with the only mention of her I'd come across in the house. But the address book had gone. Of course, the police must have taken it away the day after Damien's death. After a moment, my mind managed to drag up the fact that she'd been based in Newmarket. And Newmarket was where Samson lived too, of course, and where Maggie and Damien had bumped into him at the races. Was that relevant? And then, all of a sudden, Maggie's words came back to me: 'Damien was in an exceptionally good mood, and he'd really dressed up for the occasion too' – as though it was something out of the ordinary. Had it really been a coincidence that they'd met Samson there, or had Damien somehow known he was likely to see his brother? After all, he was local. Maggie had talked about Damien being especially affectionate and demonstrative, and not at all put out by the chance meeting. That was something to think about. Had he simply been pleased at the opportunity to rub Samson's nose in his success with women? Even if he hadn't engineered the meeting in advance, as soon as Damien spotted Samson in the crowds he might have seen his chance to make mischief.

I needed to focus on Samson. From what I knew of him, he was probably the sort to make up to any woman that crossed his path. Perhaps Damien had guessed that leaving him alone with Maggie would create exactly the scene that had occurred, and had relished the idea of her turning him down flat. I got out my laptop, and sat at the study desk, shoving the stuff the police hadn't removed to one side.

At that moment, I heard a sound: a tiny creak outside in the hall. I held my breath, and stayed absolutely still. As I watched, the study door started to move, slowly and quietly on its hinges.

And then Nate appeared. He was in jeans and long-sleeved T-shirt, as though he'd given up on the night as much as I had. He took in my face. Probably noticed my shoulders were so tensed they almost touched my ears. 'Sorry. Didn't mean to startle you. I couldn't sleep.'

I let out the breath I'd been holding. 'Same.'

'What are you up to?' He walked over to the desk, and I explained. 'That's interesting,' he said, when I passed on my theory about Damien setting up a confrontation with his brother. 'Seems to fit with his MO.'

I nodded. 'I was just about to Google Elizabeth Edmunds.'

'Imagine you'll get a lot of results.'

He was right. Facebook and LinkedIn filled my page; it was going to be like looking for the proverbial needle. I didn't think it would work, but I added 'Newmarket' into the search terms and tried again.

'Good thought,' Nate said, leaning over my shoulder. He was clearly caught up in the search. I had been too, but I couldn't help being conscious of his nearness; I could feel the warmth of him. It took me a second to click on the first hit, which was for Newmarket Racecourses. I hoped he hadn't registered the delay.

The page told me Elizabeth Edmunds was part of the racecourse's hospitality team. Her photograph beamed out of my computer screen.

'I wonder how far back her affair with Damien Newbold went,' Nate said. 'It was clearly ongoing when he died, and he surely wouldn't have had the painting done the moment he'd met her.'

'Then again ...'

'Yeah, you're right. We can't assume anything from such a screw-up. But assuming for a minute that I'm right, it suggests he must have already been involved with her when he took Maggie to the races.'

'You're right. And I agree that's most likely. I wonder if Elizabeth Edmunds saw them together at Newmarket.'

'Damien must have known it was a risk. Either he didn't care what she thought, or he was keen to make her jealous.'

'My guess is the latter.' I explained what Tilly Blake had said about the painting of Maggie Cook Damien kept on his bedroom wall even when they were at the height of their affair. 'He told her she shouldn't object to a thing of beauty.'

'God, he was a shit.'

I looked at him. 'No arguments there.'

'Would you like a drink?'

I paused for a second.

'Brandy?'

'Go on then. Sounds good.'

He was back from the kitchen in a couple of minutes.

'Even if Elizabeth did see Damien and Maggie,' I said,

taking a fiery sip, 'it obviously didn't put her off letting him stay in her cottage, or indeed agreeing to visit him on the night he died.' As the drink snaked its way down to my stomach, that led to another thought. 'Unless she had a different reason for wanting him somewhere nice and accessible.'

'Yes,' Nate said. He'd drawn a second chair up to the study desk. 'Just what was going through my mind too.'

We looked again at the photograph of Elizabeth Edmunds, and I remembered her painting on Damien's wall. I'd been thinking of her as the shy one. Could she have killed Damien?

'You can't always tell what a person's capable of from their looks,' Nate said. It was as though he'd read my mind.

Nate hadn't had the chance to share a case like this since he'd learnt his trade with Jack. He'd forgotten how much he enjoyed it. And Ruby didn't have a paunch and thinning grey hair, which was the icing on the cake. Shame she seemed to be rebounding with the tutor guy. Not that he could complain. There was no way he could approach her again. And anyway, it wouldn't be safe.

Suddenly, she turned to him. 'Do you want me to let you in on my dark secret?'

He was pretty sure she was keeping several. 'Which one?'

She rolled her eyes. 'Come on through to the drawing room.'

He followed her, and she crouched down by a floor-to-ceiling bookcase, and heaved out some photo albums. 'I thought these might help me to understand more of Damien Newbold's background, once I realised the fourth nude on his wall was his mother.'

They sat on Newbold's spindly sofa, which was definitely not created for someone of Nate's size. He heard it creak ominously as he leant back and Ruby opened the first album.

He could see why she'd become absorbed. She explained all the images in the context of what she'd found out online, blushing when she came to the albums she'd explored with the aid of a kitchen knife.

'You're thorough, I'll give you that. Possibly not cut out for regular house-sitting work though. Clients hate it when you vandalise their belongings.'

'How narrow-minded of them.'

Nate shifted and the sofa creaked again, as though it was reminding him not to push his luck. He stood up. 'Think I might be safer on the floor.' It was a shame that Newbold, like most people, didn't have more up-to-date photo albums. They might have told them something. As it was, the police had seized his computer, where he no doubt stored his jpg files. Then again, he might have kept backups somewhere the police hadn't searched. Nate got up. 'Just thought of something I might check.'

'Okay.' Ruby was still on the sofa, looking at one of the albums. She'd drawn her feet under her, and was leaning on a silk cushion, her dark hair fanned out against its lemon yellow.

Nate spent some time looking through the drawers in the study, and checking on the shelves. Nothing doing. Then it occurred to him that Newbold could have put backup disks alongside the regular music cds, which were down in the basement. But he was empty-handed when he returned to the drawing room. He opened his mouth to explain what he'd been searching for, but then shut it again. Ruby had fallen asleep.

I was confused when I woke up. Where the hell was I? Then gradually the memories of the evening gathered as I came to more fully. I was still on the sofa. The album I'd been looking at had been put on a side table, and I was covered with a blanket. The feeling of warmth intensified as I put those facts together. My empty brandy glass was next to the album. The drink had sent me off all right. I glanced at my watch. A quarter past two. Time to go to bed proper.

I got up slowly and began to fold the blanket. It was then that an unfamiliar noise caught my attention. I moved towards the hallway, and stood there, listening. For half a second, I thought maybe Nate was still downstairs, but gut instinct told me the truth was less reassuring. There was a faint scraping, like a knife on a plate, but it was coming from the study. I kept absolutely still as I tried to make sense of what I was hearing. The sound went on, still very quiet, with the occasional squeak as though something was pushing and then slipping on a smooth surface.

I felt my scalp prickle. I didn't know what to do. I hadn't got my mobile with me, and panic made me slow.

And then I realised something else was different.

It was cooler. The air was shifting, drifting through the study door towards me. I knew what the sound had been now, and felt my legs wobble underneath me. Someone had been at work, easing out a pane of glass, ready to make their entrance.

I moved forward on tiptoe, so that I could look across the hall. Ahead of me I could see enough to tell that the study curtains were drawn back. The beam of a torch swung over the room's walls.

I remembered reading an article in Saxwell's neighbourhood watch magazine about approaching burglars when they're in your house. The author had said it was crucial not to make them feel cornered. If you let them feel trapped they were likely to lash out. Heroics aside, I was quite keen not to be lashed out at. Of course, Nate was upstairs. I could try to sneak up there and warn him, but realistically, I was sure they'd hear me. If they just made a run for it that would be fine. But they might manage to grab the odd valuable item before they went. If I wanted to make myself useful in the role I'd been hired for, I needed to do something more immediate.

As I tried to think I heard a faint gasp, then a soft thud as something weighty hit the floorboards. Someone had squeezed their way in.

It was hardly heroics, but bluffing my way out of trouble seemed like the best approach.

'I know you're there,' I called out. 'And the police are on their way. I'm not coming in, but you might like to leave right now.'

Surely the person holding the torch wouldn't believe me. I sounded as phoney as hell. My voice had been shaking when I'd said the police were on their way. The intruders would probably come straight through to shut me up, and then get on with the job.

But almost immediately someone swore. 'Thought you said the ground floor was clear! I might have known.' And then came a cracking sound – perhaps part of the window frame giving way as he exited more hastily than he'd come in.

I ran through to the kitchen to try to get a look at them as they left. As the second one exited the back gate, I saw Nate hurtle out of the back door, and disappear in the same direction.

After five minutes, he was back, shaking his head. 'No good. They had a car waiting. I didn't even get their number.'

We went through to the study. It was a bit of a mess.

'I don't think they got anything,' I said. 'The thin guy had only just got inside when I called out.'

Nate nodded. 'You certainly achieved an instant response. I dashed down as soon as I heard you shout.'

'You hadn't gone to bed?' He was still in his jeans.

He grinned for a moment. 'No. Just as well or I'd have been chasing them down the street in my boxers.'

'I never thought they'd give up so easily.'

'Opportunists perhaps, rather than professionals.'

'Hell. Samson's not going to like this.'

He put a hand on my shoulder and gave it a squeeze, overriding the previous source of adrenaline. 'Nonsense. Bottom line is, you stopped them in their tracks. Samson will be forever in your debt.'

'Hmm. I think that's almost more worrying than him being cross with me.'

Nate smiled for a second. 'Yes, I see your point.'

Chapter Twenty

Nate called a twenty-four hour glazier just after he'd contacted the police. The police arrived within minutes, and he took them to the kitchen. There were two officers who pummelled first Ruby, and then him, with questions, and a couple more who gathered evidence. They'd be conscious of a possible connection with the murder so he knew they'd take the break-in seriously.

'Though any house thought to be empty following a death is a prime target,' the younger officer said. She had blonde hair, pulled back into an untidy bun. 'Any chancer who's read the news recently or seen the flowers outside might take a punt on the place being unoccupied.'

Ruby nodded, but Nate could see she was unconvinced. 'I can't help feeling it wasn't like that,' she said, her head in her hands, elbows on the table. 'From what that man said, I got the impression they knew I'd been sleeping downstairs originally, and that the arrangement had changed.'

'So you think they had inside information?' the older officer said, scratching his scalp through thinning hair.

'Maybe. I wondered whether Samson Newbold, who stands to inherit the house, might have let something slip by accident. That could be how they'd got wind of his security arrangements.'

'Though they could have sized up the situation here just by keeping an eye on the place for a couple of days,' the woman said. 'Which lights get used after dark gives a lot away.'

There was something in what she said, but still Ruby sighed.

Once the entire police contingent had left Nate turned to her. She was still slumped in a chair at the kitchen table.

'Go to bed. I'll wait up for the glazier. It'll probably be a bit noisy, but with any luck you'll sleep through it; you look as though you might. You're probably still in shock. Don't forget you had to confront them when they were still on their way in.'

She got to her feet, at last. 'Okay, then. Thanks.'

'You lie in and take no notice of me. I'll have to call Samson about all this and I'm guessing he'll want to come over and see what's happened. If so, I'll go and collect him and meet you back here.'

As she manoeuvred round the table she caught his eye. 'Thanks for the blanket earlier. Sorry I conked out.'

When I struggled back to consciousness the next morning, the first thing I did was check my mobile for the time. Bloody hell; eleven fifteen, and I had a text. Nate had written Didn't want 2 wake u. Be back with Samson at 11:30. OK?

I replied OK as I scrambled out from under the duvet and marched off to the bathroom. There was no time to prepare properly. I pulled on black jeans and a kingfisher blue T-shirt, which gave me a pallor any self-respecting Goth would have been proud of. Damn brandy and burglars, they clearly played havoc with one's complexion. I was just trying to make some blusher look natural when I heard the front door open and close, and voices in the hall.

I went to face the music. Samson's focus was on the study door as he muttered a greeting. Behind him Nate met my gaze and rolled his eyes.

We followed Samson through to the spot where one of the two men had managed to enter the house. 'I spoke to DI Johnson this morning,' he said. 'The police say we're very lucky the burglars didn't manage to get anything at all.'

'Well, I suppose the one who came inside only had a second's opportunity,' I said. 'He'd barely had time to flick a torch over the contents when I shouted out. And there are fewer valuables in here than in the drawing room.'

'Well, you've more than proved yourself,' Samson said, his eyes running over me in that well-practised way, in spite of my reduced state. His gaze made my hands go clammy. 'I gather you were on the scene first.' He glanced sideways at Nate.

'I just happened to be downstairs, because I couldn't sleep,' I said. 'I'll get us some coffee.' I walked into the hall, but Nate followed me.

'I'll do it.' As he passed me, he said, under his breath, 'I'll leave you to the love-in, Ms Flavour-of-the-month.'

'Hmm. Thanks.' I dragged myself back to the study.

'So what did our burglars look like?' Samson said.

I shrugged. 'I barely saw them.' I explained what little I'd managed to glimpse from the kitchen window. 'There was no chance of even judging their hair colour in that light.'

'So nothing that might help us to catch up with them?' He moved his lips in a dissatisfied way as he finished his question. He reminded me of a toad.

'Precious little. Nate chased them down the street, but like me, he just saw one of them was taller and thinner than the other.'

'I understand from the police that the thieves probably weren't professional.'

'That was the impression we got.'

Samson looked thoughtful. 'I've been having a spot of bother with Damien's old girlfriend, Maggie Cook. Did you know about that?'

I didn't trust myself to speak, so I shook my head instead. Going into the ethics of my chat with Maggie on the Common and her accusations of murder against Samson would seriously complicate matters.

'I suspect,' Samson said, 'that she might have reason to

break in here, or possibly to persuade her friends to do so. It might be worth bearing in mind.' He held my gaze. 'She comes out with a lot of hysterical nonsense and I wouldn't want to hear that you'd allowed her to ... shall we say, play on your sympathies.'

There was a hint of threat in his tone.

'I've no intention of letting anyone play on my anything,' I said. Not any more, anyway, and I hoped he realised that included him, revolting little slimeball.

He raised his eyebrows. 'That's good.'

Nate came in with our coffees.

Samson looked up. 'Perhaps you could take them through to the kitchen. I'll come and join you in a minute.'

I had a strong urge to hold back. Okay, so I'd already searched the obvious places for any new will Damien might have made, but what if I'd missed something? Samson would think nothing of pocketing any evidence he managed to find; there was no way he was planning on giving up his inheritance. But Nate caught my eye, and I had to follow him out into the hall.

'What's he up to?'

'No good, at a rough guess.'

We went through to the kitchen. Should I come clean? The fact that I hadn't told the police seemed all the more foolhardy, given the break-in. But both Damien and Samson had treated Maggie appallingly. Besides, I was quite sure the thieves were after the treasure trove of antiques at River House, not anything else. Looking for a missing will would take hours, and why would she entrust the job to a third party? After all, she knew the place; she'd be a lot faster than some hired amateurs. Plus, she'd still have been under the impression I was sleeping downstairs.

So I said nothing. But holding out on Nate felt wrong, even if the reasons behind it were good. A few minutes later,

Samson joined us. I looked him over but there was no way he could be concealing any significant paperwork. Even if it was only a single sheet and he'd stuffed it in his pocket I would have been able to see a corner sticking out. If he had found anything, he must have just buried it deeper in Damien's paperwork. That would lessen the chances of Maggie locating it if she happened to gain access. And even if he had discovered evidence of a fresh will he probably wouldn't be too worried. Maggie wouldn't be likely to get the chance to look for it anyway, and in a few short weeks he would have River House to himself, and all the time he liked to burn the evidence.

'I presume you're still keeping up with the cleaning,' Samson said to me. 'Once I've sorted through all Damien's junk this place'll go on the market, and it's important to make sure the house looks lived in. I'll need you to work hard to keep it in good order.'

Power games. 'Yes, I've been following the rota.'

When we'd finished our coffee, he led us out into the hall, and stood with one hand on the newel post of the staircase. 'You've had a fresh eye on the place. Have you spotted anything that's broken? Or anything you think might put buyers off?'

'I think the nudes Damien put up on his bedroom wall might raise a few eyebrows,' I said, testing him with the information to see what happened.

'Nudes?' I'd swear he perked up.

'Paintings. He's got four up there, one on each wall. Might actually endear the place to some people, of course, but if you're going to follow that TV house doctor's advice and stay nice and neutral ...'

'I think I'd better take a look.' He hauled himself up the stairs, reddening as he reached the landing, and opened the master bedroom door.

Nate and I watched him as he drank them in, one by one. He did a double take at the sight of his mother, rolled his eyes at Maggie Cook (but with a leer, nonetheless), glanced at Tilly Blake with interest, but it was his expression when he looked at Elizabeth Edmunds' image that caught my attention. There was a flash of anger in his eyes. It came and was controlled so quickly that I had to replay it in my head to convince myself it had happened. I glanced sideways at Nate, and found he was looking at me too, a question in his eyes. I hadn't imagined it then.

Chapter Twenty-One

Over the next few days mundane things happened, like a man turning up to fit a bolt to the back gate as instructed by Samson. I was pleased about that. It meant I would no longer have nightmares about him popping up suddenly in the garden like an outsized gnome. I even managed to grind through a lot of the writing for my book, though it didn't come as easily as usual.

I felt exhausted, and realised what I really needed was a dose of Steph. I hadn't told her about my run-in with Daisy, or about the burglars. I called, and when I said I had news she promptly told me she had updates to pass on too. If it was the latest on the Saxwell village scandal – local professional seduces teenage girl – then I wasn't entirely sure I wanted to hear it. All the same, we arranged for her to come over for tea.

'But you'll probably miss Nate. He's meant to be out until six or so.'

'That's a shame,' Steph said, 'but the main thing is, we can have a proper catch-up.'

So it was settled, and I went off to the newsagents on Fitzroy Street to get a paper and some more milk.

I found a bench, out by the river, and sat just across the Common, with the house behind me. As I scanned the pages for any more information on Damien Newbold's murder, I couldn't help glancing at the passers-by. Was anyone still watching my movements? Waiting until I was out of the house to strike? But the burglar alarm was set, and none of the people I saw looked like criminals. A woman with cropped grey hair walked by, three white West Highland terriers on leads fanned out in front of her. In the same moment two bronzed girls on bikes squeezed between my outstretched feet and the smallest dog, causing the woman to tut. I'm sure they didn't notice. They cycled on, laughing, dark glasses glinting in the sun, ebony hair flying out behind them.

In the paper I found a short piece on the ongoing police investigation. The headline was: 'Victim's Boss Scotches Laptop Lead.' TomorrowTech seemed to have had time to investigate the story of Damien Newbold's new invention now, and the company's Chief Executive had issued a statement saying he had no knowledge of any recent breakthrough. He suggested that the rumour, just before Damien had died, had been dreamt up by a blogger, faced with a quiet news day. But surely a technology journalist wouldn't just invent something that specific?

I put the paper down by my side on the bench where the pages rustled in the breeze. Could he still have been murdered for a new innovation that didn't exist? It seemed far-fetched. After all, if he had found anything exciting there would be no way the murderer could be sure he had the information on his laptop in the first place. And it was a rather drastic move to murder Damien on the strength of a rumour.

I was standing on the steps to River House, getting my keys out, when Emily appeared. It was the first time I'd seen her since Damien Newbold's death.

'How are you?' I asked, not knowing quite what to say.

Her eyes looked dull. 'They think I killed him.'

'I'm quite sure they don't.' It came out too sharply.

'They asked such horrible questions.' She wasn't meeting my gaze. 'And they knew things that I didn't think—' She stopped suddenly and looked at me at last. 'I saw the man who came to see you. Damien's brother.'

I nodded.

'You can tell he's a relation, but he's like a distorted caricature of the real thing. He stands to gain an awful lot, doesn't he?' Her heavy eyes lifted to meet mine. 'At first I thought ... I really thought Maggie Cook must have killed Damien. And if she had, it would have been my fault. I'd stirred things up between them, and she's got a violent temper.'

I wondered if she'd witnessed that herself.

'But it could have been Damien's brother. He might need the money. Or, even if he doesn't, it might be just greed ... or revenge for some family matter that we know nothing about. You've talked to him. What do you think?'

This wasn't a conversation I wanted to have. 'Emily, I've honestly got no idea.'

A light came into her eyes now; a new intensity that hadn't been there earlier. 'You let me down before,' she said, 'when I wanted to contact Damien. And now it's too late. I could have spoken to him before he died if you'd helped me.'

'Emily,' I began, 'you know I couldn't—'

'But you can help me now. You can find out about his brother. You can get close to him.'

Suddenly she put a hand on my arm. I thought she looked slightly crazed. 'You must understand, if Samson did it, then it wasn't my fault. It wasn't because of what I said to Maggie. And the police will know I'm innocent. Please don't let me down this time!'

'I really want to know what happened, too,' I said. 'And if I find anything out I'll take it straight to the police.'

'Will you do what you can?' She was still holding my arm.

'I will,' I said, but I had no idea what that might be.

Steph's eyes went wide when I updated her on my run-in

with Daisy Buchanan and her gang, and then I told her how Paul Mathewson had provided lemon squash and sympathy. 'He was so kind I ended up telling him everything. It felt good to offload, but I've been regretting it ever since. It would have been far better if I'd run in to you.'

'But he was nice.'

'Very. But you know how it is, he'd have done it a lot better if he'd been a woman, and better still if he'd been a woman called Steph.'

She hugged me.

I remembered again what Nate must have seen when Paul had brought me home. It had been on my mind, so I mentioned it. 'I'm just worried about what he must have thought. Probably reckons Paul and I have been making out like a couple of teenagers.' The horror of this idea made my guts squirm.

'He's broadminded enough. He might reckon you're on the rebound and out to take revenge on Luke but ...' She shrugged. '... so what? I'm sure he won't hold it against you.' Suddenly she looked up at me, a knowing light in her eyes. 'Hang on a minute ... Why are you so bothered about what he thinks?'

I glared at her. 'Because he's my employer. And because I'm human and I don't want him to think I'm so shallow that I'd walk right into an affair, just after my partner dumped me.'

She was still giving me that same look, her neatly-plucked eyebrows raised. 'Really? Sure that's all it is? Nate's one hell of a looker. I'd probably fancy him myself if he wasn't a coz.'

Mine and Nate's aborted kiss filled my head. Thank heavens there was no truth in mind reading. 'For God's sake, Steph!' I said. 'I've just broken up with my long-term partner. I was worried Nate might think I was running after

Paul on the rebound. Given he doesn't know me well, it's a mistake he might make. But you ought to understand I've had it up to here with relationships for the next decade or so.'

She put a hand on my arm. 'Sorry, Ruby! It was thoughtless of me, when you put it like that. You just sounded so anxious about what he thought, and for a moment I … Anyway, I wouldn't have blamed you, that's all.' She sighed.

'In any case,' I said, feeling horribly guilty, 'I shall be careful who I hobnob with now. Nate's got reason to be even more security conscious.' And I filled her in on the burglary.

'Heavens, Ruby, that must have been terrifying. This job seems like the worst possible thing for you to be doing at the moment.' She looked rueful. 'I wish to goodness I'd never suggested it, to tell you the truth.'

'It's been character building.'

She took her tone from me, but I could see from her pinched look that she was still worried. 'You'll be emotionally scarred for life,' she said, cutting me another large slice of the cake she'd brought with her. 'And it'll all be my fault. So how did Nate react to the burglary, on top of the murder?'

'Okay, but he's already warned me to be careful, in no uncertain terms.' I gave Steph a deliberate glance. 'And after what he's been through, that's not exactly surprising.'

She gave me a shrewd look. 'Oh my God! You've Googled him, haven't you?'

'Well, wouldn't you have?'

She made a harrumphing sound. 'Possibly.'

'It was really because you kept making cryptic little comments about his mindset. All that stuff about not wanting to let paranoia get the better of him. Everything you said pointed to some previous experience that had coloured his outlook on life.'

'So it was all my fault?'

I shrugged. 'You probably didn't do it on purpose.' I got up to make us more tea. 'I don't know why we're sitting here arguing about it anyway. I couldn't believe it when I read it, Steph. It's such an unimaginably awful thing to have happened.'

She nodded. 'Beyond what you can take in, isn't it? And we were all devastated about Susie too, of course. She was bright as a button; so full of life, and ten years younger than Nate.' She gave a sad smile. 'I hope you can see what I meant about not telling you before. Everyone who knows sees Nate as "that man whose sister got murdered".'

I nodded. 'And I can see he blames himself.'

'You talked to him about it?'

'Yes.'

'Wow. Well, it's good he opened up.' She put her head on one side. 'As far as blaming himself goes, I'm afraid you're right, and he's not the only one. Some of the villagers clearly thought he'd led Susie into danger. It even caused a rift between him and his dad.'

I could only imagine his pain. 'How awful.'

Steph nodded. 'I'm actually quite relieved you're not hung up on him. He'd be a terrible choice, given that he hasn't let anyone much get close since Susie's death; thinks it'll make them a target.' She leant forward and took a sip of her tea.

I noted the qualifying 'much', and wondered about exceptions. 'And what about giving up the PI business?'

'He can't forgive himself,' Steph said, simply. 'He says he *was* negligent, and that if he'd been competent he'd have predicted the danger. He's not prepared to offer substandard services to clients who might be hurt rather than helped by his input.'

'You're quoting him?'

She nodded. 'He said that during the only argument we've ever had. He'd never shouted at me before.' She looked up for a moment. 'It took me a long time to get over it, to be honest. I'm rubbish at confrontation.'

'So Nate's in perpetual limbo.'

Steph nodded. 'Horrible, not knowing who and not knowing why. And after all this time, I'm afraid it might stay that way. He's put his life on hold. And he's wrong.'

I looked up.

'About his work, I mean. He was a really good PI by all accounts. But it's no use reasoning with him, so it's simpler all round if new contacts just know him as the house-sitting man.'

We sat in silence and it was a good while before I remembered that she had news for me, or so she'd said on the phone.

'So what's happening in Saxwell?' I asked. 'Have things gravitated to street brawls yet? Ma Buchanan thrown any eggs at Luke?'

Steph pulled a face. 'Joking aside, it's made the whole atmosphere in the village a bit tense. Several people are cold-shouldering Robin now because they've seen him speak to Luke. And when all's said and done, he was only telling him what a prick he was.'

'Has he talked to you about his plans?'

'It's you he wants to speak to, Ruby.' Steph picked up a stray crumb of cake. 'He needs to touch base on practicalities if nothing else. His first priority's become getting out of Saxwell, so he needs to know what you want. I told him not to call you – that it was what you'd said – but he asked me to say he needs you to make contact. And for what it's worth, I reckon Daisy's friend was just winding you up. I haven't seen him go near her.'

I put my mug down. My head was starting to ache. 'I don't really care what he's been up to.' Which wasn't entirely true. 'But either way, I know I can't just stick my head in the sand.'

Steph got up and came over to my chair, crouching to put an arm around me.

I took a deep breath. 'So Luke's in a hurry now?'

She nodded. 'I know it's entirely his own fault, Ruby, but things are starting to get out of hand.'

'What's happened?'

'Someone daubed the side of your house with graffiti.'

'Bloody hell. Do they know who?'

'Some seventeen-year-old ex of Daisy's apparently. But Luke's getting it from all sides. Poison pen letters – from more than one sender by the look of it – people cutting him dead in the street, or having a go at him, according to taste.'

'Sounds like quite a cabaret,' I said.

Steph gave me a look.

'Oh, don't worry. I'll call him tomorrow.'

'It's more than he deserves, of course, but I think it might be best.'

Chapter Twenty-Two

Ringing Luke pervaded my breakfast-time thoughts, batting round and round my head like a trapped fly against a windowpane. I couldn't call him until mid-afternoon, assuming he still went out to play cricket on Saturdays. If he'd been involved in a village club he'd probably have had to jack it in, what with all the gossip, but he actually played for a team in Bury St Edmunds, because of a connection there. He was probably enjoying sneaking off somewhere where he still had some anonymity.

I was thinking so hard about calling him that I jumped like a cricket when Nate came into the room to make coffee. 'What news?'

'Samson Newbold's emailed to say he's off to London on some kind of business, so he's out of our hair for a while. He was on about Maggie Cook, wanting to know if we'd seen anything of her.'

I found it hard to look him in the eye. 'And what are your plans for the day?'

He picked up his car keys from the worktop. 'I've got to see a prospective client in Mildenhall now, and then another one in Saffron Walden, so I'll be gone for the day. Give me a call if you need anything.'

I sat on the sofa in the basement with a coffee, thinking about what Nate had said. So Samson was away in London. It was nice to know that, River House keyholder though he was, there was certainly no way he was going to turn up on the doorstep today. I imagined him sidling slimily into the London nightlife. Picking up a prostitute. I thought he was probably the type.

And then I remembered how hard Nate had said it

had been to drag him away from his local. What had it been called? Something with a colour in the title. I stared unseeingly at the French windows, trying to call it to mind. Suddenly I had it: the Red Tavern. It sounded somehow rough and smoke-filled, only it couldn't be these days, of course. I sipped some more of my drink and my mind strayed back to my last talk with Emily. *You let me down before, when I wanted to contact Damien, but you can help me find out about his brother.*

Visiting his natural habitat would probably be an eye opener.

The moment the thought was there I tried to pretend it hadn't been. The last thing I wanted was to drive over to Newmarket and attempt to waft inconspicuously around a pub full of pot-bellied blokes. I hated going into pubs on my own, even when it was just a case of having to wait for friends.

So I picked up a magazine from a side table and read about a woman who'd changed careers, giving up banking to become a sheep farmer at the age of fifty.

Of course, if I did go I might need to chat to the bartender, or whoever, to get proper background information.

I tried to focus on a photograph of a Fair Isle jumper.

And if I was going to draw attention to myself in that way, I'd need to make damn sure Samson's pub-going friends didn't report back on my presence, and enable him to identify me. No DMs. I'd told him they were part of my workaday kit.

He'd seen me demure, in a professional-looking dress, and he knew my tougher alter ego.

Before I'd mentally acknowledged what I was doing, I'd gathered up my bag and was locking up the house. There was a Claire's Accessories in the Grafton Centre, and I had an idea in mind.

* * *

The costume jewellery was perfect. Beloved of teenage girls – just what I would never normally wear. I got earrings, a bracelet and some hair clips, all with plenty of diamante, and capped the whole lot off with a pair of crazy sunglasses. They were the sort you looked at and knew had either cost five pounds or five hundred, but couldn't tell which. They too had plenty of bling down each side.

In Boots I bought scarlet false nails. My hand hovered over the false eyelashes. Was I playing at spies? Well, it would take my mind off phoning Luke, anyway.

Back at River House I Googled the Red Tavern and found it opened at midday. I'd maybe make it over there for about one. Give the place a chance to warm up a bit first. Then, once I'd got home, I'd ring Luke and afterwards reward myself for having got two nasty jobs out of the way. It would certainly mean I didn't owe Emily anything.

I was pacing up and down the hallway at River House, wondering how I could explain my presence at the pub, when there was a knock at the front door. Thank God I hadn't already got dressed up. I let out the breath I'd been holding and went to the spyhole. It was Maggie Cook again, but a very different Maggie from the one I'd seen the previous week. She was wearing a clingy, knee-length, emerald-green dress and dangly, green earrings and her eyes looked clear, her mascara unravaged by tears.

I still had misgivings as I put my hand on the doorknob, but I opened up all the same.

'Hello, Ruby,' she said, then immediately added, 'don't worry, I don't want to come in this time; I know it's not allowed. Do you fancy a walk though?'

I was curious and set the alarm before locking up and following her towards the river in the general direction of town.

'I got you these,' she said, reaching into a bag she was

carrying to reveal a box of posh chocolates. 'You don't have to take them now. I'll give them to you when we get back to River House.'

'It's very kind of you, but why?' I was striding along beside her, enjoying the sun and the light breeze that was rippling the river's surface.

'Part peace offering, part bribe.'

I think the smile I gave was a little uncertain. 'Bribe?'

'I'll come onto that. First things first. I really am very sorry I landed myself on you before, when I was in such a state.' She turned to me. 'I mean it. Whatever impression I've given, I do actually know that none of this is your fault. You've been hurled into the middle of a messy and disquieting situation. I expect you've been getting grief from all sides, and I don't envy you having to deal with Samson either.'

We shared a roll of the eyes.

'Truth to tell,' Maggie said, 'I've been on a bit of a bender ever since I heard about Damien.'

'No one could exactly blame you for that.'

She shrugged. 'I was being selfish, but I was out of it on grief and drink. That's the only excuse I can offer really.'

Uber-reasonable. I did wonder how much of this was a carefully calculated act. And yet she might have very good reasons for the performance.

We were walking past the open-air swimming pool. Through the doorway I could see a lot of people sunbathing and some nice, clear, blue water with just one bather ploughing up and down.

'How have things been for you since Damien died?' Maggie asked.

'A bit weird.' I watched her closely as I told her about the break in.

'Shit!' she said. 'I should think Samson'll want to pin that on me. I made the mistake of calling him when I was half cut and saying I'd find the will or die in the attempt. I think I put it in some dramatic way like that.' She gave me a half-smile. 'I am an actor after all.' She went quiet. 'Given that it wasn't anything to do with me, I wonder who those men could have been.'

'Whoever they were, I'm not keen to meet them again.'

'I certainly hope you won't,' Maggie said. 'Anyway, I shouldn't have added to all the aggro you've been getting. And I was also worried I must have sounded like a money-grabbing vulture, when I went on and on about the elusive will last week. I wanted to try to explain. Samson never believed in Damien's passion for me, as you know.' She turned to meet my gaze. 'I feel sure the will exists, and equally I know how much Damien hated Samson. He just wouldn't have left things as they stood.' She sighed. 'I know it's a cliché, but it's not actually about the money. I think I just want to have some evidence that the old bugger actually cared. And I really, really want to wipe the smug smile off that bastard Samson's face.'

'I can understand that,' I said, even though I knew I shouldn't.

She gave me a crooked grin. 'The money would just be an added bonus.'

I couldn't help smiling and hoped fervently that I wasn't looking at Damien Newbold's killer. 'Naturally.'

'And that's where the chocolate bribe comes in.'

'You want me to look round the house myself, see if I can find anything?'

She nodded.

'To be honest, I did give Damien's filing cabinet a quick once-over after we last spoke.'

Her face fell, and it was painful to watch.

'I can look a bit further,' I said, 'but, Maggie, how do you even know he really made a new will? I understand he told you that was what he was planning, but it takes most people months, if not years, to get round to seeing a solicitor, and getting it all set up.' I asked the question I'd skirted round previously: 'Did he explicitly tell you it was done?'

'Not exactly,' she said. 'But one day recently I could see he was mentally rubbing his hands; he just couldn't stop smiling and laughing to himself. Then he said how put out Samson would be if he knew about his latest legal adjustments.' She raised an eyebrow. 'I'm sure he was referring back to his plan to make me his beneficiary. I didn't want to make him spell it out – it would have sounded greedy, and it really wasn't important to me – but I was sure then that he'd done it.'

'The thing is, wouldn't he have left his copy somewhere obvious, if he'd wanted it to be found after his death?'

'In the normal way of things I'm sure you're right. But what if he'd only just had it finalised? He could have used a new solicitor rather than the family one. And then maybe he just put his copy aside, meaning to file it in a logical place shortly. Only he died before he got the chance.' A shadow passed over her face, the lively smile dropping as her features became still.

I didn't buy it. 'Any local solicitor would surely have seen news of his death and come forward.'

'But it hasn't made national news. And he was always down in London. Maybe he used a firm there.'

I sighed. 'I'd love to find it for you, Maggie, but somehow I just don't think it's there. Maybe he was talking about something else when he made those comments about pissing Samson off.'

'Maybe.' She turned towards me. 'But could you at least give it one more try?'

We had arrived back at the house and she handed over the chocolates.

'I'll scout round,' I said. 'But it's a big house with an awful lot of papers and books.'

'I know. All the more reason for me to be very, very grateful to you. I really appreciate it.'

She had written her number on a card that was with the bribe, and I tucked it into my jeans pocket as I carried the chocolates through to the kitchen. I'd have to sample them later, once I'd got my nasty jobs out of the way. It was time to get dolled up, but I needed to decide on an outfit. I plumped for my white linen trousers and a white blouse in the end. They seemed to offset the accessories best. I stood in front of the mirror in the attic, experimenting with the sunglasses pushed back on the top of my head, my hair clipped up at one side. Everything sparkled quite horribly. And the red nails were a great touch.

I'd just finished fixing them on when I realised Nate was standing in my bedroom doorway.

For a second Nate thought they'd got more burglars. 'Do you always dress up the moment I leave the house?'

Her cheeks turned scarlet. 'Actually, it's a bit of a first.'

The carrier bags strewn around her room and the receipts on the dressing table backed up her story.

'I didn't expect you back so soon.'

'So I see. The Saffron Walden client cancelled. So, were you feeling bored? I mean, I admit there haven't been any break-ins in the last couple of days, and the murders seem to have dropped right off.'

She was looking at her feet. The usual DMs were gone, replaced by some slingbacks.

'Okay. So, assuming you're not just having fun, I'm guessing you're off sleuthing, and don't want anyone to recognise you.' He ran through the latest developments in his head. 'Ah. The Red Tavern, right?'

She finally met his gaze. 'Steph said you were good.' She told him about her talk with Emily. 'Once I'd thought of heading over to Newmarket, going back on the idea would have felt like cowardice.'

'And it's just for Emily's sake? You're not remotely curious to find out more on your own account?'

She gave him a look. 'I suppose it's a bit of a habit. It's what I do when I write my books too.'

'But no one's likely to kill you for that research, whereas if you get a lead on Damien's murderer—'

'I know, I know. And I remember what you said. But I didn't think the risk would be too great.'

'Oh bloody hell. All right then, but I'm coming too. And don't expect me to wear any diamante.' Why on earth was he going along with her madcap plan? OK, so that was a rhetorical question.

I felt horribly self-conscious in my costume jewellery and garish make-up. It was lucky that I had to focus on the road, so I couldn't keep checking Nate's expression. The Red Tavern was on a tiny backstreet on the racecourse side of Newmarket. It looked Victorian, and definitely not as seamy as I'd expected. There were geranium-filled window boxes and the paintwork was a well-maintained Oxford Blue. The moment we walked through the door, though, I could see it had somehow established itself as a locals' pub, rather than a tourist haunt.

The man behind the bar was about fifty: ruddy-faced and wearing a long-sleeved Breton T-shirt. He'd stopped short of the beret but he had the air of someone who might slip one on without much provocation.

The place was pretty busy, but that didn't stop several people from looking round at us as we went in. Several plum-in-the-mouth voices – not unlike Samson's in fact

– halted for a second before the sea of chat righted itself again. For a horrible moment I thought Samson was there, sitting in a shadowy corner, but then I realised it was just another man of a similar type.

The man behind the bar beamed at me and nodded to Nate, whilst still somehow conveying he thought we'd probably taken the wrong turning. 'What can I get you?' he said.

'A lemonade please.'

'Nothing in it?' He was already reaching for a glass.

'Sadly not. I'm driving.'

He sighed sympathetically, then took Nate's order for a beer, and accepted the ten pound note I held out.

'To tell you the truth,' I said, 'I'm not even sure we're in the right place. Samson Newbold told me he often drinks in here – at least I think it was here – and I couldn't get any answer at his house, so we thought we'd pop in, just in case.'

The barman handed me my change. 'That's really bad luck. He's probably in here more often that he's at home, to tell you the truth.' He ran his hand through receding hair. 'Bob?'

A man just down the bar looked up.

'What did Samson say he was up to? Any chance he'll be around later this afternoon?'

'Who's asking?' the man called Bob said, then noticed me and grinned. 'Hello, there. You're a friend of his, are you? Don't look like the sort he normally brings back from the races.'

I saw the barman give him a warning look.

'We're together,' Nate said, moving closer to my side. 'My wife knows Samson from way back. Family friends.' For a moment I was distracted by the part I was suddenly playing. I made myself concentrate and took a chance. 'I didn't think he'd leave town on a race day.'

213

Bob nodded. 'You're right enough. Normally likes to see whether his horses come home in person.' He rolled his eyes. 'Though he's often disappointed about their performance. But he had to be away today.'

Another man had sidled up next to Bob now. I took stock of him as I sipped my lemonade. His mouth was set in a thin line, his head hunched forward, relative to his shoulders, like a vulture. 'What is it then?' the new man said, picking up his whisky. 'He owe you money or something?'

I tried to look shocked. 'Nothing like that. As my husband said, I'm a family friend.'

Suddenly the man leant forward and looked at me more closely. 'Really?'

I leant back instinctively. 'That's right.'

'Where from?'

Nate stepped forward, inserting some space between us.

The barman was on the case too. 'Mind your own business, Jake.' He turned to me. 'Don't mind him. He and Samson have their moments.' He leant forward and said in an undertone, 'No love lost, there, and that's a fact.'

Nate put his beer down on the bar. 'They must be on very bad terms if he lets it affect the way he deals with Samson's friends.'

The barman nodded. 'Fact is, if you were trying to collect a debt, I reckon Jake would want to make sure you realised there was a queue, and he's first in line.'

'I see.'

'Sorry.' The barman turned to polish a glass from a tray a woman had just brought in. 'I've said too much.'

I finished my lemonade quickly. 'I understand. I know him of old, don't forget.' And I gave him my best smile, but inside, I was still shaken. There'd been something about the intensity of Jake's gaze. I didn't think he'd just been warning us off.

'Can I give Samson a message for you?' the barman asked.

I made a show of thinking for a moment, then shook my head. 'Thanks, but don't worry. I'll give him a call.'

My legs felt like jelly. Nate had been right; this wasn't some kind of game. At that moment a woman came through the pub door. She was wearing a navy suit and looked hot in the fierce sunshine. And I knew her face straightaway, of course, even before I heard the barman greet her as she reached the interior.

'Liz, my darling! What can I get you?'

Elizabeth Edmunds. Nate touched my hand, and I waited for just a moment. 'Nothing unfortunately, Martin,' she said; she was still standing near the doorway. 'I'm only here to drag Tom out. There's a problem with the party from Everards Investments, I'm afraid. They're all at lunch and we need him on hand, pronto.' It was interesting to see her in person. She no longer looked shy, but organised and in control. Maybe the painting on Damien's wall just reflected how he'd made her feel.

The man who must be Tom put a half-drunk pint down on the bar, glancing at it for a moment over his shoulder as she steered him out.

Just before we left, the barman caught my eye again. 'Glad we weren't talking about Samson when Liz came in,' he said in an undertone. 'She was his lady friend not so long ago, before she switched to his older brother.' He leant forward, a look of ill-disguised relish in his eye. 'Of course, you'll know all about the tragedy of Damien Newbold's murder if you and Samson are family friends. The cottage where he was killed belongs to our Liz, and it was she that found his body.' Then he seemed to recollect himself. 'And, of course, I should extend my condolences to you.'

Chapter Twenty-Three

'I didn't much like the way that man Jake looked at you,' Nate said as Ruby started the engine.

'I wasn't overjoyed myself.'

She drove round the corner and then pulled over again. 'Sorry, but I can't wait to get rid of these.' She pulled off the red nails.

'Didn't that hurt?'

She shook her head. 'They were already coming adrift. Cheap product. So, what about Elizabeth Edmunds casting Samson aside in favour of Damien?'

'Newbold senior clearly liked to sail close to the wind.' Nate put his sun visor down as she re-started the engine and they turned west. 'I know I said I couldn't see Samson summoning up the energy to kill his brother, but I might have to revise that opinion. Damien was clearly dishing out humiliation to him over and over again. That's the kind of campaign calculated to breed hatred.'

'I agree.' Ruby pulled out to overtake a lorry. 'But would Samson have known where Damien was staying? Why would he have told a brother he loathed about a temporary change of address?'

Nate thought for a moment. 'Unless Damien told Samson he was staying at Elizabeth's cottage as part of his campaign to wind him up. He could have emailed to say how nice it would be to see her for a night or two of passion, knowing how angry that would make Samson.'

'Yes, I could imagine that.'

Back at River House, Nate took out some crusty white bread he'd bought from a bakery in Mildenhall, and he and Ruby made sandwiches with some farmhouse cheddar and chutney. 'I've thought of another possibility,' he said, as they sat down at the table. 'We'd already realised Elizabeth Edmunds had easy access to Damien on the night he was killed. She even told the police she let herself in with her own key when she found his body. Well, what if she'd secretly rekindled her affair with Samson? Maybe she'd found out about Maggie, and the way Damien operated, and had decided she'd rather have the younger brother after all.'

Ruby put down her sandwich. 'Then she and Samson could have planned Damien's murder together. They both had a grudge against him, and our trip to the Red Tavern confirms Samson was in debt. He'll be glad of the money this place will raise.'

Nate nodded, and Ruby shivered.

We were stacking the dishwasher when my mobile rang. I glanced at the screen. Sodding hell. Luke. No more putting it off then. I picked up.

'Steph said you were going to call me today,' he said. 'So I thought it would be okay to get in first, if you were planning to talk anyway.'

'She told me things were getting out of hand in the village,' I said. 'And that you wanted to sort out a move as quickly as possible.' I was conscious of Nate picking up on what I was saying, and then leaving the room to give me some privacy.

'I think whatever the future involves, I can't live it here in Saxwell,' Luke said.

No kidding. 'Right. I'll book an appointment to see a solicitor; just so we get things straight. Probably best to have someone independent to check over the arrangements we make.'

There was silence; then, 'So, that's it? Just like that?'

I had to count to ten. 'Well, what did you think I'd do, Luke? You must have known this was how it was going to end.'

I heard him catch his breath. 'It always felt as though you were holding back on committing to me, Ruby. Now you've got the excuse you needed to break free. So many years, thrown away so easily.'

Adrenaline coursed through my body. I couldn't remember when I'd last felt such fury. 'Do you really think I'm finding this easy? Do you imagine for one minute that I can just wipe the last twelve years of my life away as though they were words on a white board? This hurts, Luke. It's not easy. It's love and pain that I feel now, and I'd guess I'm going to carry on feeling for – ooh several more years to come. Doesn't alter what has to happen though.' I paused for a second to try to master my emotions and steady my breathing. 'And if we're going to talk about which of us has found it easy to throw things away …'

'All right,' he said, 'all right. We'll talk again when you're feeling better, okay?'

Unbelievable. 'You can call me to let me know who you want to have in to value the house. We should ask for at least three estimates I suppose. And I'll be in touch to let you know what the solicitor says.'

'Jesus, Ruby, I thought you'd at least want to talk.'

'We are talking. But there isn't much to say, is there?'

He paused again. 'I've been getting hate mail.'

'Steph mentioned it.'

'I just wondered …' I could hear him swallowing. 'I mean, you, out of everyone, have the most reason to be pissed off with me. So I was just wondering …'

Suddenly I got it. 'You want to know if I sent you letters?' I was speechless for a moment. 'No, Luke. Not having had a complete personality transplant I have not been sending you malicious mail.' And I hung up.

Tears of frustration and anger welled up in my eyes. Why couldn't he at least understand? I got myself a glass of water. Taking a deep breath and thinking straight I knew that, in spite of all the misery, it was better that the break up was happening now, if it was going to happen at all. What if he'd only revealed his lack of self-control when we'd already got two children?

Then at least I'd have two lovely children.

No use thinking like that now.

But what if I didn't find a partner I could love and rely on in time to have kids? Ever since we'd broken up I'd had that worry in the back of my mind. Now it pushed its way to the fore.

I took my water out into the garden, sat down on the bench and closed my eyes. Either it would happen or it wouldn't. It was only after I'd sat there seething for fifteen minutes that I realised that, in spite of what I'd said, I was currently feeling more angry than sad.

Nate stood at his bedroom window, watching Ruby sitting on the garden bench. It made him want to drive over to her old village and take her ex apart. He went down to the kitchen to make a coffee, and wondered if he should offer Ruby one, or if it was better to keep his distance.

But in a moment, she joined him inside, thanks to a distraction next door.

The raised voices at Oswald House were hard to ignore, especially with all the windows open. Neither of them spoke: they were too busy listening.

'You can bloody well pull yourself together right now.' Nate was pretty sure that was Saskia Amos's voice. He recognised the honking upper-class tone from when he'd overheard her conversation with Ruby.

There was a half-shouted reply, but the voice was indistinct, as though the speaker was crying.

'Emily,' Ruby mouthed. Nate nodded.

'You're making a real exhibition …' Again the rest was lost. Not that it made any difference. It was easy enough to fill in the gaps.

'You don't know a thing about it.' That was Emily again. 'You're too old and haggard to remember what it's like to be in love. And I don't suppose you can ever have been on the receiving end.'

Ruby raised her eyebrows.

'How dare you!' He could hear that bit all right. Nice and distinct. 'How dare you speak to me like that?'

'What do you expect when you don't even try to understand how I feel?'

'I expect a good deal more of you, young lady!'

Emily's reply was lost again and Saskia's voice grew lower now, so that the next part of the conversation – lasting for a minute or two – was inaudible.

Then Emily's words rang out again suddenly. 'That's not true! You're a lying old witch! You weave stories so that you're at the centre of everything. You think it's all about you. Well, it's not, so get over it!'

'Blimey,' Ruby said. 'What the hell's all that about?'

Then Saskia was yelling again too. 'There's absolutely no point in my staying. I don't know why I even bothered trying to help in the first place.'

And suddenly, there she was in the doorway in Nate's line of sight, followed not only by the girl who must be Emily, tears streaking down her cheeks, but also by Tutor Guy. It was a surprise, and the fact that he'd been completely silent confirmed Nate's impression of him as wet.

Saskia turned back towards the doorway once she'd descended the house steps. 'You're being a real old woman

220

about all this, Emily,' she said. 'Bitter, spiteful and pathetic. You take after your bloody father, that's your trouble. There's nothing of me in you. It's as though someone swapped my child for you at the maternity hospital.'

Nate could see the shock in Mathewson's eyes. And the other girl he'd seen around appeared too, also white-faced. Nate turned to Ruby. 'That's Fi?'

She nodded.

'And as for you,' Saskia was saying, turning to Paul. 'Haven't you got any work to be getting on with? Surely your other students need attention, or maybe you might even give your academic duties a thought. I'm certain the university must be missing you. If you carry on hanging round here like this people are going to start to talk.'

At that moment Mathewson looked up, and although Ruby and Nate were in shadow, he was pretty sure he saw Tutor Guy catch Ruby's eye. Nate made a conscious effort to unclench his teeth.

I couldn't get my head clear that night. Samson, Maggie, Damien, Emily and Saskia took it in turns to keep me awake.

And what about the would-be burglars? The crowd at the Red Tavern drifted into my head, and I imagined Samson, sitting there in the middle of them all, holding court. He'd be half cut, of course. Might he have boasted about the security at River House? I pictured him saying, to anyone who would listen, 'I was paying a girl to sleep in the drawing room to guard my stuff. She's doing all the cleaning too – very eager to please. Still, I've told her to move upstairs now, it seemed only fair.' I could imagine he'd be keen to portray himself as a proper gent. Yeah, right. And he might not even have mentioned Nate's presence. It wouldn't have added colour to the story from his point of view.

I shivered under the duvet, in spite of the warmth of the evening. If he'd said that, would one of those listening have taken special note? Decided it might not be too hard to nip in and pick up a few choice items?

Maybe Samson had bragged about all the expensive stuff in the house, too. Perhaps he'd told everyone what a rich man he was going to be. And then maybe a couple of the men he'd borrowed money from had decided to recoup their losses. And what if one of those men had been Jake, the man at the Red Tavern who'd looked at me so closely? Had he known I was lying about being a family friend because he'd been watching River House, and had actually recognised me under all that bling? If that was the case, he'd probably recognised Nate too. I hadn't worried about him going into the pub looking like his usual self. After all, we'd only been concerned about bystanders reporting back to Samson. It didn't seem likely *he'd* recognise us from the description the barman might give (husband and wife: big guy and a woman with a fondness for flashy jewellery). But if we'd come face to face with someone who'd been watching us, that was another matter.

My conspiracy theories began to spiral out of control. What if Samson needed money – a lot of money – but didn't fancy selling all those nice family heirlooms? What if he'd primed the two men to break in and stage the burglary? He could claim on the insurance, pay the men a percentage and keep the valuables.

If he was behind it, he could try again. And if that was the case, and the man, Jake, had been one of the burglars, Jake would have told him Nate and I had been snooping at the pub. But if Jake had been acting for himself, without Samson's knowledge, he would never tell, and we would be safe.

And so it was that I lay there, almost rigid, for several hours before I managed to let go, and get some sleep.

On Sunday lunchtime Paul came to see me. It was the first time I'd spoken to him since I'd poured out my woes, and I now found I was struck almost dumb with embarrassment. The fact that Nate was home also made me squirm. I didn't want him to get the wrong impression about Paul and me, even though he'd made it quite clear that we could never be an item.

'I shouldn't have tried to use my training on you,' Paul said, standing there on the doorstep. 'You can't be someone's counsellor as well as their friend.' He was wearing his off-duty gear, jeans and a navy T-shirt. 'I hope I haven't lost my chance of being one by being the other.'

I opened my mouth, ready to make some tactful comment, but he went on quickly. 'I wanted to talk to you about Emily. Any chance of stealing you away for a short time? I thought you might agree to a swift half at the Fort Saint George.'

If he'd just been there for my sake I would have made an excuse. What he knew about me weighed on my mind and I felt like a fool. Even with the Emily element I was tempted to bottle out, but at that moment Nate appeared in the hall. 'Go right ahead if you want to,' he said. He quite clearly wasn't at all bothered about me going out with Paul. It was just as Steph had said.

So I grabbed my stuff and followed him across the Common. He looked almost boyish out of his suit, his long fringe flopping forward, his clothes endearingly scruffy. Perhaps it wasn't so bad to be out and about. A change would do me good.

They were operating an outdoor bar at the pub and Paul queued up at a hatch to get us a lager each. 'Facing the river, or facing the Common?' he asked, looking at the available seats.

'Maybe the river,' I said. I could turn my back on the house and pretend it wasn't there.

He set the drinks down and grinned at me. 'Perhaps we can share a pizza sometime, under happier circumstances.'

'That would be nice,' I found myself answering, before I'd even thought about it one way or the other. I added quickly, 'You wanted to talk about Emily?'

'That's right. You probably saw something of what happened yesterday.'

'I was in the kitchen.'

'I thought I caught a glimpse of you.' He took a long draught of his pint. 'Bloody Saskia Amos.'

'I could use her to illustrate a whole book on social dysfunctionality.'

He nodded. 'I've been finding it hard to leave Emily and Fi to it, and she's been part of the reason. Emily's just got no support at home. Fi's doing her best, but she's very young. Time's moving on, but things are still hard. I think she hoped Emily would be in better shape by now, and she's finding the extended period of high emotion wearing.'

'That's understandable, I guess.'

He nodded. 'Completely. Even I didn't expect it to be like this. I've no idea how long it will take for Emily to get over what's happened, though I'm happy she's receiving more expert help now. I'm sure that should make a difference.'

'Yes.'

We paused a moment and watched a man sculling up the river, ducks scattering as he slid by.

'But my worry now,' Paul said, 'is Emily's wellbeing as all the students disappear off to summer jobs, or travelling round India, or whatever it is they're doing.'

'Will she stay on at Oswald House?'

'Would you go back to the family home?' He raised an eyebrow.

'Do you know,' I said, 'I think I'd probably forego that pleasure?'

He gave me a wry smile. 'Fi's off though. Going to stay on some farm in Tuscany with her sister. They invited Emily to go with them, but she couldn't face it. I was wondering if there'd be any chance …' He let the sentence trail off.

'Of me dropping round occasionally to pass the time of day?' I said. 'Yes, of course. I'm not sure she'll want me breathing down her neck, but I can probably find some excuses for showing up. Though it's anyone's guess as to how long I'll be here. It all depends on when Samson Newbold's allowed to sell the house.'

'Of course,' he said. 'Well, just whilst you are around, if you could stand it.'

'No problem. What about you? Do you get to jet off somewhere?'

He shook his head. 'I'm not going anywhere. I'd keep popping into Oswald House myself, but …'

'But?'

'Well, loathsome though Saskia Amos is, she does have a point about me.'

I raised an eyebrow.

'She's right that I'm not giving Emily enough space. Ultimately I do have to let her make her own way. It's just … Well, it's bloody hard to stand back when a student's having quite such a harrowing time.'

'I can imagine.' I sipped my lager. 'But I can see you've got thoroughly embroiled and I take your point. I suppose it's possible to get too involved in someone else's life. Do you always find you get this caught up in your tutoring work, or is it the peculiarities of Emily's case in particular?'

His eyes met mine and it was a moment before he

answered. 'My sister went through a similar experience,' he said. 'No murder involved, of course,' he added, quickly, 'but you know, just this thing about being led a dance by an older man. I saw what it did to her and I think that has meant I've found it harder to take a step back.'

'Makes sense.'

He paused for a moment and then looked up at me and smiled ruefully. 'To be honest though, I always do get too wound up by the troubles I see. Anyway, I'll still give Emily a call once in a while, but I'd be really grateful if you wouldn't mind looking out for her. And if you end up finding it stressful, maybe we could get together and talk it all over. I'll still be one step removed, but at least you'll have some moral support.'

'Sounds fine.'

'Do you fancy some lunch after all? I've kept you longer than I meant.' He got up and fetched one of the laminated menus from the counter.

We ended up ordering sandwiches and chips. The acidic smell of the ketchup hit my nostrils, and I suddenly realised I was well ready for some food.

'I like it here,' Paul said. 'I love watching the willows; their reflections in the river and their leaves as they're stirred by the breeze.'

It was beautiful, something I hadn't really appreciated properly since I'd arrived.

As we ate our chips, Paul said, 'Did you hear Saskia tell Emily that Damien once made a pass at *her*?'

'Bloody hell, no.'

'She said she'd turned him down, and if Damien had seriously been making a play for Emily, then he was simply doing it to get back at her.'

'What a lovely woman she is. If it had come from anyone else I'd hardly believe it.'

'I know.'

'Do you think it was just bluster? Would they have met?'

He shrugged. 'Emily accused her of lying and made the same objection you just have, but Saskia said they'd met at a party at Oswald House, whilst her husband's mother – Emily's grandmother – was still living there.'

I suddenly remembered Samson mentioning attending a party there too, whilst River House had still been tenanted. Perhaps it had been the same one. 'I suppose it is logical that any party there could have had both Saskia and Damien on the guest list.'

Paul nodded.

'And Fi said Emily's granny's living abroad now, is that right?' I asked.

'That's what they told me. Apparently one of her sons lives in Spain, and his wife's just had another baby, so she's spending some time out there to appreciate the younger grandchildren. Shame, because it's really Emily that could do with some appreciation right now.'

We got up and made our way back towards River House. Someone was walking a dog the size of a small cow on the Common. Another dog – much, much smaller – was showing an interest. Couldn't it see it might be in danger? The small dog attempted to sniff the big dog's bottom, even though it was way out of reach.

I turned back to Paul. 'When I saw Emily last she seemed not only upset, but worried. She was convinced the police seriously suspect her of having had something to do with Damien's murder.'

'Oh, I'm sure they don't really,' Paul said with a snort. 'It was just that business of her trying to track him down. But there's no evidence whatsoever that she actually managed to trace him. And anyway, can you imagine Emily doing something like that? Now if it had been Saskia we'd been talking about ...'

I shivered. 'Yes, I could certainly imagine her bludgeoning someone to death. It's the kind of thing she'd have as a hobby.'

He laughed.

'Not sure she's actually got any motive though,' I said.

'I don't think we should let that bother us. Besides, what about the business with her and Damien? What if it wasn't she that turned him down, but the other way around?'

'She made up to him and was rejected you mean?' I let the idea play in my mind for a moment. 'And now she's taking it out on Emily. Being generally foul to her and lying in order to get her own back?'

'Kind of thing I could see her doing,' Paul said.

'Certainly wouldn't be out of character. And then Damien taunts Saskia with his preference for Emily and she kills him. Perfect; it sounds watertight. Only slight problem is that it's based on stories we've made up, plus she wouldn't have known where he was staying.'

'Well, yes, but other than that ...'

'Anyway,' I said as we reached the door of River House, 'the place seems to be littered with people who might have had a motive for similar reasons. I should think the police are spoilt for choice.'

The following day, I went back to Damien's list of chores and did several, aiming to work off the chip calories from my lunch with Paul. The bath scrubbing was positively energetic.

I made up a load of washing with a few towels I found in a dirty linen basket, together with some of my own stuff, and set the programme going before mopping the kitchen floor. Outside the sun was high in the sky, and a breeze had sprung up. With the back door open, I knew the tiles would be dry soon.

Next on my list, and rather less appealing, was emailing my publisher. Jackie, in legal, needed to get a contract over to me that had to come by post because of the sequence of signatures required. Since most of our communication was by phone or email, I'd so far neglected to tell her about my change of address. Of course, I didn't have to confess why I'd upped sticks at this stage, but we were reasonably friendly, and I knew I'd have to come clean sooner or later. She'd be bound to ask after Luke when we spoke. It was one more little nudge that reminded me I would have to tackle this situation, either by keeping Luke's actions as quiet as possible, or by brazening it out.

For now, I put it off, simply sending a message to say I was staying away for a few weeks to get some peace and finish my writing.

The thought of dealing with Jackie's legal documents reminded me that I hadn't done anything else about looking for the phantom will.

I went into the study, remembering the day that Samson had visited. If he had found any relevant papers, where would he have slipped them, in order to keep them safely out of sight until he took ownership of the house?

My eyes roved over the room. There was a bookcase right next to me, reaching from floor to ceiling. The possible hiding places seemed almost limitless. I felt along the top of the books I could reach, but none of them had anything substantial tucked inside. So either I was going to spend all evening in there, nipping up and down ladders, taking out every single book just to be sure, or I could leave it until I had a bit more energy; perhaps dream up a logical plan of campaign.

I was back in the kitchen within minutes. I made myself

a coffee and took it and my laptop down to the basement, ready for a bit of gentle web browsing. I had emails from three different online clothing emporia. Clearly I'd been developing a bad habit. But rather than ordering anything new at this stage, I really needed to plan a trip back to Saxwell to pick up some of my stuff. Not appealing.

Maybe I could sneak over one day in the week whilst Luke was out at work. I knew I'd have to have a proper meeting with him eventually, but I couldn't face visiting him at Bookman's Cottage. The thought of going there at all left my insides pulled taut. My lovely home; where I'd lived happily for ten years. It was hard to think I would never sleep there again; never cook another meal or wallow in the bath.

This wasn't mood enhancing. Time to look at something else. In the end I found my browser open at the Cambridge News page, checking for anything fresh, though that was hardly mood enhancing either.

There certainly was something fresh, however. It was the top story on the homepage.

'Witness puts actress Maggie Cook at location of Newbold Murder.'

Chapter Twenty-Four

Ruby had come to find Nate in the kitchen, but now she was avoiding his eyes. Not unusual, but worrying all the same. She was holding her computer.

'Have you looked at the news today?' she asked.

'No. Why, what's happened?'

She turned her laptop screen to face him, and he read about the sighting of Maggie Cook in Little Boxham on the night Damien Newbold had been killed.

Nate went to the fridge and got them a Coke each. 'That's certainly quite significant.'

She nodded. 'Nate, I've got a confession to make.'

He pulled the ring on his can. 'Maggie told you what she was really looking for, that day when she claimed she'd left a shawl here.'

Her lips parted, and she finally met his gaze.

'I may not be a great PI, but even I didn't imagine Maggie Cook would be faffing around over a shawl.' Nate took a swig of his drink. 'Doesn't even seem likely she'd own one. A wrap, perhaps. I didn't know whether she'd confided in you or not, but it was clear you were holding something back.'

She looked down again. 'Well, you're right. And I might have messed up.'

'Care to elaborate?'

There was a pause. 'I know she's got a motive for Damien Newbold's murder.'

Nate whistled. 'Okay. And I presume that, as well as not telling me, you haven't let those interfering police in on the secret either.'

Ruby put her head in her hands. 'I was convinced that would be the wrong thing to do.'

'What did she say to you?'

The story that came out showed Newbold had pushed Maggie Cook to the limit. If she hadn't killed him, he couldn't help feeling it was only because someone else had got there first. And then, on top of all of that emotional torture, she'd had the promise of money – a lot of money – dangled in front of her.

'But when she said all this,' Ruby went on, 'I didn't think, well that's it then, Damien Newbold's murderer is sitting right in front of me. Instead I thought, does she realise how bad this makes her look? I'd swear she's not guilty, Nate. And she's been through hell and back. Rushing straight over to the police station and ratting on her just seemed wrong.'

'People who've been put through hell and back are just the kind who get tipped over the edge.'

'I can see that's logical.' She pushed her hair out of her eyes. 'But she's made of sterner stuff, I'm sure.'

'How can you be?'

She shrugged. 'Gut instinct? The way she talked? And her motive's weak really. If she doesn't even know the will was made for sure, it'd be pretty risky to go bumping him off straightaway.'

She looked down and suddenly Nate found he'd got one hand on her right shoulder and was raising her chin up with the other, so that her eyes met his. Bad move. He took his hand away again and sat back in his seat.

'When are you going to stop treating me like an enemy?' Nate said. 'I think we've established that the appropriate moment for me to throw you off this job has long since passed. So if you're not worried about losing the roof over your head any more, why can't you just tell me what's going on?'

When Nate had touched me I'd felt a jolt, a sudden

232

electric crackle, reaching far down inside me. Given the conversation we were having, it wasn't exactly the ideal moment for my body to start asserting itself like that. My face felt hot. Then it suddenly occurred to me that he'd just asked a question.

'I suppose ... Well, I suppose I knew what you'd say. And I didn't want to hear it. I've been given a lot of shit to deal with by a bloke recently, and Maggie's in the same boat. I think she's suffered enough.'

'And what would I have said?'

'Tell the police.'

'Yeah. And that's what I'm saying now. Tell the police.' He sighed, but the look he gave me was tired, rather than angry. 'I'd come with you, only I've got to go back to Saffron Walden this afternoon. The bloody woman from yesterday rearranged. And then I have to drop in at Two Wells Farm and deal with a couple of things, so I'm likely to be back late.' He waited for me to say something, and when I didn't, he carried on. 'I do understand, and you might well be right, but in a situation like this you just have to tell what you know and trust other people for a change. Especially now it's clear Maggie Cook was on the spot the night Newbold was killed.'

'She was probably over there stalking him every night since she found his address.'

He gave me a look. 'Quite possibly, but I'm not sure the police would see that as a point in her favour.'

I felt awful, but I'd have to do it, just like he said. And the police would get Maggie in, and she'd know it'd been me that had told them. I was jolted out of my thoughts by a knock at the door. I was getting better at reading the sound now, and this instance came across as angry and impatient.

Nate stood behind me in the hall as I opened up. It was Emily Amos. 'Paul came to see you yesterday, instead of me.'

She was standing on the doorstep, dressed in what looked very much like pyjamas, in spite of the summer storm that was now raging outside. I checked my watch: one fifteen. And it wasn't just her clothes that gave away her state. Her hair was matted, and she had dark rings under her eyes.

'He knows you need some space to get on with your life,' I said. 'And it was you he wanted to talk about, anyway.' For some stupid reason I glanced at Nate. I could hear myself sounding defensive, as though I was covering up, hastily making excuses. He raised an eyebrow and gave me a look that said it all. Bugger, bugger, bugger.

'He's been frightened off by my bloody mother who can't stand it when I get close to a member of the opposite sex,' Emily said.

Hell. So that was the way the wind was blowing – as far as Emily was concerned at least. It had never occurred to me that that might be a side effect of Paul's visits.

'He's your tutor, Emily. He badly wants to help, but he's got other students to see too, and he knows, really, that you've had such a hard time you need someone with a bit of extra training to look after you now.'

'If he's got other students to see, then what was he doing here with you?'

Behind me I could hear Nate start to climb the stairs. I had the urge to leave Emily standing there and go and tell him it wasn't as it looked. But why would he care, one way or the other? He was just going about his business. It was me that had the problem.

I focused on Emily and tried to keep my voice even. 'He was explaining how hard it is to see one of his students going through a difficult time. And he was hoping I'd keep an eye out for you, once your friends have gone off for the holidays.'

'He called me that? "One of his students"?'

I pretended not to understand the feeling behind her

question. 'Yes. And as for me, I'd have wanted to keep in touch anyway. You've been through so much recently.' And perhaps it was just as well it was going to be me keeping an eye out for Emily from now on, rather than Paul.

'Will he come back here to see you?' She leant against the door frame as though she was barely able to stand.

'He hasn't made any arrangement to,' I said, and then wilfully misunderstood again. 'Why, did you want me to give him a message? I'm quite sure he'll drop in on you again before too long.'

'You think so?'

'Of course.' It was probably the wrong thing to say. The dullness went out of her eyes for a moment and suddenly we were best friends again and she was terribly glad to see me. It sent a shiver down my spine.

Although I'd been cursing her arrival for my own selfish reasons, I now found it hard to send her on her way. Someone needed to take her in hand, in a practical way if nothing else. 'I can't have you in here,' I said, 'because of the house-sitting rules, but shall I come over to your place? Just for a chat?'

She nodded and I followed her through the rain to Oswald House.

It was the first time I'd ever been inside. The front door – if you could call it front, given that it was actually at the side – opened onto a large hallway with stairs turning their way up to the first floor.

Fi – complete with a mud-coloured face mask – appeared at the top and leant over the banisters. 'You're back. I didn't know where you'd—' Then she saw me. 'Oh my goodness!' she said.

'I'm sorry! Wrong moment to drop by?'

Fi laughed. 'College ball this evening. Just doing a bit of prep.'

'You're starting early.'

'Needs must. There's a lot of prep to do. Anyway, if you'll excuse the face mask I'll come down and make you some tea. And I do believe we've got some shortbread, which will give me the chance to provide for you for a change.' She was descending the stairs now, her bare feet sinking into the green carpet. 'What about you, Em? Fancy some tea and bics?'

Emily shook her head.

'Well, anyway, I'll get you some,' Fi said to me, sighing, and pushed open a stripped pine door to our right. Through the gap I could see a dresser, scrubbed kitchen table and butler sink. They must have been in that room when the row with Saskia had happened. It was opposite River House's kitchen.

'Where do you want to be?' I asked Emily.

She nodded towards the stairs and I followed her up, and into a bedroom on the left, overlooking the Common. It was hard to see my way across the floor. The curtains were still drawn and everywhere I looked there were dark shadowy mounds to negotiate. Piles of clothes and books – which were normal features of student bedrooms in my experience – as well as heaps of dirty crockery, and some food that had gone off – which ranked as taking things to extremes. Emily had clearly given up since Damien had died. Perhaps for even longer – maybe since he'd gone away.

Next to my right foot, an uneaten orange sat on a plate, half of it green and – from what I could see in the half-light – hairy. A sickly-sweet smell with acidic overtones filled my nostrils. In fact the whole room stank of a mixture of unwashed clothes and rotting fruit. It made me gag for a moment and I dashed over to pull up one of the sash windows. The room must have been building up to this state for some time, and of course Paul wouldn't have been aware of it, seeing her formally, downstairs in the sitting room. But letting the hair and clothes go seemed to be a more recent thing. I had a horrible feeling it might be in direct response to the fact that she felt Paul was now deserting her.

'Things just got too much?' I said.

She nodded. She had flopped down onto her unmade bed and was staring out of the window now that I'd pulled the curtains back, her chin resting on her hand.

'I know you've been having a difficult time with your mum, too,' I said. 'It was hard not to overhear. I wasn't meaning to pry.'

Emily still didn't turn towards me. 'She hates me.'

I tried to work out where to perch. In the end I chose a chair by Emily's dressing table, removing a pair of jeans and a dressing gown so that I could sit down. 'She's cross with you at the moment,' I said, 'which does seem desperately unfair, I know. Maybe she really does think being firm is the only approach – to help you fight your way back to normality, I mean. I'm sure she doesn't really hate you.' I wasn't a bit sure in fact. 'Maybe it was how people treated her when she was young, and it's the only way she knows.'

Emily shifted position on her bed and at that moment Fi appeared in the doorway, face mask still intact, carrying a tray with a mug of tea and the plate of shortbread. She picked her way across the room, and attempted to fit the tray onto Emily's bedside table. I helped her push three dirty mugs and a glass to one side. The glass smelled of stale alcohol.

'I could take those,' Fi began, but Emily cut across her.

'I don't want you to take them or do anything. I'm fed up with all the fuss.'

Fi made her way back to the door, catching my eye for a second as she did so and giving me a wry look.

Once she'd gone, Emily said, 'I know you're trying to make me feel better. Everyone always does. But my mother really does hate me. It's just one of those things, and it's been that way for as long as I can remember. She's a hardnosed bitch at the best of times, but if you could see how she is with my older brothers you'd know she's singled me out for unpleasant treatment.'

Possibly she was one of those women who simply don't like members of their own sex. Too much competition, perhaps, beginning when Emily was a sweet little girl with big dark eyes and bunches, and accentuated now that her daughter was – or at least had been – blossoming.

Emily was curled up on the bed now, facing away from me towards the wall. 'I came along at the wrong time, you see,' she said.

'How do you mean?'

'Just when she thought she was all done with children. The younger of my older brothers was already six when I was born. And she'd started work again – just a nothingy job, being the PA to the headmaster of some school or other. I don't even think she enjoyed it that much – but she was more independent. And then she got pregnant with me, and she had to leave, and she went back to being ankle deep in nappies and bottle sterilising equipment.'

'I met your mum briefly,' I said, 'and I did get the impression that she had a large house to run, but I imagined she might have had a bit of help with it.' She was the sort who would.

'Oh, she had lots of help with me,' Emily said. Her voice was slightly muffled by the pillow. 'They had a live-in nanny, even though my mother had given up her job by the time I was born. My father was away a lot, and she always said full-time help was essential to enable her to cope with two growing boys who needed ferrying places, as well as a screaming brat.' She turned her head for a moment, but only enough to look up at the ceiling, not to face me. 'She often tells me how much I used to scream.'

'So, do you see anything of your dad these days?' I said.

'Hardly at all since I've been here. My family's house isn't far off – between here and Ely – but I don't tend to go home much. And even before I started at Cambridge he was away working more often than not. My mother hates *him* too.'

'But they stay together.' I reached for my tea and took a sip. I couldn't face the idea of the shortbread. I mean, I'm not picky, but it was very much the wrong environment for eating things.

'He buys her a comfortable lifestyle. I'm not quite sure what's in it for him. I know she sees other men. Did you hear what she said about her and Damien?'

'I did.' I didn't admit I'd heard it second-hand, via Paul.

'I don't believe it,' Emily said. 'They probably did meet, but I think she just said it to get at me.'

'But you still reckon there have been others?'

'Oh for sure,' Emily said. 'I was at a party once with my mother and her sister. There was some bloke chatting my mother up. It was revolting. And then later I overheard my aunt say, "You get all the young, good-looking ones." My mother was grinning like the Cheshire bloody cat. It made me want to puke. And then she said, "Well, not all," and my aunt said, "You've had that gorgeous David at your beck and call for a year now. I don't know how you do it."'

'It could have just been a flirtation, I suppose,' I said.

'David came to stay once or twice whilst Daddy was away.'

Hmm. Pretty damning. 'Okay. Scratch that idea then.'

'I don't care,' Emily said. 'It just means I can't rely on any support from home, and my mother's right. I have to get tough, so nothing can hurt me any more. Maybe I have to become like she is. I don't see her hurting.'

I suddenly realised that, just like Paul Mathewson, I'd somehow hoped I could talk to her and make a difference. In fact, some vain little part of me had been thinking, maybe I'd be able to help where everyone else had failed. Because I'd written the odd book about social issues. Huh. Well, fat chance. I was already well out of my depth.

It was a relief when Fi reappeared. 'Back to normal again,' she said. Her face was flushed and shiny, now that the mask had gone.

'I suppose if Fi's out of the bathroom, you could go and treat yourself to a soak,' I said to Emily. 'It'd probably make you feel a lot better.' I could hear myself sounding like a mum. Ironic really.

Emily turned towards me slowly and dropped her legs over the side of the bed, pushing the upper part of her body to a sitting position using her hands, as though some of her muscles weren't working properly. 'Maybe.'

When she'd fetched some clean clothes to change into she padded down the corridor and I heard the bath taps running.

'Blimey,' Fi said. 'I've been gently suggesting that all morning, but she's bitten my head off each time.'

'Probably different coming from me. You automatically expect older people to be a bit bossy, and, because it's not a shock, you sometimes let them get away with it.'

'Possibly.'

'What about her room? Do you think I could give it a bit of tidy whilst she's in there, too?'

'That's territory where angels fear to tread,' said Fi. 'Another thing I've tried and regretted. But who knows? You could chance your arm. Would you like a hand?'

I shook my head. 'No need, but have you got a cloth and some antibacterial spray?'

She grinned. 'I'll go fetch.' She took a handful of mugs and I followed with the plate of mouldy orange.

'Did you see the news about Maggie Cook?' Fi said over her shoulder.

I nodded. 'On the Internet earlier.'

'What did you make of it?'

'Well, it doesn't look good that she lied to the police – or at least left information out – but I suppose she wasn't actually seen entering or leaving Damien's rented cottage, so it doesn't prove anything.'

We went into the kitchen and dumped all the crockery next to the dishwasher.

'You reckon she could have lied just because she knew being in the vicinity would look bad?' Fi said, pausing for a moment. 'Yes, I suppose that makes sense.'

'Realistically, I don't believe that could have been the first time she'd been over to Little Boxham to find him,' I said.

'Why's that?'

I explained about how Maggie had come by Damien's contact details in the first place. 'She was mad as hell when I found her in his study,' I said, 'and dead set on finding him and giving him what for. My bet is she caught up with him the very next day, which would have been Sunday; the day after Strawberry Fair. Why wait, after all?'

'You have a point.' Fi reached into a cupboard under the sink.

'Whether he let her in that first time she went round is another matter,' I said. 'If he didn't, maybe she went back on the Tuesday to have another go. Maybe he even told her to come back then. Perhaps he was already dead when she turned up and she knocked and got no answer.'

Fi handed me the cleaning stuff I'd asked for. 'Only he'd been expecting that other woman, too, hadn't he? The one who owned the cottage.'

I nodded. 'She did say they'd arranged to meet.' I thought again of Elizabeth Edmunds and her relationship with Samson. 'Assuming she was telling the truth. Hard to say, with Damien out of the picture. Anyway,' I walked towards the kitchen door, 'if Damien had invited both Elizabeth Edmunds and Maggie Cook round to enjoy his company on the same night that wouldn't surprise me. He seemed to like taunting the women in his life.'

Fi let out a long breath. 'Bit of a bugger we ended up living next door to him, really. And all the more reason for Maggie Cook to have killed him, though I agree she might not have. She does seem the type though.'

'You know her?'

'Only because of what happened after Em fell for Damien. Em had had too much to drink one night. She caught up with Maggie outside River House and told her that Damien would rather be with her. There was a bit of a slanging match.'

'I can imagine.' I dropped my voice low as we reached the hallway. 'By the way, has Emily been talking about Paul Mathewson at all?'

Fi rolled her eyes and sighed heavily. 'Just lately, and more than before? Yes, she has. I suppose it must be knight-in-shining-armour complex. She did mention that she saw you both heading off to the pub together.'

'I thought she might have. Do you think he's aware of the situation?'

'Shouldn't think so for a minute, to be honest,' Fi said. 'He's too upstanding. He'll have compartmentalised Emily into "young charge in his care" and won't have seen her as a woman at all. Men. They never get it right.'

'Oh dear.'

She nodded. 'Em's just lurching from one emotional crisis to the next at the moment. I hope she'll be okay when I go off to the ball. I'm supposed to be leaving early to meet up with my boyfriend.'

'I'd offer to stay, but I've got an appointment in town I have to keep later.' And given that I was seeing a solicitor about how to divide up mine and Luke's stuff, I wasn't sure what sort of state I'd be in when I got back.

Fi shook her head. 'Don't worry. I know she's got to go out in a bit anyway. She's seeing someone at the counselling service again. Good news that she's washing first.'

I got to work in Emily's room, piling all the dirty laundry up in the doorway, ready to take downstairs, and stacking crockery for dispatch in the same direction. Her bookcase had volumes spilling out of it in all directions, so I began to put them back. It was quite enjoyable, regaining control on someone else's behalf. So much easier than tackling my own, untidy life. I guessed Emily must be reading English. Arden editions of Shakespeare abounded, along with Sweet's *Anglo-Saxon Primer*, which nestled against *Paradise Lost*.

Gradually more of the leaf-patterned carpet became visible. One or two things had got trodden in – some make-up just under the dressing table, a bit of biscuit – but on the whole it was coming together.

Fi stomped back in, lugging the vacuum cleaner.

'Perfect. Thanks.'

As I crouched down to fish out a pair of tights that had been kicked under the bed, something weird caught my eye. A saucer, full of bits of burnt paper and ashes.

I pulled it out to show Fi, but instead of looking surprised she nodded slightly.

'Oh, yes. The remains of Maggie's letter.'

243

'Maggie wrote to Emily?'

She nodded. 'After their run-in. It was a horrible note. I mean, don't get me wrong, Ruby; Em had definitely behaved badly. Telling Maggie she should leave Damien so that they could be together was never going to make her popular. But all the same, I saw the note when it arrived, and it was vicious.'

I could imagine, having seen both sides of Maggie.

'Made Saskia look like an amateur,' Fi went on.

'Can you remember what it said?'

Her eyes drifted away from mine as she thought back. 'Some of it was similar to what Saskia said: that Damien would never look at a child like her. Then she put that Damien had actually laughed out loud when she'd confronted him about Emily and Damien's "so-called affair", and said the very idea was ridiculous.' She paused, remembering. 'That was what made Emily say she'd ruined everything. She felt Damien was bound to have said that, to calm Maggie down, whereas if she hadn't confronted Maggie, Damien would have had a chance to end it with her in his own way.'

She saw my face. 'I know,' she said. 'He never would have. And then Maggie wrote something that Emily took as a personal threat. It was something like, "If you go anywhere near him again I'll make sure you can never be together." After Damien was killed, of course, Emily became convinced Maggie had murdered him, carrying out her promise.'

'But she'd already burnt the letter by that time?'

Fi nodded. 'She kept it, but there's no way of reading the full message now.'

'Maybe I'll just put it back. Doesn't sound like something I ought to meddle with.'

I got away with cleaning Emily's room. When she came

244

back from her bath she just walked straight in as though nothing had changed.

Back at River House I could hear Nate moving about upstairs, then a few minutes later the sound of him descending to the ground floor and leaving via the front door. He must be off to keep his appointment in Saffron Walden.

I thought again about his advice earlier. I needed to go and talk to the police about Maggie. I couldn't leave it forever. But how long would it take? I imagined it would be quite involved, and my solicitor's appointment was looming. They'd managed to fit me in at five. It was only for an introductory chat, but I couldn't bring myself to reschedule.

After agonising for a bit, I came to the conclusion that I couldn't call the police to explain then, in case they insisted I went in straightaway. It would have to wait until later.

As I walked into town, I ran through what I'd found out that afternoon. I wasn't really shocked by the story of Maggie's letter. It seemed to me that Fi had been right: Emily had invited a blast of her fiery temper and got it, big time. I doubted her threats had been serious. Perhaps, after Emily had confronted her about Damien, Maggie had gone straight round to have it out with him. But had he really laughed off the supposed 'affair'? And if he'd done so convincingly, why had she still chucked a whisky glass at him, assuming that was how the scene had played out? And then why had he gone off and hidden himself away?

Perhaps he'd actually done the opposite: wound Maggie up about Emily, maybe commenting on her youth and her prettiness, so that she'd lost it with him. And then maybe he'd decided to tie them both in knots by going AWOL.

* * *

By four-forty I was already outside the solicitors' office, waiting in the street. I glanced up at the sky, which had cleared now. Clouds scudded past the top of the high-rise building and raindrops shook out of the leaves of a beech tree, scattering over my head each time the wind blew.

'The situation's quite simple in theory,' Mrs Emerson, the solicitor told me, once I'd got inside. 'You and your ex-partner are each entitled to keep your own property.' She leant back in her seat as an assistant brought us cups of coffee. 'Is your house owned jointly?'

I nodded.

'And are you both happy to sell?'

Happy. Hmm. I nodded again.

'In that case it's relatively straightforward. The trouble starts when there's disagreement on that issue. As it is, the proceeds of the sale would be divided according to strict property rights. What you also need to do is to go through your other possessions and work out who owns what. It's helpful if you can gather evidence to show how much you've contributed to any given purchase. You're entitled to take out what you've put in.'

What I'd put in. Way more than numbers on a credit card bill or a mortgage statement. As I walked back out of town towards the river it made me think of the lyrics of a Beatles tune. Something about the amount of love you give ultimately equalling the love you take. If that was true, I must be owed some.

By the time I got back to River House it was half-past six. I sent Luke an email, giving him an update and asking again about estate agents, so he knew I meant business. As for going through our stuff, I'd been kidding myself about not returning home when Luke was there. We'd have to look it all over together, whether I liked it or not.

Maybe it would still be worth nipping back whilst he was out though. That way I could cast an eye over things and make some notes, so that I could break the back of the work before we met. It would shorten the miserable time we had to spend together. And in reality there wasn't that much to divide. We weren't going to be battling for each other's CDs. It would really just be a case of totting up how much the white goods were worth and arguing the toss about how to split them.

In spite of everything that was happening in my personal life, my mind strayed to earlier in the day, and Nate's reaction to Emily's outburst. And then I thought about Maggie Cook, and the police again. I'd done my jobs for the afternoon, but the idea of tramping over to the station to rat on her was still about as appealing as climbing into a bath filled with pig swill. But I'd already put it off, and time was getting on.

I decided to have a quick coffee before calling them, and as I filled the kettle I glanced into the garden. I could take my drink out there and sit on the bench. Five minutes' peace would set me up. It was the first time in a while that I'd liked the idea of having time to draw breath.

I went to unlock the back door. The air was sweet with the scent of honeysuckle and lavender, brought out by the sun, which had made a comeback after the rainstorm ended. The paving stones had dried, and there was a fresh, clean feel to the air. I took a deep breath. At least I was starting to get some control over my own life. Emailing Luke had been horrible, but it was the first step towards moving forward. I suddenly realised that although the whole thing made me tense, it hadn't made me tearful that day.

I was gazing at the end of the garden, where a sparrow was rustling around in the clematis, when suddenly something caused it to take fright, and it flew straight out

247

of the foliage and back towards the house, making me turn my head.

That was when I saw her.

And suddenly I was reeling, my legs threatening to give way underneath me, stomach contracting, breath gone. Bile rose up, filling my mouth.

Down in the well of the stairs that led to the basement French windows, slumped against the glass, hands with fingers outstretched, her wild black hair sticky with blood and tissue, was Maggie.

Chapter Twenty-Five

'She was obviously trying to break in when she was attacked,' DI Johnson said, sitting up straight on the sofa in the drawing room. 'She'd brought a couple of tools with her: a chisel and a crowbar. Used the crowbar to force the gate by the look of it.'

I was still shaking, couldn't keep my teeth from jittering away like a pair of castanets on overdrive. 'How long had she been there?' I said, hearing the tremor in my voice.

'Two or three hours, I'd guess,' Johnson said. 'Were you at home earlier this afternoon?'

'I went off into town at around four-thirty to keep a solicitor's appointment at five, up on Castle Park.'

'Ms Cook's car's been found,' DS Brookes said. 'Parked on pay and display in Auckland Road. Time on her ticket's one forty p.m. She'd paid for the rest of the day.'

I looked across at him. 'You mean she'd arrived early, prepared for a wait?'

'Hoping you'd go out at some stage?' DS Brookes said. 'Looks quite likely. Probably forced her way into the garden as soon as she saw you head off up the river. Was the code for the burglar alarm ever re-set after she got in that time previously?'

I shook my head. 'No. Damien Newbold just arranged for the front door lock to be changed.'

'So she'd have been able to disable it, if she'd got that far.'

I nodded. There was a keypad next to the French windows in the basement.

'Do you know of any reason why Maggie Cook might want access to the house?'

I rubbed my forehead. 'She thinks – thought – that Damien Newbold had made another will. One that revoked the one in Samson Newbold's favour, and left everything to her.'

DI Johnson's eyes fixed onto mine. 'And how do you know this? It's information we'd have been interested to have.'

And if I'd made time to give it to them straight after Nate had told me to, they'd have contacted her then and there. She'd have been at the police station all afternoon, answering questions. It would have saved her life ...

I told them about Maggie's visit and her asking me to look for any new will. 'I didn't take her seriously. If I had, I would have come to you, and this wouldn't have happened.'

I saw Brookes and Johnson exchange a glance.

'We'll talk to your neighbours in due course,' DI Johnson said. 'With any luck they saw something. Most people don't just crowbar their way into someone's garden without attracting attention, even if that garden is tucked away like this one is.'

But given Emily's appointment with the university counselling service, and Fi's with her boyfriend, I had a feeling he might be disappointed.

The basement and garden were taped off and out of bounds, and when I looked out of the window all I could see were officers in white suits, picking their way over the paving stones. Although the police were finished with me, the journalists weren't finished with them, or with anyone else associated with the house. At last DI Johnson went out to make a statement and appeal for witnesses.

Nate came back. I could see him hovering behind the crowd, taller than the rest, waiting for the cameras to stop flashing. When he reached the door his face was drawn, cheeks pale, accentuating the blue of his eyes and darkness of his hair. It seemed to me that his own memories were etched on his face.

He didn't speak but followed me through to the kitchen, where his gaze rested on the scenes of crimes officers. Another reminder. And then he turned to look at me.

'You know,' I said, 'there's a hell of a lot more to this house-sitting business than meets the eye.' I don't know why I said it. Usual thing I suppose – nervous tic; a fine bit of flippancy coming to the rescue. And then I let out an awful, hiccoughing sort of laugh that was loud and high pitched. One of the SOCOs outside must have heard. He looked up at me, his eyes wide, startled and magnified behind dark-rimmed glasses, his head framed by its white hood. I looked back at him and found myself roaring with uncontrollable laughter, thrusting its way into the quiet kitchen. It was as though I was watching myself, creating this awful scene, and then suddenly, thankfully, my body realised what it was really supposed to be doing, and the sobbing took over.

Nate pulled me into a strong hug, holding me tight as I cried.

'Oh God,' I said, when I could. 'I'm sorry; and it must be so much worse for you, with all your memories. As for me, I think I'm cracking up.'

'Crack away,' he said, giving my arm a little extra squeeze as he let me go. I felt his warmth leave me as he stepped back. 'If you can't crack up under these circumstances, when can you?'

'The guffawing first was bad. That police officer will think I'm a callous bitch.'

'He won't; he must have seen the full gamut of human emotion in his time. And who cares what he thinks anyway?'

After that we talked for a long time at the table.

'I was going to go and call the police after I'd drunk my coffee,' I said. 'I thought I could arrange a time to go in and tell them about Maggie coming here, and about the possible extra will. God, I was treating it like I was scheduling in a haircut or something. I excused myself from going earlier, because I was busy with Emily, and then I had to go out. I thought I was just giving Maggie a few extra hours of peace. By being a wimp I probably cost her her life ...'

Nate clutched my hand and held it hard. 'Her murderer cost her her life. No one else.'

But he knew as well as I did that my actions had made a difference.

'I keep wondering ...' I had to pause for a moment. 'I keep wondering how long it took her to die. I mean, if I'd gone to put some rubbish out as soon as I got home, or if I'd watched the news in the basement ... Maybe she was still conscious, waiting for someone to help her.'

Shadows made patterns that moved across his face as his expression changed. He wanted to reassure me, but couldn't do so without being dishonest. He didn't know if she'd lingered. I remembered, as a child, seeing a deer once, after it had been hit by a car. It twitched and writhed whilst the driver wrung his hands. I didn't know either.

The following afternoon, Nate sent me out of the house. 'Just go off and have a change of scene. When you've had to cope with this kind of trauma, it makes sense to put some distance between yourself and this place for a while.'

I hesitated. 'What about you?'

'I'll hold the fort.' The police were still with us; they'd come back as soon as it was light to finalise their work.

But my mind had leapt to the need to go back to Saxwell to pick up some stuff. I explained. 'So could I swap your offer for some time out tomorrow?' I finished. 'I just don't quite feel equal to driving over there today. I think I need to limber up, mentally, and I'd like to call Steph and arrange to meet her too.'

'Do both,' Nate said. 'Get some fresh air now and make your arrangements for tomorrow.' He shepherded me out of the kitchen. 'Go on; bugger off!'

As I walked across the hall, another police officer entered Damien Newbold's study. I'd told DI Johnson that Samson had had the opportunity to hide the paperwork whilst he'd been in there, and they were still searching.

Nate was right, it did feel good to be out. To my right, the Common was turning a rusty brown. The summer storms we'd had hadn't been enough to compensate for weeks of drought. I avoided Midsummer Passage, with its police tape and van, and skirted round the houses in the other direction instead, watched by a few goggling onlookers. When I reached Maid's Causeway I turned right towards town. On the railings next to the Common there was a series of posters. One was advertising some kind of summer extravaganza on Parker's Piece, another a show at the Arts Theatre, and a third an art exhibition. Imelda West. There was a small head-and-shoulders shot of her grinning, her bright, bird-like eyes alive with good humour. The poster said she was a renowned ceramicist and retired head of art at the Philip Radley School. That rang bells. I spooled back through the conversations I'd had over the last weeks and, suddenly, I had it. It was the school where Saskia Amos had worked. I remembered how she'd mentioned the name, as though I ought to have heard of it and been impressed.

I peered again at the poster. The gallery was on Gwydir Street. It wasn't a long walk, and it would give me an objective. I didn't really feel like wandering round the shops.

I reached Gwydir Street from the Norfolk Street end. It was home to pleasant Victorian terraced houses – their window boxes filled with geraniums – and a couple of well-kept pubs. But at its other end the residential buildings gave way on one side to antique shops, a gallery and a cafe, all housed in a large, red-brick edifice with arched windows: Dale's Brewery. The smell of coffee from the cafe almost put me off my objective, but I dragged myself past and walked into a smallish exhibition space with Imelda West's poster on the door. Inside I recognised Imelda herself, talking to another gallery goer, which gave me a chance to look round without having to make small talk.

I thought at first that I wouldn't be able to focus, but the atmosphere in the gallery was calm, and the work was right up my street. Large, crackle-glazed bowls in deep sea greens and blues sat alongside tiny buttons decorated with fish; pendants, brooches and tiles with intricate designs, and a jug, which I immediately fell for, but which cost – hmm – three hundred pounds. The other member of the public, a tall man in a dark pinstripe, was leaving now, and Imelda looked over to me and grinned.

'Your work's beautiful,' I said, gesturing round the room.
'Thank you so much,' she said, coming over. 'What a very kind thing to say.'
'How do you get such intense colours?'
She explained to me about the processes that she used and I listened, whilst wondering whether I could afford one of her hand-painted tiles.
'And how did you hear about the exhibition?' Imelda said. 'It's always useful to find out which bits of publicity are effective.'
I explained about the poster. 'I met a woman recently who used to work at the Philip Radley School,' I said, 'so it caught my eye.'
'Oh, really,' she said, her eyes dancing. 'I wonder if we overlapped. I was there for thirty years.'

'I got the impression she wasn't there for long,' I said, 'though I only exchanged a few words with her. Her name's Saskia Amos.'

Imelda's face changed in an instant. It was like watching a landscape that's suddenly been plunged into shade by a large cloud. 'Be thankful your conversation was short!' she said, then laughed. 'There, I shouldn't have said that really. It's all a long time ago.'

'If it makes you feel better, I didn't take to her much myself.'

She laughed again, a quick, sharp bark. 'Much better. And you're spot on. She was only at the school for around eighteen months, and then only as the headmaster's secretary, so we didn't have a lot of direct contact. Goes to show how quickly she made an impression on me though.'

A blonde woman and a man with a beard came to the door of the gallery, hesitantly, arm in arm.

'Do come on in,' Imelda said to them, her voice ringing out like a bell. 'I won't bite. Look around. No need to buy.' She turned back to me. 'I must sound awfully petty, saying that about Saskia Amos after all these years, but I'm afraid she was totally unsuited to work in a school.'

'She admitted that to me.'

Imelda raised an eyebrow. 'I am surprised. Anyway, she left, shall we say, under a cloud. She could have caused a very great deal of trouble for a fine, old institution. In the end that didn't happen, so we all breathed a sigh of relief.'

The blonde woman had worked her way to the far corner of the room and was going for one of the tiles. She must be on a budget, like me.

'Excuse me just a moment,' Imelda said, and went to sort out the sale.

I went over to pick out a tile for myself.

The blonde woman was having hers tissue-wrapped and

put into a blue carrier bag when I glanced up and saw Paul Mathewson come in. He didn't see me, standing well back in the shadows, and made straight for Imelda.

'Paul!' She drew him into an embrace, kissing him on both cheeks. 'You came! You are good.'

'Wouldn't miss it,' he said. 'And I told you I'd come when we met at Julia Brockham's. You never seem to believe a word I say!'

'It's only that I know how busy you are. I do appreciate your loyalty, you know. How are those awful brothers of yours? They never come, I may say. It's been so long since I've seen Tom, I've almost forgotten what he looks like.'

'I'll have a go at him for you,' Paul said, laughing.

I decided I'd better take my tile over to the counter and make myself known, otherwise it would look as though I'd been hiding.

'Ah,' said Imelda as I drew near, 'you've chosen the one with the oystercatcher. I enjoyed making it. Did the sketch up in Norfolk.'

'Ruby!' Paul came over and gave me a quick squeeze on the shoulder. His eyes were full of concern, and his face was tired and pinched. He must have heard about Maggie. It would be all over the local news already of course, probably national too, given her career.

'Oh, how lovely,' Imelda said, unaware of any undercurrents, busy as she was with the tissue paper and sticky tape. 'I didn't know you two were friends.' She parcelled up my tile expertly and slipped it into another of the blue bags. 'If you want to go and get a drink together at Hot Numbers I won't hold it against you.' She looked up at Paul. 'Not so long as you come back and look at my work afterwards, naturally.'

Hot Numbers was the same coffee shop I'd smelled on my way to the gallery. Inside we ordered and then took bench seats at one end of a long, expansive wooden table. At the other end, a couple of students were talking about the ball they'd been to the night before.

'How are you?' Paul said. 'The news said it was you that found her. It must have been awful.'

I gave an involuntary shudder. 'It was such a beautiful evening, Paul, and I was just standing in the back doorway, looking at the birds, and the sky, and then suddenly ... suddenly there she was. And all that time I'd been thinking how idyllic it was, when in fact it was actually the most horrific of days, and I didn't even know it.'

He reached out and touched my hand for a moment, whilst I did battle with tears, threatening to show me up in front of the other clientele.

'I'm so sorry.' He reached in his pocket and brought out a business card, pushing it across the table towards me. 'Contact of mine,' he said. 'Specialist counsellor. You should see someone, Ruby, after what you've been through.'

I put the card into my jeans pocket. 'I'll think about it. Thanks.'

'You might even find it helps with all the other things you've had to deal with recently.' He let out a long sigh. 'God, what a basinful you've had. And all through no fault of your own.'

'Just one of those things,' I said. Suddenly I could see what Emily had meant. Paul seemed so sorry for me that I almost felt he was the one who needed support. 'Maggie's death is so incredible I can hardly take it in, but as far as the other stuff goes, I'm moving on. Honestly. I'm getting used to the new status quo, sorting out practicalities. I'm planning to go over to Saxwell St Andrew tomorrow and fetch some of my stuff.'

'That's good. Will you and Luke be able to talk things through?'

I shook my head. 'To be honest I'm banking on sneaking in whilst he's safely out at work, then hopefully I'll pop over to see my friend, Steph, who lives opposite, and make good my escape before he's anywhere near coming home. I can't quite face a proper discussion yet. But we've spoken on the phone, and I'll arrange a meet up soon.'

'That all sounds like good news. How was the phone call?'

'It wasn't great, to tell you the truth. I still don't think he's really conscious of what he's done.' I didn't want him to ask me any more. Sometimes talking helps, but not always. 'What about you?' I said, quickly. 'You look exhausted.'

'Work stuff. Nothing of any import. Do you feel like cake?'

I glanced down the table to where the students were tucking into enormous Chelsea buns. 'That would be good. Maybe something a bit less extreme than they're having though.'

We went to the counter to look and I chose home-made German cake.

'Have you seen Emily since I saw you last?' Paul said, when we were back at the table.

In the wake of Maggie's death I'd almost forgotten about the visit to Oswald House. 'Yes I have, Paul.' I weighed my options for a moment. 'In fact, there's something I think I ought to tell you.' And I explained about what Fi had called Emily's 'knight-in-shining-armour complex'.

'You think she's developed a crush on me?' He'd gone pale, his eyes wide, and it was clear that Fi was right. He'd had no idea at all.

I nodded. 'I'm sorry. It's quite clearly nothing you've done. I think it's just her vulnerable state at the moment. I thought I ought to warn you.'

'Dear God,' Paul said, staring into space. 'This is terrible!

I should have seen it coming. It just didn't occur to me for a minute.'

'It wouldn't.' It was awful, seeing the pain in his eyes.

'I've made things even worse for her.'

'Paul,' I said, firmly, to try to get through to him. 'You couldn't have anticipated this. When you started visiting her she was infatuated with Damien Newbold.'

I'd got his attention, but I hadn't won him over.

'Even so,' he said, 'it's the kind of thing you're meant to look out for.'

'She'll get over it. It's all part of growing up. And at least you'll be aware now, when you see her next.'

'Of course.' He took a sudden, deep breath. 'And thank you for telling me.'

I excused myself for a moment and nipped across to the ladies. While I was there, a text came through from Steph. Just heard. R U OK? RU with the police? Call if u'd like 2 talk. S x

I slipped the phone back into my pocket, but her message gave me a warm little kernel of strength.

Back in the main room of the cafe, Paul said, 'Sorry about just now. I didn't mean to go over the top; it's just a shock. And all my work with my students has been a bit difficult lately. I've asked college if I can reduce some of my duties from next term.'

'Can't be easy.'

'I just don't think I'm cut out for it. And I've got a nasty little visit I've got to make tomorrow afternoon.'

I looked across at him.

'Out the way you're headed actually.'

'To do with someone in your care?'

He nodded. 'I have to get the family involved, and I'm not looking forward to it.' He gave me a wry smile. 'I was going to make a selfish suggestion.'

I was curious. 'Go on. Put me out of my misery.'

'I was just wondering whether you'd fancy a lift over to Saxwell St Andrew. It'd be good to have company – make the whole expedition less onerous. I could drop you off at two, say, and then come and pick you up again from your friend's place at around four-thirty.'

I was torn. The timing should work okay if Steph was around. 'I'm not sure what sort of company I'll be,' I said. 'It's the first time I'll have been back home since I walked out.'

'I might not be the life and soul myself,' Paul said. He sighed. 'Perhaps we should make it another time. It was just the coincidence of us both being headed in the same direction.' He smiled for a moment. 'I bought a second-hand convertible at the end of April – an Alfa Romeo. Goes like the clappers and it's great on these hot, summer days. I wondered if we might blow the cobwebs away and forget our troubles.'

I thought of the denizens of Saxwell St Andrew twitching their net curtains to get a look as I stepped out of the sporty car, accompanied by Paul. I knew that since Luke's fall from grace they would all have been busy pitying me in a very public way. ('She was passed over for someone younger, you know. Well, of course, it often happens.') Turning up in style was quite appealing ... But, in reality, I knew I'd rather Nate took me over, even if he drove me in a tractor ... And he already thought Paul and I had something going on. I didn't particularly want to fuel his suspicions.

'It's really kind of you,' I said at last, 'but maybe it's something I should tackle on my own. I'm bound to be in a state, and you've got enough on your plate as it is.'

He nodded slowly, and then started to write on a scrap of paper. 'I understand. But if you change your mind, just call.' And he handed me his mobile number.

Either way I needed to get the visit over and done with. As I walked back along Gwydir Street I texted Steph to check she'd be around the following afternoon, and got confirmation moments later.

When I got back to River House it was late afternoon and the police had gone, both from the study and the back garden.

'Did they find anything to indicate another will?' I asked.

Nate shook his head. 'I don't think so. I didn't see exactly where they searched, but they've only just left, so I reckon they must have been pretty thorough. They were up in Newbold's bedroom too.'

He was in the kitchen, busy with various bits of shopping. 'I went to Waitrose whilst they were at it,' he said, glancing round at me, his hair falling over one eye. 'Do you fancy joining me for ...' He looked at the worktop. '... a Parma ham, black olivey, artichokey thing on pasta?'

'That sounds amazing. What can I do?'

'Is it too early for us to have a stiff drink?'

'Under the circumstances, definitely not.'

'In that case there's gin in that cupboard, tonic in the fridge and a lemon in that bag on the table.'

I could see he was a man with the right priorities. It wasn't making it any easier. I kept catching myself looking at him. A thirty-something teenage crush. Well, it might bloody well *be* a crush, but that didn't alter the potency of the effect. And somehow, it felt more significant than that.

I looked up from slicing the lemon and caught his eye. An instant blush crept up my neck. Thanks a bunch, body. He'd spot me if I didn't do something drastic. It didn't help that the chopping he was doing was making the muscles in his forearm flex. The rejected woman now has you in her sights, Mr Nate Bastable. He'd be terrified.

'I've spoken to Samson by the way,' he said, taking a large slug of his G&T.

'God. What did he say?'

'Immediately told me he was in the Red Tavern all yesterday afternoon. As you can imagine, he was also quite curious to know whether the police had found any new will.'

'Yes, I can see he might have found that topic diverting. As for the Red Tavern alibi, well, his coming out with it like that sounds like a guilty conscience. Mind you, there will be a whole crowd of people who can vouch for him, if it's true.'

'You're right there,' he said, and went back to chopping up the ham.

The food was good and so was the company.

'I never asked about your Saffron Walden woman,' I said, suddenly remembering.

'I'd be surprised if you had, under the circumstances. Fascinator though she was, she did rather pale into insignificance in the light of other events.'

'Fascinator, eh?'

Nate gave me a look. 'Not in the way you might imagine. She was wearing a long, emerald green dressing gown when I arrived.'

'Interesting, given the time of day.'

'Exactly. And she was also sporting a wig the colour of tomato juice.'

'Ah.'

'It's safe to say she doesn't carry off dressing up as well as you do.'

'Thanks. Although from what you say, it doesn't sound as though the competition was that stiff.'

'I have to confess you're right. She had a considerable

amount of curly brown hair, visible under the fake red stuff.'

'O-kay. Still, I suppose at least she'll be absent when your house-sitter takes up residence.'

'Right. But unfortunately her seven cats won't. They come with the house, and they need sitting too.'

'Oh my. Do you get a lot of requests from such, urm, individual types?'

'More than you might imagine. Still, it makes this job more interesting.' He sighed.

'But not interesting enough?'

'That's just what I would have said, until all this business with Damien and Maggie. Now I remember what life at the sharp end's like.'

He looked away, and I sensed he wanted me to move the conversation on. 'I'll stack the dishwasher,' I said. 'My turn to do something. You cooked.'

'Okay.' He took a deep breath, but then smiled. 'Though you did a good job with those G&Ts. I think mine would have floored a slighter man.'

I grinned as I put the pans into the bottom rack.

In minutes, everything had been put away, and all the dishes stacked. I looked at Nate, suddenly feeling awkward, but at that moment, his mobile went.

'Oh, Bex, hi!' he said. 'How are things at home? Speck behaving herself?' A pause. 'Really? That bloody cat, she's got such a cheek. Has there been much post?'

For a second, I hoped I'd misunderstood, but it did seem that this Bex person must be in residence at Two Wells Farm, awaiting Nate's return. Slight surprise after what Steph had said. Not especially pleasant.

'I meant to say,' Nate went on, 'I'm expecting a letter from Edinburgh. If you see it, any chance you could forward it on? Perfect. Cheers.' Then after a moment he added, 'Yeah, you too.' And he rang off, and turned back to me.

'I didn't realise you had someone keeping the home fires burning,' I said, before I'd thought how it would sound.

'Bex?' He paused for a moment and rubbed his jaw. 'Oh. I see what you mean. She's not there full time. She's feeding my cat for me whilst I'm here, and keeping an eye on the place.'

An unreasonable tug of jealousy continued to tweak at my insides. They sounded close.

He turned away, and there was a long pause before he added, 'We go way back, but she's not a girlfriend. I don't really do relationships.'

Although Steph had already told me that, him saying it made a difference. He *had* noticed the way I'd been reacting to him; this was him warning me off. Bollocks. In fact, quadruple bollocks.

'Steph mentioned that,' I said, trying to sound casual. 'I rather wish I'd stuck to the same rule.' I moved towards the door. 'I'm chilly; I'll just fetch a jumper.' And before he could reply I nipped out of the room. Upstairs, I took my time. The evening *had* turned cooler, so getting a layer was a reasonable excuse for my exit. Right. I needed to show Nate I wasn't after him; otherwise this was going to be unbearably awkward. I texted Paul. Cd I take u up on the lift 2morrow after all? The reply came before I'd descended the stairs. Certainly. I will pick you up at 2 p.m. The message was very him.

As soon as I'd told Nate my plans for the next day I felt better; hopefully he'd assume he'd been wrong all along, and that his 'back-off' messages had been uncalled for.

We were drinking coffee, and keeping our distance, when there was a knock at the door. I checked my watch. Half eight.

'I'll look,' Nate said, and went into the hall to peer through the spyhole. 'Fi from next door.' He opened up.

She looked flushed, and her eyes were damp. 'Oh, I'm sorry,' she said, when she saw Nate. 'I didn't realise ...'

'Don't mind me,' he said. 'Do you two want to use the kitchen?'

I nodded. 'Thanks.'

As we walked through, Nate disappeared into the drawing room.

'What's up?' I asked. She was close to tears; the first time I'd seen her in that state.

'It's Emily. Turns out she didn't keep her appointment at the university counselling service yesterday.'

'Oh,' I said, sitting down as I digested this. 'I see.'

'The police have been asking questions, of course, and there's no doubt at all. She did a no show. But she's being really stupid and won't tell anyone where she was. Not even me. Just says she was "walking around".'

I couldn't think what to say.

'Truth to tell, I'm worried sick,' Fi said, taking a tissue from her pocket to wipe her eyes. 'It's like I can't get through to her any more. And if she doesn't get more cooperative with the police, I'm scared about what might happen next.'

She went quiet and in the background I could hear Nate, playing blues music on the piano.

Chapter Twenty-Six

Nate had ensconced himself in the study by the time I came down to breakfast the next day, but he appeared in the kitchen to get some iced water from the fridge. After the awkwardness of the previous evening, I had the urge to get up and start busying myself at the sink the moment he appeared. 'Everything all right?'

'Just a house-sitting crisis to deal with,' he said. 'Not quite on the scale of this one, admittedly. The woman who's looking after Renstone House in Huntingdon just called to say the family's guinea pig's had babies, but they're all dead.' He sighed. 'It's right what they say about never working with animals. She wants to know if she should store the bodies in the fridge until the family gets back.'

'Hmm. That's a knotty one.' I rubbed at some imaginary limescale round the taps with my cloth.

'Would you want dead guinea pigs in your fridge?'

I glanced over my shoulder for a moment; he wasn't looking in my direction. 'You can report back that your focus group of one says no.'

'Didn't think so. I'll maybe call the vets in Huntingdon and see if they've got facilities for preserving them for a week or so.'

'They couldn't just be buried?'

I heard the sound of ice cubes dropping from the dispenser into his glass. 'We did that once, when someone's cat got run over. Big mistake. You should have heard the fuss the owner made. Exhumation was involved.'

He left the room again. In spite of my plans with Paul for later in the day he seemed intent on keeping his distance now. I must have really put the wind up him. The sinking feeling in my stomach was hard to ignore. Humiliation entwined itself with disappointment.

But Nate's focus on work reminded me of my own responsibilities. I needed to decide how to tackle the matter of an errant partner. I pressed my fingers to my temples. Someone, sooner or later, was going to notice that the topic of my book was directly relevant to my own life. I was using other people's experience of midlife crisis to make money – okay, maybe even to entertain – so I shouldn't baulk at using my own. I would make some passing reference to mine and Luke's experience, without mentioning his or Daisy's names, of course. Must protect the innocent.

With that matter out of the way, I turned my attention to visiting Saxwell St Andrew. It occurred to me that I could use the video camera on my phone to take a quick tour of my old home, enabling me to look back from the safe distance of River House, and work out what belonged to who. As far as my clothes went, I could just shove them into bin bags and take them with me straightaway.

I suddenly wondered whether Paul's convertible was the sort with no back seats and hardly any boot space. Maybe it had been a mistake to take him up on his offer. Should I call him to rearrange? It seemed too late somehow. And I knew that, if necessary, Steph would give my belongings house space until I could pick them up or she was able to bring them to me.

But then there were my books … I might as well get them out straightaway too. Perhaps I'd better just ring Paul and explain.

I dialled the mobile number he'd given me, but eventually it went to voicemail. He was probably giving a tutorial or something. And by the time he was out … I'd just have to let our arrangement stand.

I was halfway through drafting some text on my very

personal experience of Luke's midlife crisis when my mobile rang. It was Steph.

'Still on for a meet up later?' I said, hoping she wasn't calling to cancel.

'Yes, sure.' There was an ominous pause. 'Um, about this trip to Saxwell …'

'Yes?'

'I mean, I haven't told Luke or anything, of course.'

'Good.'

'But you are just coming to pick up clothes and things, aren't you?'

'What is all this, Steph? What do you think I'm going to do? I'll be in our house for about ten minutes; just enough time to shove my clothes and books into a few bags and then hot foot it over to your place for tea and chat.'

She harrumphed a bit. 'I know, I know. I knew that.'

'What's going on?'

'It's just that Luke came round to ours last night – not in the house I don't mean, but just knocked on the door.'

'Yes?'

'And he's had another one of the nastier sort of poison pens he's been getting.'

'Oh, Steph.' It was all becoming clear to me now. 'You're not telling me it's a threatening one and you think I'm going to let myself in and slash his best rugby shirt with a Stanley knife?'

'God no!' said Steph, transparent as ever.

'Luke thought I'd been writing those letters, you know,' I said. 'But you've got no bloody excuse to think it. Luke's not aware of where I am or what I've been up to, but you know what's been happening here, and what I've been doing.' I heard my voice crack, much against my will. 'Is it likely that I've been sitting round dreaming up creative insults?'

'Ruby, sweetheart, please don't take it like that.'

'You're meant to know me too well to think any such thing.'

'And I do,' she said. 'It's only *because* of what you've been through recently that I even entertained the thought for a second. In the last couple of weeks you've had an acrimonious break-up with a long-term partner, found a dead body, dealt with a grieving teenager ...' She paused to draw breath. 'You have to admit it wouldn't be beyond the bounds of possibility for you to behave out of character, under the circumstances.'

'And Luke convinced you it was me.'

'No, no, of course, he didn't. He was just worried in case it might be. He was as shocked as any of us at the idea.'

'As any of you? Good grief, how many of you were there, sitting round the cauldron?'

Steph laughed for a second and then stopped abruptly. 'Only him, me and Robin.'

'Why would Luke even think I'd bother?' I said, bitterly. 'Frankly, I haven't had the energy.'

Steph sighed again. 'Well, it was something that was in the letter.'

'What kind of thing?'

She tutted. 'He wouldn't tell me. Just said it was too personal to pass on. I thought maybe it was something to do with—'

I cut her short. 'Yes, thanks, Steph. Even my mind can conjure up the sort of personal details he might be referring to. Thing is, that narrows the field. If it's someone who knows his bedroom habits, and it's not me ...'

'You're thinking Daisy?' The words came out as though she was chewing them over, like a dog with a satisfying bone.

'Unless he's actually slept with a whole load of other

women I know nothing about, or he talks about his sexual techniques down the pub. I certainly don't ever discuss them.' The idea was horrible.

'But I could see Daisy doing it,' Steph said, ignoring my histrionics.

'Why?'

'Well, as I said to you earlier, what Daisy's friend said about Luke pestering her is a fiction as far as I can see. I'll bet Daisy put her up to it, to hit out at both of you at once. And I reckon that's actually because Luke's cutting her dead now. He's been moping around over the loss of you. What if she wanted to send a poison pen, making you look like the author?'

'To convince Luke I'm a bunny boiler and he's better off without me?'

'It's a thought, isn't it?'

Nate tried not to be prejudiced against Paul Mathewson, but he was fighting a losing battle. The guy looked as though he'd stepped out of another age, dressed in that herringbone suit with the sort of quality lace-up shoes that have real leather soles and would probably last until he was in his dotage. It'd felt weird when he'd gone to answer the door, and then given Ruby a call. Like he was her dad, seeing her off on a date with a bloke he didn't approve of. He'd stood there in the hall, fervently hoping their trip was a damp squib. Talk about dog in the manger. He'd purposely put down a marker the evening before, telling Ruby he didn't do relationships. He'd had to, before his physical feelings took over and it was too late. But it was more than just physical. He could almost taste the closeness they could share. Dangerous. He'd put her safety at stake and his sanity too if he ended up losing her.

A moment later he'd bumped back to reality. It wasn't

his choice to make anyway. In spite of the spark he kept imagining, it was clearly Paul Mathewson who'd caught her interest.

'Make sure you're back in time for tea,' he couldn't resist saying as Ruby walked down the house steps. She turned round and rolled her eyes.

Sodding hell. He needed to do something about his ego. He'd known she was keen on Mathewson all along – they'd met up in town, and been out to the pub – and yet he'd still had this instinctive feeling that she and he had some kind of connection too. It had all been in his head. He thought back to that first day he'd met her, when Steph had come out to see him off, and – he now knew – Ruby had followed them and eavesdropped. Hmm. Well, two could play at that game. Picking up his door key, he let himself out of River House, and walked in the direction that would take him to where Paul Mathewson was most likely to be parked.

Nate reached the road just in time to see Ruby sliding her long legs round and into the car. Mathewson was standing on her side of the vehicle and closed the door shut for her as though she was royalty. Perhaps he had old-fashioned gent appeal, though Nate hadn't thought that would be her thing.

He watched as the tutor neared the driver's side door. Then suddenly he stopped, paused for a moment and went back to the rear of the car, where he opened the boot. That stupid boot ... It was going to be a tight squeeze getting Ruby's stuff in there. And then he saw Mathewson reach in and lift out one of those battered, brown I'm-an-academic style briefcases. He proceeded to cast his eyes around the street, so that Nate had to take a step further back to avoid being seen. When he risked looking again, Mathewson wasn't holding the briefcase any more, and was opening the driver's door. Weird.

He watched them move off slowly, up the cramped lane, past all the nose-to-tail parked cars, and then walked round to look at the space they'd left behind.

Nate saw the briefcase immediately. Mathewson had left it on the pavement, hard up against the low wall of one of the tiny front gardens in the street. Habitual caution made him hesitate. He'd spent a lot of time investigating Damien Newbold's past, but none at all researching Paul Mathewson's. But then Mathewson had had nothing to do with the hiring of the house-sitting service. He was being ridiculous. He walked over to the briefcase and manoeuvred it carefully, so that it lay flat on its side. Then he slid the catch to release its fastening.

Nate let out the breath he hadn't known he'd been holding. Essays. The case was full of student essays. Individual names were written or printed across the top of each one: Sophie Roberts, Libby Taylor, Marcus Bland. He flicked through them, one by one. It seemed there was nothing more to tell. He fastened the case again and put it back exactly where it had been. What did it mean? Nate could imagine Mathewson being embarrassed – maybe if he'd left the briefcase in there by accident, then suddenly remembered how it was taking up half the tiny boot space – space that Ruby would need. Leaving it in there would make him look poorly prepared, but dumping the case on the pavement didn't seem like the solution of choice. He glanced around. There was a bush on the opposite side of the road. He could have put the case behind that, safely hidden, and come back to fetch it later, with no one any the wiser. Why leave it somewhere where it might be nicked, or damaged?

Back inside River House, Nate's mind was still focused on the problem. It didn't make sense. He made himself a coffee and sat at the kitchen table, not seeing what was in front of him. After five minutes of making no headway, his thoughts drifted back to Ruby again. He had half a mind to follow her over to Saxwell and offer his Volvo's boot space as spare capacity. Mine's bigger than his ... Hmm. Very mature. Perhaps not.

For a while, Paul drove me in silence. It started to feel awkward, though I could understand it. I knew he'd be preoccupied with the tricky meeting he had to tackle that afternoon.

'It's a gorgeous car,' I said, for want of any other topic of conversation.

He looked at me and raised an ironic eyebrow. 'Hell of a waste of cash really.'

'Not if it gives you pleasure. It's a real classic. I feel I ought to be wearing dark glasses and a headscarf. I'm not nearly Hollywood enough for it.' I was wearing what Steph called my 'Bolshie kit' again, right down to my boots. I felt battle gear was essential for a return to Saxwell.

Paul smiled, and there was a sadness in his eyes. 'You set it off very nicely, in my opinion. And I'm a connoisseur.'

I wasn't sure if he meant of gawky women who always wear black jeans, or of classic cars. I presumed the latter.

'Anyway,' he went on, looking back at the road again, 'it's given me a lot of pleasure over the last few weeks, so maybe you're right.'

'Do you know the way?' I asked as we reached the outskirts of the city.

'I know I need to head east. After that, I'll need your help.'

'Sure.'

The conversation flagged again, but as we turned onto the A14 near Stow cum Quy I remembered Imelda, talking about his brothers.

'What are they like?' I said to him, after drawing his mind back to the artist's comments.

He seemed to drag his attention from somewhere far away and I heard the smile in his wistful voice. 'Tom's a laugh. Life and soul of the party. He and Richard were the naughty ones when we were little. They used to play horrible pranks on visitors: licking icing off the top of my mother's cakes before they were taken up to table, sticking worms in the guest bed, that kind of thing.'

'Remind me not to come over when they're around!'

Paul laughed. 'It was always noisy at home. I'm the youngest and they'd already banded together in their war on civilisation before I was old enough to take much notice. I was in awe of them; watching from the sidelines.'

'Must have been a relief when your sister came along to keep you company.'

Again, Paul seemed to have to drag his attention back. 'Sorry?'

'I was just saying about your sister. She must have altered the balance a bit. Oh heck, sorry, I should have said, it's left here.'

'Oh yes.' He did a skilful last-minute manoeuvre round a lorry, back to the inside lane.

Once we were safely on the road towards Saxwell, he added, 'Yes, my sister gave me a good bit of moral support.'

'Are you thinking about your meeting?' I asked. Perhaps it was best to tackle it head on.

He nodded.

'Soon be over, and then you can relax. It's horrible, having to do things you're dreading, but if it's for a good cause then it'll be worth it. It's not everyone who volunteers to take on these roles; helping to put everything right when things have got out of kilter. I'm not sure I could do it.'

I saw his shoulders relax. 'Yes,' he said. 'You're right.'

He flicked his eyes towards mine momentarily and smiled. 'Thanks.'

The first sign to Saxwell was coming up and I felt my stomach lurch, causing a wave of nervous nausea. I took a deep breath. 'It's actually best to wait and take the second turning. Brings you out nearer to our house. It's in Orchard Lane.'

'Okay.' Paul cancelled the indicator and drove on.

I tried to think of something else to say, but my old life, looming nearer and nearer, made me lose all focus on everything else. It was the thought of seeing all my old stuff, sitting comfortably in its usual surroundings, and knowing I could never pick up where I'd left off.

'Right just here,' I said, 'and then our road is first on your left.' Our road.

He made the turns.

'It's double yellow lines by the houses, but you could park anywhere along this side, here by the grass.'

I got out and stood on the pavement. Scanning the homes in the road, I couldn't see any faces, staring at me from the windows. Steph's house opposite looked empty, but I knew she'd be in there somewhere, ready with tea and sympathy.

Suddenly my mobile rang, sounding loud in the quiet street. Nate.

'Everything okay?'

'I'm afraid not,' he said. 'Just had Fi round again.'

I swallowed, wondering what was coming.

'Apparently Emily's mother's been found dead.' He paused for a moment.

'You mean killed?' I asked, hearing the shake in my voice.

'Yes. Same method. And Fi says she can't find Emily.'

I could feel my heart thudding hard against my ribcage and for a moment the world around me darkened, little flecks of light pricking my view.

'Are you okay?'

'Yes, thanks,' I said, automatically. 'Are you?'

'Just wondering what's coming next. Take care, all right?' And he rang off.

'What is it?' Paul said, so I told him.

There was a long pause. 'That's sickening.'

'I don't know when it's going to end.' I closed my eyes for a moment.

Paul took a deep, uneven breath. 'I can't believe for a minute that Emily had anything to do with it. In any case, I doubt she'd be physically strong enough.' He held his hand to his head for a second. 'They'll track her down soon enough and rule her out.' He looked at me, and I nodded. I was shivering, despite the warmth of the day.

'Do you mind if I nip into your place for a moment?' Paul said. 'I could do with using your bathroom, and collecting myself before I head off.'

'Of course.' He looked as shaky as I felt.

The arrival of Fi at the door had thrown Nate off course. He'd been deep in thought about Paul Mathewson's briefcase, and whether he should bring it inside, when the knock jolted him back to reality. Her news sent his mind into overdrive. Three people dead. And there Nate was, an ex-PI on the spot, and he hadn't worked out who was responsible. Carry on much longer and there wouldn't be any suspects left.

In spite of the latest news, Paul Mathewson's briefcase still niggled too. Experience told him to look twice at any oddity, however irrelevant it seemed. The papers inside mattered to those students, represented hours of work. Why would someone appointed to help them leave them in full view like that, so carelessly?

Unless. Unless … Suddenly it hit him. Of course. Shit …

His heart went into overdrive. He could call her, but the news would be too shocking. She'd give herself away. And then she'd be in immediate danger. If she wasn't already.

Nate was in the Volvo in under sixty seconds.

As Paul put a steering wheel lock on the car I fished for my keys in my shoulder bag. They were meant to be in a little side pouch, but in my anxiety earlier I must have chucked them in carelessly. Eventually I rested the bag on the car bonnet and finally found them right at the bottom. Paul was waiting for me halfway up our garden path.

When I put my key in the front door lock the feelings of nausea got worse. In a moment, the shock at the news of Saskia's murder was compounded by trepidation over coming home. The door swung open and the familiar smell of boots and polish filled me with such a wrenching tug of homesickness that I had to turn away for a moment. Through the kitchen door I could see our oak table, battered, much the worse for wear, but loved and used.

Paul put a hand on my shoulder. 'Are you okay?'

I nodded. 'Downstairs loo's just along the corridor here. Last door on the left before the back door.'

'Thanks.'

I went into the kitchen. Luke had put my post on the dresser and I picked up the heap. It all looked so conventional, and yet around me normal life was disintegrating. Suddenly, the will to be super-efficient left me. I found I was physically shaking and sank down on to a chair at the table. For a moment I focused only on the green marks Luke and I had carelessly made when we were drawing leaves onto white T-shirts for a silly fancy-dress party. I spread my post out in front of me. So odd to see my name next to an address where I'd never belong again. Bookman's Cottage, Orchard Lane. I remembered how much I'd liked the house name when the estate agent had shown us the details. I'd tried to find out its history once we'd moved in. Who had the bookman been?

Then, at that moment, something that jarred touched the very edge of my memory. Just a tiny, warning note in amongst the white noise of a shocking day. Bookman's Cottage. Had I mentioned the name to Paul as we drove over?

Tiny, icy goosebumps raised themselves on my arms, without me being quite conscious of what my physical instincts were picking up on. I'd given him directions to Saxwell, and then told him we were on Orchard Lane, but I was increasingly certain I hadn't told him what our house was called. And yet Paul had walked from where we'd parked, past the first house on the left, and straight up the front path of my old home.

He'd known my address. Luke's address.

My mind seemed to slow as feelings of anxiety took over. If he knew ...

I got up from the table and went over to the dresser again. There was a pile of recently-opened post there too, which was the normal way of things. I snatched up the top few letters. Two different anonymous notes. One barely literate, referring to Luke as a 'pedofile', but the second ... I scanned the computer-printed words.

... you were sleeping with a seventeen-year-old girl, robbing her of her childhood whilst you and Ruby tried to create a child of your own.

I felt my breath catch in my throat. The content that Luke had said was too personal to share with Steph. Not lurid, sexual details at all, but the knowledge that Luke and I had been trying for a baby. We'd agreed to keep it secret, so only I should have known. But, of course, I'd confided in Steph, and she'd gossiped about it to Nate. Only by the time I met him, I'd moved out of Saxwell. He knew I lived on Steph's street, but probably not the house name.

With Paul, it was another matter.

I thought back to the day he'd taken me to his college rooms, when he'd found me in tears in town. I'd shown him Luke's letter, with its beautiful copperplate letterhead; he must have started the hate mail after that. The address was so memorable, in its pretty, rural way, and Paul had held on to the information.

But why had he done it? Because he felt sorry for me? Because he was falling for me? He had been pleasant when we'd got together, and solicitous too, but always as though he was holding something back.

And suddenly my mind sped up, scanning everything that had happened, looking for connections and answers. But of course, there was a direct link between Luke and Daisy's situation and Damien and Emily's. Paul had just been picking up the pieces for one sorry teenager who'd suffered at the hands of an older man, when I'd presented him with another example. The impact of the coincidence had sent him off the rails a bit, that was what it was. He must have felt there was misery all around him; misery he wanted to stop. That was why he'd sent the letters, and why he was low now. His decision to shift the focus of his work after the summer vacation showed he knew things had got out of control.

But then something else registered. On the way to Saxwell, I'd mentioned Paul's sister. When he was talking to me about his brothers it had almost seemed as though she'd been forgotten. 'I was the youngest,' Paul had said. And when I'd asked him about her, he'd taken ages to react. And Imelda had only asked for news of Paul's brothers.

I thought back. Paul had mentioned a sister when he was explaining his interest in Emily; he'd said she'd been through a similar affair with an older man. It had been just after I'd asked him if he always got so involved in his support work. Had I touched a raw nerve? Seemed too suspicious?

What if he'd just invented the sister, to make his excessive interest in Emily seem more normal? And suddenly, taking a step back, his interest in her did seem excessive. Yet I was quite sure his feelings for her weren't sexual. He'd been horrified at the idea of her having a crush on him; as though it was the worst possible thing that could happen.

And then suddenly the truth came to me.

My God, how had I been blind enough not to see it before? Now that I had the answer umpteen pieces of information suddenly slotted together to present a cohesive whole. Saskia's reference to the pupils at the Philip Radley School: 'I soon realised that those almost-adult students were very far from being grown-up.' And then Imelda West's words: 'She left under a cloud. She could have caused a very great deal of trouble for a fine, old institution.' And why had Saskia said she'd left the place? Something about 'to look after my growing family'. Even Emily had told me: 'She'd started work again – the PA to the headmaster of some school or other – but she got pregnant with me, and she had to leave.'

Cold fingers of fear gripped me.

I grabbed my phone and looked up the Philip Radley School, but I knew the answer already. It was on Huntingdon Road, the location of the private co-ed place Paul said he'd been to. I'd got the impression that Imelda was a family friend of Paul's – they were clearly in regular contact – but of course there was more to it than that. She'd been his art teacher at school.

And now even my first conversation with Fi came back to me. I'd been probing to find out if Paul had been coming on to Emily. 'Oh, no,' she'd said. 'It's nothing like that. I mean, he's old enough to be her dad or something, isn't he?'

How right she'd been.

And Saskia had used the relationship to taunt Paul openly. What had she said to Emily? Called her something like bitter and pathetic. And then she'd said, in Paul's hearing, 'You take after your bloody father, that's your trouble.'

How Paul must have hated her for it. And now Saskia was dead. And Damien Newbold had played with Emily's feelings, just as Saskia had played with his when he was a teenager, and Damien was dead. And Luke ...

Where was Paul now? I got up from the table, scraping the chair back so suddenly that it fell over.

But before I could get to the door, Paul opened it and came in. He registered my look in one second and blinked for a moment before he said, 'You know.'

Chapter Twenty-Seven

It was a statement, not a question.

He walked into the room, closing the door behind him. 'How did you …?' He let the sentence hang.

In a state of shock I picked up my phone, which still showed the Philip Radley School homepage and moved towards him. He peered for a moment at the screen, touching the casing momentarily, but I held onto it.

'I see.'

And then he reached inside his jacket and drew out a kitchen knife. 'You'd better put your phone down on the table, Ruby.' He moved towards me.

Only that morning I would have sworn that Paul wouldn't do anything to hurt anyone knowingly, but there was a new light in his eyes now. I let the blade get within eight inches, but then backed off and did as he'd said.

'Now move back further.' He reached down to pocket my phone. 'It wasn't meant to be like this.'

I stared deliberately at the knife, trying to find my voice. 'It looks as though it was.' The words came out high-pitched and unsteady. I felt as though I could hardly breathe; it was like something heavy was compressing my chest.

'Luke,' Paul said. 'The knife was for him. He was the appointment I wasn't looking forward to this afternoon.' He looked at me, his eyes sad for a moment. 'My last day,' he said. 'I can't carry on now. Sooner or later someone's going to unravel the mystery, just as you have. After I'm dead the police will know I was their missing killer, but so long as Emily never finds out I was her father she can still live a normal life. Without Saskia and Damien around to mess her up.'

'So that's why you killed Saskia?'

He nodded. 'Mainly because Emily's far better off without her. And if she'd lived, there was always a danger she'd finally tell Emily about me. I couldn't risk that, after what I've done.'

'And you killed Damien too.' I took a seat at the table. My legs felt wobbly and I didn't want to show him I was in danger of losing control.

He nodded. 'It was easy to find him. I knew from Emily where he worked. When she said she was sure he was still going in, I went and hung around outside, so that I could follow him at the end of the day. Then it was just a matter of going back one evening to progress matters.'

I tried desperately to steady my breathing. 'And he let you in without question?'

Paul nodded. 'I told him I was there because I was supporting Emily, and that I'd found out where he was staying purely because Emily and a friend had followed him home from work.'

Through my haze of fear I put all my energy into trying to focus. I needed to keep him talking. If he was telling me how it had been, he couldn't be making his next move. 'I'm surprised he wanted to speak to you.'

Paul snorted. 'People like Damien Newbold enjoy being the centre of attention. He wanted to ask me more about how Emily had been since he'd left. Hearing about her falling to pieces gave him pleasure. My visit was an ego boost as far as he was concerned.'

It was horrible, looking into his crazed eyes, yet hearing words that rang true.

'You understand, don't you?' he said. 'There's no need to say it, I know that you do.'

I felt sick. Heat washed over me. I mustn't stay silent; I needed to buy time to think of a way out of this. 'You had the attack all planned?' I said, eventually.

'Yes. I'd taken the hammer with me. And a few days before I'd sent an anonymous email to a couple of technology bloggers claiming Newbold had come up with some valuable new innovation. I thought if I stole his laptop whilst I was there, it might look as though that had been the motive for his murder. In the end it was probably overkill.'

The thought of Paul working out the details in advance, putting everything in place, was almost more chilling than anything else.

'I was a bit worried about whether I'd have the nerve when the time came,' he went on, 'but in the end it was easy.' His eyes were far away, remembering. 'When I explained about Emily's predicament, and how he should face up to her calmly, and tell her she was too young for him, he laughed. He was genuinely amused. It was just as he was reaching down to fetch a bottle from a low cupboard, and suddenly I was hitting and hitting and hitting him. Really letting him have it. It wasn't hard at all.' His eyes focused on mine again. 'In the end, it was just hard to stop.'

My head was starting to pound; my surroundings seemed to dim, and pinpricks of light disrupted my vision. Shit. Not a good time to pass out. I pushed my hands down on the table and breathed deeply, trying to regain control. 'What about Maggie?'

He sighed. 'I never meant to kill her, though after the letter she wrote to Emily I half felt she deserved it.' He leant back against the kitchen door, holding the knife in front of him. 'She'd seen me, you see.'

Of course. 'She was nearby on the night of the murder.'

He nodded. 'I think she must have seen me coming out of Newbold's cottage.'

'Think?'

'She didn't confront me, or tell the police, obviously, but I thought there was a look of recognition in her eyes when she turned up at River House that time, making trouble. Of course I didn't make anything of it then; I'd no idea she'd been in Little Boxham on the night I killed Damien.'

As he talked, I darted my eyes round the room. I knew the place; it was my own home, for God's sake. Surely there was something here I could use to gain control. But the more I wracked my brains, the more my panic deepened. There was nothing. Nothing that would protect me from a mad man with a knife.

Paul was still talking about Maggie. I remembered her asking who he was, but that didn't prove anything.

'Then my bedder in college told me a dark-haired woman had been asking questions about me,' he went on. 'And as soon as I knew Maggie Cook had been outside Newbold's cottage I guessed the truth. I still don't know why she didn't tell the police about me straightaway ...' His voice drifted off for a moment. 'But she was sure to name me once she'd been placed at the scene of the crime. It would be the obvious way of proving her own innocence.'

'So you went looking for her?'

Paul shrugged. 'I tried. I knew she must be based locally, but I wasn't having any luck. Then my search was interrupted by a call from the university counselling service to say Emily hadn't turned up for her appointment. They wondered if I knew where she was. I didn't, of course, but I decided to bike over to Oswald House just in case.'

'And you saw Maggie?' The role chance had played filled me with horror.

He nodded. 'I came round via the Common, past your place, and I was just about to cross over Midsummer Passage to park my bike when I heard a noise that didn't sound right. It must have been Maggie Cook, forcing your back gate.'

I could picture it all, with chilling clarity.

'I stood my bike against your railings instead, and crept round to investigate. By the time I realised who it was, she was quite engrossed, working out how to the force the French windows into the basement.'

'You had the hammer with you?'

He nodded. 'I'd been out looking for her when I got the call about Emily. I still wonder why she didn't report me.'

But to me, with a mind unclouded by guilt, it didn't seem so odd. The evidence that Maggie had seen Paul at all was only circumstantial, and there was nothing to say she'd actually witnessed him entering or exiting Damien's house. But Paul had begun to panic, and the emotion had eaten into him like a disease.

And now panic was taking hold of me again, too. Something told me he hadn't much story left to tell. Time was running out. A cold sweat overtook me as my eyes were drawn again to his knife. I found I couldn't tear them away.

'What about Luke?' I said. But though I still wanted to keep him talking, I realised I was inviting him to finish his story.

'I was going to take him with me. I'd decided to end it today, and I thought I might as well wipe one more pervert off the face of the earth whilst I was at it.' He ran his tongue over dry lips. 'It made the act seem more meaningful; strengthened my resolve.' He moved towards me a couple of steps. 'You were never going to be harmed, Ruby. I know you'll believe me.'

'What were you going to do?'

'I'd made up my mind to talk my way into your house, simply so that I could arrange to get back in later, once you were safely over with your friend. And that part of the plan worked. I pocketed your back-door key after I'd used your cloakroom.'

'And then you were going to come back to wait for Luke?'

He nodded. 'I was going to call you and tell you that my afternoon appointment was overrunning, and please could you make your own way home. I was sure Steph would take you; you wouldn't want to wait around until Luke got back from work.'

'And whilst we were driving back to Cambridge ...'

'I'd stay here and finish everything off. I planned it for you, Ruby,' he said. 'And for the girl Luke slept with, and for every girl like her that he might have molested in the future.'

'Luke didn't molest Daisy.'

'She went into it willingly, her eyes wide open?'

'Far more, I'm certain, than Emily did.'

'But what does anyone know when they're seventeen?' His eyes, I'm sure, saw nothing of what was in the room. They had that faraway look that told me his mind was in the past, looking back on his own schoolboy self. After a long pause he said, 'It's up to the adults to take responsibility for their actions. Luke deserves to die.'

'You're very bitter.'

He suddenly flared up. 'It's behaviour like Luke's that's made me bitter. Have you any idea how hard it is to watch your child grow up controlled by a woman like Saskia, with no way of getting close to her? No hope of ever having any involvement, and then having to stand back and watch whilst another selfish over-sexed adult runs amok with her emotions?'

'Weren't you ever tempted to tell Emily who you really were?'

'It was my love for her that stopped me. Saskia was at pains to point out what would happen if the truth got out. Emily's "dad" is a very rich man. That house where she's living now belongs to his mother. Saskia said he'd disinherit Emily if he ever found out. And though he's hardly ever there, Emily's told me herself that she loves him. Whereas she's terrified of her mother. I'd have been ruining the one good relationship she has.' There were tears in his eyes now.

'But it hurt,' he said. 'Still hurts, that another man has that adoring, daughter's love.'

I could hardly bear to ask my next question, but I had to know. 'What are you going to do now?'

He looked at me through wet lashes. 'I'm sorry, Ruby, but now I'll have to take you with me, not Luke.'

I felt my mouth turn dry.

'The most important thing is that my secret is kept, and now it's only you who could give me away.' He bit his lip. 'As it is, the police will assume I was in love with Emily. They'll think I was yet another older man who couldn't keep his hands to himself, and that I killed Newbold out of jealousy.' He shuddered. 'But that's the way it'll have to be. Better that, than letting Emily grow up knowing her father was a murderer, four times over.'

I realised he was already counting me as one of the number.

'Do you want to get yourself a glass of water?' Paul said, looking at my face.

I felt like laughing insanely at this. 'I don't think so,' I said at last.

'Emily will believe the police,' Paul said, returning to his original theme as though he'd never left it, 'because she's developed this awful crush on me. She'll just feel she was right all along, and I was interested in her. So interested that I killed for her, and then died for love of her.' He paused and I saw his Adam's apple move as he swallowed. 'She'll be right in one way.'

He was completely sure of his ground. My mouth was as dry as ashes, but I had to speak. There had to be some way of shaking his conviction. 'But what about killing me? That won't fit.'

He shook his head. 'I don't know what they'll make of that, but I think it's unlikely they'll decide it means I'm Emily's father.'

God, nothing was going to work, the look in his eye told me that. The light I could see there was born of zeal. He had decided what needed to be done in a noble cause; end of story. Quite literally. I sought desperately for another tack. 'But if she believes you loved her,' I said, 'how will she cope, thinking she was the object of such an obsession?'

'She'll get over it. And in the meantime she'll know she was special.'

'Special? Paul, for God's sake, the way you're seeing this situation is totally skewed.' I knew I was talking to save my life. 'Don't you see that if you do this you're treating her just like Damien Newbold did?'

Paul's eyes shot up to meet mine, a flash of anger flaring in them like the sudden lick of a snake's tongue, shooting out towards its prey.

'You're affecting her whole life by your actions and assuming she'll just throw it off, and that having someone kill for you is actually quite flattering? Is that really what you think?'

But it was no use, he had already become calm again, resolved. 'I'm making the best of a bad job,' he said. 'Whatever she thinks, I believe she will recover, but not if she finds out I'm her father. That's not something she'd ever be able to run away from, is it? With that information she'd always know I was a part of her, running through her being.' He shook his head. 'That would never do.'

And then he walked over to our cooker, still facing towards me. 'I brought the knife, instead of my hammer, so it would be easier to end it all, after I'd killed Luke. But I don't want to do that to you. There's a better way for both of us.' He was side on to the stove now, and he began to turn the gas taps on, one by one. Then he picked up the packet of matches that lay, as of old, on the shelf above the toaster.

Chapter Twenty-Eight

Paul stood there, leaning against the cooker. The smell of gas had already reached me where I sat at the table. I began to raise myself out of my chair.

He immediately took a step forward, knife at the ready. 'Don't try anything, Ruby. This is too important to me. I know I said I didn't want to stab you, but I won't hesitate if you interfere.'

So I stayed where I was. At least I was standing now, but the heavy table still blocked the way between us. Panic rose up inside me. I tried to focus, but the hissing sound of the gas taps filled the air.

I watched the matchbox in his hand. It couldn't be long now before he'd be ready to make the explosion. How would it work? If I was lucky, he'd put the knife down to strike the match, but even then, I'd have no hope of reaching him before he made that crucial first spark. Shit. If I'd said yes to the water I might have been able to throw it over the matches ... Too late now.

My only plan, my only hope, was to move, very, very gradually, round the side of the table, so that I could try to lunge at him as he switched his focus from me to the matches. Tears pricked my eyes as I shifted a few millimetres at a time. It was never going to work. This was actually it.

Then suddenly there was a series of knocks at the front door.

For just a moment Paul jerked his head and I managed to move forward a foot or so, but then his eyes were fixed on me again. 'Just ignore it,' he said. 'And don't move any closer. I know it's hard to wait, but we're almost there now.'

A second later I could hear Steph's voice, echoing through

the letterbox, muffled by the closed kitchen door. 'Ruby? Are you in there?' Then there was a pause. 'Ruby! What the hell are you doing? Turn that gas off, for God's sake.'

It was just enough to distract Paul, and for a crucial second he looked instinctively towards the kitchen door. I'd already made ground, and now I kicked upwards, aiming to cause him maximum damage in the area that would hurt the most. My right DM smashed close to his crotch but not close enough. He dropped both the matches and the knife, which went skidding off towards the window. I didn't have a hope of getting both; he'd recover too quickly. I'd have to take my chances with the knife. Whilst Paul struggled to regain his feet I took the matchbox and plunged it into a half-full bowl of washing-up water Luke had abandoned.

But Paul, still cursing and obviously in pain, had thrown himself towards the knife and now held it fast again. He was standing between me and the door. The smell of gas was overwhelming, making me gag.

'I'm sorry, Ruby,' he said, 'but there's no way out of this. Steph probably thinks you're going to kill yourself because of what happened with Luke. One false move and she knows this place will blow sky high. Even if she calls the police, they'll just try to talk you out of the house. They won't dare to intervene directly, in case it makes you panic.'

And I knew he was right.

Steph was standing in the street outside what must be Ruby's house when Nate got to Saxwell, and he felt a chill run like iced water through his veins at the sight of her. Mascara was cascading down her cheeks, and her skin was the colour of chalk.

'It's Ruby,' she said, without questioning his presence. 'I think she's ...'

What was she trying to say?

291

'I can't believe it,' Steph said, starting again, 'but I can smell the gas from the front doorstep. I think she's planning to blow up the house, with her inside it.' The last words came out in short bursts, as she gasped for breath between sobs.

He took a long, deep breath. For a second he'd thought he was already too late. Not that he'd had any idea what to expect. Nate shook his head. 'She's with Paul Mathewson. He's our murderer. And it'll be he who's turned on the gas.'

'What?' Steph blinked wet eyelashes. 'I don't—'

'I don't get it either,' he said quickly. 'But he's always seemed overly close to Emily Amos. Maybe he had some pre-existing obsession with her, and killed Newbold for mucking her about.'

'God. Ruby said there was something odd about their relationship.' Steph rubbed her eyes. 'I just teased her for being nosy... but how did you come to think—?'

As she spoke Nate dragged his mobile out from his jeans pocket and called the emergency services. Yes, he told them, he did want all three. And he wanted them to come in very quietly indeed. They were dealing with a man who could blow a woman sky high if he was alarmed in any way... And quite possibly even if he wasn't.

After Nate had rung off he explained to Steph as briefly as he could, so she'd stop asking questions, and he could think. 'Mathewson left a briefcase full of student essays on the pavement when he drove off with Ruby this afternoon. I spent ages trying to work out why. Then it suddenly came to me. He wanted them to be found and returned to their rightful owners. Because, murderer though he is, he cares about his students. And if he wasn't going to be able to return them himself, it meant he wasn't coming back. I figured maybe he was making a run for it. Perhaps taking Ruby with him – as a hostage, or for entertainment. But—'

he looked up at Ruby's house, feeling nauseous, '—I didn't imagine he had anything this final in mind.'

Steph was crying again. 'What are we going to do?'

'I'm not sure,' Nate said, 'but I'll think of something. One thing we do know: this guy Mathewson's mad, but only north by north-west. He still cares about his students. That scrap of humanity means he's got a chink in his armour.'

Although Paul was armed again now, the knife didn't represent the same split-second threat that the matches had. But if he found another way of creating a spark we'd both be killed instantly. It was only luck that the automatic lighter on the cooker had conked out a while back. I needed to clear the room of gas. But how? The windows were double glazed, the sort that weren't going to yield, even if I threw a saucepan at them. And I couldn't get at the saucepans anyway.

I was just going to have to hope that some other idea came to me before Paul found a second source of ignition.

At that moment I heard a very faint sound, a tiny click. Paul didn't seem to notice. His eyes were darting left and right, looking for what he needed. Then suddenly they fixed on the light switch. My legs started to wobble. I'd read that operating one could be enough to make a spark; knew you should never turns the lights on in the event of a gas leak. He reached out and put a finger on the switch.

It took me a moment to realise that the light wasn't coming on. Someone must have cut the power. And then the gas stopped hissing too. Paul let out a howl that sounded far more animal than human. It sent shivers down my spine.

For a second I breathed a sigh of relief, but there was still no way to dissipate the gas, and Paul's anguish had triggered an even higher level of desperation. Still facing me, and holding the knife high, he opened the kitchen drawer next to the cooker, darting his eyes down for a moment to scan the contents. I could see he'd noticed something that interested him.

Then suddenly, I was aware of another faint sound from outside the kitchen door. A second later it opened and Nate walked in.

I gulped in a great lungful of gas, retching as the smell engulfed me all the more completely.

Paul only took a second to react. Before I was able to move he'd leapt behind me, and had the knife to my neck. 'Don't come any closer.'

'I'm not going to.' Nate held up a hand. 'I just wanted to talk. You need to know that the police are on their way. I wanted to find out the situation in here.'

'You're not involved,' Paul said. 'I don't have to kill you. Leave now. Close the door behind you.'

He shook his head. 'I'm not interested in going anywhere without Ruby.'

'Then close the door anyway, if you don't want to see her hurt.' Mathewson tightened his hold.

'Okay.' Nate did as he'd asked. The air was only marginally changed, right by the door. As soon as he returned to where he'd been standing the smell of gas was sickening. Ruby must have been trying to reason with Mathewson all this time, but Nate had to give it a go too. 'I found the students' essays you left behind. I know you care about innocent people; you don't want them to suffer, even in a small way.'

He saw Mathewson swallow, but he didn't speak.

'Well, Ruby's also innocent.' Surely he could get through to him. 'I don't believe you really think it's right to hurt her; whatever your reasons may be.'

Mathewson's eyes were swimming with tears, his hair

flopping down over his face, but he still held the knife hard against Ruby's neck.

Nate took a tiny step forward. 'Let Ruby go, Paul.' His mouth was so dry he could hardly get the words out.

Mathewson's eyes were wild. 'No! I told you, don't come any closer.' The tears were stopping; he was regaining control. 'Walk with me towards the drawer, Ruby.'

She shifted awkwardly towards the cooker, just in front of him. The drawer to its right was already open.

'Get the knife sharpener out.'

Shit. 'That'll never do the job.' But Nate wasn't sure. It was an electric one that ran on battery. Even if the blade didn't spark, the motor might.

'Take a knife from the block.'

Nate saw Ruby's hands shake as she reached forward.

'Put the knife in place. Won't be long now. Nearly over.'

He couldn't risk it. Nate was going to have to use his last resort. 'Paul.'

Ruby's hand, holding the knife, hovered above the sharpener.

'There's no way you'll get a spark out of that. Not with a knife of that quality. Cooking's a hobby of mine. By the time you've finished the police will be here, and maybe they'll risk storming the building. I'd already guessed you were having trouble making the explosion – why the delay otherwise? They'll know you're stuck, without any means of igniting the gas. You'll be left without any options. Is that what you want?' He put his hand into his jeans pocket, and took out the lighter Steph had dashed to find for him, once he'd guessed the type of bargaining chip he might need. 'I'll give you this, in exchange for Ruby.'

Mathewson hesitated, but at that moment someone called through a loud hailer, and his eyes widened. 'Okay. But you come and take her place. Bring the lighter.'

'Nate, don't.' Ruby's eyes held his for a moment.

'All right, Paul. I'll do that.' Nate walked over to his side. 'Now let Ruby go.'

Mathewson released her, and turned his knife on Nate, but he was tensed and ready. Holding on tight to the lighter, he swung a punch at Matthewson's stomach. The tutor bent double, but Nate didn't have time to get out of the way as his arm jerked up. The knife sliced him from elbow to wrist and he dropped the lighter.

They both dived for it, but Mathewson landed first and Nate watched, almost unable to react as he took it in his hand.

It was only then that Nate realised Ruby was still in the room. 'Shit, Ruby – get out!'

Mathewson's thumb was on the lighter's wheel, pushing down. And then, at that moment, something collided with his head. A cast-iron skillet.

Nate felt as though his reactions were in slow motion. And time wasn't a luxury they had. Mathewson was reeling. Down but not out. Blood streamed from his nose.

Nate grabbed Ruby, who was still staring at the damage she'd done to Paul, and propelled her towards the door. From the hall he heard Mathewson calling: 'Never tell her, Ruby. Please, never tell her.'

They had just reached the road when the explosion came.

Chapter Twenty-Nine

The day after Paul died, I stood outside what was left of Bookman's Cottage, crying. Luke was next to me, but I think he understood it was the house, and our past, that I was mourning.

'We were happy here, weren't we?' he said, putting a hand on my shoulder for a second.

'We were. For a long time. I'd been feeling the years had been wasted, but I suppose they weren't really. They were good while they lasted.' I looked at him then and he nodded.

'I was the biggest fool, but I never thought my actions would put you in danger. I'm glad you're okay.'

'Yeah,' I said. 'And I'm glad you are too.'

I was wrung out when Steph had me in for coffee, after Luke and I had said all we had to say. But in spite of that, I also felt more peaceful than I had since I'd moved out of Saxwell. It was hard closing the door on the past, but it was what I wanted.

'I still can't believe you thought I was going to blow up my own house,' I said as Steph put my drink in front of me.

'You'd already said you didn't belong there any more.'

'It was hardly going to increase the sale value, though, was it?'

'I thought you'd gone crazy.'

'Well, thanks very much. That makes it just fine then.'

She cut me a piece of the cherry cake she'd bought. 'Will you shut up, and just be grateful you're still alive?' she said.

'Hmm.' I picked up the slab she'd put on my plate. 'You have a point.'

'Thanks. Where's Luke staying?'

'A B&B in Bottisham. Even I have to admit it's a bit rough on him, though maybe it's nice to be out of the village. I wonder if having your house exploded by a murderer is covered by standard buildings insurance. At least we won't be arguing over the white goods after all, and I think it's safe to say the oak table's no longer up for grabs.'

She snorted, accidentally shooting cake crumbs off her plate. 'Have you seen the newspapers? It's made the nationals. They're reporting on your starring role. Here.' She handed me one she'd got with her. It implied that I'd worked out the details behind the three murders before the police, but that I was refusing to comment, making me sound dignified and modest.

'Well, of course,' I said, 'their information is correct. The instant Paul Mathewson tried to blow me up in my own kitchen I knew he was the killer.'

Suddenly, she came round to my side of the table and put her arm around my shoulders. 'I understand why you're being flippant, Ruby. You've always used it as a defence mechanism. But you'd better let everything out sooner or later, sweetie. It's not good for you otherwise.'

'What do you mean?'

She sighed. 'I know you and Paul were getting close. What happened must have knocked you for six.'

My mind took a moment to latch onto what she'd said. She was right about being knocked for six of course, but the rest? 'Excuse me?'

'Well, it was obvious you'd started to, you know, like each other.'

'You mean, in *that* way?'

'Of course,' Steph said. 'Nate mentioned you'd been spending a lot of time together, pub trips and so on.' She gave me a look. 'You might have let me in on that one. I had no idea.'

I turned to her. 'Steph, look at me.'

She did.

'Now think. Think very carefully, was Paul Mathewson, in your lifelong experience of my tastes and habits, my type?'

She opened her eyes wide. 'No. Well, no, of course not. I thought that straightaway. But you might have been acting out of character, under the circumstances. And Nate said it was a fact, so I assumed—'

'That he was right? Nope. One hundred per cent wrong. You should trust your instincts.'

'Well, my instincts told me you were sweet on Nate, but you put me right quick enough on that one.' She was giving me that look of hers, all pleasant speculation.

'Ah, yes,' I said. 'I remember that.'

I had one more visit to make before I went back to River House. Fi had asked me to drop in. Both she and Emily wanted to talk. I was a bit anxious about it, but it had been the prospect of the initial police interview that had chewed me up the most. Paul's dying plea not to give him away had rung in my ears, and the desperate, devastated look in his eye haunted me.

I, too, wished that Emily need never know, but, of course, I couldn't keep back the fact that he'd been her father. And it turned out that Paul's old teacher, Imelda West from the art gallery, had beaten me to it, anyway. She'd told the police the whole story about Saskia Amos's affair with Paul, and the fact that the staff had always wondered whether he might have fathered her youngest child. She would have spoken up sooner, only she'd liked Paul Mathewson very much, and had had no idea that Emily Amos and Damien Newbold had any connection. It was only when Saskia Amos was found dead, that such old history seemed potentially relevant.

After I'd arrived at Oswald House I sat in the kitchen with Fi. She told me that Saskia's husband was coming over to look after Emily, and that her grandmother was on her way back from Spain too.

'Between ourselves, Ruby,' she said, looking at me with sleep-deprived eyes, 'he's talked to Emily about it, and he says although it's possible she's not his, it's by no means certain. When you think about it, he and Saskia must still have had an active sex life when she got pregnant, otherwise he'd have been asking questions at the time.'

'True.'

'Emily wants to get a paternity test done,' Fi went on. 'She says it would be too horrible for her dad otherwise, not knowing whether he's got a cuckoo in the nest.' She sighed. 'Or, as Emily put it, the daughter of a psycho in his house.'

'So will they do that?'

'I think so,' Fi said, 'because Emily won't rest until she knows for sure, and her dad wants what's best for her. He's told her it won't make a difference, whichever way the results go. As far as he's concerned she'll always be the same daughter he's known since babyhood. And I have a feeling he'll stick around a bit more now, so they'll get to know each other better.'

'That's good news.'

But we both knew the effect it would have on Emily if she did turn out to be Paul's child.

A few minutes later, Emily herself turned up. She wanted to hear everything that Paul had said in detail. It wasn't a conversation I wanted to have, but there was nothing for it. It was when I got to the bit about Maggie that her eyes seemed to grow in size, filling with tears. She said, in a small voice, 'It was me.'

'I'm sorry?'

'Me,' she said again. 'At the college. The woman with long, dark hair asking questions about Paul.'

Another bit of the jigsaw I'd thought was secure shifted and slotted into its correct place.

'I'd …' she paused, raising her right hand to her forehead '… well, you know, I'd got a bit of a thing about him. I suppose because he'd been helping me through a tough time. I started to think that maybe he was the one for me instead of Damien. Only suddenly he didn't seem to be coming round to see me quite so often, so I dolled myself up and slipped over to his rooms. I thought I could invent some reason for suddenly needing his support; only he wasn't there and his bedder was. I told her I was looking for him, and asked about his timetable. Might he be around that evening or did he tend to go out? But when she asked my name I bottled it and said I'd contact him later. If I hadn't done that …'

I couldn't think how to respond. 'Paul was convinced Maggie had recognised him anyway,' I said at last, hearing the lameness in my tone. 'It wasn't just the business at the college.'

Emily looked at me, wanting to believe.

'It was Paul that did all this,' I said. 'No one else.'

'She's right, Em,' Fi said, and crouched down by her friend's chair to give her a hug.

Ruby looked wiped out when she got back to River House.

'Would you like tea?'

She nodded. 'I would fight anyone who stood between me and the kettle.'

They went into the kitchen. 'You won't get any argument from me. Not after seeing you in action with that skillet yesterday. Talk about saving the day.'

'Just a contribution. If you hadn't come in and persuaded Paul to let me go, I'm pretty sure I'd be dead by now.'

He saw her shiver. And he knew she'd been doing the rounds, tackling one emotionally difficult situation after another. He might as well face her with the latest bit of news immediately, and get it over with.

'I've just had a call from a solicitor's firm in London. Damien Newbold did make another will.'

She turned to him, her face pale. 'I can't believe it. In Maggie Cook's favour?'

Nate put teabags into mugs. 'Seems not. He left the lot to the Actors' Benevolent Fund. When he told Maggie Cook he was going to make sure she had a comfortable future that must have been what he meant. One last laugh.'

'My God. He really did hate women, didn't he?' The kettle had come to the boil, and she poured the water out.

'I'm afraid so. It's the same attention to detail he showed when he sent you the phone and the message in the attic, only on a much grander and more hurtful scale.'

She bit her lip. 'I hate the way he managed to read me.'

But Nate shook his head. 'He didn't know for sure you'd open the packet, or move up to the attic bed. He just thought it would be amusing if you did. I think it was like a game to him. He couldn't control his mother, so he set out to manipulate every other female in his life. He was sick.'

She nodded. 'Why was the news of the new will so delayed?'

'As well as hating women, Newbold hated his brother. He left a sealed letter with his family solicitors to be sent to a London solicitor's premises two weeks after his death. The family solicitors had no idea what was in it, apparently, or even that they were sending it to a rival firm. Newbold hadn't put the company name on the envelope, just a name and the address, so it looked like a personal letter. In fact, it was a message to the London firm saying if you've received this then I'm dead, please notify my family solicitors and

302

Samson Newbold about my new will, which you hold.'

Nate poked at the teabags with a spoon.

'He went to all that trouble simply because he wanted Samson to have the chance to gloat over his gains before having the rug pulled from under his feet?'

He nodded. 'And think how Maggie Cook would have felt, if she'd still been alive.'

Ruby closed her eyes for a second. 'So I presume this place and everything in it will be sold ASAP, for the benefit of all those actors.'

'That's right. I'll know in a day or two whether the new executors want us to carry on overseeing this place, or if they'll make their own arrangements.' And that would be that. Nate took his tea upstairs to his room feeling empty.

Nate had cooked supper the night before; tonight I was determined I'd do it. I'd amassed all the ingredients I wanted, but still hadn't plucked up the courage to turn on the gas. Instead, I stood there looking at a load of chorizo, garlic, onions and peppers. The pasta was still on a plate on top of the scales. I'd been in the same situation for about five minutes when Nate walked into the room.

I saw him glance at the elaborate preparations, the oil in the cold frying pan, the pasta water cooling in the kettle. Then he looked at the hob. He bloody knew; knew exactly why nothing was underway.

He picked up the matches from where they sat, on the shelf next to the herbs, and put them into my hand. I could feel my fingers shaking as I made to strike the light. He turned the gas knob as I leant towards the cooker, and then within a moment the oil was heating, and I had tipped in the onion.

I couldn't look at him. 'Thanks.'

'Not a problem.'

'I was going to add in some of the rosemary you bought, too.'

He went to the windowsill to take a couple of sprigs from the pot it was growing in. Without looking at me he said: 'I never asked how things were in Saxwell.'

'It felt odd. Like finally closing a door that's been ajar. But somehow it was a relief.'

Now he did cast me a quick glance. 'Must have been harrowing to see your house like that.'

'Yes, but I'd already been mourning it before it was destroyed. I knew I could never go back.'

He rinsed the rosemary and brought it over to me to chop. 'I'm glad Steph was there to give you a coffee after you'd met with Luke.'

I smiled automatically. 'She's one in a million, your cousin. Although we had a moment of awkwardness.'

He was reaching for a bottle of wine to the left of the cooker, but glanced at me and raised an eyebrow.

'She was under the impression I'd had a crush on Paul Mathewson, and would need to talk things through. To be fair, if she'd been right, I'd certainly have needed to unburden.'

'You mean you and he weren't—'

I gave him a look. 'No. I don't tend to go in for men like Paul. I'm not really a herringbone-suit-and-intense-personality sort of girl. Bloody good thing, as it turns out.'

'Can't argue with you there.' I noticed he was smiling as he uncorked the Rioja and poured us each a healthy glass. 'Want me to lay the table?'

'Thanks.'

'I would have been down to help sooner, only Samson Newbold called,' he said.

'I bet that was an interesting conversation.'

'It was quite ...' He paused for a moment to reach for

some plates. '... lively. I did have one bit of good news for him though.'

'Really?'

'The London solicitors are happy to cover our fees for sitting this place, so he won't have to cough up.'

I tipped the chopped peppers into the hot oil and onions. 'I'm guessing that wasn't quite enough to make his day?'

'Very astute of you.'

I stole a glance in his direction. His hair had fallen forward as he worked. I took in the dressing on his arm. The scar would be a long one. Peering at him was a mistake. Did he have to make a thing of looking so rugged? I dragged my attention back to the cooking.

'I might have a lead on our burglars too,' he said.

'Really? I thought perhaps we'd never know.'

'Maybe we won't for sure, but Samson's had a break-in now, at his own house.'

'Interesting.'

'Yes. Apparently it was the night after he'd had the news about the will. He'd been down in the Red Tavern as usual, drowning his sorrows. Sounds like he'd had a skinful. Said one of the regulars there who's not normally his greatest fan was being really sympathetic, buying him more and more drinks.'

'And that clearly didn't ring alarm bells at the time, thanks to Samson's unshakeable belief in himself.'

'Got it in one. Anyway, at the end of the evening Samson was so far gone that the landlord of the Red Tavern and the drink-buying bloke had to lift him into a taxi. He doesn't remember how he got out at the other end, or anything else until the following morning.' Nate raised an eyebrow. 'He told me he was convinced the guy at the pub had spiked his drinks.'

'Doesn't sound as though much spiking would have been required, given the quantities.'

'I thought it would be tactless to point that out. Anyway, the next day he found he'd been robbed and he's convinced the guy at the pub was behind it. I'm not sure how far he'll take it with the police; he might just consider they're quits now, if this was one of the people he'd borrowed from. And he did admit he'd mentioned the security arrangements at River House in the pub. He wondered if the same guy was responsible for both break-ins, so he wanted to see what I thought.'

'Well,' I said, 'it sounds quite possible, and it's good to have things tidy. I like knowing the answer to these little mysteries.'

He reached across to get the pepper grinder from the work surface by my side, accidentally brushing my arm. His warmth and the contact sent shivers through me. They shot round to all the most relevant areas in an alarmingly intense way. I flicked a glance at him.

He gave me a crooked smile. 'Sorry.'

Suddenly I was very conscious of how close he was standing; that and how it still wasn't close enough, as far as I was concerned.

'Shit, Ruby,' Nate said.

'You say the nicest things.'

'It's just that …' He moved closer still, until I was aching for him to touch me.

'What?'

'Since I met you, I've started to feel alive again. I never thought I'd get that back after Susie died.'

I felt goosebumps rise on my arms. Tears pricked my eyes as I turned to face him properly.

'But what happened to her is the very reason we shouldn't be together.'

I turned off the gas I'd bravely managed to light. 'Do you have any idea who killed her?'

He shook his head. 'The one thing I'm sure of is that it was someone who was out to get *me*. She'd never have made such a ruthless enemy.'

I wondered. Not everyone with enemies deserved them. You only had to look at Damien's mother to see that.

'Her killer's still out there,' Nate went on, 'and for all I know they're planning their next move. Their target might be me. Or, if we start a relationship, it could be you.'

'I'm willing to take the risk. I don't want to play it safe if it means us being apart.'

He took my hand in his and interlaced his fingers with mine. 'I didn't mean to fall in love with you. Certainly didn't mean you to find out.'

I looked up at him quickly and the tears threatened again. 'Same.'

We were both silent for a moment.

'Nate,' I said at last, 'why did you come and get me, when I was with Paul, and you knew you could be killed? You put yourself in harm's way then.'

He looked at me. 'That was different.'

I shook my head. 'Uh-uh. That was the same. Except you were putting yourself in certain danger, whereas in this case, it's harder to know what we're dealing with. I'm just making the same choice you did.'

He was a centimetre from me, his eyes serious. 'But are you sure you want to make it?'

'Never been surer.'

And, at last, he let go of my hand, and took me in his arms.

Thank You

Thank you so much for reading A Stranger's House. I do hope you enjoyed following the first Ruby Fawcett and Nate Bastable mystery as much as I enjoyed writing it!

I also hope you found Cambridge an interesting setting. I've lived here for years now and worked at the university centrally, as well as the colleges where the students live. To me, the city seems like the perfect backdrop for crime fiction. It's a place of great contrasts, where worlds collide thanks to its compact nature. On a five-minute walk you can see drug dealers on the commons as well as choirs singing madrigals from punts on the river. And given that it's home to multi-million pound businesses, as well as academics with world-class reputations, it's not hard to imagine the sort of rivalries that might sometimes boil over!

One of the things a writer's always after is feedback. It's invaluable to know whether our stories strike a chord. (And if the response happens to be good, it can make a huge difference to the profile of a book and author too!) If you have time to leave a brief review, either on a retailer's website or somewhere like Goodreads, that would be amazing. I also love hearing directly from readers. You can contact me via my website, Twitter or Facebook, using the details in the 'About the Author' section. It would be lovely to hear from you.

Thank you, and happy reading!

Clare x

About the Author

Clare Chase writes mysteries set in London and Cambridge featuring crime-solving couples. She fell in love with the capital as a student, living in the rather cushy surroundings of Hampstead in what was then a campus college of London University. (It's currently being turned into posh flats ...)

After graduating in English Literature, she moved to Cambridge and has lived there ever since. She's fascinated by the city's contrasts and contradictions, which feed into her writing. She's worked in diverse settings – from the 800-year-old University to one of the local prisons – and lived everywhere from the house of Lord to a slug-infested flat. The terrace she now occupies presents a good happy medium.

As well as writing, Clare loves family time, art and architecture, cooking, and of course, reading other people's books.

She lives with her husband and teenage children, and currently works at the Royal Society of Chemistry.

A Stranger's House is her second novel with Choc Lit. Her first was *You Think You Know Me*.

www.twitter.com/ClareChase_
www.clarechase.com
www.facebook.com/ClareChaseAuthor

More Choc Lit

From Clare Chase

You Think You Know Me

Book 1 – London & Cambridge Mysteries

Sometimes, it's not easy to tell the good guys from the bad ...

Freelance journalist, Anna Morris, is struggling to make a name for herself, so she's delighted to attend a launch event for a hip, young artist at her friend Seb's gallery.

But an exclusive interview isn't all Anna comes away with. After an encounter with the enigmatic Darrick Farron, she is flung into the shady underground of the art scene – a world of underhand dealings, missing paintings and mysterious deaths ...

Seb is intent on convincing Anna that Darrick is up to no good but, try as she might, she can't seem to keep away from him. And as she becomes further embroiled, Anna begins to wonder – can Seb's behaviour be explained away as the well-intentioned concern of an old friend, or does he have something to hide?

Visit www.choc-lit.com for more details, or simply scan barcode using your mobile phone QR reader.

One Dark Lie

Book 3 – London &
Cambridge Mysteries

**The truth can hurt, and
sometimes it leads to murder …**

After becoming embroiled in
a murder investigation, Nate
Bastable and Ruby Fawcett
have decided to opt for the
quiet life. But crime has a habit
of following them around.

When her work dries up, Ruby
finds herself accepting a job researching and writing about
Diana Patrick-John, a colourful and enigmatic Cambridge
academic. Simple enough. But then there's the small fact that
Diana was found dead in suspicious circumstances in her
home – the very place where Ruby has now been invited to
stay.

As she begins to uncover Diana's secret life, Ruby's sleuthing
instinct kicks in, leaving her open to danger and retribution.
But can she rely on Nate to support her? Especially when
his behaviour has become increasingly distant and strange,
almost as though he had something to hide …

Read an extract of the first two chapters overleaf.

Visit www.choc-lit.com for more
details, or simply scan barcode using
your mobile phone QR reader.

Introducing Choc Lit

Preview
One Dark Lie

by Clare Chase

CHAPTER ONE

When Quentin Patrick-John asked me to write about his sister, the offer came just at the right moment. Of course, there was more to the proposition than met the eye. A lot more.

Quentin seemed to sidle out of the shadows on King Street. I'd been up in the new flat I was renting there, above Claudio's restaurant. It was tiny, and the smell of garlic and pizza dough started to drive me crazy hours before my proper dinnertime, but it was warm and mostly watertight.

Seven o'clock on an early December evening. Nate had been with me, lounging on my bed. We'd got together six months earlier, after confronting a homicidal maniac who'd blown up my house. Long story: suffice it to say, said maniac had been strongly inclined to blow me and Nate up too, which had proved to be a bonding experience. The moral is, if you get involved in a murder investigation, be prepared to take the rough with the smooth. Nate did warn me about this at the time, but I got curious.

Now the dust had settled we were taking things slowly: seeing each other often, but still keeping our own space.

Nate's mobile rang, and I watched as he talked. He was wearing a soft, thickly woven charcoal grey shirt over jeans, his long legs stretched out in front of him.

He glanced in my direction, and for just a moment his

blue eyes met mine. Then he got up, turned away and wandered to the other side of the room. 'Yeah, sure,' he said. 'But I'll need to call you about it later.'

I walked to the window overlooking the street, as though turning my back would give him more space. Pushing the curtain aside I felt the draft from the sash and pulled my hoodie more tightly round me. Outside, lamplight only emphasised the dark alley opposite. Someone leant against the wall there, and lit a cigarette. The scene was lonely, but the noise from the crowd downstairs was reassuring.

Frost coated everything in my line of sight. A spider's web hung from the lamppost, looking as though it had been encrusted with sugar.

Behind me, I was conscious of Nate's low voice. There'd been a lot of these sorts of calls lately; ones where he told the caller he'd have to speak to them later. To be fair, there was no privacy in my flat – the only door, apart from the entrance, was the one to the loo.

'Okay,' Nate was saying. 'See you then.' He cut the call and came over to me, turning me round to face him. I think it's his eyes that do it. That blue gaze gets me every time. Thoughts of quizzing him still hovered, but his look pushed them to the edge of my brain until I couldn't quite think what they were doing there.

'Don't tell me. You have to go.'

He gave me a crooked smile, and his unruly dark hair fell forward as he bent towards me. 'Nearly right.' He put one warm hand on my shoulder, and one on my waist, making me shiver. 'I have to go, soon.' And he drew me towards him. My last thought was that I ought to have pulled the curtains closed again.

But, of course, a little while later, he really did leave. Moments afterwards, I realised he'd forgotten his scarf. I grabbed it from the back of the chair, where it had become submerged under some of my outer layers, tugged on a pair of Converse and dashed down the stairs. After hurtling along the corridor that led to the street, I pulled back the front door. I slipped a little on the pavement in my haste to reach Nate before he found his car and drove off. In fact, I might have gone right over, if it hadn't been for the well-dressed man in front of me, who brought me to a halt, standing there in his black wool overcoat and rust coloured scarf. I'm pretty tall and we were evenly matched; it was lucky I hadn't knocked him flying. I took a step back but all the same, I could smell his cologne; a man who liked to advertise his expensive tastes. He looked familiar, but I was distracted, and shelved the task of trying to place him for a moment.

'I'm sorry,' I said, automatically, whilst looking over his shoulder to try to see where Nate had parked. Too late. His ancient Volvo was way down the street, its indicator winking as he prepared to pull out.

'No need to apologise.'

Something about his upper-class drawl jogged my memory. Nate had introduced us once, when we'd bumped into him in a bar in town. He hadn't provided many details though; an ex-client was all he'd said. The atmosphere had been rather strained, as far as I could recall, but I'd never found out why.

The man glanced over his shoulder for a second, following my gaze. 'I was hoping to catch you after our friend Mr Bastable had left, as a matter of fact.'

I raised an eyebrow. 'That sounds ominous.' I was still trying to remember his name; something double barrelled?

He gave me a fox-like smile. 'He wasn't too keen on me talking to you, I must say.'

I shivered in my indoor clothes, and folded my arms

across my chest. 'That might mean I'm not keen on the idea either.'

'I had a feeling you'd want to make up your own mind.'

He had me there, of course.

'I suggest we pay a visit to the Champion of the Thames. I can buy you a drink and explain, and then you can ask me more, or tell me to go to hell as the mood takes you.'

I thought for a moment. I'd been planning to order one of Claudio's takeaways and hole up. But naturally, I was too curious to refuse. 'Just let me get a coat and lock up.' I went back indoors and nipped up the stairs to my flat. As I grabbed my outer layer from a hook by the door, his name came to me. Quentin – that was it. Quentin Patrick-John.

When I got back to the street he was standing bang in the middle of the pavement, just as before. A gang of students, heading for warmth and garlic bread, were forced to swarm round him, but he seemed oblivious.

We must have looked like a strange pair, heading into the pub; I in my jeans and donkey jacket, and he in his precisely tailored clothes.

He stood at the bar, his dark hair shiny in the glow from the open fire. I wondered if he dyed it; he looked more than old enough to have had some grey streaks by now.

'Whisky?'

I shook my head. 'I'll get my own.' I asked the barman for an IPA.

Quentin laughed as he took a sip of his drink. 'I can see why you and Nate are together. Same habitual caution. Though that suits his profession.'

It's true that an incautious PI would probably get into trouble pretty quickly. Not that he was doing PI work any more. Or at least, not as far as I knew. His life had been torn apart a couple of years earlier. That was when he'd swapped detection for running a house-sitting outfit. He was a good businessman, and it brought in the money, but I could see it bored him.

Quentin motioned me to the one free table in the tiny bar and I peeled off my outer layers as the warmth began to penetrate. The logs on the fire crackled and popped and the whole room smelled of wood smoke.

Opposite me, he loosened his scarf and eased out of his coat. 'Well, there's no need to be quite so much on your guard. I'm here with an offer of work. No pressure.'

I raised an eyebrow.

'My sister died earlier in the year. She was a world-renowned academic and I'm after someone to write about her life. I'd like it to be you.'

It wasn't what I'd expected. Thinking about it, my career had come up briefly when Nate had introduced us. He must have looked me up after that, for whatever reason. I took a sip of my beer and waited.

He gave a small smile. 'I didn't expect you to bite my hand off, and you're not disappointing me. Here's my proposition: I know your books sell well; you're good at capturing the public's attention by writing about experiences people can relate to.'

He didn't need to remind me about that. He might as well have said, 'I know you capture the public's attention by writing about topics that give people a voyeuristic kick.' I was out of love with my work. I'd finally come to see it for what it was when I'd written my latest book on mid-life crises. In the middle of it all, my partner Luke – now very much ex – had chosen to have a fling with a seventeen-year-old neighbour. To cap it all, we'd been trying for a baby at the time. I went from browsing books on pregnancy to walking out on him, at double-quick speed. So, there I'd been, nicely on the receiving end, in just the same position as the subjects I'd been interviewing. Yes, if someone had turned up to ask about my experiences just then, I'd probably have been delighted to tell them all the gory details. It would have been a great way to get back at him. I'd have regretted it afterwards though, when it was all too late. I wondered how many people wished they'd never let Ruby Fawcett into their lives. Not a good feeling. Still, it had been an eye-opener.

'I think your name, and your writing style will draw in readers for the book about Diana. You'd get a lump sum for the work.'

On the face of it, it sounded like a good opportunity to move away from the pulp non-fiction I'd come to despise. And a lump sum could work all right if it was decent. I didn't imagine the book would sell in vast numbers, so the lack of royalties might be okay. 'And you want a life story, bringing in her ideas and academic achievements, rather than a scholarly appraisal of her work?' Then I pulled myself up and gave a hollow laugh. 'Well, of course you do, or you wouldn't be asking me.'

He nodded. 'There's lots more detail I can give you, but I wanted to sound you out first.'

'Fair enough.' I took a swig of my drink. 'But why did you go through Nate, instead of coming straight to me?'

He glanced up and met my eyes, but didn't say anything.

'What?'

'You're not going to like it. I assumed you'd already know the background to Diana's death, but if you did you'd have answered your own question.'

I took a long breath. 'You wanted Nate's help too? There were suspicious circumstances?'

He gave me a look. 'You could say so. She was found strangled in her sitting room six months ago. The police haven't found her killer.'

CHAPTER TWO

Nate turned off the A14, moving away from the orange glow and sea of headlights to quieter roads. As he turned towards Little Nighting the streetlights gave way to darkness; expanses of inky fields stretched out left and right. The moon was hidden behind a cloud and he switched to full beam. Once, he'd enjoyed the move from the hubbub to the peace that meant he was nearing Two Wells Farm and home. All that had changed two years earlier. He could still remember the acrid smell when he'd returned to his house that night, and the haze of smoke drifting across the lane. An echo of the hollow feeling of fear that had gripped him then took hold of his insides every time he came home now. Friends were always asking why he didn't sell up, but he couldn't leave the place. It would seem like a betrayal. All the more so, when the business was unfinished.

He glanced at his watch for a second, pressing the button to illuminate its face. He still had time to spare. Overshooting the village, he took a right towards Faddenham, which made no sense. Didn't stop him doing it though, every time since he'd found out the truth. They'd be in The Feathers. Squire was a friend of the landlord, which seemed to mean the place had escaped being shut down on no less than three occasions. He was a man who could pull strings in countless circles.

Nate pulled up between a BMW and a Merc. His knackered Volvo would stick out like a sore thumb, but he wasn't staying. He could already see them through the leaded window. Squire laughing, holding court; the rest of the gang currying favour; queuing up his drinks. Mel was there too, slinking around, perching for a moment on his lap. So that meant her dad, Tony Dukes, Squire's right-hand man but also his main rival, must be absent. As Nate watched Squire's haughty face, he felt his heart rate increase. He was conscious of the almost painful thudding in his chest, and of the blood pumping in his ears. It hurt to sit there, powerless, looking at the man who'd ordered the murder of his sister. Yet somehow he couldn't stop. Any opportunity and he'd be there, however useless it was.

But it was time to go. He turned the car and set off back in the direction of Little Nighting, his mind on Ruby. He'd been scared to start a relationship with her back in the summer; worried he might be putting her in harm's way. But at that point he hadn't known what he was dealing with. For a long time he'd just been up against the bald facts, hitting him with force and shock like mentally slamming into a concrete wall at breakneck speed. Someone had torched his house. Just beforehand, his sister had come to stay unexpectedly and he'd been called out, also without warning. She'd been upstairs, alone, when someone had walked round, dousing the perimeter of Two Wells Farm with petrol, shoving soaked rags and then fire lighters through the letterbox. She must have been sleeping when the fire was set. She was only wearing a T-shirt when she was found, and the sheets on the spare bed had been rumpled. Nate had pictured what must have happened so many times. She'd have woken and smelled the smoke; heard the crackle of the fire as it tightened its hold on the building. Maybe she'd looked out of the window, but escape that way would have seemed impossible. The thatch that reached down either side of it would already have been alight, as well as the thick ivy clinging to the wall below. So, already coughing, breathing in far too much smoke, she'd have looked for a way out through the house.

She'd died of smoke inhalation. The firemen found her body at the top of the stairs; her way out would have been blocked by the fierce flames below. He could only imagine the terror she must have experienced.

For many months he'd been convinced the attack had been meant for him. After all, he'd collected plenty of enemies in his work as a PI. But as time went on he'd made no headway in identifying the killer from amongst the criminals he'd crossed. And at last he'd started to think the unthinkable; that maybe his kid sister – cheerful, impish Susie, ten years his junior – had been the killer's target after all.

And then, just after he'd got together with Ruby, he'd found out he was right. And the potential danger now was far worse: Squire had to be brought down. But he was the kind of man who'd stop at nothing. If he once worked out Nate was onto him, he'd use any means to control matters, and that included using Ruby. His possible methods didn't bear thinking about ...

Even before he'd found out the truth, Nate had refused to let Ruby stay at Two Wells. If someone had been out to get him, they might also target anyone he loved. He'd done his utmost to minimise the chances of her being seen by the wrong people. Limiting their relationship to her flat in Cambridge just about worked, but matters would come to a head, sooner or later. He could tell her patience was wearing thin. But now he knew the truth, it was all the more impossible to let down his guard. And worst of all, he was keeping his knowledge from her. The longer he did that, the bigger the lie became, but there was no other way. If she found out what was going on she'd want to be involved, and that risk was just too great.

An owl flew across the Volvo's path, bringing him abruptly back to the here and now. The pinewoods that swallowed up the countryside this side of his village loomed into sight, making the dark night even darker. The track where walkers normally parked was on his right now, but he kept going, pulling in a little further on, down a narrow rutted avenue where the trees crowded in on either side. He glanced behind him and cut the engine. The road was barely visible at this distance. He clambered out, feeling the frost-hardened earth under his feet, and trod through the trees. An ice-coated pine needle carpet replaced the dirt of the main track, giving as he made each step. In summer he loved the smell of the pines, but in weather this cold you could hardly detect it. The harsh night air caught at his throat. After five minutes, he registered movement: a faint shifting of shades of indigo between the trunks. Steve. He must have left The Feathers soon after Nate had.

As usual, Nate had mixed feelings on seeing his thin, shivering silhouette, revealing hunched shoulders and lank hair. There was pity, combined with the pull of some kind of bond, born out of familiarity and shared experiences. But there was always anger too – not fair, but something he couldn't damp down entirely – and a plunging feeling of regret that tugged inside his chest. Steve met his eye for a moment, then looked at the ground, as though reading Nate's mind. Without looking up, he took a cigarette and lighter from his pocket.

Steve was the link – the unwitting key to the tragedy. Three years earlier, the boy's uncle and aunt had asked Nate to find him. He'd been living with them for six months since his parents had died, but after a spate of trouble at his sixth-form college, and a few run-ins with the local police, he'd taken off. His uncle had reckoned he was somewhere in East Anglia; he'd let that much slip to a schoolmate.

Nate first met Steve's relations at their tidy two-up, two-down in Swansea. He'd felt for the boy's aunt, Mary, with her red eyes, prematurely lined face and exhausted complexion. 'We've failed Steve's parents,' she'd said. 'We only wanted what was best for him, but we've driven him away. I took time off work, so I could meet him straight after school – but that turned out to be the final straw. What eighteen-year-old would want that? I should have known.' He'd watched her knuckles whiten as her hand clenched round a tissue that was in shreds.

Steve's uncle, Len, had put a large, ruddy hand on her shaking shoulder. 'It wasn't your fault, Mary. The boy had been through too much. He needed to kick back at life, and that included us.'

Nate could empathise: he'd lost his own mother when he was twenty-five, and even in full adulthood he'd pretty much stopped functioning for a couple of months.

When he'd got up to leave Mary and Len's home, Len had glanced up, and Nate had seen his eyes glisten for a moment before he'd looked away. 'We're hoping someone's shown Steve some kindness,' he'd said at last. 'You know: taken him under their wing. But whatever's happened, we really want him to know we'd love him back. He's my brother's son.'

Someone had taken Steve under their wing all right. Unfortunately, that someone had been Squire: one of the most ruthless and charismatic crooks in the region.

It hadn't taken Nate long to find the boy. Armed with the photo supplied by Len and Mary, just a few words to key connections had confirmed Nate's worst fears. It so often worked like that with runaways. No doubt Steve had exhausted what little cash he'd set out with, and had started looking for a quick way to earn more. Enter Squire. Nate could imagine how he would have portrayed himself: the big boss of a close-knit team, interested in Steve personally, despite his youth. Flattery went a long way when you felt vulnerable and alone. And after that, Nate knew how the slippery slope worked; he'd seen it before. By the time you realised what was going on, you were in too deep to turn your back.

At last he'd managed to meet the boy, through a friend of a friend. Very gradually, over a number of weeks, he'd started to get to know him. When at last the moment came for Nate to admit that Steve's uncle and aunt had sent him, it went smoothly. The boy didn't fly off the handle or refuse to see him again – but he wouldn't return home, either. By that stage, Squire had made Steve aware that working for him was a one-way street. Leave, and his oh-so-charming boss could turn nasty.

'And he'd get away with it, of course,' Steve had told Nate. 'He's clever like that.' His eyes were wide – a combination of fear and a grudging admiration that still lingered, Nate reckoned. 'And he'd go after my uncle and aunt if I left. I know he would. It's the kind of thing he's done before.'

Nate had pointed out that Steve's uncle and aunt were in Wales, and that it would give Squire far more hassle to go after them than to let things lie. But the boy hadn't believed him; Steve was a small cog in Squire's machine, but he was convinced his boss would do anything to hang on to him.

And Nate's current knowledge had left him questioning his own gut instinct about how far the man would go. It all depended on how bothered Squire was. Nate was willing to bet he'd move heaven and earth to get revenge if he was seriously riled.

Nate shivered and shoved his hands deeper into his jacket pockets as Steve moved closer, puffing on his cigarette.

'Pleasant evening at the pub?'

'Yeah, right. Two hours in Squire's company isn't something I enjoy.'

'Sorry I had to cut you short earlier. I can't talk when Ruby's around. There's no way I want her knowing about any of this. And you want to make damn sure no one overhears you calling me.'

Steve looked up at him, his eyes in shadow, arms folded against the cold. 'I understand that. After what happened, you don't exactly need to explain.'

Nate nodded, but still he worried. Steve was twenty-one now, but a naive twenty-one. 'So, what have you got?'

His demeanour changed. Suddenly Steve looked like a happier version of the teenager he'd been when Nate had first traced him. 'Bit of a breakthrough.' He handed over a small, empty plastic pill bottle. 'Squire's getting Melanie hooked on something, I reckon. Earlier this evening I heard her tell him she'd run out of the "present" he'd given her. And just before that, I saw her chuck that in the bin.' Nate glimpsed his smile broaden. 'I fished it back out again when no one was looking. Don't know what was in there; packaging's plain, but I doubt it was vitamin C. It's information that could get Tony right where we want him. You know what he's like about Melanie.'

Tony was overprotective of his only daughter. Coupled with that, he was known for his short temper and skill with a hammer – or indeed any other blunt instrument that came to hand. The image of his large, ruddy face flicked through Nate's mind. It must have shown in his expression.

'It's no use looking like that, mate. We can't hope to pull off this kind of stunt without Tony on our side. Besides, you know we can sort him out later. You want to take the bottle and see if you can find out what was in it?'

Nate nodded. Much as he hated the thought of promoting Tony's cause, what Steve said made sense. There was no other way. The relationship between Squire and Tony was already uneasy, but Nate wanted them at daggers drawn. It was a dangerous game.

He put a hand on Steve's shoulder. 'You know what I'm going to say, don't you?'

He heard him let out a breath. 'Yeah. I'll watch myself.

And, I know: I can go home any time, and you'd prefer it if I did. But my uncle and aunt would be in danger if I backed out. Besides, I can help you, being on the inside. Your sister was good to me, and it's my fault she met Squire in the first place. I'm not leaving until this is over.'

Nate watched as Steve ambled off through the pine trees.

He remembered the day that had changed everything: the day he'd arranged to meet Steve at Two Wells for the very first time, to get him to talk to his aunt on the phone. They'd been in the kitchen together, drinking coffee, when Susie had turned up. She'd come without calling ahead, just as she had on the day she'd died. He'd heard her Fiat 500 screech to a halt in his driveway and known who it was before she'd pounded on his door. She'd got halfway through telling him about the job she'd landed, working for a local paper, before she'd pulled up short at the sight of Steve, sitting in the shadows. Nate hadn't even paused for thought before introducing them. Then Susie had helped herself to coffee and they'd all congregated around his large oak table. Steve hadn't been keen to call his aunt; it was Susie who'd talked him round, sympathising and recounting her own wild times. She hadn't been much older than him, and had also known what it was like to lose a parent in your teens.

So thanks to his sister, the boy had called his aunt, and it had gone well. Mary had been in floods of tears – the good sort this time – to know that he missed her and Len, even if he didn't feel he could go home.

Nate had been vaguely aware that Susie had given Steve her number, just in case he wanted to talk more. But Steve had never mentioned her again, nor she him. A few weeks had passed when none of them had been in touch. His task to persuade Steve home had reached stalemate and Susie was busy with her new job.

And then there'd been the night of the fire. Susie had arrived mid-evening, and he'd been pissed off with her; she'd turned up unexpectedly as usual, and made him late for an appointment that had been arranged at the last minute. They'd exchanged a sentence or two at most.

And then his world had collapsed.

It wasn't until two months after his sister's death that he'd managed to get it together enough to check in with Steve. And it was then that he'd realised their friendship must have progressed after that first meeting at Two Wells. Steve felt her loss strongly; that much was clear. Of course, he hadn't known then that his own boss was responsible. Now that he did, he was risking everything to help Nate bring Squire down.

Even though Susie had met Squire through Steve, the boy was wrong about her death being his fault. It was he, Nate, who'd allowed Susie and Steve's paths to cross; he who'd never asked about any future meetings they'd had. He simply hadn't seen the danger.

Coming soon!
Visit www.choc-lit.com for details.

Gripping edge of your seat reads!

More from Choc Lit

If you loved Clare's story, you'll enjoy the rest of our selection.
Here's a sample:

Visit www.choc-lit.com for more details